DEVIL'S NIGHT

Katerina St Clair

Devil's Night

Author: Katerina St Clair

Edited by: Sydney Miller

Cover Art: Anatolii M/ Ceren (Paperbacks)

Cover Art: /Anatolii M/ Ceren (Hardcovers)

Interior Art: Anatolii M

Trigger Warning List

Please Read Carefully Before Proceeding:

- Stockholm Syndrome

- Consensual Non-Consent

- Non-Consensual Sexual Actions

- Branding

- Blood Play

- Anal

- Cum Play

- Bondage

- Kidnapping

- Torture

- Graphic Violence

- Graphic Sex

- Gun Play

- Knife Play

- Breeding Kink

Playlist

You're So Pretty- Sombr

Scream My Name- Thomas La Rosa

Poison In My Veins- Elvis Drew

Sick & Twisted- Chris Grey

Let Me Fall- Ex Habit & Bury

F*ck- Mandrazo, Sebabrazy & Kiyashqo

P*rnstar- Nessa Barrett

Feel- Beneld & Bury

Make Me Feel- Elvis Drew

The Wall- PatrickReza

Same Old Song (S.O.S Part 1)- Two Feet

For all my dark romance girlies who would rather read
my books than go to therapy.
This fucked up tale is for you.

1

WE'RE ALL A LITTLE MAD

ECHO

I have never felt as if I were meant for anything good.

Not love. Not peace. Not grace.

I was born with blood on my hands, learning to stop flinching at the sound of death long before I could even spell my own name.

I have taken a man's last breath and felt no remorse. If anything, I reveled in it—in the silence that follows a death rattle, in the final flicker of defiance behind a man's eyes as he realizes he's not walking away from me.

While other children were learning nursery rhymes, I was learning how to cut arteries. The sound of lungs filling with blood is not something you forget.

It gurgles like a broken machine.

The screams that come after are never whole.

Rasping, choking, begging for mercy I don't believe in.

Those sounds used to haunt me.

Now, they help me sleep.

God has never looked in my direction.

And I never once begged for his light.

Because what good would it do to ask for redemption, when damnation is all I've ever known?

No.

I have never been deserving of good things.

And maybe that's why I like this job so fucking much.

"I don't know anything, I swear!"

The man cries, voice quivering, his hands shaking so violently I wonder if his bones might splinter.

His face is a ruin with blackened eyes swollen shut, lips split open, and his jaw clicking slightly every time he sobs too hard.

He's young. Barely thirty if that.

Still has the softness of someone who's never been truly broken.

But that's the problem, isn't it?

Boys like this who are sons of monsters, grow up thinking the world will never touch them.

Isaac Romanov.

A name that carries weight in certain circles.

Money. Power. Immunity.

A sick, twisted little fuck who built his empire on broken children; their cries echoing through halls lined with imported marble and velvet drapes.

He wore his last name like armor.

Walked around like his father's money made him untouchable.

But he forgot one thing.

Even gods can *bleed*.

And tonight, Isaac Romanov is going to learn that monsters like me don't knock when we come calling.

We just tear the door off the hinges.

I know the nicknames they whisper when they think I'm not listening.

The Shadow.

Death.

The last thing a man sees before he's dragged to God's doorstep and forced to knock.

They say I'm the devil's errand boy, the one who comes when your sins finally outweigh your soul.

And maybe they're right.

Isaac Romanov had that look about him when I first walked into the room. Relaxed, smug, convinced that his money, his name, the strings his family pulled behind closed doors, would get him out of Catalyst's walls unscathed.

He truly believed himself untouchable.

He isn't the first. He won't be the last.

But now?

Now he's curled on the floor like a kicked dog, bound and trembling.

His wrists are rubbed raw from hours of struggling against the restraints. Skin torn, flesh split, bruises blooming like rot beneath his pale, shaking arms.

And he's crying.

Begging.

As if mercy is something he has ever deserved.

Every breath he takes comes out jagged.

Every word, a plea to a god that stopped listening the moment he touched his first victim.

But I'm not here to save Isaac.

I'm here to make him remember every name he thought he could forget.

It's all pain now.

The pain we've inflicted.

The pain I've perfected.

And the truth is, I don't look away from it. I savor it.

In the heat of it, I catch the subtle curl of my lip when the first drop of blood spills.

The way my pulse quickens, like a drug every time a cry gets louder, sharper, more desperate.

And in their last moments, I see it. Not just their fear, but the reflection of my smile, the gleam of my satisfaction shining in their final gaze.

I am the closing chapter.

The final face they see before the void takes hold.

The last flicker of light before they're swallowed whole by the dark.

"Pull another one," I mutter, my voice low and even.

Isaac flinches at the command, his broken sobs catching in his throat.

His feet claw at the dirt beneath him like it might save him.

It won't.

He looks up at me, and for the first time, I think he understands.

There's no escaping the reckoning.

Not when I'm the one holding the scales.

"No," he gasps, like the word might shield him. Like that single syllable could somehow stop what's already coming for him.

"No-"

"Yes."

My smile is slow, deliberate...cruel.

"You don't get the luxury of having an option."

"I told you everything I know!" Isaac screams, desperation cracking his voice in half. The sound bounces off the walls of the holding cell, swallowed by the cold stone and steel around us.

He's hoping the echoes will make him sound more convincing.

They don't.

"I know that," I scoff. "But that doesn't change a goddamn thing, does it?"

Stepping closer, I let him feel the weight of what's next before I even lay a hand on him.

"What you've done. What you *would* continue to do if I let you walk out of here in one piece..."

I pause, studying the way his eyes twitch, the way his mouth curls inward like he's trying to swallow the truth.

"What was the youngest you took from their mother?"

His lips clamp shut.

His silence says everything.

"Five... was it?" I ask, voice low and steady, like a loaded gun.

He doesn't answer.

He doesn't need to.

The heat rises in my chest. Not rage. Not anymore.

Just purpose.

Shaking my head, I snatch the pliers from my man's outstretched hand, metal clanging softly against my palm.

Isaac flinches.

Grabbing his wrist, I yank it forward—hard. The movement is sudden, brutal. He yelps, trying to pull away, but he knows better. There's no escape now.

"It was a job," he hisses, spitting blood as he speaks.

"I was following orders. Just like your men blindly follow you now. She was nothing. A means to an end in my father's eyes."

There it is.

His father.

Dimitri Romanov.

The root of this entire cancer.

Catalyst's most hunted parasite.

Every vile act I've traced... every life ruined... every child broken... all roads lead back to him. To a Romanov.

"And what happened to that five-year-old girl?" I grind out, each word like acid on my tongue. "How much did your father make off the innocence he sold to the highest bidder?"

Isaac's lips tremble. He's fighting to stay silent.

Coward.

"Not talking now? Fine."

Tightening my grip, I force the pliers down again.

Another nail.

Another scream.

This one shatters something in him.

And something in me... likes the sound.

"She died!" he finally wails. "She died, okay?! They used her, and when they were done, they *killed* her!"

"They?" I echo, the word crawling out of me like poison. "You say that as if you weren't there. As if you weren't part of it."

He sobs, loud and ugly, the sound bubbling through broken ribs and a shattered conscience. Blood smears his face, a mix of red snot and tears, and for a fleeting moment I wonder...

Is this what fear feels like to him?

Because if it is, it's not even close to what he made that little girl feel.

The heavy metal door creaks open, hinges groaning like the cell itself is protesting what it's seen. A flood of sterile LED light spills in, bleeding across the blood-stained floor in jagged streaks. The room smells like iron and violence.

"Echo?"

Like clockwork.

Right on cue.

The voice of reason.

The conscience I never asked for, dressed in black and burdened by his badge of morality.

"Roman," I murmur, lips curving into a smirk as I watch him hesitate in the doorway.

My closest ally. My reluctant anchor.

He takes in the sight: Isaac Romanov slumped in chains, the floor slick with blood, fingernails missing, face a grotesque canvas of what pain looks like when it's earned.

Roman's jaw tightens, his fingers brushing against his watch.

"Your interrogation of Mr. Romanov was only supposed to last an hour."

I cock my head, feigning surprise. "I don't remember asking you to delegate my time."

He bristles, just slightly. The Roman I know is always walking the razor's edge between approval and horror.

Still, he answers.

"Yes. They still want him back. Alive."

"Perfect."

The word drips from my mouth like poison dressed as honey.

Before he can finish his next breath, my hand moves.

Quick. Fluid. Without hesitation.

I draw my Glock from its holster, the motion so fast, so rehearsed, it's practically instinct.

The barrel finds Isaac's forehead, right between the eyes, the sweet spot where cowards finally meet consequence.

The shot cracks through the air like thunder.

A single, brutal punctuation mark to everything he's ever done.

Blood sprays in a crimson arc as the bullet tears through bone. Isaac's body twitches violently, muscles seizing in those final involuntary spasms.

Then stillness.

True, blessed stillness.

"Send them the body," I say, stepping over the corpse. "Courtesy of Catalyst."

Patting Roman on the shoulder as I pass, the gesture is casual, almost affectionate, but his eyes are elsewhere, fixed on the spreading pool of blood, his mouth a tight, silent line.

"There are some things we need to discuss," he says finally, voice clipped, unreadable.

"There better be bourbon," I reply, riding the high like it's laced with something illegal.

Because it is a high.

The world has one less monster in it.

And for the first time today, it feels like justice actually bled.

Gazing out the window of my office, I watch as fog coils through the forest like smoke from a freshly fired gun. The pines outside stand tall, but blurred, drowned in thick clouds, like ghosts haunting the treetops.

It's quiet here.

Still.

The kind of silence that follows a justified execution.

Bourbon warms my throat, every sip a slow burn, every drop a reward. I let it settle in my stomach, grounding me.

For a moment, I savor the peace, until Roman's voice cuts through it.

"You just killed Dimitri Romanov's first heir," he says from behind me, like I'm unaware of the weight in the trigger I pulled.

I don't turn.

Can't even get five seconds to enjoy the end of a monster without Roman dragging me back to his high ground.

"That little shit was trafficking children, Roman," I say, flicking my eyes toward the fog again. "Worse than a certain Faulkner we both once knew."

Glancing over my shoulder, I meet the iron edge in his gaze. He's too serious. Always is.

"Have you forgotten how we handle problems like that?" I ask.

"I haven't forgotten," he growls. "But have *you* forgotten what kind of message that sends? Blood like this, Dimitri's blood, doesn't dry quietly. I have a family, Echo. *Little girls*. And Noah, he's got a family too-"

There he goes again.

Preaching.

Challenging.

The glass slams against the edge of my desk before I even think to stop myself.

It shatters beneath my hand, crystal shards slicing into my skin.

Roman flinches, not at the sound, but at the blood.

The red runs thick, warm, down my palm.

But I don't feel it.

Pain is a language I no longer translate.

Instead, I turn. Slowly. Deliberately.

He sees it in my eyes, that glint of something feral, something that doesn't ask for permission.

"Do not question me, Roman," I warn, voice steady as thunder. "I brought you into Catalyst because you're one hell of a man. You served with me in the army. You've bled with me. Followed me into fire. But don't think, not for one *goddamn* second, that I don't know what I'm doing."

Moving toward him, my steps are calm and measured, the blood from my palm pooling at my fingertips.
One droplet. Then another.

"I told you, I protect my people. Always. What you're doing now?" I press my finger, bloodied and unflinching, into the center of his chest. "That sounds a hell of a lot like *doubt*."

Roman's breath catches, his jaw tightening.

But his eyes never leave mine.

"Do you doubt me, Roman?" I whisper. "Do you doubt my *authority?*"

His lips press into a firm line. Then, a slow shake of his head.

"No, sir."

"Good."

The word lands like a verdict.

As if summoned by tension itself, three knocks strike the office door, sharp and precise.

A pause. A breath.

"Come in," I call, wrapping my tie around the bleeding hand, watching the red soak through the cloth like ink in water.

The door opens, and in strolls Noah Ackerman, Catalyst's all-seeing eye, arms stacked with files and curiosity as he steps into the tension like it's a second skin.

"Sir," he says carefully. "I have that file you requested-"

He trails off, eyes darting between me and Roman, sensing the aftermath of something heavy.

"Did I come at a bad time?"

"No, you're fine, Noah," I snap. Too sharp. Too soon. But I don't apologize.

"You're bleeding-"

"He said he's fine, Noah," Roman cuts in, voice gravelly but loyal.

"What's the file?"

"Open it," I say, gesturing toward the folders with my wrapped hand.

Noah passes one to Roman.

I tap the cover twice, slow and sure.

"Issac wasn't the only heir of Dimitri's that I've had my eyes on."

I smile now, calm, assured, the high of vengeance still simmering beneath my skin.

"Issac was a problem."I lean forward, voice dropping into something darker."But *she*... she's leverage."

A pause.

A beat.

Blissful fucking leverage.

2

Blood, Sweat, and Bloodlines

Katya

"Again!"

Her voice cuts through the room like a blade, and a moment later, Maria's foot does too.

Maria's leg slams into my side, the sharp strike knocking the wind from my lungs. Pain blooms beneath my ribs as I hit the floor, the impact jarring, my body already begging for rest. But there's no room for mercy here.

Not in this place.

Not under *her*.

Before Maria's satin-covered foot can come crashing down on my chest, I roll, sweat-slick palms slipping against the polished floor. I lash my leg out in a last-ditch attempt to sweep her ankles and bring her down with me.

But Maria moves like smoke, graceful and elusive.

The blade in her hand flashes under the studio lights, and I feel the whisper of its edge graze far too close to my skin. Instead of the floor, the tip of her knife nearly finds my arm.

I suck in a breath, sharp and ragged, my muscles trembling from fatigue.

"You'll have to be quicker than that," Maria taunts, her voice sugarcoated in mockery.

She stalks forward, feline and poised, and with a flick of her wrist, she drags her blade across my cheek. Not deep, but deliberate. A reminder. A signature. A threat.

I recoil instinctively, blood blooming warm against my skin. Lifting trembling fingers to my face, I trace the cut, crimson now painting my pale cheek in a thick, angry smear.

"Get up, Katya!"

Mrs. Pavlov's voice is a hissed command, sharp as broken glass.

Her hair is coiled into its usual severe bun, not a single strand out of place. Her eyes are reptilian, cold, watchful...unblinking. In her hand, she clutches the thin metal rod that's already kissed my back more times than I can count.

Every mistake. Every hesitation. Every falter is met with steel. Punishment is as much a part of the routine as the steps themselves.

"It is all about *grace,* ladies," Mrs. Pavlov says, circling like a vulture. "Your movements must be beautiful... and lethal. You are not girls. You are weapons. Remember that."

Maria steps back as I slide my knife toward her.

She doesn't flinch.

Her feet glide effortlessly, body moving like she was born in rhythm with violence.

There's no pain in her eyes. No fear. Only satisfaction.

My back throbs, raw and striped with welts. Maria's skin remains untouched, unpunished. Of course it does.

Gritting my teeth, I force myself upright. My feet scream in protest. The tips of my pointe shoes are soaked with blood, the fabric fraying, skin inside torn and raw. Each step is agony.

But I push through it, because to fail again means another strike. Another mark. Another smirk from Maria.

Maria watches me with the grin of someone who knows she's already won.

"Katya," Mrs. Pavlov purrs, stepping close enough for her cold perfume to burn in my nose. "Run through your routine again."

I swallow...hard.

My body is already collapsing beneath me: legs shaking, toes throbbing and my vision hazy.

But I raise my arms, set my position, and lift to a pointe.

I turn.

Once.

Twice.

Three times.

Each one shakier than the last. My form falters, balance slipping as pain sears up my legs.

"Grace," Pavlov snaps.

The rod comes down, slicing across my shoulder blades.

"Poise."

Another strike. This time across my lower back.

"*Dignity.*"

The third blow sends me to my knees.

"Stop!" I cry out, the word torn from my throat.

My knees crack against the floor, my feet crumpling beneath me. My toes scream within the confines of bloodstained satin. Finally giving in; I collapse, my body broken and trembling.

And yet, I know this isn't the end of it.

Not here.

Not with *her.*

Behind me, laughter bubbles like poison. Snickering, Maria tilts her head and shakes it slowly, her golden braid swinging behind her like a noose.

The other girls join in with twisted smiles, their eyes gleaming, not with pity, but with pleasure.

They love watching me fail.

They feed on it.

"It would seem the rest of you value the money your families have put into your training," Mrs. Pavlov says, her voice thick with disdain.

A sneer clings to her face as she paces past them, her heels clicking against the polished floor like gunfire. "You are all excused for today."

She waves her hand, as if dismissing insects.

The girls scatter like the well-trained, well-fed wolves they are, casting smug glances over their shoulders as they leave. Maria lingers the longest, soaking in my humiliation like it's sunlight, basking in it.

Trying to push myself up, my arms tremble beneath me. The pain in my back is a low roar, my knees raw from the cold, unforgiving floor.

Crack.

Her rod lands again, slapping across the fresh bruises on my spine. I let out a dull whimper, my voice barely more than a breath. Then she crouches beside me, quiet and cold.

Lifting my chin with the metal tip of her rod, she forces my eyes to meet hers.

Her gaze is merciless.

The look of someone who's made a life out of sculpting killers.

"You think because your father is *Dimitri Romanov* you get it easier?" she hisses, her lip curling.

No warmth. No softness. Only ice.

"You think being a Romanov means you're above this?"

She leans closer, her breath venomous. "Your father is the very reason those girls get to sleep in penthouses. The reason they eat. The reason I have a villa in the South of France. *He pays for their comfort.* And you..." Her rod presses into my throat now, just enough to remind me how easily she could crush me. "You are supposed to carry that legacy."

She pulls back, standing tall again, like I'm not even worth the breath it took to dress me down.

"The Romanov empire will not survive on the back of a weak, spineless girl. *Stand up.*"

I do.

Somehow, I do.

Despite the screaming of my bones.

Despite the swelling in my ankles and the blood soaking through my shoes.

Despite the way my entire body feels like it's being stitched together by willpower alone.

"You will run through the routine," she snaps, turning her back to me. "*Until your body gives out from exhaustion.*"

"And if you do not beat Maria tomorrow..." She pauses, looking over her shoulder, her eyes narrowed, dead and hungry. "I *promise* you, Katya, you will learn what *real* pain feels like."

My throat tightens. My vision swims. My pulse thunders like it's trying to break out of my chest.

This is the cost.

The unspoken price of being *his* daughter.

The price of being a *Romanov*.

3

SPARE THE ROD, KILL THE ROMANOV

KATYA

"Thank you," I say flatly to the taxi driver, barely mustering the energy to sound polite. The exhaustion from training clings to me like wet cloth, heavy and suffocating. My muscles ache beneath my uniform, skin raw beneath the layers. I press my spine against the seat for one final moment of stillness before forcing myself to step out onto the gravel path leading to my father's home.

I expect quiet. Darkness. Maybe one of the guards at the gate and nothing more. But instead, three of my father's men are waiting for me on the front steps, their silhouettes sharp under the exterior lights. Their posture is off. Too stiff...too alert. Glancing around instinctively, I half-expect to see him standing with them, arms crossed, ready to issue a cold critique on whatever bruises I've brought home this time. That's usually the routine. He meets me after class, assesses the damage I couldn't avoid, then adds his own punishment to the tally. When he's satisfied, I'm sent home to lick my wounds in silence. It's methodical. It's familiar.

Tonight is not.

"Where is my father-" I start as I climb out of the cab, adjusting my bag higher on my shoulder despite the burning ache in my muscles.

"Your father and mother have requested your presence immediately. It's urgent," one of the guards replies without hesitation.

His tone is clipped, rehearsed. My stomach knots. My father never sends men to retrieve me, not unless something has gone horribly wrong. He's always warned against displays of force that draw attention, saying discretion is what keeps us alive. But now, not only have his men been sent to fetch me, they're on edge. Their hands hover near their weapons, fingers twitching like they're expecting a shootout on the doorstep.

As I limp across the foyer and into the house, I try to find my footing. The pain in my ankles are sharp and constant, radiating from beneath the blood-stained satin of my shoes. Every step reminds me of today's failures, of Maria's blade slicing across my cheek, of Mrs. Pavlov's rod snapping down again and again. I ache everywhere, and the last thing I want is to be dragged into some family crisis.

"Has Isaac made it home yet?" I ask, hoping for something normal. My voice cuts through the silence, but none of them answer. Not even a glance in my direction. Just more quiet.

"Is that a no?" I push again, but the silence holds.

I clench my jaw, resisting the urge to scream. All I want is to sleep, soak in a hot bath, and maybe feel human again for five minutes. But the way they're guiding me now, tight formation, watchful eyes, it feels like I'm being led into something much colder.

For a long time, I let Isaac carry the weight of our legacy. He was always the one to sit at the table, to issue the orders, to dirty his hands in front of the family while I bled behind closed doors. I've tried to play my part, quiet, obedient, efficient. Not a daughter. Not a sister. A tool. A weapon they could shape into whatever the Romanov name required. I've never fooled myself into thinking we're good people. Our empire is built on blood, drugs, guns, hitmen, women sold and silenced. There are truths I know, and others I've trained myself not to look at too closely.

Still, I was born into this life. I didn't choose it. No one gave me the option to be anything else.

Reaching for the handle of my father's study, my hand trembles slightly—not from fear, but from sheer physical exhaustion. The doors swing open, and immediately, the temperature shifts. The air is warm from the roaring fireplace, but everything else feels frozen.

My father stands with his back to me, staring into the flames as if they've spoken some private revelation. My mother is seated in his chair, her posture stiff, her gaze distant. She doesn't turn to look at me. She doesn't blink.

Lining the room are men I know too well, my father's closest confidants. The fathers of the girls I train with. Business partners. Men who have orchestrated empires of violence from behind polished mahogany desks. Each of them clutches a glass of bourbon like it might shatter in their grip. No one speaks. No one acknowledges me.

Something is wrong.

"Right this way," one of my father's men whispers, his voice barely audible over the pounding in my ears.

Following without a word, the air in the estate grows heavier with each step I take. The deeper we move into the house, the more suffocating it becomes, like the walls themselves are pressing in around me. The low hum of murmured conversation dies as I step into the study, the room thick with tension and the scent of aged liquor and woodsmoke.

One of the maids approaches quietly, a glass of dark red wine already in her hand. Without waiting for permission, she presses it to my lips.

"Drink, Ms. Katya. You will need," she urges in a hushed accent, her voice trembling as if she already knows what I'm about to see.

She tilts the glass until the bitter liquid spills past my lips, forcing me to drink until the wine trickles down my chin and stains the front of my shirt. I wipe my mouth with the back of my sleeve, blinking away the sting of alcohol and confusion.

"What... what is this?" I ask, my voice barely above a whisper. "Dad?"

At the sound of my voice, the entire room turns in eerie unison. The heads of every man seated around the room, my father's most trusted associates, the same men who have watched me grow from girl to weapon, shift to look at me.

Their expressions are unreadable. Cold. Their silence louder than any scream.

My father stands behind his desk, hands braced on the polished wood, knuckles pale. He doesn't speak immediately, and when he finally does, it's without warmth.

"Come here."

His voice is low and stern, meant to be obeyed. The tap of his finger against the desk is sharp, final. There is no room for hesitation.

Slowly moving toward him, each step is more reluctant than the last. My gaze drifts to my mother seated beside the fire. She hasn't moved. Her face is a stone mask, eyes locked on the dancing flames as though they're the only thing keeping her anchored.

"Mom," I whisper, "what's-"

The words stop.

A scream builds in the back of my throat, but it dies before it ever reaches the air. My breath catches violently, torn into ragged fragments as my vision tunnels in on the nightmare before me.

There, sprawled on the floor beside my father's desk, is Isaac.

Or... what's left of him.

His face is frozen mid-expression, eyes wide, clouded over with death. A perfect, round bullet hole is bored into the center of his forehead, the wound so precise it almost looks surgical. But the mess around it isn't. Blood pools beneath his skull, soaking into the Persian rug. His nails are jagged, torn as if he clawed at something, or someone, before the end. His arms are bent at unnatural angles. Bones protruding from his wrist like white shards of porcelain.

I can see *inside* his skull.

And the worst part is that no one is moving. No one is weeping. No one is yelling.

This is... expected. Controlled.

My knees buckle. I turn away, bile racing up my throat as my stomach twists violently.

Don't vomit. You've seen a dead body before. This isn't new. You've seen worse. You were trained for this.

But it's Isaac.

Oh my god. It's Isaac.

Don't vomit. Don't-

My body betrays me. I double over, retching hard, the acidic burn clawing its way up my throat. The contents of my stomach splash across my bloodied ballet shoes, the sharp scent of wine mixing with vomit and sweat.

Gasping for air, I brace a trembling hand on the wall, my vision blurring with tears I refuse to let fall.

"Jesus Christ," I choke out, wiping the back of my hand across my mouth, my voice raw. "What the hell is going on?"

But no one answers.

And the silence, again, is louder than anything else.

I barely register the sound of my father's men stepping toward me. Everything is muffled now, distant, like I'm underwater. The only thing that cuts through the haze is his voice, cold and clipped, void of anything resembling comfort.

"Let her deal with it," my father commands, waving off the instinctive movement of his men. "Do not coddle her." His tone is sharp, each word slicing through the air like a blade. "She needs to *see* it. She needs to see what they did to her brother."

Terror swells inside me, flooding every inch of my chest. "What the fuck happened?" I rasp, my voice shaky with rage and disbelief. My hands are trembling, my knees threatening to buckle again. My heart is pounding so loudly I can barely think.

My father doesn't answer with words at first, only action. He tosses back the last of his drink, the clink of glass echoing through the silent room. Then, with a fury barely restrained, he marches toward Isaac's body, crouching low like he's about to discipline a child instead of mourn a son. He grabs Isaac by the hair and lifts his head, holding it up like a trophy gone to rot.

"Your brother was *careless*," he barks, giving the body a violent shake. My mother sobs behind him, but he doesn't even flinch. "Your brother was *ignorant*," he snarls, before spitting directly onto Isaac's slack, bloodied face. He lets go, and Isaac's head hits the floor with a sickening *thud*.

I want to scream.

I want to reach for him, *not my father*, but Isaac. The brother who once swore he'd never let this life touch me. The brother who promised he'd carry the Romanov name so I wouldn't have to. But now he's nothing more than a body in my father's study, discarded like garbage.

From his coat, my father pulls a bloodstained envelope and shoves it into my chest, pressing it there until I have no choice but to take it. His breath reeks of liquor, rage rolling of him in waves.

"And now," he says, voice low, eyes wild, "we all have a common enemy."

Staring down at the letter, my fingers trace the familiar emblem on the front. The blood has dried around the edges, leaving a crusted border that flakes beneath my touch. My stomach turns violently.

I know this symbol.

I've seen it before.

"Catalyst," I whisper, nausea clawing its way back up my throat.

"Catalyst," my father confirms, the word bitter in his mouth. "The same Catalyst your brother was supposed to have handled. A job he assured me was finished. That their CEO had been taken care of. That there were no loose ends." He gestures toward Isaac's broken corpse, lips curling. "Well, I suppose *this* is the loose end now."

The room falls silent again, but this time, every eye is on me. Waiting.

I swallow hard, bile still thick in my throat. "Now what?" I ask quietly, hating how fragile I sound.

My father steps closer, eyes narrowing with a look that could shatter glass. "Now," he says, almost in a whisper, "you don't fuck up."

He turns to his men, his voice rising again. "She goes nowhere alone. She attends every lesson. She misses *nothing*. I want her involved in every family decision from this moment forward." Stepping close, he grips my chin tightly between his fingers, studying me like a puzzle he doesn't trust to stay intact. His eyes are filled with expectation. Fury. Fear, maybe, but it's buried beneath so many layers of control it's impossible to reach.

"Don't disappoint me," he murmurs.

He nudges my chin away like I'm something disposable, and I turn back toward Isaac. My brother's lifeless gaze meets mine again. My father's spit still glistens on his face.

"I want him in the crypt," my father growls. "Not that he deserves it."

Glancing toward my mother. I wait for her to speak up. To cry out. To say something.

But she doesn't.

She doesn't even look at me.

"You're excused," my father mutters. "You have a busy day tomorrow. Go home."

I don't say a word. My legs move before my mind catches up, guiding me toward the door. As I step out of the study, I nearly slip on my own vomit, slick, sour, still fresh from the horror of earlier. The door shuts behind me with a deep, final thud, sealing the room, and everything inside it, away.

Standing there, frozen, I struggle to catch my breath. It's the first real inhale I've managed since I entered this godforsaken house. But it doesn't feel like relief.

It feels like drowning.

My father's men are already waiting in the hall, their expressions unreadable, their eyes hollow. They'll drive me home, like always. Pretending nothing happened; pretending the world hasn't just shifted beneath my feet.

And as I stare past them into the darkened hallway, the weight of it all settles over me like a second skin.

All I want to do is scream.

But I can't.

Not yet.

4

ESPRESSO AND DECEIT

ECHO

Coffee. Every morning.

Espresso…black, bitter, unforgiving.

No sugar. No cream.

The kind of drink that leaves an aftertaste, sharp and lingering, much like the woman who sips it.

She's disciplined, that much is clear. Every calorie accounted for, every indulgence denied. She eats just enough to stay upright, never enough to be noticed. Not too thin to draw concern, not too full to be criticized. It's a delicate balance, one she's learned to master. Because in her world, attention is a weapon. And being a target? Fatal.

Two men trail her movements, always nearby but never directly beside her. Well-dressed shadows playing the role of disinterested bystander, though their eyes scan every corner, every face that dares come too close. They're protection, of course, but also a warning.

Katya Romanov is never alone.

She sits bundled outside the café, despite the rising heat of summer, her body cocooned in oversized layers. A thick wool coat despite the sun. Dark designer shades hide her eyes, and her inky black hair is pulled back in a sleek knot. Her skin is pale, untouched by light, porcelain behind a veil.

She looks fragile at a glance, silent, delicate, and still. But watch long enough, and you'll see the tremble in her fingers. The way her shoulders flinch ever so slightly each time someone walks too near. Her gaze drops quickly, hiding behind the rim of her espresso cup. She doesn't speak to anyone. She doesn't linger long. She lazily sips her coffee, watches and waits, then, reacts.

Is she mourning? That's the question that keeps circling.

Mourning *him*—her brother. Isaac Romanov.

But how does one mourn the death of a monster?

I study her from the safety of my car, engine off, the windows tinted black. The file Noah compiled rests on the passenger seat beside me, thin and frustratingly vague. There isn't much to go on, no real dirt, no confirmed crimes. Just rumors. Whispers. Her name scattered across transaction logs and social events, her presence always surface level. Never bloody. Never provable.

Katya Romanov. Twenty-five. Second-born. Publicly less involved in the empire than her brother, but no less dangerous, according to our sources. She's not the blade. Not the hand that strikes. She's the face of the deal, the one they send when they want to appear clean.

The file lists her upcoming engagements, appearances, and family gatherings.

And then it's there.

Sworn to be wed to Nikolai Sokolov.

Tapping my fingers along the steering wheel, the name sits bitter in my mouth like acid.

Nikolai. That smug little bastard. The same one who torched a whole operation last year and left two dozen of my men in body bags. Charming. Vicious. Loyal to a fault. And now he's been promised Katya?

"So... Little Butterfly," I mutter under my breath, watching her rise from her table, tucking her chin low as her guards circle close. "Daddy wants you protected. And Nikolai wants your cunt." I scoff, shaking my head, smirking despite the gravity of the situation.

You can wrap her in velvet and keep her behind glass, but she's still part of the machine. Still a Romanov. Still leverage.

Especially now.

Watching her leave, her guards are suddenly more alert. My little gift from last week must've rattled them. A threat delivered without a sound. A warning stitched into the envelope that arrived on their doorstep.

She may not know it yet, but she's already part of the game.

And I'm done watching from the sidelines.

"Seems like you're perfect after all," I murmur, eyes following her until she disappears down the block. "Delicate, obedient, untouchable."

A butterfly pinned beneath glass.

Let's see how long she stays that way.

Pulling out my phone with shaking hands, my fingers move before my mind can even catch up. There's no time to hesitate, not when every second feels like it's working against me.

"Call Noah," I mutter, pressing the device to my ear, my fingers tapping out an uneven rhythm against the dashboard as it rings. Once. Twice. Three times.

"Shit, man, it's not even seven yet-"

"I don't pay you to bitch," I snap, voice sharp with edge. "You said Dimitri was transferring funds to a warehouse downtown. What's the address?"

There's a pause, followed by the muffled groan of someone else, his fiancé, most likely, grumbling in the background. Noah sighs, clearly half-awake, but not stupid enough to test my patience further.

"Aren't you supposed to be off?" he asks, tone groggy but pointed.

"The *address*, Noah."

Another beat of silence. I can hear the sound of fingers flying across a keyboard now, the quiet click of urgency in his movements.

"I'll send it over," he mutters. Then, hesitating, "Does Roman know you're working-"

"Have a good day off, Noah," I cut him off, ending the call before he can finish. I toss the phone onto the passenger seat, the screen lighting up a second later with an incoming message. The location. The coordinates. The confirmation that I'm not just chasing a ghost.

The adrenaline surges now, hot and blinding. It floods my veins, sharpening my focus, dulling the exhaustion I hadn't realized was clinging to the corners of my vision. My hand shakes, just barely, the phantom of hesitation tracing across my thoughts.

Glancing down at Roman's contact on the screen, my thumb hovers over the call button. A single name, one tap away. The rational part of me, the one he helped build, knows I should tell him. Loop him in. Be smart.

But it's just a quick peek. A look.

Nothing more.

Reaching down, I yank my sidearm from its holster, popping the magazine free with a practiced flick of my thumb. I count the bullets, one by one, more out of habit than need.

Fully loaded.

No safety net. No backup. Just me, and the truth waiting to be uncovered.

Reinserting the magazine with a sharp click, the sound is like a promise in the silence.

No need to call Roman.

Not for this.

Not when I know damn well, there's no rest for the *wicked*.

5

Fool Me Once, Pay The Price

Katya

"Did you come to play today?" Maria sneers, eyes narrowing with mockery, voice thick with venom.

The sting in my feet is relentless, but I push through it, letting the harsh melody of Mrs. Pavlov's piano drag me into rhythm. Each note slices through the haze of pain, grounding me in movement. The sharp, deliberate chords mask the aches of last week, the bruises, the shame, the memory of Isaac's lifeless face.

"What's wrong? Gone mute?" Maria presses, circling closer. "Can't think now that big brother is-"

My arm lashes out before her sentence finishes. Steel bites through skin, and the red that blooms across her arm is instant. She stumbles back, clutching the wound, surprise flashing in her eyes. The sight of her faltering fuels something buried deep inside, something desperate and unrelenting.

Momentum carries me forward. Spinning hard on the ball of my foot, I drive my leg into her wrist, sending her knife clattering to the floor. Blood drips freely now from her arm, painting a trail as she staggers, her body barely holding form. The skin inside my shoes burns raw, every pivot cutting deeper. Still, movement doesn't stop. It *can't*.

Mrs. Pavlov circles like a shark, eyes sharp, expression carved from stone. With no hesitation, she brings the metal rod down on Maria's back. The sound of it cracking against flesh echoes through the studio.

"Pick it up," she hisses. "You're not done."

Maria trembles as she bends to retrieve the blade. Fingers slick with blood, she lifts it toward me again, her face pale, her eyes never leaving mine.

"He is dead," the words leave my lips before I can stop them, low, steady and dangerous. "But I'm not."

"Shame," she breathes, her voice shaking just enough to betray her. "Would've been doing the world a favor."

Grace.

Poise.

Humility.

The words echo in my skull, Mrs. Pavlov's pillars of control, etched into us like commandments.

And yet, none of them have ever belonged to me.

Not grace when survival demands brutality.

Not poise when blood slicks my hands.

Not humility when every day is a war.

Just pain.

Discipline.

And the fire that's finally starting to burn back.

The knife clatters to the floor, forgotten. Grace no longer matters. Precision, poise, control, none of it survives the heat flooding through my veins. The rage that's been simmering beneath the surface boils over, breaking through the carefully constructed shell they've forced me into. Every welt from Mrs. Pavlov's rod, every sneer from my father, every moment Isaac's lifeless body was paraded like some grotesque warning, it all crashes into me at once.

All because of my name.

Romanov.

A legacy soaked in blood, and now it's bleeding out of me.

"You fucking *bitch*," the words rip from my throat, sharp and unfiltered, right before my fist connects with Maria's jaw.

The impact is solid, satisfying. Her head snaps to the side as she tumbles backward, hitting the floor in a graceless heap. A chorus of gasps erupts from the girls around us, the room falling into stunned silence. Even Mrs. Pavlov yells, the sharpness of her voice barely cutting through the static in my head.

Maria scrambles to sit up, blood pouring from her nose, her eyes wide with a mixture of shock and fear. Another blow lands, this one harder, fueled by years of swallowing everything that should've been screamed.

"My *brother* will hear about this!" she shrieks, her voice cracking.

"*Tell him*," I hiss, towering over her. "Tell him his delicate little bride-to-be just beat the shit out of his cunt-whore of a sister."

The words hang in the air like smoke, filthy and thick, impossible to ignore.

A hand clamps around my wrist before the next punch can land. Mrs. Pavlov yanks me back, her face twisted in disgust, eyes wide like she's staring at a wild animal she no longer recognizes.

"My girls do not fight like men," she snaps, her voice trembling with rage. "*Stand up.*"

Breathing hard, I pull away from Maria, chest heaving. The girls who once giggled behind raised hands now rush to Maria's side, lifting her to her feet with hesitant touches, as if being near her might invite the same punishment.

"You were sent to me to be sculpted into graceful weapons," Pavlov continues, circling me now. "Not turned into rabid dogs. What do you think your father will say when he hears of this?"

A slow smile spreads across my face as I glance toward Maria, her once-perfect features marred with bruises and blood.

"I don't know," the words slide out with ease, "but I know that felt *fucking* amazing."

Dragging my wrist from Pavlov's grip, I spit on the floor, letting it land like a final insult between us. Her lips twitch with fury, but she doesn't speak. She doesn't have to.

The other girls part as I walk past, their wide eyes following me like I've become something else entirely. Not Katya the Romanov daughter. Not Katya the dancer. Something new. Something dangerous.

And for the first time in what feels like years, I don't feel like a puppet on a string.

I feel *alive*.

6

There Is No Running From Your Shadow

Echo

"I'd say this is far from fucking abandoned," the words come out low, almost to myself, as I crouch behind the tree line, peering through the scope at the mess of blacked-out SUVs crowding the lot.

The building ahead is falling apart, brick chipped, windows cracked, graffiti scrawled across the face like scars, but the vehicles tell another story. The way they line the perimeter with tactical precision, their engines still warm, the way the drivers remain seated, eyes alert, none of this is accidental. This place is active. Alive.

And dangerous.

Men and women gather just outside the rusted double doors, puffing on cigarettes with a nonchalance that doesn't match the weight on their hips. Each one strapped with a handgun, some with rifles slung casually over their backs. These aren't hired thugs. They move with training, with purpose.

Romanov inner circle.

Wherever my Little Butterfly has gone fluttering off to, she's not alone. Her father's friends, and their spawn, all present and accounted for. Familiar faces. Recognizable scars. Kids who grew up in this empire like it was a birthright, like the blood on their hands was always just ink on a ledger.

Security, no doubt. Watchdogs with sharp teeth.

And yet... careless.

Multiple entrances remain unguarded, side doors rusting on broken hinges, windows large enough to crawl through, blind spots easy to exploit. A ghost could've slipped in and out without so much as a whisper. Hell, *I* could've slipped in already.

They think proximity to the Romanov name makes them untouchable. That just being born into the inner circle grants them immunity from consequence.

No wonder Isaac was so easy to get to.

Complacency like this is a cancer.

And I'm here to cut it out.

That's the beauty of it, isn't it?

They'd never expect a strike this early. Never imagine I'd be bold, or reckless, enough to move this close to their territory. They're still licking their wounds, still scrambling to make sense of Isaac's death, still pretending their empire isn't crumbling at the edges.

Roman would call this careless.

Noah would say it's uncalculated, a decision fueled by emotion instead of reason.

But to me?

This is opportunity.

Every guard outside that building. Every pair of eyes distracted. Every vulnerable opening left unchecked. It all spells one thing: a chance to bleed them from the inside.

How many could I take out before they even knew I was there?

How many could I break before one of them finally leads me to her?

The building itself is nothing special, an aging fortress hidden behind rust and broken glass. But the blood money that keeps it running flows directly from the Romanov empire. Owned and operated under the guise of performance training, it's run by Genivive Pavlov, a name I know too well. An assassin trained in ballet and brutality alike.

What better cover than a stage?

What better grooming than dance?

Young women from the Romanovs' inner circle are shaped here, refined like porcelain, polished to perfection. Poised and elegant in public, but sharpened beneath the surface. Killers dressed in silk. Blades hidden behind ballerina smiles.

It's always the same with them.

They talk of legacy while hiding rot beneath the floorboards. a rot that spreads, infects, and destroys.

Isaac? He was just the beginning. A taste. A warning. A promise written in blood.

When I'm finished, there will be nothing left of their empire. No heirs. No handlers. No survivors to rebuild what they think they're entitled to.

Every demon Roman's faced. Every ghost lurking in Noah's closet. Every ruined life, every trafficked soul, every whispered scream in the dark, it all leads back here.

To them.

Catalyst wasn't born to challenge the Romanovs. It was forged to end them.

They smuggle. They manipulate. They break.

And I've seen what that leaves behind.

I remember the children.

The faces. The fear.

Tiny hands wrapped around my finger, desperate, pleading.

"Don't let go."

Not again.

Not this time.

Never again.

Never-

"What took you so long?" a voice breathes from the shadows, low and hushed.

Someone's already here.

A flicker of motion catches at the edge of my vision.

Lifting my head just enough to track it, I spot the hooded figure jogging toward a parked car just a few feet away. From my place on the bench across the street, half-shadowed beneath the branches of a dying tree, I watch in silence. The hood is drawn low, movements hurried but not uncoordinated. This isn't panic. This is intention.

The figure leans into the driver's side window. The voice that answers from inside is high, impatient, distinctly feminine.

"You caught me in the middle of something. Do you wanna go or not?" the driver snaps.

"I didn't ask you here for no reason," the hooded figure bites back, tossing something through the window. A small white pouch lands with a soft thud in the driver's lap before the girl, yes, girl, pulls back, her feet already moving.

She turns, heading my way.

Heart knocking against my ribcage, I lower the brim of my ball cap, keeping my head down just enough to stay invisible. She walks past without pausing, unaware that every step she takes has me gripping the edge of my seat.

Without raising suspicion, I tilt my phone upward, angling the camera just enough to catch her through the screen. A breath catches in my throat as the lens sharpens around her face.

Katya Romanov.

Blue-green eyes. Skin like porcelain. That same cold, unreadable gaze that's haunted the profiles I've studied a hundred times. But no photo, no surveillance footage has ever done her justice like seeing her now, flesh and blood, walking free under the open sky like she doesn't carry the weight of an empire on her shoulders.

There's a reason her family keeps her on a leash. A reason she's always guarded, always hidden beneath layers of silk and shadow.

And yet, here she is.

Alone. Hooded. On the move.

My grip tightens around the phone.

Where are you running off to, Little Butterfly?

And more importantly, who are you running from?

Passing your driver a pouch of coke just to slip past your own bodyguards?

Must be important.

That's not the kind of move someone makes on impulse. That's desperation, or something damn close to it. Whatever Katya Romanov is running toward, she doesn't want anyone from Daddy's inner circle knowing about it.

Her hand trembles as she reaches for the door handle. Mangled. Bruised. Blood still crusted along the knuckles. A little scuffle inside Genivive's fortress must've gone sideways fast. From the look of her, it wasn't much of a fight, at least not one she walked away from unscathed.

So, she's a fighter now?

Interesting.

Let's see how long that lasts.

The car engine hums to life, low and efficient, and she climbs in without looking back. I catch a clear view of the license plate before it merges into traffic, disappearing into the current of early morning chaos. Her trail won't stay warm forever, but it's warm enough for now.

Tapping the side of my phone, the screen is still lit with Noah's last text:

> Anything yet?

He's expecting silence. He knows today's my day off.

But that's the thing, isn't it?

Today's the perfect day *not* to follow the rules.

With one flick of my thumb, I kill my location. The GPS blinks out. No more breadcrumbs.

Noah can wait.

Roman can keep pretending everything's under control.

Because for the first time in weeks, the game has shifted.

And me?

I've got a trail to follow and no leash to hold me back.

Time to have a little *fun*.

7

THE PATH LESS TRAVELED

KATYA

"**Y**ou look like fucking shit," Nikolai laughs, the sound dry and grating as he fumbles with his house key. His fingers, jittery from whatever he took earlier, move quickly, not toward the door, but toward his next fix.

With practiced ease, he dumps a fresh line of coke onto the key's flat edge, snorts it without flinching, and exhales like it's the only thing keeping him standing.

"You can thank your sister for that," I mutter, flexing my bruised knuckles, watching the cracked skin pull tight over split bone. The sting is dull now. Familiar.

"Maria?" He arches a brow, shaking his head with a scoff. "Don't tell me you finally laid into her."

"More like... I finally stopped listening to Mrs. Pavlov."

He lets out a low whistle, running a hand through his already disheveled hair. "You know your father's gonna lose his mind when he hears about that. This isn't the time for you to start going rogue, Katya. Not after Isaac. Both our families are on edge. They're expecting us to be flawless."

I glance at him sideways, voice flat. "You only came to pick me up so you could check off a box on your family's weekly Romanov PR tour. Make Mommy and Daddy think you give a shit."

"It's all about the money, Katya dear," he sneers, mimicking my father's favorite phrase. "Our parents didn't marry for love, and neither will we. It's legacy. Power. That's all it's ever been. The least we can do is pretend, spare a few civil moments together so the time we're forced to share doesn't feel like outright war."

"Oh yes," I smile bitterly, "me, you, your coke lines, and your limp cock...a Romanov fairytale."

His eyes narrow, the grip on the wheel tightening as he exhales through his nose. The tension between us shifts, colder now, but not unfamiliar.

"My cock will be fine," he snaps, holding the bag of coke up between two fingers like a trophy. His gaze locks on mine, sharp and petulant. "So long as the Romanov drugs keep flowing my way."

My hand trails slowly across his thigh, deliberate and unhurried. Fingertips graze the soft fabric of his pants before slipping beneath, dancing lightly over the weak bulge hidden behind his boxers. No teasing, just intention. A firm grasp, a slow, calculated massage. Enough to get a reaction.

His breath catches, body stiffening beneath my touch. For a second, his eyes widen, not in pleasure, but in panic. There's no hunger in his expression, no heat. Just tension.

Coke cock.

The realization is enough to make my lips twitch with amusement.

He swats my hand away, too late to hide the embarrassment creeping up his neck. His cheeks flush red, and he fumbles with his pants, trying, and failing, to recover whatever dignity he thinks he has left.

"I have my doubts," I murmur, voice soft but loaded, watching him struggle.

His scowl is immediate. "You know," he snaps, still adjusting his waistband, "you really are a bitch."

A smile curls at the corner of my mouth, unfazed. "You're not betrothed to me for my *kind* attitude," I reply smoothly, leaning back, letting the silence stretch long enough for the humiliation to settle between us.

He doesn't answer.

He can't.

Because we both know the truth.

This arrangement was never built on compatibility, just power, inheritance, and appearances.

Eyes locked on Nikolai's GPS, I narrow my gaze. The route displayed on the screen winds deeper into forest than it should.

Less city. Less light. More trees. More isolation. The map shows us frozen in place, the icon of the car unmoving even as the tires hum beneath us.

Nikolai taps the screen with growing agitation. Nothing changes.

"What the fuck?" he mutters, leaning closer. White powder still clings to the edge of his nostrils, smeared like war paint. His high is wearing off, and with it, the illusion of control.

"I thought you were taking me home," I bite out, sitting up straighter.

"Traffic," he shoots back, almost defensive. "This way was supposed to be quicker-"

But something isn't right.

"Brakes," I say sharply, gaze darting to the road ahead.

Nikolai flinches but slams his foot down, jolting us to a hard stop. The tires screech against damp asphalt, and we both lurch forward.

Just ahead, an older SUV idles sideways in the middle of the lane, hazard lights off. A lone figure stands near the front of the vehicle, hunched under the lifted hood, his features obscured by a ball cap and shadow. At first glance, he looks harmless, one man, working on the dead engine.

But something feels... wrong.

He steps away from the hood, slowly, deliberately. Broad shoulders, tall frame, dark light brown curls that peek out from beneath his hat. Dressed in a black hoodie and dark jeans, he blends into the early evening like smoke. Hard to place his age, early thirties, maybe.

With a casual wave, he signals toward us and begins walking in a steady line toward Nikolai's side of the car.

Nikolai tenses beside me. His hand drifts low, curling around the grip of the pistol in his holster. His instincts are predictable, pull the gun, play the tough guy.

"What the hell is he doing?" he whispers, voice tight.

I swat his hand before he can fully draw. "His car's just broken down," I say under my breath. "Don't be a jackass. Roll the window down and try not to look like a paranoid cokehead."

Nikolai grits his teeth, then reluctantly pulls his hand away from the weapon and hits the window switch. It rolls down halfway, but the man is too tall, his torso blocks the view entirely, his face still obscured.

"Hey, man," the stranger says, his voice low, deep, and strangely smooth. "Got jumper cables? Battery's toast."

"This is a Tesla," Nikolai scoffs, rolling his eyes as he leans out the window.

"Which has a battery," I cut in. "Get out and help him. It's not like he can call for roadside out here. Signal's trash." Without waiting for a response, I swipe Nikolai's coke bag from the center console and hold it up like a prize.

His eyes snap wide.

"No more goodies," I smile coolly.

The switch flips in his face. Nikolai bares his teeth, practically growling. "You better get your entitled ass out and help," he hisses, throwing his door open with a loud metallic *creak*.

Rolling my eyes, I mirror the motion, stepping out into the crisp bite of the autumn air. Leaves scatter across the pavement, the quiet crackle beneath my boots louder than it should be. The air smells of pine, cold metal, and something else I can't name yet.

The man's still standing at the front of the SUV.

He hasn't stopped watching us.

"Do you have jumper cables?" Nikolai asks, his tone clipped, posture stiff.

"In my trunk," the man replies, motioning casually behind him. "I can grab them-"

"No," Nikolai snaps, cutting him off before he can finish. "I got it."

Without waiting for a response, he rounds the car toward the back, his gait sharp, erratic. The coke still has him on edge, short fuse, shallow breathing, every nerve fraying. He's one wrong word away from turning this into a shootout.

And just like that, I'm left alone with the stranger.

Only now do I really look at him. Really see him.

Golden-brown curls tousled under a ball cap. Skin sun-warmed and dusted with stubble. A thick scar cuts down his right cheek, catching just enough light to be noticed. His eyes are dark, unreadable, but not empty.

Tall. Broad. Older.

Up close, he could pass for a model in a rugged kind of way, like one of those fashion campaigns that tries too hard to look effortless. But there's something sharper beneath the exterior. Controlled. Coiled. A stillness that doesn't belong on someone stranded by a dead battery.

His eyes flick to mine, and my stomach dips.

There's weight in his gaze, like he's not just looking at me, but into me.

"What did you do to your hands?" he asks, voice low and steady.

I blink, instinctively curling my fingers before shoving both hands deep into pockets.

The skin on my knuckles is still raw, bruised and cracked from training, from Maria, from every time I stopped pretending to be someone delicate.

His question lands strange. Not condescending. Not amused. Just... curious. Which, somehow, is worse.

"Why does it matter?" I reply, tone flat.

"Just looks painful," he says, his gaze lingering. He doesn't push, but he doesn't look away either.

"It is," I admit after a beat. "Still, none of your concern."

His expression doesn't change, but something tightens in his jaw. He glances down the road, then toward the trees, like he's scanning for something.

Or someone.

"A lot of old money around these parts," he mutters, arms crossing over his chest. "Really nice car for two faces as young as yours to be driving."

There's something loaded in the way he says it. Not quite accusatory, but not casual, either.

"You ask a lot of questions," I whisper, voice low, fingers curling tighter around the hilt of the blade hidden in my pocket.

The metal is cool against my skin, grounding.

His gaze shifts back to me, expression unreadable.

And for a moment, the air feels like it's holding its breath.

"Do I?" he echoes, head tilting ever so slightly to the side.

There's something eerily calm about the way he says it, as if he's humoring me, drawing out the moment like a cat toying with a mouse.

"Nikolai?" I call out, louder this time, stepping back instinctively as the man takes a deliberate step forward.

No answer.

My heart stutters. No footsteps. No voice. Nothing.

The man nods slowly, that half-smile tugging again at the corners of his mouth. It doesn't reach his eyes.

Glancing toward the back of the car, the color drains from my face. Nikolai's body lies motionless near the open trunk, slumped across the gravel. Hands still wrapped around the jumper cables, his knuckles pale.

No rise and fall in his chest.

No twitch.

Just stillness.

Oh no.

My stomach twists. Adrenaline roars through me as I jerk my blade from my pocket, the hilt biting into my raw palms. The man lunges just as I slash, steel tearing across his palm in a quick, clean line.

He hisses, but the sound is amusement, not pain.

That smile returns, only now it's twisted. Unhinged.

He takes a step back, admiring the blood trickling from the wound like it's an offering. I hold the knife out between us, feet planted, ignoring the ache in my heels and the scream in my tendons. Pain has no place here now.

Only survival.

Who the *fuck* is this man?

"Fentanyl on the cables," he says casually, flexing his bleeding hand as he looks down at Nikolai's crumpled body. "Narcan's in my car. He might live. Might not. Honestly?" His eyes cut back to mine, voice dropping to a snarl. "He's not the one I came for."

Another step closer.

My grip tightens, blade steady, breath ragged.

"Step the fuck back before I show you what your insides look like," I growl, steel meeting steel in my voice.

His grin widens.

"This?" he asks, lifting his bleeding hand. "I *let* you do this Katya. I let you see me bleed."

And then, *God help me*, he drags his tongue slowly across the cut, licking the blood like it's some kind of ritual.

My stomach lurches.

What the actual *fuck*.

"You're sick," I spit. "How the hell do you know my name?" I seethe.

"How do I know your name?" he muses, ignoring the insult completely. His tone is taunting now, teeth bared in a smile that doesn't belong on a sane man. "How do I know *his* name? How did I reroute your Tesla's GPS without ever stepping inside it?"

He leans in, eyes gleaming.

"Who has all the questions now, *Katya?*"

It's the ink that gives him away.

A dark, inky tattoo etched into the underside of his wrist, revealed for the briefest moment as his sleeve shifts. But I know that mark, have memorized it in the nightmares that followed Isaac's death. It's more than a symbol. It's a signature.

Catalyst.

Everything inside me unravels at once. Thought dissolves. Training, instinct, grief, they all merge into one blinding surge of rage. I don't hesitate. My body moves before my mind catches up, launching forward as my voice rips out raw and venom-laced.

"You killed my brother!"

The knife flashes in my hand, silver catching in the fading light as I strike again and again. My aim is precise, but he's faster. He ducks every swing, his body moving like he's already memorized my rhythm. There's something calculated in the way he avoids each blow, not defensive, not panicked. Almost... entertained.

His hand shoots out, wrapping around my throat, not with the intent to strangle, but to command. One smooth motion and I'm driven back, slammed against the hood of the Tesla. The metal shudders beneath me, the impact rattling down my spine. My breath catches in my throat, but I don't cry out. I grit my teeth, refusing to give him the satisfaction.

Pain pulses behind my eyes. The blood, his, mine, I can't tell anymore, smears across my cheek and jaw. Copper thickens the air, seeping into my mouth. He leans over me, body heavy, posture relaxed as he rips the blade from my hand. My back arches against the cold metal of the car as he pins me there, his presence pressing down like a storm.

The knife, now in *his* hand, drags along the curve of my waist. Not hard enough to cut. Just enough to remind me he's in control. I try to shift beneath him, but he anticipates it, adjusting his grip until every part of me is locked into place, beneath him, beneath *this* moment.

"You're fast," he says, voice low, smooth. Almost admiring. "But sloppy."

I hate the way my breath hitches. Hate the heat that prickles across my skin despite the cold. I hate the way his eyes stay fixed on me, on my face, my lips, my throat, as if he's mapping the entire geography of my fear and fascination in real time.

And I hate how much he sees.

"So much fire," he murmurs, leaning in. His breath brushes my lips, warm and maddening. The sound of it makes the space between us feel intimate in a way that shouldn't be possible, not like this, not *now*.

Before I can respond, before I can twist away or scream or sink my teeth into his neck, he pulls something from his pocket. I see the blur of movement, and then the cloth is over my mouth.

A sickly sweet scent floods my nose and burns its way through my skull. Chloroform. I try to thrash, to turn my face away, but it's already too late. The fight drains from my limbs. The air thickens, my head spinning as his voice drips into the hollow space left in my mind.

"I did kill your brother," he whispers, not with regret, but with purpose. The blade in his hand lowers, slowly, tracing down the front of my body with unbearable slowness. Not to harm. To *mark.*

"And now, Little Butterfly," he says, his mouth so close to my ear it sends a chill racing down my spine, "I'm going to kill you."

Darkness claws at the edges of my vision. The last thing I feel is the scrape of the blade halting just above my waistband, daring, lingering. The last thing I see is the curve of his mouth, something between a smirk and a promise.

And then everything disappears.

8

Can You See Me Now?

Katya

A sharp, rhythmic pounding echoes behind my eyes, each pulse of pain like a drumbeat inside my skull. The throb won't let up, won't fade, it anchors me in this haze of nausea and confusion. Rolling onto my side, I brace myself for the familiar. The softness of silk sheets. The faint scent of lavender or rosewood candles burning on my bedside table. Warmth. Safety. Home.

But the second my palm hits cold concrete, reality slams into me.

This isn't my room.

The air is damp, murky and thick with the scent of mildew and stone. There's weight on my wrists, heavy and biting. Metal digs into my skin, and when I try to move, resistance jerks me backward with vicious force. Panic creeps in, slow and suffocating.

Then it all comes back.

The GPS reroute. The SUV. The knife. The rag over my mouth. The man with the ink on his wrist and blood on his hands.

A scream tears its way from my throat before I can stop it, raw and strangled. I bolt upright, pain splitting down the back of my skull, and I finally see it, stone walls on all sides, a barred window filtering in pale light from above, and a floor so clean it feels like a taunt.

Chains scrape against the concrete as I move, metal clinking like a warning bell. I glance down at the thick iron cuffs lock around my wrists, bolted to the wall like I'm some kind of rabid thing.

Still wearing the same black sweats and grey hoodie. No signs of blood or violation. But my feet, God, my feet are still crammed into my ballet shoes. The fabric is soaked through, the faint pink now a dark, rusted red. My toes throb, swollen and split.

A shallow bowl sits in the center of the room. Stainless steel, filled to the brim with water.

Like I'm a dog.

Thirst scrapes down my throat, a dry, aching canyon. I crawl toward it instinctively, desperation overriding dignity. The chains drag loudly behind me, the sound making my teeth clench.

"Don't."

The voice stops me cold.

I turn sharply.

Nikolai sits slumped against the far wall, his wrists shackled like mine. His shirt is torn, barely clinging to him, and his chest is streaked with deep red gashes, angry and fresh. His eyes are wide, glassy with pain and exhaustion, but still burning.

"He put something in the water," he says, his voice hoarse. "Hoped I'd drink it."

I stare at the bowl, then slowly lean back, retreating from it like it's acid. My stomach knots. My mouth stays dry.

"What the hell is happening?" I whisper.

Nikolai's laugh is humorless, cracked and sharp. He yanks against his restraints with a metallic rattle. "What the fuck does it *look* like? The same psychotic fuck who got Isaac? He got us too."

I look at him again, really look. The wounds across his torso aren't old. They're fresh, raw, still bleeding in places. Angled like they were done with care.

"What did he do to you?" I ask, voice shaking.

Nikolai swallows hard, his Adam's apple bobbing. "After he gave me the Narcan... he found the coke in your pocket. Thought it'd be fun to watch me choke on it. Shoved it up my nose, down my throat. Then he held me down, like I was a goddamn child, asking about Isaac, about your father. My father."

"The drugs. The laundering. The fucking hits-" My voice rises with each word until-

A sound.

We both freeze.

Boots scrape against the stone just outside the door. That sound, slow and deliberate, dragging something heavy.

We fall silent at once.

Then he appears.

The man who killed my brother. The man with the Catalyst tattoo. The one who watched me bleed and smiled.

He walks in with the kind of quiet that makes your skin crawl, not trying to intimidate, not trying to announce himself.

Just existing like he belongs here. Like this is *his* house, and we're just inconvenient furniture in the basement.

A Glock is tucked casually into the waistband of his jeans. My own knife gleams at his hip. In one hand, he drags a metal chair behind him, the sound shrieking against the floor until he stops just short of the dog bowl.

He turns the chair around and sits, straddling it backwards, arms folding across the top like this is a dinner party and we're late to the table.

"Glad to see you're both awake," he says, voice calm, soothing, even.

Like he didn't just dose me, beat Nikolai, and chain us to a dungeon wall.

Like this is just the beginning.

Nikolai still won't look up. His chin hangs low, his posture all shame and silence, like if he stays small enough, maybe the monster in the room will forget he's there.

The monster, however, notices everything.

"I see the two of you have had time to talk," the man drawls, his voice smooth, as if he's discussing the weather.

My pulse quickens. "What did you do to him?" I bite out, unable to stop myself. My voice shakes with fury as my gaze locks onto his.

A smirk curls on his lips. He turns his head just enough to cast a dismissive glance in Nikolai's direction.

"His skin was too clean," he says coolly. "A last name like his, walking around unscathed? No. He needed a few... advancements."

"*Advancements*?" The word stings as it leaves my tongue. I crawl forward, ignoring the way the chains tug at my wrists, the cuffs slicing into already-raw skin. "What the fuck is wrong with you-"

The slap lands like fire.

No warning. No buildup. Just heat and bone and skin.

My head snaps to the side, hair whipping across my cheek as I gasp. A strangled yelp tears from my throat, my vision flashing white for half a second. Stunned, I go still. My cheek pulses beneath the bloom of red-hot pain. Fingers tremble as they reach to cradle the sting, warm spit already trickling from my lip.

Across from me, the man doesn't flinch.

"Clearly," he says, tone laced with amusement, "she hasn't learned the rules yet. Has she, Nikolai?"

The silence is answer enough.

With the toe of his boot, he nudges the metal dog bowl toward me. The water inside sloshes slightly, catching the dim light.

"*Drink.*"

I stare at it. Something swirls beneath the surface. My own reflection ripples in the bowl, distorted and broken. I think of Nikolai's warning. I think of his wounds. And then I think of the heat still buzzing on my cheek.

"I'm not drinking that," I mutter.

The tension shifts instantly.

A whisper of steel brushes the back of my neck. Cold and unmistakable.

My knife.

His voice is barely audible. "It wasn't a request, Katya."

The tip of the blade drags along the curve of my neck, featherlight but threatening. It travels down the slope of my spine, slow and deliberate, making every hair on my body rise. I suck in a breath, my chest trembling.

"I'm not your dog," I whisper.

He leans closer, his breath warm against my temple. "No," he murmurs, "but you'll still obey."

My lips part, the heat between us thickening into something else. Something terrifying.

"If you want to cut me..." My voice is raw, reckless. "Then cut me."

The knife digs in just enough to draw a bead of blood. But it's not the pain that makes my skin buzz, it's the way he watches me. The way his eyes drink me in, as if each drop of defiance only adds to his hunger.

There's a shift in his mouth, not a smile, not quite. A pull. A curl.

Not admiration.

Possession.

Reaching for the bowl, fury burns through my veins. My fingers wrap around the rim, and with all the strength I can muster, I hurl it at him. The chains pull me back before I can follow through, but the bowl clatters to the ground, water splashing his front.

He doesn't blink.

Rising slowly, he's like a storm cloud brewing just beyond the horizon. He's calm, calculated, but beneath it, something simmers.

"To think," he says, eyes flicking to Nikolai, "I was doing you a kindness."

Then his gaze returns to me, hungry, dark, and deliberate.

"Eyes up, Nikolai," he mutters. "You'll want to watch this."

Chains rattle as I'm yanked backward, my spine scraping against the cold concrete. Nails claw at the ground, shoes slip, and every inch I fight is met with brute force, each slam of my back into the floor driving the air from my lungs.

"That bowl," he growls through clenched teeth, dragging me like a disobedient pet, "had a sleep aid in it." His voice vibrates with irritation. "Something to help you sleep through his screams tonight."

He glances down at his soaked shirt, drenched in the water I refused to drink. A sigh escapes him, slow and sharp.

"But since you were feeling defiant..." He clicks his tongue. "I guess you'd rather *clean it up*."

A hand clamps around my throat and pins me to the cold floor, the weight of his body hovering above mine. I gasp, legs kicking uselessly beneath him. His grip is punishing, just enough pressure to blur the edge between restraint and something more dangerous.

"The more you fight, the worse it will hurt," he warns, eyes dark as tar. His voice drops a note lower. "Stop fighting me."

"Fuck you," I spit, the words slipping from my lips even as my vision pulses with heat.

The slap is brutal. It doesn't just sting, it slices. My head jerks to the side, pain blooming across my cheek like a brand.

"You really don't know when to shut that smart little mouth, do you?" His tone is cruel, but it carries something else. A charge. A current. Something unreadable that simmers just beneath the surface.

I don't answer. Not with words.

He jerks me up by the collar of my hoodie. I drop to my knees, forced to tilt my head up. That's when I feel it, cold steel pressed against my temple. A tremor ripples through me.

His Glock.

He stands over me now, shirt clinging wet to his torso, his waist at eye level. Water darkens the fabric, drawing my gaze to the way it molds against his skin. My pulse skips. Not from fear. From something I don't dare name.

"Clean it up," he commands, pressing the gun just a little harder. "Not a drop hits the floor."

Humiliation floods my chest, thick and bitter. He knows exactly what this is. What it feels like to kneel for him, to be forced to obey in this way. He's reveling in it.

But my throat is raw, lips cracked. I'm thirsty. And there's no telling when I'll get water again.

Reaching up, my chains dragging behind me, I curl trembling fingers into his shirt. The fabric is warm, soaked with water, yes, but also with his body heat, his cologne, the sweat clinging to his skin. As I wring it out, droplets slip through my fingers and land on my tongue.

Salt. Leather. Him.

His body remains still, but I feel the way he watches me. As if every breath I take is a dance performed solely for him. His presence buzzes beneath my skin like a phantom touch.

"I said drink it, *Katya*." My name in his mouth sends a shiver down my spine.

The water slides past my lips and down my throat, each drop tainted with him. I drink it. Not because I want to, but because I have to. Because I *need* to survive.

When the shirt yields no more, I retreat, dragging my chains with me, wiping my mouth with the back of my hand. The taste of him lingers.

"*Good girl,*" he purrs, the smirk that follows aimed not at me, but at Nikolai.

I turn, heart seizing.

"Ready to play?" he says, his voice laced with cruel promise as he stalks toward Nikolai like a predator.

Nikolai shrinks against the wall, eyes wide, body trembling.

"No," I whisper, straining against the chains. "Wait."

My arms are useless, pinned behind me, body collapsing from exhaustion. I can't reach him. Can't protect him. All I can do is watch.

He unlatches Nikolai from the wall, dragging him by the hair toward the door. He pauses, just long enough to turn and look at me.

He drinks in the sight of me slumped and broken, kneeling, my breath ragged.

"Who..." I wheeze, knees giving out. "Who are you?"

His smirk cuts deep.

"You'll know..." he says, tugging Nikolai through the doorway, "when you wake up."

Darkness pulls me under before I can reply.

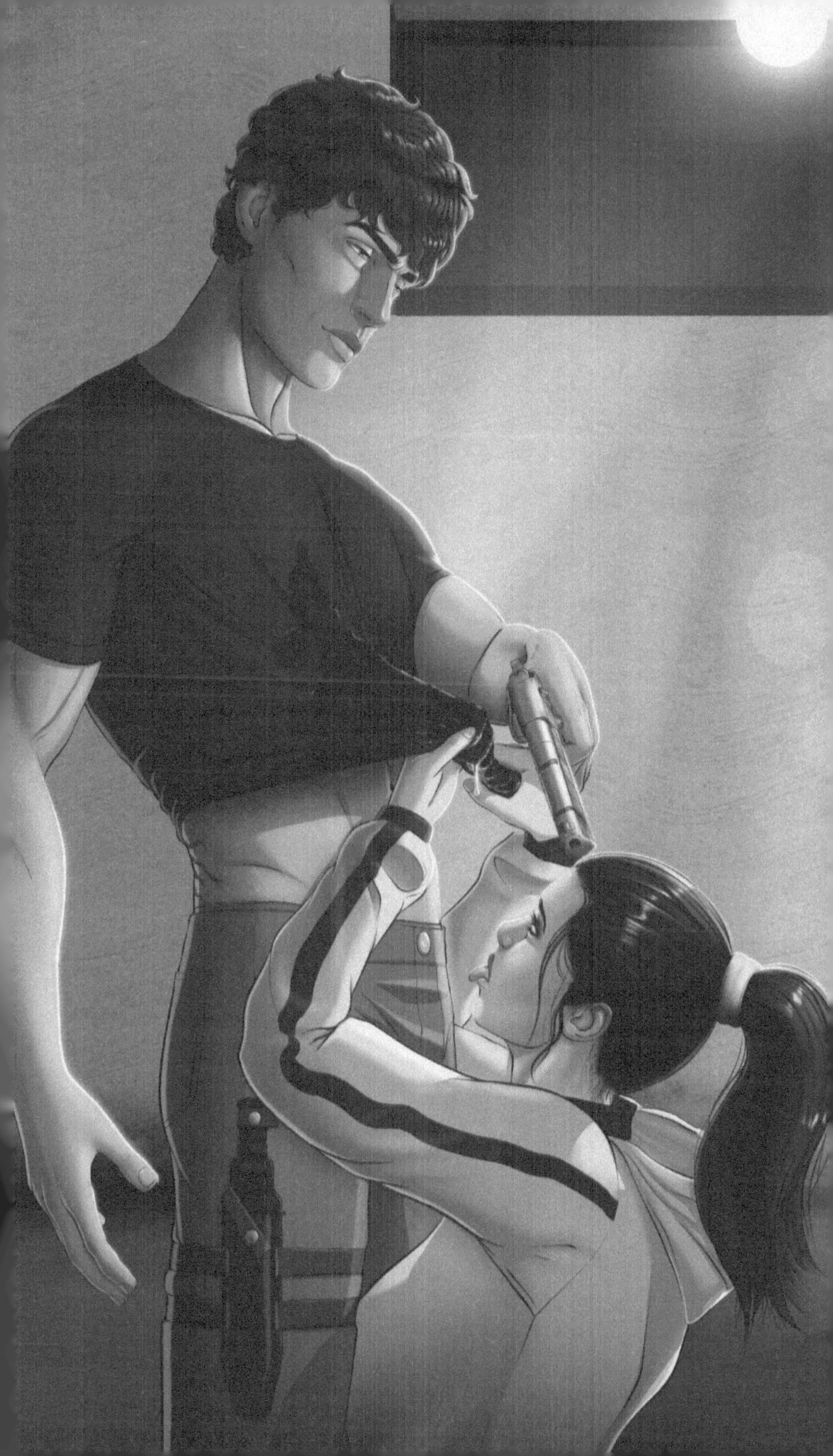

9

The Best Sokolov Is A Dead One

Echo

"How many more children?" The words leave like venom as another pitcher of water crashes over his face.

His body thrashes under the deluge, the soaked cloth muffling any attempt at a scream. Strapped tight to the chair, his muscles flex and spasm, wrists rubbed raw from struggling against the restraints.

Yanking the cloth away, the gasps that follow are desperate, almost comical. Wide, bloodshot eyes blink up at me, as if surprised I haven't already ended him.

"I already told you," he pants, choking out the words between coughs. "She and I, fuck, we didn't know anything about the kids. That was Issac's shit, all of it. Dimitri...my parents... they never pulled Katya or me into that side. It was just the usual, drugs, hits, status. That was it. All I had to worry about was looking good, killing when needed, and where to score my next bump. Hell, a week ago, the only thing on my mind was marrying her. Maybe even throwing a baby in her-"

His sentence cuts off in a scream as I snap one of his fingers back without warning. The crack is sharp. The sound of his pain? *Bliss.*

"That's not what I asked," comes the cold reply, watching him weep like the spoiled little son of a tyrant. "You think I dragged you both down here just to confirm what I already know? Issac, for all his failures, at least gave me something useful before he bled out."

Breathing hard, his gaze darts around the basement. "And I'm supposed to believe this is Catalyst?" His voice trembles with disbelief, but not nearly enough fear.

My hands slide casually into my pockets. "Let's just call it a... *passion project.*"

He laughs, or tries to. It comes out cracked and bitter. "You fucked with the wrong families, man. That girl upstairs, the one you've been torturing for sport? If she ever gets loose... forget Dimitri. *She* will be the one to kill you."

A smirk pulls across my lips, slow and sure. "I'm counting on it."

Silence stretches between us, thick and suffocating. Blood drips from his broken hand. His breath comes in ragged pulls.

"But in the end," I murmur, stepping closer, letting him see the gleam in my eye, "you all end up in the same place."

Lowering my voice to a whisper, I let the words settle like final rites.

"In the hands of God."

Fingers trail slowly across the worn metal tray, brushing past bone saws and pliers until they settle lovingly on the scalpel. The blade gleams under the basement's flickering light, thin and precise, hungry for skin.

"What exactly do you think she and I have done?" Nikolai snaps, his voice strained from pain, but laced with disbelief.

"You misunderstand," the response is calm, measured. "It's not about what *you've* done. It's about who you are. I know what your families have built. The Romanovs. The Sokolovs. Fifteen years of trafficking children, laundering their names and blood through foundations, false adoptions, and pharmaceutical fronts. You were born into it. Raised by it. Whether you watched or participated doesn't change the truth, you are their legacy."

Nikolai jerks against the restraints, his eyes locked on the scalpel now glinting just inches from his feet. "Killing us won't stop anything," he growls. "You think you're some kind of savior? You're not. You're just another monster-"

"No," the word cuts through the air like the blade itself. "Issac's death was a warning. You, Nikolai? You're a message."

A slow smile spreads as the scalpel is raised, not yet striking, just teasing the space between threat and promise.

"And Katya..." The name rolls from the tongue like something forbidden, savored. "She's my leverage."

Pacing begins, slow and deliberate, the scalpel gliding through the air with each step. The space between them grows heavier, charged with anticipation.

"So," my voice lowers to a whisper, silk-wrapped steel. "Which toe would you like to lose first?"

Dragging Nikolai back into the cell, I ignore his groans as his legs give out beneath him. His fingers are wrapped crudely, and blood seeps through the gauze. Across his arm, the word **TRAITOR** is freshly carved, raw and angry, a punishment and a reminder all in one. I chain him up against the far wall, watching his chest rise and fall as he pants, too weak to curse me, though the hatred still simmers in his eyes.

I toss him a bottle of water. He fumbles it at first, then devours it like an animal, drinking too fast, too desperate. For a moment, he looks like he might cry again, but he doesn't. He swallows it all down; water, pride, and whatever pain still has claws in him.

Katya's curled on the floor, small and still, her chest barely moving. The few mouthfuls she got earlier were enough to knock her out. She's quieter like this, softer. The hard lines of her jaw have relaxed, the crease between her brows smoothed. For the first time, I see the parts of her she tries to hide, the exhaustion, the fragility.

Even in sleep, her body is tense. One hand clutches her hoodie near the hem, as if protecting herself even now. My eyes trace the length of her, bruises on her ankles where the pointe shoes dig in and dried blood crusting around the seams.

"Who the hell still wears ballet shoes after they've bled through them?" I mutter under my breath, more to myself than Nikolai, but he hears me anyway.

"You want to know why?" he rasps, tossing the empty water bottle toward me with a glare. "It'll cost you another."

I ignore the bait.

Instead, I crouch beside her, staring at the contrast between her pale skin and the black hoodie bunched around her waist. My fingers hover above her before finally pressing into the fabric. I push it up carefully, revealing her abdomen inch by inch. Her stomach is flat, toned, unmarred by scars or bruises, so unlike the rest of her. My fingertips drift along her hip bones, brushing the edge of her ribs, trailing lower until the curve of her waist deepens into something intimate.

"Touch her again, and I swear to God-" Nikolai's voice cuts through the quiet.

"I'm not raping her," I growl, teeth clenched as I shoot him a look over my shoulder. "So shut the fuck up."

Reaching into my belt, I find the scalpel, its edge gleaming under the overhead light. My hand doesn't shake. It never does. With calculated precision, I press the blade to the skin just below her navel and carve the letters slowly...deliberately. E. C. H. O.

Blood beads along each letter, thin trails weaving toward the waistband of her pants.

Staring at my work, my heart pounds harder than I expected.

She asked for my name.

Now she'll always know it.

Against my better judgment, I swipe a thumb through the blood, then bring it to my tongue. The familiar taste of the metallic, warm liquid spreads, but something else is there.

Something that lingers.

Fuck.

I hate the way my body reacts. The pulse in my groin, the ache in my chest. She's unconscious. Vulnerable. And still, the sight of her, the scent of her, blood, sweat, that faint perfume clinging to her hoodie, it makes my control slip.

Pulling the hoodie down, I smooth it over her skin. But just as I go to move away, my hand brushes against something rough. I frown, then slowly turn her onto her side.

The sight knocks the breath from my lungs.

Her back is a canvas of pain. Scars slash across her skin, some healed poorly, others fresh, barely scabbed. They vary in width and depth, but all are brutal, unmistakable in origin. Rod lashes. Dozens of them. Some cross over each other, layering pain atop pain.

My hand hovers above her spine, trembling now. I've seen this kind of cruelty before. I've inflicted it. But this? This was drawn out. Repeated. Designed to break someone.

A dry laugh chokes from Nikolai's throat. When I look at him, his expression is grim.

"You thought the Romanovs spared their daughters?" he says. "You thought Katya got to be soft?"

The taste of her blood still lingers on my tongue, and now it turns bitter.

"What did they do to her?" The question leaves me sharper than I intend, thick with something I don't want to name.

Nikolai lets out a bitter laugh, dry and sharp. "You mean what did she do to herself?" He leans his head back against the wall, eyes bloodshot, voice rough with exhaustion and spite. "You're looking at the cost of failure as a Romanov."

I glance down at her, still unconscious on the floor her body barely rising with each breath. Nikolai's words loop in my head: failure, cost, Romanov.

"The shoes you were asking about," he continues, voice low. "Mrs. Pavlov doesn't just train women. She breaks them. Katya dances on sprained feet."

Moving to the edge of the mattress, I kneel beside her. My hands hover above her ankles, hesitation crawling down my spine. Carefully, I unlatch the slippers, each movement slow, deliberate. The fabric clings to her skin, stiff with dried blood and sweat. When the shoes finally come off, I stare in stunned silence.

Her feet are mangled. Swollen. Raw. Bruised in places that should never be bruised. Red welts bloom around her toes, skin cracked and torn. She's been dancing on these?

"She sprained her ankle a week ago," Nikolai mutters, watching me from across the room. "Courtesy of her loving big brother. My sister nearly shattered the other one not long before that. Her father told her to toughen up or face something worse. The scars on her back? Pavlov's doing. Discipline for losing a combat match."

I swallow hard, my thumb grazing the edge of her ankle. She doesn't stir.

"A lady's back," he continues, his voice distant now, almost reciting, "is never seen if she's dressed modestly. A woman shall serve her husband. Not like he has much use for her back, or her feet, for that matter."

The words taste foul in my mouth.

Romanov women aren't meant to rule. They're meant to breed. To bleed. To serve.

"To them, she's not a person. She's an asset. A baby factory, a chess piece, a pretty little puppet with a blade in her sleeve. And me?" Nikolai chuckles darkly. "Well, I'm just the sperm bank. So congratulations, Catalyst. You kidnapped their breeding pair. Dimitri won't care. He'll just make another. Another heir. Another obedient girl. One who hasn't started biting back."

My hands curl into fists. I want to deny it, want to say she's more than that, that she's nothing like what he's describing. But that would mean admitting I've started to care. And I can't. Not here. Not now.

"She didn't know what Issac was really doing," Nikolai adds after a moment. "And if I'm being honest... I think a part of her was relieved when he died. You're not the first person to hurt her…and you won't be the last."

The words echo in the silence, slamming into me harder than any blade ever could. I stare at her small, bruised frame. She looks so young like this. So small. And yet, every inch of her tells a story. The calluses. The welts. The bruises. She's been serving someone her whole life, family, duty, expectation. And now me.

I shift back, rising slowly.

"What's your plan for her?" I ask, the question more loaded than I mean it to be.

Nikolai gives me a long look. Not hateful. Just… tired. "I think I just told you."

Turning away from them both, I move toward the door, heart pounding so loud it threatens to crack my ribs. My hand hesitates on the handle, but I don't look back. The moment the metal door slams shut behind me, the air tightens around my chest.

I shouldn't care.

But the way her blood looked with my name carved into it… the way she breathed my command like it was gospel…

It's already too late.

10

My Secret Addiction

Katya

Pain lingers like an old friend, nestled deep in my feet, my spine, and now curling into the fragile curve of my torso. Groggy, aching, I roll to my side, my fingers grazing beneath my hoodie and freezing the moment they land on a bandage pressed above my hip bone.

"What the fuck..." The whisper falls from my lips as my eyes dart down, the stark white wrap standing out against the grime of my clothes.

Shifting again, I brace for the familiar pull of chains. But they never come.

Instead, what greets me is worse, stranger. A plate rests just inches from my reach. Eggs. Bacon. Still steaming.

And beyond that? Him.

He sits silently, eyes locked on me, watching. Measuring. Waiting.

My body moves before I can stop it, legs scrambling backward across the mattress, instinct flaring. But his boot strikes hard and fast, colliding with my chest and sending me crashing back down, air knocked from my lungs as the mattress catches me.

"Sit," he commands, voice laced with cold indifference.

The gleam of metal follows, my knife, drawn casually from his belt like it belongs to him now. Gloved fingers flex around the hilt. He points it toward me, not as a threat, but a directive.

"We both know you're too weak and too groggy to do anything right now."

His tone cuts like a scalpel, clinical, bored, but watchful.

A groan pulls my attention sideways. Nikolai lays slumped across the far wall, water bottles placed beside him like some kind of peace offering.

"He's not dead," the man mutters, catching my glance. "He wanted water. I wanted silence."

My gaze snaps back to him. "Why did you unshackle me?"

He doesn't answer. Just nudges the plate closer with the tip of the knife, as if feeding a feral dog.

"Eat."

Pulling up my hoodie, I press gently near the bandage. The pain is faint, dull...managed. My stomach churns with more than hunger.

"What, need me to eat so you can keep harvesting my organs?" I spit, eyes narrowing.

His lips twitch in faint amusement, or annoyance, I can't tell.

"If I wanted your organs, sweetheart, you'd already be dead and drained on the floor. This? This is me being nice. Now eat. You look like shit."

"Well, being held captive does tend to ruin one's glow," I mutter, my voice dry.

His stare doesn't waver. "Don't bullshit me. You looked like shit before I ever took you."

The words hit harder than I expect.

He leans forward slightly, the air between us thick with something too intimate to name. "Your ankles are sprained. Your back looks like a fucking chopping board. Your feet were bleeding through your shoes."

Glancing down, I notice they're gone. I hadn't even realized.

"You touched me," I say flatly, the accusation resting heavy in the space between us. "While I was unconscious. Just like him."

His jaw tightens. "I moved you off the cold concrete and gave you a mattress. Would you rather I left you to freeze?"

"And you just so happened to take off my shoes? Look under my clothes?"

The accusation hangs in the air, daring him to respond.

He stands slowly, that blade still in hand, his steps silent but deliberate. Looming. Controlled. Dangerous.

"Careful with your tone," he says, voice low, sharp enough to draw blood. "Don't mistake this for mercy. You're still mine. And if I say eat, you fucking eat."

For a breath, neither of us moves. The heat between us could burn the walls down.

But my body, weak, starved, aching, knows better than to keep testing the fuse.

Still, I keep my eyes on him as I reach for the plate, teeth clenched, rage and something far darker roiling in my gut. Hunger gnaws at me, but it's not just for food.

It's for answers.

It's for vengeance.

I shovel the food down like it might be taken from me, each bite more about survival than satisfaction. The plate is cleared within minutes, the gnawing hunger in my gut easing only slightly.

He watches without saying a word.

When I push the plate toward him, his hand moves. Not to reach for it, but to casually sheath my knife back into the waistband at his hip. His next move is slower, more deliberate, he pulls a bottle of water from his jacket pocket, then a small plastic bag filled with pills.

My eyes narrow, breath catching just slightly.

"What are they?" The question is low, wary.

"Painkillers," he answers. "For your ankles. And for the gift I left under that little bandage on your side."

Something tightens in my chest.

My fingers drift to the edge of the hoodie, just above my hip, brushing the gauze lightly. My heart skips, my voice sharpened by dread.

"What's under the bandage?"

He doesn't miss a beat. "My name."

For a second, my world narrows to the sound of blood roaring in my ears.

"You put your fucking name on me?" My whisper is brittle, shaking, venom laced with disbelief.

"A good reminder," he murmurs, leaning forward, his voice a low hum of amusement. "You don't belong to the Romanovs anymore."

His breath fans over my jaw, sending a shiver down my spine. "You're mine now."

My pulse spikes. Every nerve ending inside me is on fire. Whether from rage or adrenaline or something more dangerous, I can't tell. I don't think I want to.

Everything inside me fractures.

Without thinking, my body moves. I lunge at him, teeth bared, fingers clawing through his hair as I throw my weight into his lap. His back slams into the floor as we crash to the mattress in a blur of limbs and heat. My hand scrambles for the knife at his waist while his hand closes around my wrist.

He's strong, too strong, and even dazed, he overpowers me with little effort.

But I fight.

I twist and thrash and grind against him, and somewhere in the middle of it, our bodies lock into each other, breathless, panting.

Then I feel it.

The cold press of steel slipping past my lips.

My eyes widen.

The Glock.

His Glock.

It pushes deeper, the barrel gliding slow and steady along my tongue until it kisses the back of my throat. My gag reflex flares. My body stiffens.

His weight pins me down, one hand twisted in my hair, the other steady on the weapon.

His smile is the most dangerous thing I've ever seen.

"Do I have your fucking attention now, butterfly?" he whispers against my cheek, voice so low it's almost intimate.

The gun slides deeper, suffocating. Humiliating. I can't breathe, can't think, but I feel everything.

Heat coils low in my stomach. Shame and fury twist together, and I hate the way my body responds, hates the way part of me trembles not just from fear, but from how devastatingly close he is.

"You wanted your knife back?" His mouth brushes the shell of my ear, his tone dark and wicked. "Fine."

He pulls the gun back from my mouth, slow and deliberate, watching every second of the recoil in my body as oxygen floods back into my lungs.

I gasp. Cough. Swallow the burn in my throat.

Lying beneath him, I feel like a live wire.

And I know, from the way he's looking at me, from the tension in his body against mine, he feels it too.

Whatever this is between us, it's not clean.

It's not sane.

And it sure as hell isn't over.

"Take off your pants."

The command lands like a crack through the air.

My breath hitches. "No." The word barely escapes, a trembling murmur as my eyes widen in disbelief.

He leans closer. Slow. Unyielding. The air between us turns colder.

His voice lowers, just above a whisper.

"Take off your pants, or I'll shoot Nikolai in the head right now and make you clean it up."

My stomach drops. The world narrows. My gaze darts to Nikolai, still slumped nearby, silent but alive. For now.

The threat isn't empty.

Every inch of me screams not to move, to fight, to run, but there's nowhere to go, no one to save us. My fingers tremble as I reach for the tie of my sweats. Fumbling with the knot, I blink away the burn rising behind my eyes.

Don't give him the satisfaction.

But I do. I have to.

Yanking the waistband down, I strip them off, teeth clenched, leaving myself in nothing but my underwear. The cold air hits my legs like ice, prickling my skin, but it's nothing compared to the heat of his stare.

He watches every movement.

Not like a man admiring a woman, but like a predator savoring the way his prey obeys.

With casual ease, he tucks the gun away. The tension in the room only thickens.

Then his hand is on my throat.

The leather of his glove bites against my skin, not squeezing, not yet, just holding, reminding me who holds the power here. I suck in a breath, heart hammering against my ribs.

His other hand moves with precision.

He yanks free the knife from his side, my knife. The same blade he took from me. The same one he used to mark me. His fingers trace the hilt like it belongs to him more than it ever did to me.

Pinned in place, barely clothed, heart thundering and throat wrapped in his hand, I can feel it, this isn't just punishment.

It's control. Ritual. Possession.

And the worst part?

Part of me is still burning beneath the terror.

"Slide over your panties," he purrs.

The sound of his voice coils down my spine like smoke, heavy with something too smooth, too dangerous. My stomach turns, knotted with dread and something far more shameful. Something I don't want to name.

If I refuse, I know what he'll do. I've seen what he's capable of. Felt it.

My breath falters.

With trembling fingers, I reach beneath the hem of my shirt. The elastic clings to my hips like it knows it shouldn't be moved, like it's trying to protect what little dignity I have left. But I slide it aside anyway, slowly, hesitantly, baring myself without baring everything.

That's when I feel it.

Warmth.

Wet.

A slick heat pooled between my thighs.

It hits me before I can hide from it, the damning proof that my body has betrayed me. That somewhere, beneath the fear and the hate and the humiliation, something in me is... responding.

To him.

To this.

My breath catches in my throat as my fingertips brush over the damp cotton. Shame burns hotter than anything he's done to me yet.

I don't even look up. I don't want to see his face.

But I feel him lean in closer. Like he already knows.

"Open your mouth for me," he whispers, the command as intimate as it is violating.

My lips part before I can stop them.

I don't know if it's obedience... or survival. Maybe both.

He holds the blade steady in his gloved hand, turning the hilt slowly, deliberately, before lifting it toward my lips.

I hesitate, but his eyes don't waver. That look, the one that says he'll make me regret disobedience, burns into me like a brand.

My lips part, unsure whether it's defiance or dread that's keeping me from trembling more.

Cool metal grazes my tongue.

He slides the hilt past my teeth, letting it linger too long, the cold unforgiving taste of steel dragging along my tongue, deeper... until it taps the back of my throat. Tears prick at my eyes from the pressure, and only then does he pull it back, slow and measured.

"Want it back?" he murmurs.

His hand shifts, tightening around my throat, not enough to choke, not yet, but enough to remind me who's in control.

I say nothing.

My fingers tighten around his wrist before I even realize I've moved. The leather of his glove creaks under the pressure of my grip, my nails sinking into it, not to push him away, but to *feel*. The space between us crackles, like a wire pulled taut between violence and something far more dangerous.

His breath brushes my skin, hot and slow, and when he speaks again, his voice is a caress dipped in cruelty. "Hmm?"

Then the hilt slides lower.

The sound, slick, obscene, stills everything. The air. My breath. *Him*. It hits us both. The confirmation. The truth.

I'm wet.

And not from fear.

Heat blooms across my chest, radiating up my neck as I freeze, unable to look at him, unable to *hide* what my body has already admitted. Confusion coils with the shame, the fury, the dark, aching hunger I've fought to ignore.

He leans in, impossibly close, his mouth grazing the shell of my ear.

"That wasn't part of the plan," he murmurs, voice rough, like gravel and heat, each word digging beneath my skin, lodging there.

"You're already wet," he breathes, more stunned than mocking, as if the admission slips out before he can reel it back.

My lashes flutter open, locking onto his stare. There's no cruelty in his expression now, just something darker. Confusion. A reluctant hunger. Like he's trying to make sense of the thing pulsing between us.

As if *I'm* supposed to explain the betrayal of my body.

"You-"

The word barely escapes before I shift. Just enough to press my leg against him. The contact is brief, but undeniable.

Heat flares through me.

Because I feel it. The pressure beneath his pants. The stiff response he's trying, and failing, to ignore.

His eyes widen, just a flicker, but it's all I need. My voice drops, velvet laced in venom.

"And you're already hard-"

His hand tightens around my throat, just enough to make my breath stutter, just enough to remind me he's in control. The weight of him, the force of his presence, settles over me like a storm ready to break.

Then he moves, driving the hilt into me with a dark kind of reverence. The hilt presses against me again, not gentle but not cruel, dragging a gasp from my lips before I can stop it. I shouldn't feel this. I shouldn't want this. But my body arches anyway, traitorous and aching.

His gaze never leaves mine. It's sharp, devouring, filled with something primal. And when he sees the way I respond, despite the defiance still burning in my eyes, his lips curve into a smile that makes my stomach clench.

"You hate this," he murmurs, voice low and smug, "but your body... your body knows better."

The next thrust is deeper, pulling another sound from my throat I can't swallow fast enough. My hands fist his shirt, my skin flushed and burning. I bite down on my bottom lip, hard, but it doesn't stop the heat spiraling through me.

Each breath is shallow. Each movement of his hand calculated. Controlled.

"You want to hate me," he whispers, his mouth brushing the shell of my ear. "But you want this more."

And god help me, because in this moment, he's right.

"Being fucked by your own knife, my hand around your throat, my name carved into your skin..." His voice is low, not a growl, not a whisper, but something between, like a prayer and a curse. "Your pussy wet before I ever truly touched you, Katya. That's the truth. That's the part that haunts you."

My body burns with shame, with betrayal, not by him, but by my own skin. It responds to him against my will, hips rocking instinctively with each cruel thrust of the weapon. I hate it. I hate *him*. But I can't stop. Warmth coils deep in my stomach, and I bite down hard, stifling the sounds clawing their way up my throat.

His hand tightens just a little more. Not enough to choke, not yet, just enough to remind me who holds the reins.

"Your silence is louder than your screams, you know," he murmurs, almost fascinated. "And still... your body *answers* me."

It's unbearable , the way he watches, the way he *knows*. Every thrust, every reaction, every flutter in my breath. He isn't just breaking me physically. He's unraveling something inside me, piece by jagged piece.

Spitting at him feels like the only rebellion I have left. It lands squarely across his cheek, a line of spit trailing down his face. His movement halts, not in anger, but surprise. Then, slowly, the edge of his mouth curls, not with rage... but with something close to pride.

"You finally fought back," he says, wiping his face with the back of his gloved hand. "Took you long enough."

He pulls the knife from between my thighs, and for a second, I swear I feel colder without it. Hollow. Empty.

I recoil from the thought, grabbing my pants and yanking them up, my fingers trembling as I cover myself. On my feet now, my breathing is shallow, unsteady. We just stare at each other.

Two predators caught in the same snare, unsure which one is actually bleeding.

He holds up the knife, turning it in the low light. Something glistens at the base of the hilt. undeniable, shameful.

"You came," he smirks, quieter now. "Imagine if it was my cock."

Panting, chest heaving like a caged animal, I glare at him through a haze of adrenaline and shame. My heart thunders, every beat a war drum against the walls of this prison.

"Let me out of here," I growl, voice hoarse, barely tethered to sanity.

He steps closer, his eyes gleaming with something unholy, hunger, yes, but something more twisted. Reverent.

"After that?" he murmurs, and before I can recoil, he drags his tongue deliberately across the hilt, slow and taunting, tasting me, tasting power. The sight shouldn't make my breath hitch. It shouldn't root me in place. But it does. God help me, it does.

As if savoring the moment, he licks his lips, watching my every flinch like it's the first spark of something sacred.

Then, with a flick of his wrist, he tosses the blade to the floor, the metal clattering like a gunshot in the silence.

"Your fear," he breathes, his voice dangerously soft, "is my addiction, Little Butterfly."

And I realize, too late, that it's not just my body he's claiming.

It's every piece of me I thought was untouchable.

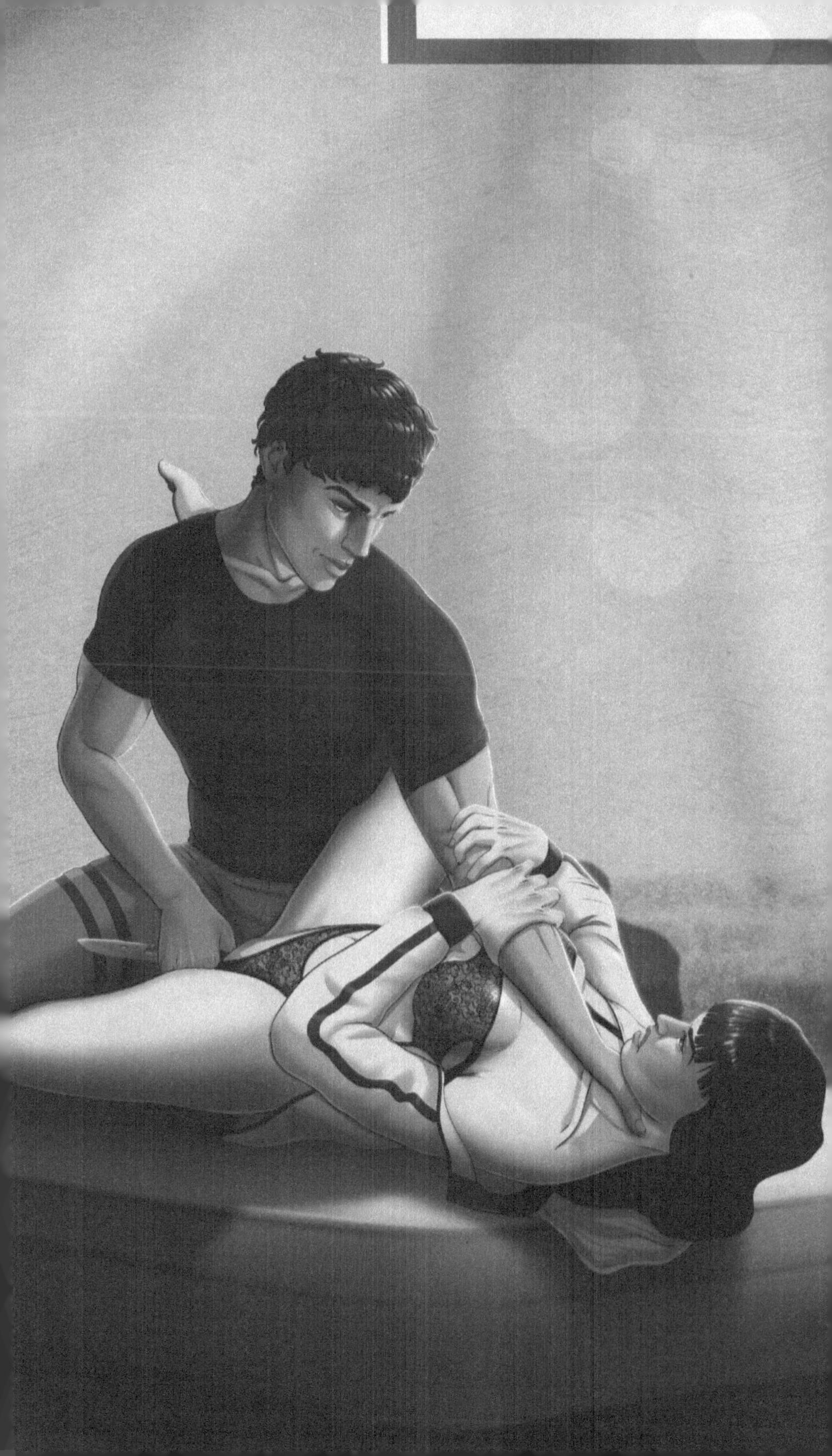

All Is Fair in Sin And War

Echo

"Echo?"

A voice cuts through the thick silence, but it barely registers.

"Echo?"

The second time it hits harder, dragging me out of the fog. My eyes pull from the window, the glass still fogged where my breath had been resting.

"What?" The word comes rough, low, like gravel stuck in my throat.

Roman's watching me, that unreadable look on his face. "I asked if any of our men have given you updates on Nikolai or Katya."

Katya.

The name tastes like sin.

Heat flares low in my stomach, uninvited and impossible to ignore. My jaw clenches as the memory floods back, her trembling breath, the sharp sting of the blade between us, the way her release coated my tongue like a fucking drug.

And I didn't want to stop.

Didn't want to pull back. Didn't want to let go of that knife.

I wanted to drive it in her harder, just to see if she'd still moan the way she did when I dragged it out, slow and relentless. I wanted to kiss her with blood on my hands, make her bite back another scream until she couldn't anymore.

She should've been terrified.

But she wasn't.

Her body arched into it. Into me. Her lip, already bruised from trying to silence herself, was begging to be torn free. To be sucked, bitten, claimed.

In that moment, it stopped being about control.

It became need.

Dangerous, primal, sickeningly deep need. I thought I was breaking her, showing her who held the power. But what I saw in her eyes, the way she looked at me like I was both the threat and the answer, *fuck*, that did something to me.

Her fear would've been easier to handle. Predictable.

But this?

This want, the way she opened for me, the heat rolling off her, the way her breath caught when my mouth hovered just above her skin, it's carved into me now.

She's carved into me.

Roman's voice is distant now, irrelevant. All I can feel is the phantom taste of her, the burn in my veins, the growing ache between my hips every time I replay the sound she made when my hand slid between her thighs.

I didn't want to torment her.

I wanted to fuck her until she forgot her own name.

Wanted to leave her wrecked, soaked, shaking...mine.

Katya isn't just under my skin. She *is* the skin. And every second I'm not inside her feels like another slow death.

Roman's still talking, but I'm not listening.

Because I'm already gone.

Already thinking about the next time I get her alone.

But God, when she touched me...

When her knee grazed my cock and reminded me just how easily my body betrays me, I *had* to silence her.

A warning. A distraction. Something to kill the heat rising far too fast.

I should've left. Should've pulled away before it got that far.

Should've never let it happen.

Fuck.

What the fuck was I thinking?

But then came the taste of her.

That sweet, sinful taste that hit me like a drug. Warm. Intoxicating. Coating my tongue and burning its way into my bloodstream.

Her eyes, locked on mine the whole damn time, didn't waver.

And her nails?

Raked down my front like she owned me.

Her hips moved like she was born for it, like she knew exactly what she was doing, driving me to the brink, dragging me down with her.

And I let her.

No, I *welcomed* it.

Since that night, I've never touched myself so hard, so desperate, in the dark.

Like a fucking addict.

Fist clenched tight around my cock, trying to recall the way she sounded, the way her skin felt under my hands, the way her breath hitched when I pressed into her just enough to make her ache.

Even now, right fucking now, just the thought of her stirs something low.

Heat pooling beneath my waistband. Blood thickening. Body remembering.

She's not even in the room and she still has this hold on me.

I bring the mug to my lips, hoping to mask the tension. "No one's seen them," I mumble, voice gravel-coated and tight.

"We've known that," Noah replies, rubbing the exhaustion from his face. "Our men have done what searches they can, the ones not watching the Romanov operations. Before the weekend, Katya was last seen leaving Pavlov's. Nikolai was tracked to his family home. His Tesla was found dumped, GPS fried, cameras wiped. Dimitri's already called a hit on whoever took her-"

"She could've run away," I snap, harsher than intended.

"Romanovs don't run away," Roman sighs, voice low with finality.

"How much is Dimitri's bounty up to?" My question cuts through the silence.

"Five million," Noah says, tapping the end of his pencil against the edge of his laptop. "Each day that passes, the number climbs. A lot of Romanov allies invested in the union of Katya and Nikolai. No union, no empire..."

"No money," Roman finishes with a bitter edge.

Five million.

That's what she's worth on paper.

But the girl I saw, the bruises on her thighs, the scars mapped across her skin, the way her ankle was already healing wrong beneath the restraints, she didn't look like a princess.

She looked like a survivor.

A fractured, discarded thing.

Not the polished bride of a legacy empire.

"Genevieve Pavlov," I mutter, watching both men closely. "Did either of you know what she was doing to her students?"

They share a look, unreadable and silent.

"The instructor?" Roman finally asks.

"Yes," I push, jaw tight.

"She's got a record," he admits. "Did time in a Russian penitentiary for smuggling. Caught selling a few of her students off to Dimitri. Burned down her family's home in her teens. Rumor has it, she killed three before she was seventeen. That's how she got noticed by the Romanovs. It's why they let her train their women and the daughters of their associates."

"And no one ever thought to ask what that training looked like?" My voice lowers, sharp and unflinching. "Did you know she was beating the girls? Mutilating them?"

"How the fuck would we know that?" Noah snaps, frustrated.

I lean back, forcing my spine straight even though the tension coils deep.

"Rumors," I mutter, though I know they're more than that.

Roman shrugs. "So what? All pieces of the same rotten puzzle. If Pavlov laid into them, that's one less problem for us down the line. You've seen it. The overdoses. The weapons. The children trained like dogs. Wherever Katya is right now, my hope is that she's in a shallow grave. One I can piss on as I send Dimitri the footage-"

The mug shatters in my hand before I even realize I've clenched it.

Glass explodes across the table, slicing through skin like paper.

"Fuck." Blood pools fast, a dark red line racing down my wrist. My breath catches, sharp and ragged.

Roman startles. "What the hell, man?"

Gripping my wrist, I glance at the lesion. Deep. Clean. Sharp. I yank my tie free and start wrapping it tight.

"I'm fine," I mutter, voice flat, jaw locked.

Roman takes a cautious step forward.

"Echo-"

"I said I'm fine," I snap, cutting him off, voice dark enough to end the conversation.

Let them think it was an accident.

Let them believe it was anger.

But they don't know the truth.

It wasn't the bounty. Or the mission.

It was the image of her in a grave.

And the way my entire body *revolted* against it.

Roman and Noah hesitate at the door, lingering just long enough to make me wonder if they sense what's shifting beneath the surface. But eventually, the door clicks shut, and the silence that follows feels heavier than it should.

Lowering myself into the chair behind my desk, I let the weight of the room settle around me. It's too quiet now, just the faint hum of the building and the slow burn crawling beneath my skin. My hand moves before I can stop it, dragging my phone from my pocket.

I don't check texts. I don't respond to emails. Opening the security feed, I hover over the camera app. One tap and the screen blooms to life, pulling up the basement.

And there she is.

Katya.

The hoodie's gone, tossed to the floor like it never mattered. What's left clings to her body, tight black fabric stretched across her chest, exposing just enough to set my jaw. The tank top reveals too much, and yet not enough. Every curve, every bruise, every scar is on display, and I can't fucking look away.

She's hunched over, tearing the shredded remains of her hoodie into strips. Her fingers work with a strange kind of rage, methodical and silent as she wraps the fabric around her raw, bleeding feet. Even half-starved, she moves with purpose, refusing to fold.

And still, it's not her that makes the anger rise.

It's him.

Nikolai sits too close, leaning in, whispering low in her ear like he's earned the right. His hand grazes her thigh. Her body tenses, but she doesn't move away.

My stomach tightens.

I unmute the feed, needing to know, needing to hear what he's saying to her. The words spill out in thick Russian, sharp and fast. Their voices blend together, a conversation meant to shut me out completely.

It's the way he looks at her, bruised and bitter, but still full of something dangerous, that makes my hand shake. She cups his face like she pities him. Like he deserves her sympathy.

Like I'm the fucking monster.

Nikolai leans forward, eyes narrowing as something shifts in his tone.

"If I'm going to die," he snaps, "I should at least know if your dirty cunt was worth it."

I stop breathing.

Katya tries to respond, but he's already moving. One hand curls into her hair, yanking her closer until their foreheads nearly touch. The chains rattle violently as he drags her between his legs, wrapping them around her hips like she belongs there.

The chair beneath me screeches across the floor as I bolt upright, the back of it slamming into the windowpane behind me. My heart thunders, but my eyes don't leave the screen.

He's holding her still. His hand travels under her shirt. She flinches, eyes wide, body twisting as she tries to get away.

And he laughs.

"Now you're afraid, Katya?"

There's nothing left in him but madness. Hunger. Desperation.

She's exhausted. Dehydrated. Barely able to stand. And yet, she still fights him, still finds the strength to resist.

He is unrecognizable now. No longer a prisoner, but a creature, feral and collapsing in on himself. A monster of my own making.

Maybe I should let him do it.

Let it spiral. Let them destroy each other and call it justice.

But then I see her face, see the fear flash across it, and everything in me locks into place.

Katya isn't his to torment. Not his to humiliate. Not his to put his hands on.

She's mine.

And I'll tear this place apart before I let anyone else touch what belongs to me.

12

The Monster Behind The Mask

Katya

"**N**ikolai," I gasp, voice cracking as his rough hands shove beneath my shirt. The cold touch of his fingers against my skin makes my body jolt, but he only presses down harder, his legs pinning mine in place as I writhe beneath him.

There's no room to move. No space to breathe.

His calloused palms slide over my breasts, and then he pinches, hard. My back arches from the sting, a dull whimper escaping my throat, unbidden. Pain ripples through me, sharp and fast, but nothing compared to the aching between my legs, the lingering throb where another man already claimed me.

I still haven't had the courage to look beneath the bandage.

I can feel it there. Burned into me.

His name.

Branded like a possession.

"What, Katya?" Nikolai breathes, voice mocking as he yanks my shirt higher. "Can't you give me a little bit of fun?"

His eyes are wild now, bloodshot and glazed. Madness lingers just beneath the surface.

My body, bruised and used, can barely keep up. My muscles scream with every shift, but the strength I need to fight isn't there. Whatever fight I had is slipping through my fingers, and he knows it.

Pressure digs into my ankles. My knees. He uses his weight like a weapon.

Panic burns hot in my chest.

"You're fucking losing it," I whisper, trying to wedge my hands between us, to pry him off me, but it's no use. His nails drag down my torso, scraping across raw skin, tearing the edge of the bandage as they go.

I flinch as the adhesive gives way, and pain flashes white behind my eyes.

"Captivity will do that," he spits, leaning closer. His breath reeks of rot and rage. "Turns men into animals."

The world feels too small. Too loud. My heart pounds like it's trying to claw its way out of my ribs.

He laughs, unbothered.

And then, just for a second, I find an opening.

Slamming my elbow into his chest, I hear the dull thud of impact. He stumbles, exhaling sharply as the air leaves his lungs in a broken grunt.

It's not much. Not enough to stop him.

But maybe... enough to stall him.

Even if just for a breath.

Seizing the moment of distraction, I lock my fingers together, tighten my fists, and slam them down into his knee with everything I have left.

A sickening pop echoes through the basement, followed by Nikolai's scream of pain. His grip on me falters, his hands releasing just enough skin for me to squirm free, my body twisting out from under him like smoke slipping through fingers.

I crawl across the floor, hands scraping against the ground, pain lighting up every inch of my body. Chains rattle behind me as his voice erupts in a furious, inhuman yell.

My arms tremble, my knees threaten to collapse beneath me.

Where is my fucking knife?

"You stupid little bitch," he snarls.

"Fuck you," I hiss, dragging myself further, every movement igniting fresh pain that claws up my spine.

But I don't make it far.

Fingers clamp around my ankle and yank me back.

I scream, nails clawing at the floor, but his body is already climbing over mine again, his weight crushing, suffocating. There's no air. No space.

"Now I'm really going to let you fucking have it," he spits, venom dripping from every word.

He forces me onto my back, and his hand cracks across my face, blinding me in white-hot pain. My head spins. His fingers fumble at the knot of my waistband, tugging, pulling, while I claw at his face, at anything I can reach.

I thrash beneath him, desperate.

"Get the fuck off of me!" I scream, the sound raw and broken. Sweat drips from his forehead onto mine, his eyes wide with frenzy, detached from any trace of humanity.

"Does it not feel good, Katya?" he sneers, pressing his hand hard against me through my clothes. My stomach rolls, bile threatening to rise.

His breath hits my cheek, hot and fast.

"It'll be quick," he growls. "You can be useful for a few fucking minutes, can't you-"

Suddenly, he's gone.

His weight is ripped off my body in a blur of motion. I gasp, my lungs seizing as they finally draw in a full breath. My vision swims.

Nikolai's body slams against the wall, the sound of chains clanging as his skull cracks against concrete. He crumples in a heap, groaning, barely conscious.

Across from him stands the man with shaking hands and a Glock clenched in a white-knuckled grip. His chest rises and falls in shallow bursts. His eyes are fixed on Nikolai, empty and unreadable.

I sit up slowly, the cold floor grounding me. My head turns just enough to see the door behind them, open, wide, waiting.

My knife.

It lies near the threshold, just out of reach.

My wrist.

No longer chained.

"I wasn't-" Nikolai starts, voice cracking.

The gunshot is deafening.

He doesn't get to finish.

The bullet tears through his thigh, dropping him to the ground with a blood-curdling scream. He grabs at the wound with both hands, tears streaming down his cheeks, sobbing like a child.

The man doesn't speak.

Doesn't flinch.

He doesn't look at me, doesn't acknowledge the open door or the chaos swirling around us.

He just points the gun.

Staring.

Frozen, I remain on the ground, body stiff and paralyzed. The door is right there. My knife within reach. My legs scream at me to move, but fear holds them hostage.

The world tilts on its axis as I force myself to rise.

I don't know if I'll make it, but I have to try.

Making a break for the open door, my foot lands wrong.

Pain explodes through my ankle as it buckles beneath me, sending me crashing down hard. My knees skid against the concrete, the sound of skin tearing beneath me drowned out by my own scream. I barely make it past the threshold, my hands clawing at the floor, reaching into the dim hallway beyond.

The air shifts.

Gone is the stale rot of the basement, replaced by something warmer...drier. The faint scent of wood polish and leather. A hallway meant for people, not prisoners.

For a moment, I freeze.

The idea of going back into that room, back into that cage with Nikolai, is worse than whatever this new hell might hold. My chest heaves as I take a shaky breath, trying to hold onto the sliver of freedom just inches away.

But I feel him behind me.

Not close. Not yet. But near enough that his shadow stretches long across the floor in front of me, dark and thick like a noose.

"If you're going to shoot me too," I whisper, not bothering to turn around. "Just get it over with."

There's no answer. Just the sound of something heavy hitting the ground beside me. The thud echoes through the corridor, cold, metallic and final.

Leather.

Thick. Worn. Soft where the chains were sharp.

A collar.

"Put it on," he commands, voice like ice.

My stomach twists. "I'm not-"

The crack of his palm colliding with my ass steals the breath from my lungs. The sting spreads fast, raw and humiliating. It isn't about pain, it's about control.

"Put it on," he growls, his hand curling into my hair, yanking my head back until my eyes are forced to meet his.

My mouth clamps shut, rage trapped behind clenched teeth.

He releases me, and I hesitate for only a second before my fingers tremble around the collar. Wrapping the leather around my neck, I fasten it, flinching as his hands take over, tightening it without hesitation. Not cruelly, but tight enough that I feel it every time I swallow.

"Move," he orders, his voice low. "All the way out of the doorway."

I drag myself forward, inching into the hallway. The light here is dim, the stairs ahead lit only by the faintest glow. Behind me, the door slams shut with a steel groan, and I hear the lock engage, heavy and final.

When I look back, he's tucking the gun away, his eyes raking over me. Not with lust. Not even with rage.

Just calculation.

"Now what?" My voice is bitter as I glance down, breath catching at the sight of blood soaking the front of my shirt.

The bandage is loose. Torn from Nikolai's hands. Barely holding.

With trembling fingers, I peel it back, slow and reluctant, bracing myself for whatever I'm about to see.

Four letters.

Carved deep into my skin. Still raw. Still red.

They don't make sense at first. I stare at them, confusion giving way to horror as the letters align.

E-C-H-O.

Recognition slams into me like a freight train.

His name.

It's his name carved into me.

Not a threat. Not a warning.

A fucking claim.

"Echo," I mutter, tasting the name like acid as it leaves my mouth.

He winces, barely, but enough to know he heard it. Like the sound of it coming from me unsettles something beneath all that cold calculation.

"You need a bath," he mutters. "Only way that happens is if you listen. And behave."

My lip curls. "So I've upgraded from hostage to pet?"

Fingers twitching, I tug at the collar.

"Have to make sure you don't run again," he murmurs, crouching in front of me. "Now don't I?"

He grabs a lead from a wall hook, thick leather, matching the collar, and a black mask. I go still.

The snap of the clasp is final.

The leash is real.

His hand connects it to the collar, and my eyes widen, pulse spiking in my throat.

"Until those ankles are healed," he adds, standing. "This is how we'll move."

He slips the mask over my face, blinding me to everything but his voice and the press of his fingers as he tugs the lead.

And just like that, he walks.

And I follow.

Up the stairs. One slow, humiliating step at a time.

Like a dog.

A servant marked, bound, and trembling beneath her master's grip.

13

What Of Us Remains?

Katya

S team coils thick in the air, blanketing the room like a second skin. The scent of vanilla mixes with something deeper, something masculine and sharp. It clings to the tile, to the porcelain, to me.

Water rushes behind me, filling the tub to the brim, the sound almost soothing if not for the tension knotted in my spine. I sit stiffly on the edge, arms wrapped tight around my legs, trying to ignore the damp press of the mask against my face and the leather collar snug at my throat.

He hasn't said anything for a while.

But I can feel him. Standing just out of reach. Watching.

My thoughts spiral, sharp and chaotic. If I could find his gun, I'd end this. I'd drown him in the tub, watch the bubbles go still. I'd run. I'd survive.

But I don't know where he's hidden it.

And worse, I don't know if I want to move yet.

His voice finally cuts through the fog. Low. Measured. Unyielding.

"Take off the mask."

I don't flinch. Don't look at him. My lips part in a bitter smile, a scoff escaping before I can hold it back.

"You gonna point your gun at me if I don't?"

There's no answer.

Only the heat of his body drawing closer, the soft brush of fingers along my jaw as he peels the mask away like he's stripping the last bit of control I had left. Light floods back in, too bright. I blink through it, vision clearing just in time to see him standing over me.

His shirt sleeves are rolled to his elbows. The top two buttons undone. His black tie wrapped carelessly around his right hand, veins flexing beneath the tension in his grip. There's no gun holstered at his waist. No badge. No sign of restraint.

Only Echo.

Only the locked door behind him.

This isn't a temporary place.

It's lived in. Sharp suits hung by the door. A toothbrush in the holder. This is his.

"You don't take prisoners home," I murmur. "This isn't a sting house."

He doesn't respond.

Doesn't have to.

His silence says everything.

When he speaks again, it's not a suggestion.

"Take off your clothes."

I tense. The words sink into my skin like heat. Not loud, not cruel, but final. Unmoving.

"I'm not doing it with you in here."

"I'm not leaving."

We stare at each other, unmoving.

"I'm not stripping with you watching."

His smile is slow and arrogant.

"Funny. Fear made you spread your legs easily enough."

The words should make me flinch. Should make me burn with shame.

But instead, the air between my legs shifts. Warmth stirs. Unwanted. Treacherous.

I hate him. I hate how my body reacts to him.

"Turn around," I mutter, eyes narrowing.

"No," he answers, taking another step forward. "I'm not careless enough to do that."

His hand hooks the collar, and before I can resist, he's pulling me up, slow and deliberate. My legs wobble from the pressure on my ankle, and I reach for his shirt instinctively, palms flattening against the firm wall of his chest.

His heartbeat is steady beneath my fingers. His breath warm at my temple. He doesn't move. Just watches me fall apart.

"I fucking hate you," I breathe, words thick with exhaustion and fury.

His voice dips, soft and cruel all at once.

"Why do you think you're here, Little Butterfly? You think I brought you here because I like you?"

I don't answer.

I can't.

My fingers move to the waistband of my sweatpants, and slowly, I push them down my hips. They fall in a whisper, pooling around my ankles, leaving me half-naked in front of him.

"You're no better than the rest of them," I whisper, lifting my shirt over my head and keeping my back turned. "You're just another man who gets off on control."

Heat radiates behind me before I feel his hands.

They land heavy on my hips, warm and possessive, fingers splaying wide as he presses forward. His chest brushes my back, the hard ridge of his cock grazing my ass through his slacks.

My breath catches. My thighs clench.

"You keep talking like a victim," he growls, his lips brushing against the shell of my ear, "but you're dripping down your legs."

"No, I'm not," I whisper, even though I know the truth. My body betrays me in every way that counts.

In the mirror, I see it. My bare body flush with his, arms wrapped around my chest to hide what I can. But nothing is hidden. Not from him.

"Pity," he mutters.

His fingers slip down, curling into the waistband of my underwear. He doesn't hesitate.

One brutal yank.

The lace tears down my thighs, pooling at my feet like a final humiliation.

I'm completely exposed.

Back arched.

Breasts heaving.

Ass brushing the hard length of him that he makes no effort to hide.

He doesn't touch me again. Doesn't push. Just stands behind me, watching the way I tremble.

My arms instinctively stay crossed over my chest, but I can feel his eyes on every inch of me. Branding me.

Then comes the command, low, deep, and final.

"Put your arms down."

I swallow hard, throat tight against the collar.

This isn't a request.

This is a choice.

To fight.

Or to surrender.

I don't move.

His hand glides up my spine, slow and possessive.

"You want to get clean?" he asks, voice softer now. "Then show me what I own."

My jaw clenches as his hands find my wrists, guiding them down with slow, unshakable control. I don't fight him. I can't, not now. My balance falters, and I instinctively grip the fabric of his shirt to stay upright, the pressure of the collar at my throat a constant reminder of just how little power I hold in this moment.

He circles me like a predator sizing up his prey, the air between us thick with steam and something darker, something primal. My breaths come shallow and uneven, chest rising and falling as I try to keep hold of whatever fragments of dignity I have left.

"Open your eyes, Katya," he commands, voice low, dangerous.

The tug on my collar is sharp, yanking me forward a step. I stumble into his chest, and the breath leaves me in a rush. Slowly, I lift my gaze, forcing my eyes open just as his settle on mine.

He doesn't look away.

Neither do I.

His grip shifts to my hips, grounding me, anchoring me. I'm bare, exposed, trembling beneath his stare, but all he does is hold me there, like he's waiting for something.

The worst part?

He doesn't have to touch me for my body to betray me.

My pulse pounds. My thighs ache with heat I didn't give permission to exist.

I glance toward the mirror, just for a second.

And my eyes fall. Traitorous. Curious.

My breath catches.

He's hard. Straining against his slacks, the evidence of his arousal painfully obvious, the sight flooding warmth through my core like wildfire.

I can't look away.

The tension in his jaw sharpens as he follows my gaze.

"If I wanted you to look at my cock," Echo growls, his hand snapping up to grab my face, his fingers tightening around my cheeks, "I would've told you to."

His grip is firm...commanding. His voice just as dangerous.

"You're naked," he breathes, leaning in closer. "I've tasted your cum. You're still clinging to my shirt like you want me to hold you. I know the exact pitch your whimpers hit when you're close. I can see your breasts, your nipples are already begging, and I'd bet my life if I reached between your thighs right now, you'd be wet, just from seeing what you did to me."

My heart pounds. My legs tremble. There's no escaping the truth of what he's saying, no room to argue when my body pulses at every word from his mouth.

His grip eases, just slightly.

"But let me make one thing clear, Katya," he growls, reaching down to the floor. "You're not here for what you want."

His hand finds the discarded fabric, my underwear, soaked and ruined from everything he forced out of me earlier. Balling them in his fist, he raises them slowly, like a gift, like a sentence.

"You're here because I'm going to torture you," he says, his voice dropping lower, darker. "Not the way Nikolai got it. Not the way Isaac begged for it. No, you get a different kind."

His fingers press the fabric against my lips, and I hesitate.

Just for a breath.

And then I open.

He slides the underwear into my mouth, pushing past my resistance, until I'm gagging on the taste of my own shame, pain, release, and humiliation thick on my tongue.

I stare at him, wide-eyed, heart racing.

He doesn't blink.

Just pushes me down to my knees with a steady hand, bending me forward over the rim of the tub. The porcelain is warm beneath my face, heated by the water still running behind me, filling the air with more steam than I can handle.

His voice is a razor.

"This is the kind of torture that bends you," he whispers into my ear. "Breaks you. Makes you forget you were ever anything but mine."

His hand slaps down on my ass, hard and unrelenting. The sting ricochets through me, and I scream, the sound muffled by the fabric in my mouth as my hands claw at the edge of the tub for something, anything, to hold onto.

Another stroke of his hand follows, not as hard, but slower. More deliberate. His palm traces the scarred skin of my back, and I shudder.

"The next time you get the chance to run," he murmurs, "you won't want to."

Fingers hook into the sides of my gag. He pulls the ruined underwear from my mouth, dragging them past my teeth. I gasp for air, chest heaving as oxygen returns in sharp, greedy bursts.

He tosses them aside like they don't matter.

Like I don't matter.

"Why are you doing this to me?" I croak, turning to look at him, barely able to keep my voice steady.

His expression doesn't change. His eyes don't soften.

"Get in the water, Katya," he says coolly. "You don't get to ask questions tonight."

I hesitate, knees weak beneath me. My body still burns from the slap. My throat aches from the gag.

"I won't be your pet," I whisper, eyes narrowing.

He leans down, voice brushing over my lips like smoke.

"We'll see."

And then, sharper..final.

"Now get in."

The water laps softly around me, the scent of vanilla and salt clinging to the steam as I lean forward, staring down at my reflection. It's distorted in the ripples, fractured like everything inside me. But for once, the heat soothes instead of scorches. My body, bruised and aching, finally finds something close to relief. The burn in my ankles fades to a dull throb beneath the weight of the bath, and for a moment, I let myself breathe.

I scrub at my hair longer than necessary. Not because it needs it, but because I don't want to get out. I don't want to move. I don't want the spell broken.

Across the room, Echo sits with one leg crossed over the other, the pages of *War and Peace* flipping steadily in his hand. He doesn't speak. Just reads. Occasionally glances up.

The silence between us is suffocating.

Thick and full of everything neither of us will say.

I watch him more than I should. The way his jaw flexes when he reads something he disagrees with. The way his thumb taps the edge of the book in rhythm with his breathing.

Maybe... maybe there's still something human in him.

"Can I ask you something?" I whisper, voice barely above the water.

His page freezes mid-turn. He doesn't look at me right away.

"Ask," he says finally.

"How old are you?"

He closes the book slowly, resting it on the counter before drawing in a long, thoughtful breath. His eyes meet mine, unreadable.

"How old do you think I am?"

A question with a question.

Typical.

I raise a brow. "Old enough to know kidnapping is illegal."

Something dangerously close to a smile flickers at the corner of his lips. Not warm. But real.

He moves, rising from the chair and crossing the tile in slow, unhurried steps. The sound of his movements echoes against the walls as he kneels beside the tub.

"Thirty-eight," he answers, voice low and smooth. "Lean back."

My muscles tense. "Why?"

"I'm going to help you with your hair."

That throws me.

My fingers twitch beneath the water. The collar still rests snug around my neck, a physical reminder of who he is and what he's done.

"Take it off," I whisper, quieter this time. "Just while I'm bathing."

He starts to rise.

Panicking, I reach out, curling my hand around his wrist. My fingers wrap tight, pleading without words.

"You can put it back on after," I say, barely holding my breath. "Please."

He stares at me for a long moment. Too long.

And then, he does it.

The collar slips from my neck with a soft pull, the absence of it both freeing and terrifying.

I lean back, slowly, letting my body melt into the heat as his fingers thread gently through my wet hair. The sensation is startling, almost tender. He works the soap through with practiced ease, his touch careful. Methodical.

For the first time, he doesn't feel like a captor.

Just a man.

"You already know how old I am," I murmur, closing my eyes beneath his hands.

"Twenty-five," he says. "Five foot two. One hundred and ten pounds. Allergic to strawberries. You hate being watched while you sleep, but you do it with your mouth slightly open. Should I keep going?"

My breath catches. His voice is calm, but the words wrap around me like a noose.

"I know everything that matters," he adds.

He finishes rinsing the soap from my hair, his touch lingering longer than it should. Carefully, he helps me sit upright again, a strong hand steadying my back as I shift.

My fingers brush his cheek.

A scar, faint, but present. My thumb grazes it softly, before I can think better of it.

"How did you get that?" I ask, my voice a thread of breath, too intimate to take back.

His entire body stills.

The softness vanishes.

"I think we're done," he says, pulling away like I burned him.

The moment snaps.

Just like that.

He reaches for the collar, and before I can protest, it's back around my neck. Cinched tight. Familiar and cruel.

The bath is over.

The warmth of his hands replaced by cold absence.

And as he rises and walks toward the chair, he doesn't look back.

The man who touched my hair, who let me breathe, is gone.

Only *Echo* remains.

And as he lifts the mask, sliding it back over my eyes, I realize that something far worse than fear has begun to take root inside me.

I miss the man more than I fear the monster.

14

THE DEVIL'S DESIRES

Katya

The mask slips from my face with a slow, quiet pull, and for a moment, my eyes burn with the rush of light.

When my vision clears, I stare.

The room is massive, moonlight flooding through a barred window and stretching across dark hardwood floors. At the center sits a bed that doesn't belong in a place like this, wide, elegant, draped in black silk sheets that shimmer under the pale glow. Above it, a canopy frames the mattress, thin veils cascading down like a stage set for something meant to be watched.

The air is colder here, untouched by the steam of the bath I left behind.

I shiver.

The fabric I'm wrapped in is Echo's. The oversized dress shirt hangs loose off my shoulders, brushing against my thighs with every step. His boxers barely cling to my hips, the waistband sitting low, too low. My damp hair clings to my back, sending chilled rivulets down my spine as I clutch the shirt tighter around me.

"You're not putting me back down there?" My voice is quiet, unsure if it's hope or fear that colors it more.

Echo turns toward me, his jaw tight, his tone sharper than steel. "Do you want to go back down there with Nikolai?"

I flinch at the name before shaking my head.

The collar is tighter than before, or maybe I'm just now noticing how much it presses into my skin when I speak out of turn.

The bed looks so warm.

So inviting.

Too soft for a place like this, too much like a trap.

"There are meds on the side table. Water, too. Take them. Drink. Rest," he instructs, voice clipped. "There'll be food in its place by morning. The windows are barred. No neighbors for miles. Door will be locked. You can try and get out, but it'll be a waste of your energy."

As I begin to glance around, his hand snaps out, gripping the collar and tugging hard. My body stumbles forward, a gasp caught in my throat as he yanks me closer.

"You see that?" he hisses, turning my head toward the far corner of the room.

A red light blinks above the curtain rod, just barely noticeable.

A camera.

"I am watching you. Always," he says, lips brushing the shell of my ear. "Try anything stupid, and I will know. Even if I'm not here, I'll find out. And you know how I deal with disobedience."

His grip tightens, then releases.

The mark of his control lingers even after his fingers are gone.

"And if I don't listen?" I whisper.

Echo lets out a low, dark laugh as he circles me. "You want to end up like Isaac?" His hand lifts, and his finger presses hard to the center of my forehead. "Cold. Lifeless. A hole right here, blood dripping down your pretty little face?"

My breath catches, body frozen beneath his touch.

"Or," he continues, tilting his head, "do you want a shot at survival?"

"You're never letting me leave," I murmur, pulse rising.

"Maybe I will. Maybe I won't." He smirks, stepping away. "But what's the fun in letting Nikolai be the only one who gets to break you?"

His words are venom, each one coiling around me like a chain I can't shake. He's cold again, his voice, his movements, everything about him sharp and dangerous. But as he walks toward the door, I catch a flash of something beneath the hem of his shirt, dark streaks of something jagged, ink or blood, marring the skin of his back.

It doesn't fit.

It doesn't match the perfection he's crafted into armor.

"Light," I whisper, the word slipping from my lips before I can stop it.

His hand stills on the doorknob. "What?"

"I can't sleep without some light." The truth feels too vulnerable, but I say it anyway. "Just a little. Please."

He taps his foot once. Glances around.

Then scoffs. "That's not my problem."

The door shuts with a heavy thud.

And I'm alone.

Utterly, completely alone.

The silence stretches, so deep and all-consuming it buzzes in my ears. The camera blinks from the corner, watching. Waiting.

My eyes fall to the bed, the black sheets glowing silver under the moonlight. They look soft. So soft.

Too soft for a prisoner.

Katya Romanov.

What the hell are you going to do?

Echo

"Rise and shine," I sing sweetly, voice dripping with mock cheer as I tip the bucket forward.

The icy water crashes over Nikolai's body, soaking through the bloodied gauze wrapped around his thigh. He jolts, gasping like he's been shot all over again, limbs kicking uselessly against the restraints as his chest arches from the floor.

A low groan tears from his throat as his hands instinctively go to his leg. The wound is messy, but non-lethal. I made sure of that. Pain is more useful than death.

He pants heavily, hair clinging to his face, breath coming in uneven bursts. The rawness of it all, the desperation in his chest, the way he bites down on a scream, fills the room with something almost tangible.

"Well..." I drag the chair closer and drop into it lazily, legs spread, arms resting on my knees. "More like good night."

He doesn't respond, just continues to gasp like a beached animal, body writhing in the puddle he's now trapped in.

I smile, slow and mean.

"So. Let's try this again."

I lean forward, resting my elbows on my thighs as I study him like a specimen.

"You and I? We've gotten to know each other pretty well at this point. You've pissed me off, I've returned the favor. I think-" I reach out and press two fingers into the edge of his bandaged thigh, "-you know by now just how far I'm willing to go."

The scream he lets out vibrates through the floor, and I can't help the smile that curls across my face.

"There it is," I murmur. "Music."

He collapses back, soaked and trembling.

"How can I take down Dimitri Romanov?"

"I told you," he growls between breaths. "I don't know-"

"I don't believe you."

Rising slowly, I circle him like a vulture with too much time on its hands.

"Your family has always been close with the Romanovs. Marrying his daughter? That doesn't just *happen*. That's strategy. Eldest son. Groomed from birth. Your father whispered things to you he wouldn't even write down. Sworn to secrecy, playing the loyal dog... but what use is loyalty when your body's rotting in a ditch?"

His lip curls. "As useful as Katya would be."

I still.

"You killed her, right?" he pushes. "That was the plan, wasn't it? Break her. Bleed her. Toss her aside when she served her purpose?"

I tap my boot against the floor and stare at him. "Would it matter if I did?"

He says nothing, so I press.

"Doesn't seem like her father had much use for her. I've seen fathers cling tighter to ash than he clings to her memory."

"You don't understand," Nikolai mutters, eyes darkening. "Dimitri was *afraid* of Katya."

That gets my attention.

He sees it. Smiles through the pain.

"Afraid of what she could become. What she'd do if she ever got the full picture. Katya was always... dangerous. Nontraditional. Watching throats slit and not blinking. Passing trays when the coke was lined up. Turning her head when punishments were handed out. She never bought into the system, she just danced around it."

"Soft," I murmur, testing the word on my tongue.

"Soft in all the wrong places," Nikolai snaps. "And *ruthless* where no one needed her to be. She cut my sister, *cut* her, for talking back. Threatened Pavlov for working the girls too hard. Fought her own brother like he was a stranger. And the men who disrespected her mother?" He huffs. "Gone. Just... disappeared."

He leans forward, jaw clenched tight.

"She moved like a shadow. Quiet. Vicious. Always watching. Tell me, how does a woman like that learn the truth about Dimitri's operations and *not* burn it all to the ground?"

My fists curl.

"She needed to be broken," he continues. "Dimitri knew it. Isaac knew it. Even her mother fucking knew it. My job as her husband was to keep her in line. To keep her *ignorant*. Killing her? That would've been a relief for Dimitri. A burden lifted."

My face must shift, just barely, but he sees it.

And it makes him laugh.

"Is that shock I see, Echo?" he breathes, bloodied teeth flashing.

I say nothing.

Because for the first time, I don't know what I feel.

Nikolai keeps going, voice lower now, like he's twisting the knife. "The worst part? She's not dead. She's with *you*. And that? That scares him more than anything."

He licks his split lip, watching me unravel.

"His daughter. His shadow. The one thing he's always been able to control... now gone. And completely out of his reach."

"You're lying," I whisper.

"Maybe," he shrugs. "But you'll never know, will you?"

His smile is all teeth and blood, and for a moment, I think I might actually kill him.

But I don't.

Because now... I *need* to know if she's still his.

Or already mine.

15

Sins Hide In The Shadows

Katya

Make it stop.

A pillow muffles the sound of my ragged breathing as the darkness pushes in on all sides. Silk sheets twist around my limbs like restraints, clinging to sweat-slicked skin as memories of the day coil tighter around my throat. The room is too still, too quiet. The kind of silence that amplifies every breath, every thought, every unrelenting echo of him.

Moonlight no longer graces the floor.

It's buried behind thick, unfeeling clouds, leaving me suspended in pitch-black nothing. No glow. No stars. No escape. Just cold air, the faint scent of his cologne lingering in the fabric, and the unbearable weight of knowing he's always watching.

Seven days.

Seven nights alone in this room, the camera blinking in the corner. No visitors. No escape. Only his voice on the intercom, the pills he leaves on the table, and the quiet understanding that sleep comes at a price.

Tonight, the sleep aids remain untouched.

Chest heaving, legs unsteady, I slide out of bed. Pain flares in my ankles, but the pills dull the worst of it. Bare feet pad across the floor as I stagger to the door, the knob icy against trembling fingers.

Locked.

A familiar curse leaves my lips as I rattle it, twisting hard. "Come on," I whisper, voice breaking. "Come on, come on...fuck-"

The door swings open mid-struggle, and I stumble forward.

Straight into him.

Hard muscle catches my fall. Warm hands press against my arms, steadying me just as the door slams shut behind us with a sharp, final *click*. The lock turns.

He's here.

And the room suddenly feels smaller.

"You're supposed to be asleep," Echo mutters, voice low and hoarse with whatever dark thing he's been drinking.

"The light-" My breath trembles. "I told you I can't sleep without it."

A hum escapes his throat. Not quite sympathy. More like amusement.

Keys hit the nightstand with a metallic clatter.

He steps closer, slow and deliberate, until his shadow consumes the sliver of space between us. The heat of him rolls over my skin, soaking through the thin fabric of his shirt that I still wear like it belongs to me.

"Come here," he says.

Not a command shouted.

A promise whispered.

Feet move without permission, drawn into his gravity. The air between us crackles, heavy with things unspoken.

Fingers brush the buckle at my neck. The collar loosens and drops. But his hand doesn't leave. It curls around the nape of my neck, thumb stroking softly along the tender skin of my throat.

That slow, deliberate touch sends a shiver down my spine.

"Does it hurt?" His breath is warm at my cheek. "Your skin?"

"A little," slips past my lips, barely more than a breath.

The smell of whiskey clings to him.

"Why are you here Echo?" The question barely escapes.

"You say my name," he murmurs, voice deepening, "like it means something."

His touch lingers for one second too long.

Then, it's gone.

The absence burns more than the contact.

He moves to the bed without another word, muscles shifting beneath the loose fabric of his shirt. The mattress dips beneath his weight as he sits on the edge, sleeves rolled up, neck exposed.

His presence radiates through the room, thick and oppressive, a pulse in the dark.

Behind him, the collar lies beside the keys.

Within reach.

But so is he.

Heat pools low in my belly, shame curling in its wake. There's a choice hanging in the air, suspended between the silence and the tension threatening to snap.

Keys.

Or him.

Safety.

Or something that feels like danger wrapped in silk and the low growl of my name on his lips.

"You did cut it into my skin," the words slip out, barely a whisper, the sting still echoing in my flesh.

"That I did," he drawls, voice low and careless, like he's proud of it. "And to answer your question, I'm here to help you sleep."

Sleep.

The laugh that nearly escapes me dies in my throat.

Twisting to glance back at him, hesitation creeps in.

"There's still no light."

A slow smile curves his mouth. "I don't need light to make you sleep."

He pats his thigh, the invitation clear. Commanding.

Not a request. A warning.

"Collars off, Butterfly," he says, each word like silk laced with threat. "Don't make me drag you over here by your hair. I could have you at my feet before you even reached those keys. Now, come."

My pulse roars in my ears as I take a breath that doesn't settle. Stepping forward, the sharp ache in my ankles makes each movement feel like a punishment. There's no dignity left in the way I crawl onto the bed, knees sinking into the mattress. The weight of his gaze burns into me.

Straddling him.

Close enough to feel the heat rising off his skin. Close enough to feel his thick, hard cock beneath me pressing right where I'm starting to throb.

The contact steals the air from my lungs.

We're nose to nose, breath to breath, but he doesn't kiss me. No, he just watches. Watches like he's already won.

His hands find my thighs like they've always belonged there, dragging over the skin in slow, deliberate strokes. Then, nothing. He leans back, hands falling away, a cruel smirk twisting his lips as he lets me sit there, needing more.

"What are y-you doing?" The words stumble from my mouth, almost accusing, but far too breathless to sound like protest.

"Nothing." His voice is the kind of soft that scrapes. "You put your hands on me. You climbed into my lap. You put yourself on my cock. All I did was ask you to come over here."

A game.

That's what this is.

And I've already lost.

"You-" My palm slaps his chest, frustration and something far darker swelling inside me. But it's not anger that drives the motion, it's desperation. Because moving only grinds me harder against him, and the friction sends heat spiraling up my spine. My breath hitches. His doesn't.

That smug bastard doesn't even flinch.

His cock pulses against me, thick and unrelenting, teasing every inch of where I ache the most.

He's not touching me now. That's the worst part.

He doesn't have to.

His nose brushes mine, eyes locked on my face like he's reading every dirty thought that's racing through me.

"I what, Katya?" he purrs, voice dipped in sin. "Say it. I want to hear you choke on it."

And God help me, I almost do.

"Can you touch me?"

The words fall out like a sin, soft and reckless. A whisper I should've swallowed.

His silence stretches, thick and knowing.

Then, finally, his hands are on me.

Rough palms glide up my thighs, calloused fingers claiming the skin inch by inch, and the moment he touches me, something deep inside ignites. Not a spark. Not a flicker. A fucking blaze. It licks up my stomach, down between my legs, spreading until the ache is impossible to ignore.

I should stop this.

I could stop this.

He's drunk. The keys are right there. I could run. I know how to fight. I've brought men twice his size to their knees.

But I don't move.

I just burn.

"How else did you think I was going to make you sleep?" he murmurs, voice low and sinful, like he already knows he's won.

When his fingers hook the waistband of my boxers, I lift my hips without thinking. No resistance. No hesitation. He slides them down my legs slowly, savoring it, dragging the cotton over my trembling thighs like it's a ritual. By the time they hit the floor, I'm already soaked with anticipation.

He falls back against the mattress, but there's nothing idle in the way he moves. It's deliberate, calculated and possessive.

And then he pulls me with him.

His grip on my thighs is firm, almost bruising as he drags me up his chest, positioning me exactly where he wants me, hovering over his face, knees spread on either side of his head. I can feel the heat of his breath against me, and it's like every nerve in my body snaps awake.

He hasn't even touched me there yet, and I'm already falling apart.

My fingers find his hair, tangling in the wild curls like it's the only thing anchoring me to reality. But the moment I try to shift away, try to slow this down, he growls. A sound low and primal, vibrating right against the place I need him most.

"You're not running now," he mutters against me, lips brushing my skin. "Not after asking me to touch you."

His fingers dig deeper into my thighs, spreading me wider, locking me in place. His mouth is so close I can feel the warmth of his tongue just before it makes contact.

And then, he licks me.

Slow. Torturous. Claiming.

A strangled sound tears from my throat as my head falls back, every ounce of shame drowned beneath the heat of his mouth. He doesn't tease. Doesn't ease me in.

He devours.

His tongue works me open like he's starving, like this is his reward and punishment all at once. Each flick, each curl of his tongue sends lightning through my veins. My hips roll without permission, chasing more, needing deeper.

"Fuck," I gasp, my grip in his hair tightening as he groans against me, the sound sending vibrations through my core.

"You taste like sin," he growls, licking me again. "Like you want to be ruined."

And maybe I do.

Maybe I already am.

Because I can't remember why I ever wanted to run.

"You're done when I say you are."

The warning curls from his lips like smoke, sinking into my skin and making my heart thunder so violently I swear he can feel it. There's no room to speak, no room to think, not when he grips my thighs and forces me down harder onto his face.

A gasp rips out of me, sharp and guttural.

The heat of his mouth crashes into me, and suddenly I'm nothing but sensation. His nose is buried deep between my folds, tongue moving with ruthless precision, slick, strong, devastating. He doesn't ease in. He attacks.

Every stroke of his tongue is deliberate. Every suck, every press, is a silent promise to ruin me.

He licks up every inch of me like I'm the only thing that's ever mattered. Like he's been waiting his whole life to taste me and now that he has, he's never letting go.

My hips move on their own, grinding, rocking, chasing the high he's dragging out of me with his mouth. Wet, obscene sounds fill the room, echoing in the silence like sin. His tongue slides along my entrance and circles my clit, and the moment his lips close around it, hard, I cry out.

Louder this time. Shameless.

Fingers tangle in his hair, tugging so hard I know it must hurt, but he groans against me like he likes it. The vibration rips through me like lightning. My own hair brushes the small of my back as I lean forward, gripping onto the headboard, needing something to hold onto.

His scent. His taste. His control. It's all I can feel.

Fuck, what am I doing?

He's vulnerable like this. Exposed. Drunk.

And still, he's completely in control.

Because I can't stop.

The heat coils tighter and tighter until it snaps, and when it does, I break over his mouth like a wave. Shaking. Writhing. Cuming hard.

But he doesn't stop.

He keeps going, dragging every last ripple of my orgasm out until I'm trembling and soaked, until my cum is coating his face, his jaw, his mouth—until there's no room left for shame.

Only pleasure.

Only his name.

The more I cry out, the more I come undone, the harder he grips my thighs, holding me down as his tongue laps me clean like a man feasting at the altar of something sacred.

This isn't gentle. This isn't soft. This is worship.

And I let him.

Because I've never been devoured like this.

Never been ruined so sweetly.

Never wanted anything more.

He sits up without warning, keeping me straddled across his lap like a throne he refuses to relinquish. My cum glistens along his face, lips, chin and cheekbones, catching the silver glow of the moonlight through the bars on the window like a crown made of sin.

And fuck, he wears it proudly.

Fisting a hand into my hair, he yanks me closer with a sharp tug that forces a gasp from my throat, my body jolting against his in response. The look in his eyes is absolute.

The demand slices through me like a hot blade.

My release, *my* mess, shines along his perfect, ruined features, and still, he doesn't wipe it away. He *wants* me to do it. He *needs* me to.

And I do. Without question. Without shame.

With a breath that trembles on the edge of obedience and obsession, I lean in, my tongue dragging slow and heavy along the sharp line of his jaw, tasting the raw, warm tang of my own arousal smeared across his skin. It coats my tongue, sweet and electric, fueling a heat that hasn't gone anywhere, only deepened.

Every breath, every lick, feels like surrender.

His cheeks. His nose. His lips. I clean him like it's a ritual, a worship, and in some sick, twisted way, it *is*. He made me cum, and now he wants every trace of it gone by *my* mouth. So I drag my tongue over the bridge of his nose, lapping up every drop like I'm starving, like I've forgotten anything outside of him exists.

My hips start to move, slow, desperate rolls over the thick hardness pulsing beneath me. It presses right against where I'm still wet, still trembling, still aching for more.

His hands dig into my waist, gripping me with bruising force, holding me there, teasing me with what's beneath me but giving me nothing.

The stretch. The size. The very thought of him inside me is *terrifying*.

Unthinkable.

I want it anyway.

Want to feel him split me open.

Want to hear him groan against my throat as I fall apart around him all over again.

He says nothing as I keep licking him clean, like he knows I'm falling deeper with every stroke of my tongue. Like he's giving me just enough to ruin myself on him, slowly, willingly, helplessly.

And he hasn't even fucked me yet.

Once I've finished licking every last drop of myself off his face, he doesn't speak. Doesn't give praise. Doesn't offer softness.

He just lays me back.

My spine meets the mattress, cool against my sweat-slick skin, and then his hand is between my legs, *again*, like I haven't already shattered for him once tonight.

Two fingers slip inside with zero resistance.

The stretch is sudden, knuckle-deep, and brutal in its precision. My body jerks, a cry catching in my throat as he pumps them hard, relentless, like he's trying to wring another orgasm out of me just to prove he *can*.

Gasps fill the air between us, sharp and ragged. My lip trembles as I reach for something, *anything*, but there's only him. Only the lewd, wet sound of my slick coating his hand with every brutal thrust.

I'm so soaked he could fit his *entire* hand in if he wanted. The thought alone sends heat lashing through my abdomen, tightening like a noose around my sanity.

"You will not leave," he whispers against my skin, his voice like a prayer dipped in violence.

Then a third finger slides in, stretching me even wider.

"You won't leave," he continues, biting the shell of my ear, "because you *won't want* to leave."

The moan that leaves me is part denial, part surrender.

"You're wrong," I gasp, even as my body arches into his touch like it's begging for more.

A dark laugh rumbles in his throat.

"We'll see," Echo mutters, dragging his tongue down the column of my neck, slow and deliberate, before his teeth sink into my skin hard enough to leave a mark. My breath stutters, eyes fluttering closed, and then just like that, he pulls his fingers out of me.

Too soon. Too cruel.

I whimper from the loss, every nerve still lit like firecrackers.

And then, I watch.

I *watch* as he lifts his hand to his mouth, licks my taste from his fingers with a lazy smirk, and walks away from the bed like I didn't just fall apart for him. Like I'm not still trembling. Still open. Still needing.

"You could've killed me," I say, voice cracking in the dim silence. "Strangled me. Locked me in here and made me disappear."

"But you didn't, Echo. Why?"

He pauses in the doorway, fingers still glistening with my slick.

"You could've strangled me. Shot me like you did Nikolai. Left me with nothing." I swallow hard, hating the rasp in my voice. "But instead... you came in here and let me ride your face like a whore until I came."

The words hang heavy in the dark.

He doesn't respond.

Just closes the door behind him, leaving me in silence, the echo of his touch still pulsing inside me.

Only when the click of the latch sounds does my body finally give in.

Eyes closed. Breathing shallow.

And this time, I sleep.

16

PRIVATE PROPERTY

ECHO

Fucking stupid.

No, worse than stupid.

Debilitating.

What the fuck was I thinking?

She was right. I should've tortured her. Should've kept her in the dark, locked up and broken beneath Nikolai, right where Romanov scum belong. Let her rot in the filth she crawled out of, remind her what she is.

And yet, here I am.

I let her out. Let her breathe my air. Sleep in my sheets. Bathe in my water. I dressed her in my clothes like she belonged here. Like she hadn't come from bloodlines soaked in betrayal.

What the fuck is wrong with me?

Nikolai's story doesn't matter. None of it matters. I can't trust a single goddamn word out of his mouth. I know that.

But her?

Fuck.

The way she tasted, God, the way she tasted. Sweet, like sin and surrender. The way she looked at me while I licked her clean, the way she curled into my lap like she was made for it, like she'd been waiting to crawl back to me. There was no fear in her eyes. No hesitation.

She came to me.

Needed me.

Her thighs spread, her fingers twisted in my hair like she'd rather die than let me stop. Her hips grinding against my mouth, using me, riding me until she shattered all over my tongue. And when it was over, when her cum was still dripping down my face, she licked it off like it belonged to her. Like she wanted to wear her filth on her tongue just to make me proud.

There was no shame. Just heat. Hunger. Desperation.

And I should've stopped. I should've walked away.

But I didn't.

Because I didn't want to.

I wanted to ruin her.

I wanted to bury myself so deep inside her pussy, she wouldn't know where she ended and I began. I wanted to hear her scream my name when I ripped her apart. I wanted her to bleed around me, to cry and beg and still come undone like she was grateful for the pain.

All my sickest fantasies. All my worst, filthiest fucking desires.

I wanted to break her.

She should've run. Should've taken the first chance she got and disappeared into the dark.

But she didn't.

She stayed.

Why?

Why the fuck didn't she run?

The question clawed at the inside of my skull all night.

Why didn't she run?

The collar had been off. The keys were right fucking there. No chains, no threats. Nothing but her and the door. I gave her every reason to leave, every opportunity, and still, she stayed.

And for the life of me, I can't figure out why.

There's no comfort in this place. No softness in me. I've done nothing but remind her who holds the leash. Nothing but use her, test her, push her closer to the edge.

Last night was supposed to be a test.

A way to see what she would do when the cage was cracked open.

But now, hours later, in the dull, hungover haze of morning, the real problem settles in like rot: I don't even know what answer I wanted.

Would I have been satisfied if she ran?

Would I have hunted her down just to punish her for proving she could?

Or was I hoping, deep down in some sick, twisted corner of myself, that she'd stay? That she wanted to?

The thought sours in my stomach.

I take a long, bitter swig of my coffee, letting the burn coat my throat. It doesn't help. My head's still fogged from last night, her taste, her sounds, the way her body moved against mine like it had done it before. Like it was meant to.

Normally, I don't take days off. Work is routine. Structure. Control. But the idea of walking into that office, sitting through one of Roman's probing conversations, pretending I'm not unraveling from the inside out?

I'd rather set the whole place on fire.

The house is too quiet.

Katya's door remains shut. No sound, no movement, no breath I can hear. The silence presses against my ears like cotton soaked in gasoline, suffocating and ready to ignite.

Every curtain is drawn, every window blocked. This house was designed to isolate, to keep things in. Out here, miles from civilization, surrounded by trees and thick forest, even if she did run, she wouldn't get far. Two miles on foot through woods she doesn't know. No phone. No car. No one to hear her scream.

The worst part?
She knows that.

And still, she stayed.

My foot taps against the tile floor, a slow, agitated rhythm. I can feel the mistake before it forms in my chest, before it rises up through my throat and pushes past my teeth.

My gaze drifts to the plate I set out for her, untouched. Cold now. Pointless.

A stupid gesture.

And still, something in me lurches.

Why the fuck did I do that?

"Fuck," I hiss under my breath, raking a hand down my face.

She's in my walls now. In my head. In my goddamn bloodstream.

And I don't know how to get her out.

Making my way to her door, I slide the lock open with a soft click, revealing the girl on the other side.

Her expression is clouded with confusion, lips slightly parted, eyes darting toward the kitchen like she's waiting for the next blow, the next command. Not trust. Not warmth.

I follow her gaze toward the plate of food I'd been about to bring her. It sits on the counter, untouched. A silent offering I'm no longer sure I have the right to make. Without a word, I leave it there and step back, watching her cautiously emerge from the room.

When she crosses the threshold, I nudge the plate toward her. My jaw tightens.

It's impossible not to see her as she was last night.

On her knees.

In my lap.

Breathless and wrecked and mine.

But now, now she's guarded, controlled, studying the plate like it might bite.

Her eyes flick to the utensils, fork, knife, like she's calculating, like she doesn't know whether this is another test or a trap. She hesitates, fingers brushing the metal. Then finally, after several seconds that feel like an eternity, she picks up the fork.

Without a word, she sits at the kitchen island and begins to eat.

I watch every movement. Every swallow.

"Is it true?" I ask. My voice is low, heavy with something I haven't named. "What you feel... about your family's work?"

She glances up at me through her lashes, pale skin tinged with a flush that spreads slowly across her cheeks. Shame? Anger? Guilt?

"What did Nikolai tell you?" she counters, leaning into her hand, feigning nonchalance.

But I see the shift in her. Something in her walls cracks, just a little.

Right now, like this, I don't see the killer Noah wrote about. I don't see the Romanov heir carved from steel and blood. I just see her.

"Do you know what Dimitri does?"

A bitter laugh escapes her lips as she nudges the plate aside, appetite vanishing like smoke.

"My father lies. Kills. Manipulates. Blood paved the way to every inch of his success," she murmurs. "I've killed for him. Sold myself to his vision. Used drugs, power, whatever he needed. I was a weapon he forged with his bare hands."

Her voice is distant. Detached. Too calm for the things she's saying.

"But you didn't follow blindly."

Her eyes flick to mine, and for the first time, her voice softens.

"Not always. I saw what he didn't. I saw the cracks. The corruption. When the people he called allies turned out to be monsters, I didn't protect them. I eliminated them."

Her jaw tightens. "It made me an enemy in my own house. Pavlov's punishments became worse. My father's grip turned to chains."

A silence falls, thick and suffocating.

"The children," I say, before I can stop myself.

She goes still.

Her face drains of warmth. "What children?" The words fall unevenly from her lips.

I look away.

Guilt crawls beneath my skin like ants. I didn't mean to say it. Not like that. Not now.

"This is a game," I mutter, jaw clenched. "And I'm fucking losing."

Her chair scrapes sharply as she stands. She moves fast. Faster than I expect.

I turn to see her hand wrapped around something silver and bright.

A knife.

"What the hell are you talking about?" she spits, the blade trembling in her grip as she raises it between us. Her eyes are wild, not calculating. Panicked.

I don't flinch. I look down at her.

She's not faking.

This isn't an act.

The knife shakes in her hand, not because she's weak, but because she's rattled. She's desperate for the truth. And I just tore open something she wasn't ready to face.

"Put it down, Katya," I say, my voice flat, but not cold. "You're not going to hurt me."

Her lips quiver. "I need answers."

"Not like this."

Her flush deepens. Her frustration burns through her restraint.

Grabbing the back of her neck, my fingers slide into the heat of her hair, holding her steady. Her breath hitches. Her pulse pounds under my palm. I grab her wrist, squeezing hard enough to make the blade drop to the tile with a sharp clang.

Pulling her closer, I feel the fury thrumming off her skin.

But underneath it?

Is confusion.

Fear.

Need.

"That's enough questions for today," I hiss, my lips brushing the shell of her ear.

Her breathing staggers.

"Maybe it's time you went back to your room."

And this time, when I guide her back toward the hall, she doesn't fight me.

She follows.

Her jaw tightens like a warning, eyes sharp and unreadable. Then, without a word, her free hand moves.

Cold fingertips graze the edge of my waistband, delicate but deliberate, the icy trail of her touch igniting something primal just beneath my skin. My muscles tense, the air stilling around us as her fingers slide just under the fabric, teasing, testing...threatening.

I should stop her. I want to stop her.

But I don't.

Because my heart is already slamming against my ribs, blood rushing so hard it drowns out reason. The ache between my legs surges instantly, heat pulsing, blood thickening, everything below my waist demanding more.

Then, she yanks her wrist back.

My stomach clenches, breath caught.

Her narrowed eyes lock onto mine like a challenge, a dare, and then she sinks. One slow, calculated motion until she's on her knees in front of me.

My throat dries.

Both hands grip the edge of my waistband now, knuckles pale from tension, her fingers curling into the fabric like she owns it.

"Katya-" My voice is hoarse, strained. Not angry, but desperate.

When I move to stop her, she strikes fast, sinking her teeth into the flesh of my hand, hard.

I flinch, stunned, staring down at the crescent indents she leaves behind. Her mouth. Her bite. It's still tingling, burning, marked.

Fuck.

She tugs on my belt with slow, agonizing precision, the metal clinking in the silence between us. Each motion is a threat laced in seduction, every second dragging my sanity closer to the edge. The blood flow between my legs shifts from ache to pressure, thick, pulsing and impossible to hide.

The strain in my pants is visible now, undeniable, twitching beneath the weight of her gaze.

But I still say nothing.

Can't.

Because her fingers are at my zipper now, dragging it down inch by torturous inch. The sound is deafening.

Her knuckles brush the bulge in my boxers, and my entire body jerks, heat flaring as her touch ghosts over the hardest part of me.

My hands grip the edge of the island like it's the only thing keeping me grounded. The marble is cool under my palms, unlike the fire raging everywhere else.

Katya doesn't speak. She doesn't have to.

Her silence devours me.

And I let her.

Because right now, in this moment, with her on her knees and that look in her eyes, I've never felt more owned.

Then, warm.

So warm it borders on sinful, her lips press to the base of my cock, soft and slow, kissing up along my length like she's worshiping it. The contrast between her cool fingers and the heat of her mouth makes my knees want to buckle. Every inch she traces with her lips tightens the coil in my gut.

My hand finds her hair, curling into those silken strands as I look down.

Her eyes flick up to meet mine, wide and wild, and the second she sees just how much I've been keeping from her, there's a flicker of something, shock, awe, maybe even challenge, lighting up behind those lashes.

Yeah, okay, Katya. Let's see how long that silent treatment really lasts now.

I hook my thumbs into my boxers and drag them down, slow and deliberate, letting my cock spring free right in front of her face. Her breath hitches, the sound almost imperceptible, but I hear it. I feel it.

My fist curls tighter in her hair, tugging her head back just enough so I can stroke myself in front of her. Long, slow pumps, teasing the tip with my thumb while I keep my eyes locked on hers. Her lips part slightly, her tongue slipping out to wet her bottom lip like she's imagining the weight of me there.

And fuck, so am I.

She stays on her knees, hands dragging up my thighs, slow as sin. She grips the backs of them, grounding herself like she already knows she's about to be undone.

I groan, the sound raw, broken, as I take in the full picture, Katya, on her knees, mouth open, gaze locked on my cock like it's the only goddamn thing in the world.

Her spit glistens as she leans forward, a trail of it slipping from her mouth onto my tip. She spreads it with her tongue, slow and torturous, dragging it down my shaft in one long, wet line.

My grip tightens, yanking her closer, and her head bumps softly against the island cabinets behind her. She doesn't flinch. Doesn't pull back.

She fucking smirks.

"Oh, you're still upset?" I ask, breath low, rough, my hand cradling the side of her face as her lips part.

And then, she takes me.

Warm. Wet. Perfect.

Her lips wrap around my head, tongue circling the crown as her eyes flutter. I twitch against her tongue, every nerve ending burning as she sinks down farther, inch by inch, swallowing me like she's starving.

She nods, barely, mouth full of me, eyes glassy with that defiant heat.

Silent treatment intact.

But her mouth says everything I need to hear.

My hips start slow, just the tip pressing past her lips, easing down her throat inch by inch.

She gags.

Beautifully.

That perfect little throat can't take all of me, not yet. Her hands, delicate and trembling, grip the backs of my thighs like she's hanging on for dear life, fingers curling into my skin as her body fights to adjust to my size.

My hands cradle her face, fingers splayed over her flushed cheeks, thumbs brushing over wet lashes already clinging together.

Each thrust pushing deeper.

Each gag is music.

Her throat spasms around me as I press just a little farther each time, a slick, wet vice that threatens to drag me to the edge far too fast. Her spit starts to pool at the corners of her mouth, dripping down her chin in thick, messy ropes, coating my cock with every brutal stroke. Her eyes water, wide and glassy, a silent plea mixed with something darker, something I don't think she even understands.

I do.

I fucking do.

My pace shifts from slow torment to something meaner, more possessive. Her head knocks into the cabinets behind her with every thrust, the thud dull beneath the wet, relentless sound of me using her mouth like it's mine.

Because it is.

Her throat is mine.

Her gagging, choking, drowning in me, it belongs to me.

Her nails dig into my skin now, sharp little crescents pressing deeper the harder I go, the rougher I grip her face, the more I force her to take what I know she can't handle.

And God help me, I can't stop.

I don't stop.

I drive myself deeper, harder, fucking her mouth like it's the only thing tethering me to sanity. The slap of skin, the sloppy suck of her lips trying to hold on, it's all building, all boiling beneath the surface, release clawing its way through me with every passing second.

I shove a hand behind her head and hold her there, make her take it.

She gags violently, choking on every inch, spit bubbling down her chin, dripping onto her bare thighs.

She's trembling.

Barely holding it together.

And I love her like this.

Unraveled. Ruined. Still full of fucking fire.

Something inside me snaps.

The urge to finish like this, to mark her, to own her completely, it pulses through me like lightning.

But I don't.

I won't.

"I'm not cumming in your mouth, Butterfly," I growl, voice thick with restraint and something darker, something possessive enough to swallow her whole.

I pull out with a wet pop, a thick trail of spit still connecting her swollen lips to the slick head of my cock.

She gasps for air, coughing, tears running, lips red and raw, and somehow...somehow, she still lifts her chin and smirks.

Grabbing onto me, eyes glowing with something feral, she breathes, "That's all you've got?"

That fire...

That defiance.

Oh, Katya.

So this is the torture you want?

I grab her without hesitation, lifting her over my shoulder like she weighs nothing.

She kicks. Pounds into my back with those small fists, but it's all for show. Her body gives her away, hips grinding against my shoulder, wet heat bleeding through her boxers and seeping into my skin.

My free hand slides beneath the fabric.

Fuck.

She's soaked.

Dripping.

Needy.

So fucking ready for this and she doesn't even realize it.

All mine.

I palm her slick cunt once, just to feel how ruinously wet she is, then slide her down, letting her feet barely brush the floor before I shove her forward, my hand wrapping tight around her throat.

With one commanding push, I bend her over the back of the couch, her face buried in the cushions, her ass perfectly presented in the air. She squirms, not in protest, no, but in anticipation. That little shiver crawling up her spine betrays her.

Dragging down her boxers, I expose her inch by inch. Her skin glows in the low light, flushed and trembling. My hand drags across her ass, slow and deliberate, fingers digging into the softness before I deliver a firm slap, more a warning than a punishment.

She whimpers, but not from pain.

It's hunger. Desperation.

She's right where I want her...where I need her.

Bent. Silent. Mine.

"A dirty fucking whore like you, Katya..." My voice is low, teeth clenched around the growl building in my throat. "I think you deserve my cock buried in your ass. Don't you?"

She freezes.

That gorgeous body goes still, muscles tightening beneath my hand. Her head turns just enough for her flushed cheek to press into the couch cushions, eyes meeting mine over her shoulder.

"I've never-"

I cut her off without a breath of hesitation.

"It wasn't really a question."

My hand tightens around her neck, pressing her down just enough to remind her who owns this moment. Her chest rises and falls beneath me, ragged and uneven, and the way her thighs rub together tells me everything I need to know.

She's scared.

She's overwhelmed.

But she's drenched.

She wants it.

And she's about to learn exactly what kind of man she's given herself to.

I spit, slow and thick, watching it trail down the crease of her perfect ass.

It drips between her cheeks, shining as it mixes with the slick still coating my cock from her mouth. The way she took me down her throat... fuck, I can still feel the ghost of it wrapped around me.

Now it's her turn to feel all of me.

Spreading her thighs wider with my own, I line myself up, tip barely nudging her tight, untouched hole, and just hover. Teasing. Letting the threat of what's coming stretch out until her moans dissolve into low, choked sobs against the cushion.

Then I press in.

Slow.

Deliberate.

Cruel.

Her body tenses, trembles, clenches, but still, she takes me. Inch by inch, her ass devours my cock, the pressure unbelievable. The tightness... goddamn. My jaw clenches as I push deeper, her cries muffled by the couch, her fingers clawing into the fabric like she's trying not to fall apart.

But I want her to fall apart.

Her moans shift, rising higher, warping into screams when my hips finally meet her ass, burying myself fully inside her. The stretch is brutal. She's not used to this. Her body isn't ready. And still, she's taking it.

I start to move.

Slow at first, just enough to let her feel the shape of me, the way I drag against every nerve ending inside her. Her screams echo through the house, raw and uncontrolled, blending with the wet slap of my hips crashing into her. My cock throbs inside her, impossibly hard, the tight grip of her body making it feel like I'm going to lose control far too fast.

Her tears soak into the couch. Her nails dig deeper. Her body tries to crawl forward, but I've got her locked in place, one hand gripping the back of her neck, the other slamming her hips right back into mine.

Every thrust is harder.

Deeper.

Mine.

She gasps. She cries. She aches for me now.

"E-Echo," she sobs, voice cracking in the air, the sound a perfect blend of pain and pleasure.

I groan, the weight of her ass wrapped around me enough to drive me fucking insane.

"I-I won't leave," she cries, her voice muffled in the cushions, broken and soaked in desperation.

The second those words hit my ears, I lose whatever restraint I had left.

I fuck her harder.

Like I'm trying to brand it into her.

"Won't leave who?" I growl, leaning over her, teeth grazing the shell of her ear. I'm seconds from exploding inside her.

"You," she gasps. "I-I won't leave you."

My hand slips from her neck to her jaw, tilting her head back, forcing her to feel every thrust, every word.

"I thought you knew," I pant, hips jackhammering now, on the edge of losing every ounce of control.

"You're mine, Little Butterfly."

And I'm going to fuck her like she finally believes it.

With a final, punishing thrust, I bury myself deep and release.

My cock pulses, spilling into the tightest part of her, my hips slamming into her ass as she screams, a sharp, raw sound that echoes like a war cry through the walls of the house. It's not pain. It's not pleasure.

It's everything.

Her body spasms beneath me, trembling as I grind in deeper, forcing every last drop into her. I want it to stay. I want her to feel it for days.

Only when the waves subside, when her moans turn to shallow, ragged breaths, do I slowly pull back.

My eyes stay locked on the sight below me, her ruined body trembling, leaking, marked.

My cum slips from her ass in thick trails, painting her thighs, mixing with sweat and streaks of blood, slick, raw proof that she's been claimed. Her legs are shaking. Unsteady. And still, she grips the back of the chair like it's the only thing keeping her tethered to reality.

She's wrecked.

Perfectly.

Blood still coats my cock, a mix of her body surrendering and my brutality, and fuck, it only makes her look more like she was made for this.

For me.

I should leave her like this.
Used. Filled. Trembling.

But I don't.

I can't.

Something dark and possessive coils in my gut as I slide an arm beneath her, lifting her broken body into mine. She doesn't fight it. Doesn't speak.

She just breathes, shallow and uneven against my chest, leaking me down her thighs, skin flushed and sticky.

She's mine now. Every inch of her knows it.

Carrying her through the quiet hall, I don't head back toward the room she's been locked in.

I take her to my bed.

And I don't know which part of my blackened soul has latched onto this girl... but it's done.

There's no going back.

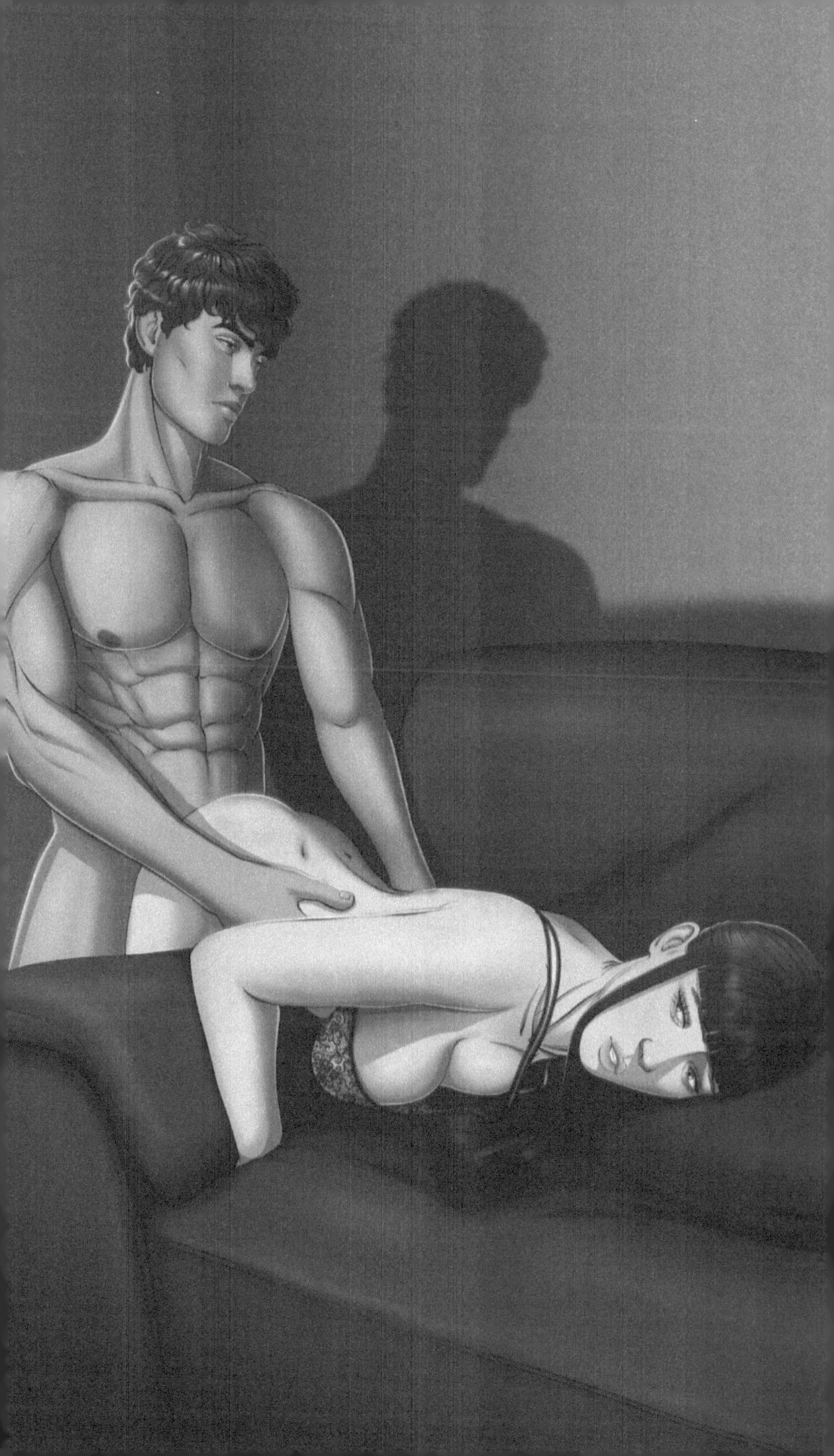

YOUR TIME IS UP

ROMAN

Smiling at the photo on my desk, my thumb drags slowly across the glass, tracing the faces I'd do anything to protect. Eden, smirking with her signature defiance, and our girls, caught mid-laugh, arms tangled, wild curls flying in every direction. For a second, the weight of the world dulls beneath the image of them.

But peace doesn't last long in this job. It never does.

The silence of my phone draws my attention next.

Still blank.

Still no word.

Not a single message from Echo. Not even the usual, vague-ass check-in.

He's been off for the past week. Off in ways that don't sit right. Leaving work early. Calling out last-minute. Ignoring protocol.

Echo doesn't do things wrong. He bends rules when it suits him, but outright disorder? That isn't his language.

The air in the room is tight, like it knows something I don't.

The creak of the office door pulling open draws my gaze toward the hallway. Noah steps inside without knocking, something in his face drawn tight. Dark rings under his eyes, posture coiled like he hasn't truly slept in days.

"Hey," he says, voice hoarse, trying to play it casual. "Are Ana and I still good to come to your place this weekend?"

Dropping into the chair across from me, he exhales sharply, fatigue radiating off him like heat. He's trying to keep it together. The effort shows.

"Yeah, of course," I nod, leaning back in my chair. "The girls have been hounding me all week, wondering when they'll see Ana again."

The corners of his mouth lift just slightly, but his eyes stay locked on his phone.

And then, like clockwork, the frown returns.

"Still no word from Echo," he mutters, more to himself than to me.

My stomach sinks.

"No," I answer, jaw tightening. "You neither?"

A slow shake of the head. "Nothing."

A beat of silence settles between us.

"Something's been off with him lately..." I finally say it aloud.

The words hang in the air, tension lingering just beneath the surface.

Noah shifts, visibly uncomfortable the moment they leave my mouth. His leg bounces once, twice, then stops. He doesn't meet my eyes.

"What?" The question is sharper than intended.

"It's probably nothing," he says too quickly, gaze flicking to the wall, to the window, anywhere but me.

"Noah." My tone drops.

He sighs, scrubbing a hand down his face. "I shouldn't say anything."

"You've got about three seconds to start talking," I tell him evenly, "or I remind you that you still owe me for getting that mess in Germany off your record. And, unless you forgot, I am your superior, so if something's going on with Echo, you will tell me."

A muscle twitches in his jaw. Whatever it is, it's not just speculation. It's something he's been sitting on. Something big enough to make even him second-guess speaking it aloud.

And now, I can't breathe right.

Because whatever's about to come out of Noah's mouth, it's not nothing.

It's something I won't be able to ignore.

"A week and some days ago," Noah starts, his voice measured, but it's clear he's been sitting on this information too long, "Echo came in on his day off. Claimed he was just tying up loose ends."

I tense.

Noah glances up at me, something darker moving behind his eyes. "He went to check out Pavlov's establishment. Alone."

The air stills.

"Not even twenty-four hours later," he continues, "Katya Romanov and the Sokolov boy both go missing."

The implication cuts through the silence like a blade.

My brow furrows. "We don't have anyone in our confinement. We would've flagged it."

"I know," Noah replies quickly...too quickly.

"So what are you insinuating?" My voice sharpens, narrowing in like a spotlight. "That Echo had something to do with their disappearance?"

Noah doesn't answer right away. He doesn't need to. The hesitation in his expression already tells me what he's afraid to say out loud.

I lean forward. "Do you think he's capable of something like that? Kidnapping two people in broad daylight?"

The question feels wrong coming out of my own mouth. I want to shut it down, dismiss it outright, tear Noah apart for even suggesting it, but the silence that follows says everything.

Because deep down, I do know what Echo is capable of.

He trained me.

I covered his first body.

And there's a reason we keep him off the books when things need to disappear.

Before either of us can speak, the office intercom buzzes to life, our receptionist's voice shaky through the static. "Mr. Briar...

there's someone in the lobby waiting to see you and Mr. Ack-erman."

My gaze darts to the intercom speaker. Noah straightens be-side me, instinct kicking in.

"Send them in," I say, already on edge.

Noah exhales through his nose. "Regardless of what we think... something's going on with him. Calling off in the middle of a week like this? That's unheard of for Echo. Something's wrong."

The words barely leave his mouth before the office door swings open.

Both of our hands move in tandem, guns drawn, fingers tensed, aimed without hesitation.

The man standing in the doorway doesn't flinch. He stands tall, flanked by two others in tailored black, his eyes sweeping the room with a familiarity that makes my skin crawl.

Dimitri Romanov.

Smirking and alive, standing in our headquarters like he owns the goddamn place.

I rise from my chair, gun locked in on his skull. Noah does the same, stepping around the desk, stance wide and steady.

"How the fuck did you get in here?" The question tears out of me before logic can catch up.

Dimitri's expression doesn't falter. "I walked through the front door."

My grip tightens.

"Your men knew better than to start showering bullets without a reason," he adds casually, stepping farther into the room as if we hadn't both already made the decision to put him in the ground.

Noah and I lock eyes, just long enough to confirm neither of us is breathing easy.

"Roman Briar. Noah Ackerman," Dimitri says, each name like a toast as he slowly eases into Noah's chair, the gall of it borderline suicidal. His men remain standing, silent, posted directly behind him like they were carved from the floor itself.

"In the flesh," he muses, smoothing his jacket. "It really is an honor. Though, I admit... I was hoping to feast my eyes on another."

My stomach knots.

"Echo, is it?" Dimitri tilts his head. "Echo Kane."

He smiles, cold and sharp, like the steel of a blade just before it's buried between your ribs.

No one moves.

And for the first time in years, I wonder who's actually in control of this room.

Boots slam against the tile as I reach the door, the sound of drawn weapons echoing through the hallway. Our men are locked and ready, but they're late. The moment's already passed. Dimitri Romanov stands inside Catalyst headquarters like he's been here a thousand times before, like this place belongs to him.

My hand shoots up. "Stand down."

The command leaves no room for hesitation. They obey, reluctantly, weapons lowering by inches.

Mine doesn't.

Dimitri doesn't blink. Doesn't flinch. His lips tug into a slow smirk, eyes watching every move like he already knows how the rest of this is going to play out.

"What can we do for you?" The question leaves my mouth sharp-edged, my Glock steady at my side.

He doesn't answer, just snaps his fingers.

The man beside him moves instantly, pulling a photo from inside his jacket and tossing it onto my desk like it's just another fucking formality. It lands face up—blurry, grainy, low-resolution. A man in a baseball cap, head tilted just enough to obscure his features. Could be anyone.

But it's not.

Even through the distortion, I know that frame. That posture. That deliberate way of holding back weight like he's always ready to strike.

It's Echo.

Noah's breath hitches beside me. He doesn't say a word, but I feel it. He knows too.

Dimitri watches us both with the satisfaction of someone who's just won a game we didn't realize we were playing.

"This," he says, motioning lazily toward the photo, "is the last known person to see Nikolai and my daughter before they disappeared. The image is... inconveniently unclear. But I can see it on your faces."

His voice lowers.

"You know who it is."

The tension in the room tightens like wire.

"All I need is a name."

"That's not how this works."

He tilts his head, amused. "Oh, but it is now. See, unlike Echo, you two leave footprints. You have jobs. Reputations. Families."

A cold weight settles in my chest.

"Let's talk specifics," he continues, gaze flicking toward Noah. "Noah Ackerman. Fiancée. Anastasia Burns. Works in this very building, doesn't she?"

Noah's grip on his weapon tightens.

"And Roman Briar. The infamous vet turned priest. A wife and two daughters, both in Spokehaven. Quaint little house with a white fence and a swing in the yard."

My hand curls tighter around the Glock. One wrong word and I'll end him.

"All very much alive... for now."

The breath in my lungs freezes. "Are you threatening our families?"

His voice drops even lower. "No. I'm warning you what happens if I don't get my daughter back. I want Katya alive. I want Echo Kane gone. If those things don't happen-" he shrugs, "-then you'll understand pain on a very personal level."

Before I can speak, there's motion from the hall.

Ana.

She steps into the room with her gun drawn, jaw set, posture locked. She's ready to shoot.

Dimitri turns toward her like he's already planned this too. "Anastasia Burns," he says, smiling like the devil. "Even more stunning in person."

Noah shifts fast.

Dimitri's fingers snap again.

His man moves quicker than I can raise my gun.

Ana slams into the wall with a sickening thud, her weapon hitting the floor. A thick arm wraps around her throat, lifting her off the ground. Her boots kick wildly, lips parting in a strangled gasp, nails clawing at the forearm crushing her windpipe.

Noah lunges. So do I.

Dimitri lifts a single finger.

"One move," he says softly, "and she dies."

Ana's eyes lock with mine, desperate and burning. She can't breathe.

Her body jerks, boots scraping against the wall, lungs fighting for air she won't get unless we play by his rules.

This isn't just a threat.

It's a demonstration.

And if Dimitri Romanov doesn't get what he wants, this is only the beginning.

Ana flails, her boots skidding along the wall, hands clawing at the forearm locked around her throat. Her eyes are wide, wild, desperate for air. Every second ticks louder, Noah on the edge of pulling the trigger, rage blazing beneath his skin.

One shot. That's all it would take to start a war we're not ready to end.

And Dimitri knows it.

"My daughter," he says smoothly, voice silked with venom. "Consider this a gentle warning."

He snaps his fingers again.

The man obeys, releasing Ana without hesitation. She hits the floor hard, body crumpling in a heap. The air wheezes back into her lungs as Noah drops to his knees beside her, hands on her shoulders, murmuring too low for me to hear.

Dimitri doesn't wait for a thank-you or a reaction.

He just leaves, vanishing with his men like they were never fucking here.

Fury ignites in my gut like a lit match dropped into gasoline.

"Get them out of the building!" I bark, my voice shattering the stunned silence. "Double security. Now. I want eyes on every hallway, every blind spot. If one Romanov so much as breathes wrong on Catalyst property, I want them dropped."

The room scrambles into motion. Fear and urgency thick in the air. No one dares ask questions.

"I want eyes on my house. On Noah's. Twenty-four seven. Round the clock until I say otherwise."

My blood pounds in my ears.

"Now get the fuck out of my face!"

Slamming the door behind me, I barely register the sound of files shifting on my desk or the slight rattle of the blinds. Everything feels tight—my fists, my chest, my fucking skull.

Ana's still on the floor, cradled in Noah's arms, her face pale and damp with sweat. Her glossy eyes lift to mine, throat already bruising, skin blotched with trauma. She looks like she wants answers.

So does Noah.

He glares up at me, fury laced with something worse...fear.

"What the fuck, Roman?" Ana rasps, her hand shaking as it clutches her throat.

Noah doesn't wait.

"Where the hell is Echo?" His voice is ice.

I say nothing.

Not at first.

Because I know what I saw. That photo, blurry or not, was Echo. The posture, the way he carries weight, the stillness behind it. There's no fucking doubt in my mind.

He was there.

He's done something.

And now we're all caught in the blowback.

"I don't know where he is," I growl, jaw clenched so tight it aches. "But I do know this..."

My hand slams against the edge of the desk, the sound splitting the room.

"His day off is fucking over."

18

Every Last Drop

Katya

His breath ghosts over my skin, each exhale like smoke dragging across my collarbone. He lingers at my throat, lips brushing the pulse there, slow and possessive, before he sinks his teeth into me again, this time harder. I feel it in my spine, the way he sucks, like he's pulling something out of me more vital than blood. Like he's feeding on the fact that I let him.

My wrists stay pinned above my head, trapped beneath the strength of one hand. He doesn't ease up, doesn't shift his weight, not even when I arch into him, silently begging for contact, for pressure, for him.

He wants to feel me struggle.

His mouth moves again, trailing down my chest, lips hot and open, tongue tracing the line between my ribs and my hips. He bites once, low, right above my pelvis and I flinch, but the sound that escapes me isn't a protest.

It's a moan.

"Look at this," he murmurs, dragging two fingers through the slick heat between my thighs, pulling them apart with just enough force to make me whimper. "You're soaked. And for what? A few bruises and the way I hold you down?"

He chuckles darkly, the vibration rippling against my skin.

"You're mine," he says, almost to himself. "You were made to break for me."

And I am.

I fucking am.

He circles my clit with slow, merciless precision, not to bring me relief, but to taunt. His fingers press down just enough to make me ache, to make my thighs tremble, then slip lower, down to my entrance, already dripping with our mixed release.

"Still hurting?" he asks again, his voice like smoke and iron.

I nod, biting my lip so hard I taste blood.

And then, more.

He slides two fingers in, all the way, curling them as he leans in to whisper against my jaw.

"You know I don't stop just because it hurts, Little Butterfly."

A third finger joins the others, stretching me, fucking me deep with claim. My breath catches in my throat, body caught between pain and white-hot pleasure.

"But that's the part you like, isn't it?" he growls. "You want it to hurt. You want me to split you open again. Fill you till it spills out. Make you scream so the walls know who you belong to."

I try to speak, try to beg, but all that comes out is a choked sob of need.

He pulls his fingers out and presses them to my lips.

"Suck."

I don't hesitate. I wrap my mouth around them, tasting myself, tasting him, moaning around the thickness of his fingers as I swirl my tongue over them like I would his cock. His eyes darken as he watches me.

And then, he lets go of my wrists.

My hands fall limp.

But before I can even think to touch him, he's on me.

His mouth crashes into mine, his tongue sliding between my lips with a hunger that's all teeth and need. One hand grabs my jaw, the other snakes beneath my thigh, lifting it high against his waist as he grinds his cock against my cunt.

Still hard. Still pulsing. Still denying me.

"You want me to fuck you?" he growls against my mouth, hips grinding, cock dragging through my soaked folds.

"Yes...please-"

"Beg better than that."

"Echo," I cry, nails digging into his back, dragging down his spine, "please, I need you inside me. I need you to fuck me until I forget my own name-"

He growls, low and violent, and then he slams into me.

One stroke. Deep. All of him.

I scream, loud, raw and feral. He doesn't stop. His hips snap into me over and over, relentless, merciless, pounding me into the mattress like he's trying to fuck his name into my bones.

Every inch of him stretches me open, claiming every part of me, dragging another orgasm up from the pit of my stomach like he owns it.

"Say it," he demands, thrusting harder. "Tell me who you belong to."

"Y-you, Echo, fuck, I'm yours-"

He leans down, biting my neck, thrusting so deep I nearly black out.

"That's right," he breathes. "You're mine. And I'm never letting you go."

"Once won't be enough," he growls, sweat dripping from his brow onto my chest. "A hundred times won't be enough, I'll ruin this pussy until it's molded to my cock."

His nose brushes mine, eyes wild, blood rushing under his skin like a predator too far gone to pull back.

And something snaps inside me.

"You own me, Echo," I whisper, the words shaking in my throat, breathless, broken, true.

"Now fucking breed me."

His eyes darken instantly, jaw twitching like I just set off a bomb in his chest. His grip slips on my wrists, stunned for a heartbeat and I take it.

I lunge up, crash my lips against his, all tongue and teeth and hunger. My hands tear at his shirt, ripping the fabric like it offended me, dragging it off his body, tossing it to the floor with a desperate cry. My nails scrape down his chest, his abs, his hips, leaving red trails he'll still feel tomorrow.

He grunts, grabbing me, flipping me onto my back so hard the bed shakes. His mouth never leaves mine, devouring my moans as he yanks his boxers down. I reach between us, gripping his cock, thick and angry in my palm, stroking it like I own it even though we both know I'm the one who's owned.

No hesitation. No teasing. Just the slick heat of me guiding him in, raw, unprotected, soaked from him and already ruined.

He slams into me.

One brutal, bottomed-out thrust that makes me scream into his mouth. My legs fly open, knees pressed high to my chest as he shoves himself in deeper, like he's trying to fuck straight through me.

His cock stretches me wide, fills me past the point of pain, and still I want more.

I need it.

He pistons his hips, ruthless, relentless, pounding into me like I'm just a hole to be used. His voice is a broken rasp against my neck, hot and breathless.

"Gonna fuck a baby into this cunt," he growls, one hand sliding between my legs to press down hard on my stomach, feeling how deep he is. "Gonna fuck you so full of me, you leak for days. Gonna make you beg for it."

I can barely breathe. Barely see.

All I know is him.

The stretch. The sting. The sound of my wet, ruined pussy clapping around him, slick with his spit and my arousal, soaking the sheets. My thighs shake with every thrust, my nails dragging down his back, drawing blood that only makes him fuck me harder.

"My pussy," I cry, "My fucking pussy-"

"No," he snarls, slamming into the hilt. "Mine. My pussy. My cum. My fucking hole."

I clamp around him at the words, body betraying me, chasing my climax like a drug. My legs wrap tight around his waist, locking him in place, needing to feel every drop when he unloads.

"I want it in me," I moan. "Want to feel you spill. Want to watch it leak out-"

That's all it takes.

He rips himself free with a filthy, wet sound, grabs the back of my neck, forces me forward, and slams my face down toward where I'm stretched open and twitching.

"Fucking look at what you've done to me," he growls, stroking himself furiously.

His cock throbs, and then, he explodes.

Hot ropes of cum shoot across my pussy, my thighs, my entrance, dripping into me, soaking me, filling me like he wants to claim my womb. He groans, loud and broken, watching every second of it pour from me.

Then, before I can even catch my breath, he grabs me by the hips and drags me to the edge of the bed.

He spits on my pussy. Spreads it with two fingers. Watches it drip.

Then, slowly, he bends down and licks.

Licks his own cum out of me like it's dessert.

Licks like he wants it all back.

His tongue drags one last time between my thighs, collecting every drop of the mess he made—thick, hot ropes of cum still leaking from my overstretched cunt. He moans into the taste, savoring it, swallowing it like it's divine, like this is what he was born for: to wreck me, to consume me, to feed on what he forced out of me. When he pulls away, his lips are slick, glistening with his own mess, and he doesn't wipe them. No, he wants me to see it. To see him, feral and dripping, reduced to a beast by the taste of his cum spilling from the hole he broke open.

Then, he leans in.

Cock hard again, spit shining on his tongue, and lets it fall from his mouth into mine, slow, heavy drops of white ruin, a secondhand offering I don't dare reject. I open without being told, jaw slack, throat already aching, and let his seed coat my tongue like holy oil. It clings to the roof of my mouth. It sticks to the back of my throat. It owns me. When he growls, "Swallow," I obey instantly. I choke it down without flinching, the bitter warmth sliding into my gut like a brand.

He watches me with something dangerous in his eyes. Something twisted. As though every act of filth only confirms what he already knows, that I'm his, not just in body but in soul. That he can fuck me, fill me, use me, and I'll still crawl back to him hungry for more.

"You look better like this," he mutters, tracing his fingers over my slick mouth, across my jaw, down my throat. "Dripping. Full of me. Mouth open and brain empty."

I nod, dazed, ruined, eager. I want him to see it. I need him to.

Without warning, he drags me down off the bed, my knees hitting the cold floor as he flips me onto all fours. I whimper from the sudden impact, but he doesn't soften. He grabs my hips, spreads me wide with brutal hands, and spits again, right onto my already swollen, dripping hole. The sound of it, the heat of it, makes me flinch, but before I can even process it, he's there. Hard and thick, lined up again, shoving in with zero resistance.

He doesn't ease in. Doesn't ask. Doesn't care.

He's using me.

And it's perfect.

His cock slides through the slick mess inside me with ease, buried to the hilt in one violent thrust that punches the air out of my lungs. I scream, forehead pressing to the floor as he begins to move with brutal, punishing thrusts that shake my entire body forward, my tits bouncing with every impact, my thighs sticky, spread and trembling.

He fucks me like he hates me. Like he needs to break something.

His grip bruises my hips. His pace is merciless, tearing moan after moan from my throat, loud, feral, shameless. Every time I gasp for air, he fucks it right back out of me. The room is filled with the wet slap of our bodies, the disgusting, beautiful sound of my cunt being destroyed for the second time, slick from his cum and my own slick, pouring out of me like I'm nothing but a vessel for him to ruin.

"You like this," he snarls, yanking my hair back so he can hiss into my ear. "You need to be fucked like this. Used like the little hole you are."

"Y-Yes...fuck...please-"

"You're going to keep it in this time. I'm going to fill you again, and you're going to hold it like a good little cumdump."

I scream as he slams into me deeper, harder, faster. My body breaks apart beneath him, my arms collapsing, my head hitting the floor again, drooling, crying, cumming on him without even realizing it. My body betrays me, clenching, milking his cock like it's desperate for every drop. I want it. I need it. I want to feel him empty again inside me, feel it spill, feel it stay.

And he knows.

With a broken, vicious groan, he slams in one final time, cock pulsing so violently I feel it with every twitch. He unloads inside me, deep, messy, choking on his own moans as he forces his cum in so far it burns. His hands never leave me, gripping my ass, spreading me open, watching every second of it leak back out.

But this time... he doesn't pull out.

He stays.

Buried inside.

His cock softening inside me like he wants to keep it there until I forget what it's like to be empty.

"This pussy," he breathes, barely human anymore, voice cracked and animalistic, "was made to be my fuckhole."

And I nod, forehead to the floor, cum dripping from my thighs, throat raw and a smile on my lips.

Because he's right.

And I'll let him do it again.

He stays inside me, buried deep, our bodies locked together in sweat and arousal, in something far too dark to be called intimacy, but it is. His breath slows against the back of my neck, hot and heavy, chest rising and falling with a quiet, satisfied violence. The scent of sex coats everything. The air. The sheets. My ruined cunt, still dripping around his softening cock.

I don't move.

I can't.

And he doesn't let me.

One of his hands snakes around my waist, pulling my limp body upright, forcing me to sit on his lap, his cock still inside me. My head lolls back against his shoulder, my body trembling, exhausted, used. A mess of spit, sweat, blood, and cum.

But he holds me there.

Not gently.

Possessively.

"Good girl," he murmurs, dragging his tongue along my jaw like he's tasting the sweat there, like he's cleaning me with his mouth. "So fucking perfect like this. Stuffed full of me. Broken open."

His fingers trail down to my thighs, where his cum has started to leak again. He growls low in his throat, as if the sight alone offends him.

"No," he breathes. "You don't get to leak without permission."

He shifts under me, lifts me just slightly, just enough for his cum to slide forward, and shoves two fingers back inside my cunt, pushing it all the way back in. My body jolts. A strangled sound claws from my throat, but I don't resist.

I thank him.

"I'll keep it in," I whisper, voice raw and wrecked. "Please let me keep it-"

"You will," he snaps, pressing his palm to my lower belly, hard. "I'll make sure of it. You don't get to waste a single drop of what I gave you."

He lifts me fully now, only to drag me back into his arms, pressing my naked, ruined body against his chest as he carries me, limp, wet, still spread open, out of the room. I don't ask where he's taking me. I don't need to know.

Because wherever it is, I belong there.

He lowers me into the tub, still clothed from the waist up, still entirely in control. The water is already warm, he must have turned it on before he fucked me raw, and now, he washes me. But not like a man tending to wounds.

Like a man reclaiming territory.

His fingers glide over every bruise he left, every bite mark, every sticky trace of his release. He doesn't wipe it away in shame.

He rubs it in.

Massage. Branding. A reminder.

His cum still oozes from me in lazy trails beneath the water's surface, and he watches it with reverence, like he's watching paint peel from his favorite canvas.

"You'll never be clean again," he says quietly, brushing his lips along my shoulder. "Not after tonight."

I nod, cheeks flushed, body aching, throat raw, and I don't cry.

I smile.

Because I don't want to be clean.

Not if it means losing this.

When he dries me off, it's not gentle, it's thorough. He kneels in front of me like he's worshiping, but I know better. He's checking me. Reaffirming his mark. Claiming every inch all over again. When he finishes, he puts a plain black collar around my neck, soft leather, unmarked except for a single ring in the front.

No padlock.

Not yet.

But the promise is there.

"You're going to sleep with me now," he says, voice like smoke curling in the dark. "In my bed. With my cum still inside you. With my scent all over your skin."

"Yes, Echo," I breathe. "Please." I whisper, letting him guide me under his sheets .

He climbs in behind me, pulling me into his chest, one arm locking around my waist.

"If you leak onto my sheets," he growls, dragging his teeth across my earlobe, "I'll wake you up just to fuck it back in."

My fingertips trail lazily down his back, nails dragging over the bruises and claw marks I left behind, some still fresh, angry, red. Others faded into permanent ghosts on his skin. He barely flinches.

But I notice it.

That tiny hitch in his breath.

The way his body tenses just long enough to betray a memory he wasn't ready to revisit.

"What is it?" I whisper, legs still shaking, the ache between them a dull throb I've grown addicted to.

His hand slides along my thigh, slow and warm. A silent distraction.

"You should rest," he murmurs, voice low, like he's trying to tuck the moment away, smooth it down with gentleness he doesn't know how to hold for long.

But I don't let him.

"Tell me something," I plead, lifting my face toward his jaw. "Not about me. About you. Please."

There's hesitation. I feel it in the quiet stillness of his chest, in the way his fingers pause for half a second before moving again. Then, with no warning, he scoops me up, lifts me like I weigh nothing and pulls my legs around his waist. His hands anchor beneath my thighs as he begins walking, slow and aimless, like his body needs movement to keep from unraveling.

Is he holding me?

Or clinging to something I can't see?

"When I was thirteen," he begins, voice barely a whisper, "my mother died of an overdose. Needle still in her arm. Blue lips. Eyes open."

The words land like broken glass, shards that somehow cut through both of us at once.

He keeps walking.

"When I was fifteen, my father drove drunk into a telephone pole. Killed himself. Killed the woman in the passenger seat. He was never supposed to be driving. He was never supposed to be a father."

His grip tightens on my thighs, and suddenly I realize how close I am, how he's holding me like I might be the last real thing in the world.

"After that," he continues, quieter, "I got passed around. Drunken uncle. Timid aunt. He used to say hitting me was 'building character.' That pain would 'make me a man.' It's good for you, Everett, he used to say. You're too soft, Everett."

Everett.

The name hits like a bullet.

I don't speak. I don't move. I just breathe against his shoulder, my body clinging tighter around his waist as the weight of it all hangs in the air between us.

"I knew what pain was before I ever understood what love felt like," he says. "So when I turned eighteen, I signed the first papers I could. The military took me. Took the name too. Everett didn't survive basic. Echo came out the other side."

He stops walking.

We're in front of the mirror now.

He doesn't look at it, but I do.

His back to the glass, the massive black tree spanning across his shoulders and spine, roots digging into flesh like veins. And now that I see it up close, I can make out the tiny details I missed in the dark. Each leaf is shaded by hand. The bark, textured in black and gray. The grooves of his back move with it, like it's alive. Like it's growing out of him.

My nail marks are everywhere. Bright red slashes across the branches. Along the trunk. A storm carved into something sacred.

"In Iraq, Roman and I found a local doing tattoos," he says. "Cheap. Barely sterile. All by hand. Roman got his vines. I got this. It was the only thing I remembered about her."

"Your mom?" I ask.

"She loved trees. Reading under them. Watching the seasons change. She said they reminded her that even the worst parts of life had to make room for something new."

My chest twists. I reach for his cheek, drag my fingers along his jawline, and tilt his face toward mine.

"And that?" I whisper, nodding toward the scar settled on his cheek. A jagged cut just below his left eye.

He smirks, but there's no humor in it.

"Last piece of my father," he mutters. "Sharp. Crooked. Always too close to the fucking throat."

My breath catches. There's something unspoken between us now, raw, vulnerable, and terrifying in how quietly it bleeds through the room. Something that's more than pain. More than lust.

It's recognition.

I press my forehead to his. I don't say I'm sorry. I don't say anything at all.

Because Echo doesn't need pity. He needs silence.

My head drops to his shoulder as he carries me toward the bed, his bed, and I let myself sink into the heat of his skin, still flushed from everything he just did to me. I stare at the mattress, at the cool sheets, at the place I know he sleeps alone every night. And I ask the only question that matters.

"I can really stay here tonight?"

His arms tighten around me, just enough to make it feel like he'd rather bleed than let me go.

A beat of silence.

Then a soft exhale against my temple.

"I didn't put a nightlight in here for me," he whispers.

And in that moment, an unsettling reality clouds my mind.

I'm sleeping in my cage.

And I've never felt safer.

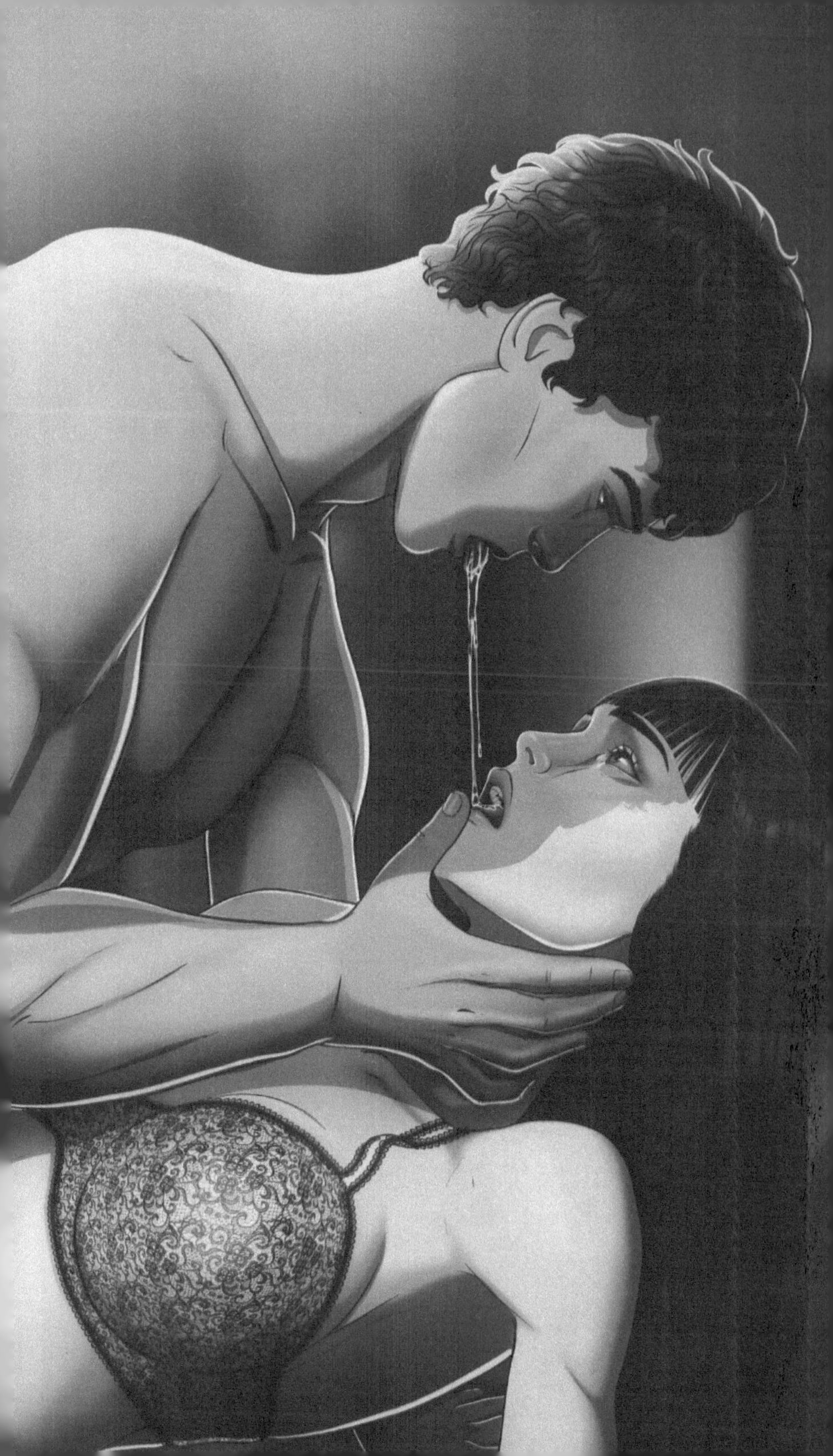

19

Salvation Is Not For Sinners

Katya

His arms cage me like a vice, but his touch is anything but harsh. His chest rises and falls beneath mine in a slow, almost hypnotic rhythm, like I haven't spent days choking on the chaos he breathes. His heartbeat is steady, too steady, like none of this touches him. Like breaking me apart was just a ritual... and now, I'm the altar he rests on.

His fingers trace my waist with the gentleness of a lover, not a captor. Lazy, languid strokes that burn hotter the longer they linger. My skin prickles under his touch, my thighs still slick from what he did to me, from how thoroughly he fucked me. Used me. Tasted me. Ruined me.

"What are you thinking?" His voice is low, each word wrapping around my throat like silk meant to strangle.

I don't answer right away. My breath stutters, shaky and shallow. My fingertips glide across his palm, brushing over the deep grooves, the stories carved into his hands. Hands that held me down. Slapped me. Spread me open. Made me scream.

"Nothing," I whisper. A lie. A dangerous, desperate lie. "Nothing at all."

He hums, like he knows better. Like he's proud of the silence he's taught me to keep.

His fingers roam higher, dragging over the raised scars on my back. I stiffen. My nipples graze his chest, bare and aching, the friction maddening. My nose brushes his, breath mixing with the heavy tension between us, heat and hesitation fighting for dominance.

"What are you thinking, Everett?" I breathe, his real name curling around my tongue like something forbidden.

His eyes flicker. His entire body stills.

And then he cups my face, thumb ghosting across my lips, that mouth he made filthy just hours ago. His mouth hovers over mine, not kissing. Not yet. He wants me to beg for it. To need it.

"Will you really stay, Katya?" he murmurs, and the way he says my name, like he owns it, makes something deep inside me clench.

He buries his face in my chest, curls brushing my skin, his mouth dangerously close to my nipple. I feel his breath there. Hot. Measured. Claiming. My thighs instinctively squeeze tighter around his hips, like my body's already made the decision my mind is still trying to outrun.

How am I here?

How am I this close?

Why does it feel right?

He fucked me like I was nothing. Less than nothing. Made me choke on him, ride him, cry for him. Used me until my body went limp and still kept going. And I let him.

And now... now he holds me like I'm his.

He looks so human like this. So real. But that's the trick, isn't it? That's how monsters keep their prey.

I rake my fingers through his hair, tugging just hard enough to make him growl into my skin. He shifts beneath me, and I feel him, hard again. Ready. Like he hasn't had enough of me. Like he never will.

The moment stretches, thick with heat and silence and things I'll never say.

"Yes," I whisper. The word slips out too easily.

It's not a lie.

It should be, but it's not.

I mean it.

And I don't know why.

Why, after what he did to Isaac. After the blood. The screams. The way he made me watch.

I should hate him.

But instead, my body presses closer. My hips grind down. My breath catches. My throat burns with the need to stay.

I want him.

I want the monster.

And maybe that's the most broken part of all.

He wraps his arms around me like he's anchoring something untamable...me, maybe. Or himself. There's no space left between us, no breath I take that doesn't brush against his chest. His skin burns into mine, every inch of him molded to every inch of me, like we were made to fit this way. Made to collapse this way.

His chest presses against mine, his skin hot, flushed from everything we just did, from everything he took from me and everything I gave him willingly. Our bodies are still slick with sweat, still vibrating from the echoes of what we became in those sheets. My heartbeat pounds against his like we're one organism, fused by lust and something far more dangerous. Something I don't have a name for. His breath is warm against my cheek, his scent wrapping around me like a drug. Every inch of me is tangled in him, claimed by him. I can still feel the ache between my thighs, the sting of where he grabbed me too hard, bit too deep, thrust too far. And yet, even now, with my body bruised and used, all I want is more. More of him. More of this madness. I am completely his, torn open and willingly stitched together by the hands that destroyed me.

"Will you let go?" I whisper, barely able to form the words as his lips drag over the sensitive skin of my throat, slow and possessive. His mouth is lazy, like he's savoring me. Like he has no reason to rush because he knows, he owns me now. His teeth scrape over the curve of my shoulder and I gasp, hating how my body arches into him on instinct, craving the hurt almost as much as the heat.

"No," he breathes, the word spilling from his mouth like a sacred promise. It's not just a refusal, it's a binding oath. A threat. A confession. And I don't know whether to feel safe or scared. Maybe both.

Then...

Ding-dong.

The sound slams into the room like a detonation. We freeze. The haze of post-ecstasy fractures instantly. My heart spikes. His eyes snap to the door. In a single breath, everything about him shifts. The heat drains from his body and is replaced with something colder. Sharper. More lethal. He moves like a machine, ripping the sheets up to cover me with one hand while the other reaches for his clothes. His mouth is drawn tight, jaw clenched, that soft look he gave me just seconds ago burned away like it never existed. "Stay," he snaps, and the command cuts into me with a precision that leaves no room for defiance. He's gone.

I scramble into his clothes, tugging on a pair of his sweats that hang loose on my hips, and one of his old band tees that still smells like his skin and sex and sin. My legs feel shaky beneath me, my body sore, raw, and somehow still wanting. I follow him at a distance, blood roaring in my ears, drawn to the storm like a moth to the flame that's already singed my wings. I shouldn't be doing this. I should hide. But I can't stop moving toward him.

His dresser drawer is cracked open. A glint of steel catches my eye. My knife. I grab it without thinking. Without hesitation. My fingers wrap around the handle like I was meant to hold it.

I stay low in the hallway, peering through the crack in the bedroom door as Echo undoes lock after lock, four in total. His fingers move with practiced urgency, each click echoing like the tick of a countdown. He's done this before. This isn't paranoia. This is preparation. A life lived expecting enemies. And now, they're at his front door.

The moment he swings it open, the man standing there storms in without waiting. Tall. Broad. Drenched from the rain, with a presence that screams power. He knows Echo. Knows him well.

"Come on in, Roman," Echo mutters dryly, but the sarcasm is forced, brittle.

"Save it," Roman snaps, eyes raking over Echo's appearance. The half-buttoned shirt, the flushed skin, the damp curls. My fingerprints are probably still etched into his hips. And Roman sees all of it.

Echo leans against the kitchen island, arms crossed, trying to look relaxed, but he's already calculating. His body is wound tight, like a trigger pulled halfway. "What?" he says. "I take one fucking day off and now you're breaking into my house like a jealous ex?" He grabs his gun, places it on the counter, deliberate. Measured. A message: This is my house. My territory. You don't call the shots here.

"You take a day off," Roman says, voice cold, "and Dimitri Romanov walks into Catalyst." The name makes my stomach lurch. I stagger back a step.

Dimitri.

My father.

Echo straightens, that mocking glint in his eyes flickering out. His jaw tightens. "What did you just say?" Roman doesn't flinch. He steps closer, his fury barely restrained.

"You heard me. Dimitri. In my office. With his men. Threatening my wife. Putting hands on Ana. In front of Noah. Wrapped their hands around her fucking throat and we couldn't stop it."

I see it. The exact second something inside Echo snaps. His entire body tenses like a wire pulled too tight, ready to whip back and cut something open. Then he moves—fast. Violent.

He shoves Roman, hard, sending him back a step. "Careful," Echo growls, voice low and trembling with rage.

"No," Roman shouts, pushing back. "You've been absent. Distracted. And now Dimitri's flashing pictures, proof, Echo. Proof that you were one of the last people to see Nikolai Sokolov alive. And with Katya Romanov."

My name slams into the room like a death sentence.

I don't even have time to react before Echo explodes.

He lunges, hand clamping around Roman's throat and slamming him flat on his back with the kind of force that shakes the floor. Roman chokes, gasping for air as Echo towers over him, wild-eyed and unhinged. He pins him down with one boot to his chest, hard enough to bruise.

"Do not forget who the fuck you're talking to," Echo hisses, voice vibrating with something primal and unstoppable. "Now tell me, what pictures did Dimitri show you?"

And all I can do is stand there, frozen.

This man, this monster, was just inside me. His breath still lingers on my skin. His cum is still dripping down my thigh. I let him hold me. I let him kiss me. I let him whisper that he wouldn't let go.

And now he's about to kill someone.

Because of me.

Because of us.

And the worst part?

Some twisted, broken part of me doesn't want to stop him.

Roman's eyes blaze as he yanks something from the inside of his jacket, his movements sharp, furious. The sound of paper crumpling under pressure fills the space just before he throws the documents at Echo's chest like a challenge. Pages scatter mid-air and float down between them like ash from something already burning. Echo catches the edge of the top sheet before it hits the floor, his eyes scanning whatever Roman has brought him. Something in his shoulders shifts. Tension loosens, not entirely, but enough to make the air feel less suffocating for a moment. Without looking at Roman, Echo turns on his heel and walks toward the living room, the paper held loosely in one hand like it's already telling him something he doesn't want to hear.

"Grab yourself a drink if you want," he mutters, voice calm again, deceptively smooth. "Let me explain."

Roman grunts, pushing off the floor with a hiss of pain and pride. He brushes off his jacket, jaw tight, but he doesn't argue. The tension between them sizzles but doesn't explode. Not yet. They move like men who've fought before. Men who know the rhythm of rage and when to pull back just before blood spills.

Their voices drop to low murmurs, lost in the space between kitchen and living room, and yet my heart thunders like a drum against my ribs. I can barely hear what they're saying, but it doesn't matter. I can feel what's coming. Something worse is circling. I feel it tightening around us like a noose. My father is closing in. And if he's coming for Echo, if he's trying to get through him to me, then there's no line he won't cross. No life he won't crush beneath his boot to make a point.

I barely have time to finish the thought.

Movement, quick, sudden, and silent, catches my eye like a flash of silver in a dark room.

I freeze.

My gaze shifts away from the two men talking, my focus narrowing on the hallway just beyond the kitchen. I squint, holding my breath, my instincts screaming that something's wrong. The hallway is dim, shadowed, but I see him.

A body.

Wrecked.

Barely standing.

Nikolai.

He's slumped against the wall, one hand pressed against his side, the other wrapped tightly around a jagged shard of glass. His knuckles are white from the grip, and blood trickles down his arm, staining the floor beneath him. His face is swollen, almost unrecognizable. One leg is heavily bandaged, the fabric soaked in red. His shirt hangs from his body in tatters, soaked with sweat and agony.

But it's his eyes that haunt me.

Wide. Wild. Alive.

And in his hand, draped from trembling fingers, is a single key.

My stomach drops.

His wrists are free. The shackles Echo kept him in... they're gone.

Oh no, Echo.

My eyes dart to the dresser. The ring of keys. The one Echo always keeps close, the one that never leaves his sight, it's missing.

I don't even breathe.

Nikolai looks up, and our eyes meet. There's a second, maybe less, where something passes between us. Recognition. Rage. Desperation. Then his gaze shifts past me. Past the hallway. Toward the living room.

We both see it at the same time.

Echo's gun.

Still sitting on the kitchen island where he placed it earlier. So casual. So careless.

He didn't see Nikolai. Neither did Roman. They're too deep in whatever war is brewing between them to notice the storm already here.

I watch in horror as Nikolai's fingers twitch, the glass slipping from his grip as his hand inches forward, reaching for the weapon.

My legs move before my brain does.

I don't think. I can't think.

There's no time to scream. No time to weigh right or wrong. No time to call out a warning.

I lunge.

The sound that follows splits the world in half.

A single gunshot.

Louder than anything I've ever heard. Louder than war. Louder than pain.

And in that moment, nothing else exists but the sound of it ringing through Echo's house like a death knell, and the certainty that everything is about to burn.

20

Fool Me Once

Katya

I don't hesitate, I can't. The second Nikolai's fingers graze the gun, I slam into him, tackling his broken, blood-soaked body to the floor with everything I have left in me. The sound that explodes from the barrel as his finger pulls the trigger is deafening, the shot firing into the ceiling in a flash of heat and smoke. I force his arm up, twisting it, trying to wrench the gun away, but I'm not strong enough. Not fast enough. His head snaps forward, skull meeting the bridge of my nose with a sickening crack. Pain explodes behind my eyes. I gasp, stunned, the metallic taste of blood already coating the back of my throat. My grip slips. I shove him back with all the strength I can muster and roll away, disoriented, blinking through the daze. But he's not done. His hand fists in my hair like a leash, yanking me back toward him with enough force to make my spine scream.

"Jesus fucking Christ!" Roman bellows, his boots pounding the floor. He and Echo rush toward us, but they're seconds too late. I'm already locked in hell.

My fingers dig into my pocket, fumbling through fabric until they close around cold metal. *The knife.*

Without thinking, without hesitation, I rip it free and drive it downward, burying it in Nikolai's stomach with a sharp, savage thrust.

His scream cuts through the air like a demon being exorcised, but he doesn't let go. Instead, his teeth sink into my shoulder, clamping down with feral desperation. My scream rips from my throat, raw and blood-soaked. The pain blinds me. Blinds everything. And then I feel it, cold, hard steel pressing against the side of my skull.

Echo's gun.

He still has it.

"Both of you fuckers stop right there," he growls, voice slurred but full of venom.

Roman and Echo freeze mid-step. The tension in the room thickens like a noose pulling tight. Roman's chest heaves. Echo's eyes flicker, calculating, ready to kill, but not yet. Not if it means killing me in the process.

Nikolai laughs, a low, vicious sound that vibrates through his chest and into my spine. He's enjoying this.

He wants this.

"Mmm... your friend doesn't know about your little slut, does he?" he sneers, dragging the words out as he presses the gun harder against my temple. "Get up, Katya," he hisses, blood dripping from his mouth, his wound leaking all over the floor.

I don't move. I can't breathe. My body shakes, my shoulder pulsing with pain, blood soaking the collar of Echo's shirt.

Roman lifts his gun slowly, aiming it straight at us, rage burning in his eyes. "I will blow both your fucking filthy heads off," he growls.

But Nikolai doesn't even flinch.

"No, you won't. Right, Echo?" he mutters, voice rough and mocking. He angles the gun higher, the cold barrel digging into my temple, smearing soot across my skin. "If he shoots me, I'll fucking kill her first."

Roman's eyes flick to Echo. He doesn't lower the weapon, but he doesn't fire either.

"Good," he mutters, like this is a game he's willing to lose.

"Do not pull that goddamn trigger," Echo snaps, voice low and lethal, the fury barely contained. He takes a step forward and slams a hand against Roman's chest, stopping him. Roman looks at him like he's lost his mind, but Echo's voice is absolute. "Dimitri wants her alive."

At that, Nikolai grins, blood curling at the edges of his mouth like paint on a dying canvas. "Sure he does," he wheezes, eyes glassy. "Then open the door."

"I'm not letting you leave this house," Roman snaps, his voice slicing through the tension like a blade. His stance is rigid, gun still raised, his eyes locked on Nikolai with lethal focus. The words aren't a warning, they're a line drawn in blood.

Echo doesn't respond at first. He barely glances at me, his face unreadable, his eyes cold. I can feel him calculating, weighing every option, every risk, every consequence. One wrong move and someone dies. Maybe all of us.

Behind me, Nikolai breathes heavily, his body shaking, soaked in blood and sweat. But even on the verge of collapse, he's holding the gun with terrifying confidence. The barrel is pressed to my head, his grip in my hair like a leash. His body is failing, but his spite is alive and thriving.

"Step aside," Nikolai rasps. "Or I'll paint your wall with her skull. I'll drag her outside, and I'll put a bullet in her mouth before either of you can blink."

Roman doesn't budge.

Echo finally speaks, voice low and measured. "Let him go."

Roman's head whips toward him. "What the fuck did you just say?"

"I said let him go," Echo repeats, eyes narrowing. "He's dying. He won't make it far. Let him think he's escaping."

"You're handing him a loaded weapon and Dimitri's last living heir," Roman hisses, rage coiling beneath his words. "You've *lost it.*"

"He's not taking her," Echo growls. "He can barely stand. He's bluffing."

Nikolai chuckles behind me, the sound wet and broken. "Am I? Or did she just beg me not to leave her behind?"

Roman's expression twists, disgusted. "What the fuck does that mean?"

"Oh, you don't know?" Nikolai sneers, dragging me back tighter against him, his mouth grazing my ear. "Your golden boy didn't tell you what he's been doing with your precious little Romanov? Didn't tell you he's been fucking her in that bed of his like she's nothing but a mouth and a hole?"

Roman's entire body stiffens. His face blanks for a beat, like his brain short-circuits trying to make sense of what he just heard. And then, his eyes go wide, his voice cracks through the space like thunder. "*Echo?*"

"He's lying," Echo says too quickly. "He's delirious, he's bleeding out. He doesn't know what the fuck he's saying."

But Roman is already looking at me. And he sees it.

The way my eyes flinch.

The way I don't deny it.

The way my silence screams louder than any confession ever could.

"Jesus fucking Christ," Roman mutters, stepping back like the air's been knocked from his lungs. "You slept with her?"

Echo's jaw clenches. "It wasn't like that."

Roman rounds on him. "She's a hostage. You tortured her."

"It was torture, not pleasure," Echo bites out.

"That's not better!" Roman shouts. "You're supposed to be watching her, not crawling between her legs while her father lines up hits on our people!"

"Oh come on," Nikolai drawls, voice slurring, "Don't be mad. She liked it rough. Don't you, Katya?" He jostles me, hard, and the gun shifts against my skull again.

Roman's gun rises again, this time with more fury than control. "Let. Her. Go."

"Shoot me and I shoot her," Nikolai grins. "We all go down. How's that for balance?"

Echo moves fast, hand on Roman's arm, holding him back. "Don't. Not here. Not like this."

"Not like *this*?" Roman hisses. "You already made *this*."

Echo doesn't respond. The guilt in his eyes flickers for a second, but then it's gone. Walled off. Buried. He turns to Nikolai, voice steel. "You walk out. You take the car. You *don't* take her."

"I'm not asking," Nikolai mutters. "She's my leverage. She's my fucking insurance."

"You'll be dead before you make it to the next street," Echo says. "Take the car. Walk away. You touch her again, and I swear to God-"

"What, Echo?" Nikolai rasps, pushing the barrel hard into my temple. "You'll kill me? Get in line."

Then suddenly, without warning, he *shoves* me forward. Hard.

I stumble and fall, hitting the floor with a grunt, my shoulder screaming from the impact. I twist onto my back just in time to see Nikolai lurch toward the door, bloody and limping, dragging himself like a corpse with a heartbeat.

The keys jingle.

The car door slams.

Engine roars to life.

Echo and Roman don't move. They just watch him drive away, red taillights disappearing into the black.

Silence swells between the three of us.

I lie on the cold tile, heart pounding, throat raw, vision swim-ming.

Roman stares at Echo like he doesn't recognize him.

Echo stares at the door like he's already planning the next kill.

And me?

I stay where I am.

Because no one's coming to help.

How could I have been so delusional?

How could I ever have believed there was more beneath Echo's touch than possession? That the way he held me meant some-thing, that the heat, the chaos, the aching softness buried be-neath his violence was *real*? Maybe it was always just in my head. A sick fantasy I built around a man who used my body like a weapon, a reward, a distraction. Maybe he never saw me as anything but another broken thing to bend to his will. Maybe he *would've* let Nikolai shoot me. Maybe he wouldn't have blinked.

The question burns in my throat as he looks at me now, stone-faced and silent, his expression unreadable. The same eyes I once thought held depth now feel bottomless in the worst way. That same stare from the basement. That same hollowness that watched me cry, watched me break, and never flinched.

"Are you hurt?" he asks flatly.

The words feel like a slap. Not concerned, just protocol.

Before I can respond, Roman speaks, voice low and ven-om-laced.

"Katya Romanov," he mutters, pacing slowly behind me. "Quite the fucking mess you've made."

Then he moves, hard and fast.

The air is ripped from my lungs as I'm slammed back onto the tile floor, the shock of it stunning me into silence. Cold steel clasps around my wrists, the sharp *click* of the cuffs biting into my skin. My knees scrape against the ground, my shoulder burning from the earlier fight. My hair spills around my face as I'm forced down, body pinned like prey.

I look at Echo. I *stare* at him, eyes wide with horror, mouth trembling, a scream stuck in the back of my throat.

"E-Echo?" I sob, the sound jagged and small.

Do something.

Say something.

Stop this.

But he just stands there. Watching. His throat bobs like he's trying to swallow words that won't come, like there's something crawling beneath his skin, but he doesn't move. He doesn't speak.

Roman isn't finished.

"You're lucky I don't put cuffs on *you* after what I just saw," he spits at Echo, shoving my cuffed wrists behind me. "I already texted Noah. Our men are on the way. So why don't you tell me what the fuck is going on here? Was Nikolai right? Are you fucking her? Have you been keeping her here like a goddamn pet?"

The words feel like acid. I squeeze my eyes shut, heart slamming against my ribs, trying to disappear into the tile beneath me. Roman's voice is too loud, too real. Echo's silence is worse.

"E-Echo?" I whisper again, voice cracking, tears streaking down my cheeks.

He steps forward. My eyes flick open. For a moment, I think he's going to stop this, that he'll shove Roman off of me, that he'll kneel beside me and finally, finally be the man I imagined in the dark.

But he doesn't.

He just cocks his head, eyes icy, jaw tight, his expression hard and void of the man I thought I saw in that bed.

And then he speaks.

"No..." he says quietly, almost thoughtfully. "It was just business."

The words slice through me like a blade, clean and deep. I blink once. Twice. I can't breathe.

That's all I remember before his knuckles find my chin.

A flash of pain. The crack of bone on bone.

And then,

Darkness.

21

Who Is Really The Monster?

Echo

What the fuck have I done?

The thought hits like a hammer to the skull, again and again, as I pace the narrow confines of the observation room, my fists clenching at my sides until my nails draw blood. The goddamn key ring. I *left it out.* Left it in plain fucking sight like a rookie, like some lovesick bastard too caught up in her scent to remember that monsters like Nikolai don't die easy, they wait. They *watch.* I should have known. I should have seen it coming. That little shit had eyes even when his mouth was bloodied shut. And now Katya's paying the price for my weakness.

"She hasn't said a word since we brought her in," Noah says beside me, voice flat, almost clinical.

I can't answer. I don't have the words. I'm too focused on the image in front of me, her, on the other side of the glass. Bruised. Silent. Bound to a steel chair like a prisoner of war. Her wrists are still red from the cuffs, her face swollen where my fist met her chin, where *I* put it there.

I want to throw myself through the glass. I want to grab her, cradle her face, apologize with every breath I have left. I want to beat myself bloody for what I did. For what I didn't stop.

She hasn't looked up once. Hasn't moved. She just sits there, a shadow of the girl I had in my bed, the one I fucked into oblivion and called mine like I had the right. She's not screaming. She's not crying. That silence is worse. She's gone inside, and I did that. Me.

If I had been honest with Roman from the beginning, maybe I'd be locked in that cell beside her right now, stripped of every right I once held, but at least I'd be close. At least I'd know she wasn't alone. That no one else would hurt her. That I could watch. Protect. Bleed if she needed me to. But now? Roman's watching me like I'm next in line to be interrogated, and maybe I should be. I tortured them both. That's the truth. And I didn't stop when I should've. I didn't want to.

"How long?" Roman asks, his voice sharp.

"Long enough," I mutter, jaw tight, refusing to look away from the glass.

"Why the hell would you do it in your own home?" he snaps, pacing now, frustrated beyond measure.

Because no one would stop me there. Because the walls knew the screams. Because I could make it something else entirely.

"The kind of torture they deserved..." I start, voice low, weighted with things I'll never admit.

Roman turns toward me, brows furrowed. "What does that even mean?"

I close my eyes, jaw trembling with the war I'm still fighting inside myself. The kind of torture I gave them, gave her, wasn't just blood and bruises. It wasn't just pain for pain's sake.

It was intimate. Controlled. Slow. The kind of torment that had her trembling, not from fear, but from how badly she wanted more. I touched her like a weapon. I used my mouth like a blade. I broke her down, inch by inch, and instead of begging me to stop, she opened her legs wider.

"Beyond our capabilities here," I finish, and the words taste like sin. Because they are.

Roman recoils slightly, not fully understanding, and I hope he never does.

Because if he knew, if anyone knew, what I did to her, how I needed her, how I fucked my obsession so deep into her body she moaned my name through pain... they'd bury me beneath this building.

And the sickest part?

I don't regret it.

I only regret that it ended like this.

Why hasn't she said anything?

Why hasn't she asked for me?

The silence from the other side of the glass is more deafening than the scream she let out the first time I laid hands on her. I can still hear that sound. Still feel it etched into my skin like a scar that never healed. But now... now there's nothing. No glance. No glare. No whispered plea. Just silence.

"She stopped Nikolai from harming you," Roman says, pacing like a caged animal. His voice grates against my nerves. "She stopped him from putting a bullet through one of us."

He pauses, eyes narrowing on me, dragging his gaze across my posture like he's peeling back layers. "Was she in your room?"

The question is accusatory.

My jaw tightens.

"Interrogation," I mutter. "One-on-one. Let her feel like she could trust me. Let her think I was someone safe. Someone close."

It's a lie.

A flimsy, transparent fucking lie. And he knows it. I know it.

But it's the only version I can say out loud.

Because the truth is worse.

The truth is, I *was* someone she could trust. I never should've been, but I was. I held her when she cried. I kissed her wrists where the shackles dug in. I watched her fall apart and I *let* her, because I was there to catch her. I didn't knock her unconscious. Not at first. Not until the line blurred so badly I couldn't see straight.

It wasn't just business. Maybe at the start, but not after the first time she touched me like I was more than a monster. Not after the first time she moaned my name like a prayer and a curse all at once.

I let it go too far. And now I don't know how to undo it. I don't even know if I want to.

"She was protecting her captor," a voice cuts in sharply.

I turn, facing Ana, Noah's fiancée.

She steps into the room like she belongs here, neck bruised, throat purpled and swollen from what Dimitri's men did to her. And yet, her voice holds no weakness. Only sharp, clinical certainty.

"Her *savior*," she adds, eyes narrowing as she stops beside Roman.

My stomach churns.

"Stockholm Syndrome," she clarifies, nodding toward the girl on the other side of the glass. Katya. Still unmoving. Still silent. Her head bowed beneath the flickering fluorescent light, hair tangled around her shoulders like a veil.

"No," I breathe, shaking my head. "No. That's not it."

"It *is*," Ana snaps. "You don't see it because you don't want to see it."

I move closer to the glass, fists clenched at my sides, trying to will her to look up. To see me. To *say something*. But she doesn't move. Doesn't flinch.

"Katya Romanov is a killer," Ana continues. "A killer who knows nothing but vengeance. The only thing she's ever known is blood, control, and power. You had her unchained. Untethered. *Free* in your home. And she didn't hurt you."

"She *protected* you," Roman adds, arms crossed. "And now she's shutting down. That gives me all the answers I need."

I can barely breathe. The walls feel like they're closing in.

"She feels betrayed," Ana says, more gently now, as if offering an autopsy rather than a judgment. "Whatever fucked-up manipulation you used on her, it worked. You convinced her you were something else. Something better. And then you hit her. You threw her back in a cell. You proved every lie right."

I press my palms to the glass.

"She's not broken," I whisper. "She's not-"

"She's *hurt,* Echo. She's confused. And right now, she thinks *you* are the enemy. And the only person she might talk to is the one who shattered her."

I watch her.

Blank. Emotionless.

Her head hangs low, too heavy for her neck to hold. Her arms rest limp at her sides, fingers twitching only slightly when she exhales. She's not screaming. Not resisting.

She's *gone.*

And I don't know if I'll ever get her back.

"And my car?" I ask, though I already know the answer. The question's a formality, something to say while my mind races, while guilt coils tighter in my chest.

"Just as you suspected," Roman says, folding his arms across his chest like he's holding the whole damn world together by sheer force of will. "At Dimitri's estate. Nikolai ran straight to the Romanov manor."

Of course he did. Straight home. Straight into the arms of the devil who made him.

Just perfect.

"We'll make sure there's extra security at your place," Roman adds, his voice clipped. "Let them think you're still there. We'll keep Catalyst quiet."

"Good," I reply, already strategizing. "Let them believe I'm home. Let them waste their energy hunting shadows. I'm staying here tonight."

I don't even look at Roman when I say it.

"Here?" he repeats, eyes narrowing. "With her?"

"Yes," I snap. "Nikolai thinks she's still at the house. Dimitri made threats. It's about time we start making a few of our own."

More lies.

Layer after layer, burying me in the hole I dug with my own hands. This whole operation is rotting from the inside out, and I'm the infection that spread it. But the worst part is, I don't care. Not enough. Because she's still here, and if staying by her side is a risk, I'll take it.

God help me, Catalyst is the safest place she can be now.

And that says everything.

My gaze drifts to the glass. She hasn't moved in hours. Her head hangs low, shoulders slumped, wrists limp in the restraints. But then, slowly, deliberately, her head turns. Her bloodshot eyes lift, locking on the one-way mirror like she can feel us watching.

"Is he in there?" she whispers.

The first words she's spoken in hours. Her voice is like sandpaper, raw, scraped clean from the inside. It's not a question meant to be answered. It's a death sentence, waiting to be carried out.

Roman presses the mic button, his voice steady as ever. "You'll have to be more specific, Ms. Romanov."

Her eyes don't blink. Her gaze burns.

"How many of you are watching me?" she mutters. "How many of your people are you letting watch me, Echo?"

The way she says my name twists something inside me. It used to sound like a secret. Now it's venom.

I move forward, nudging Roman aside.

"Answer their questions, Katya," I order, voice hard. "Behave."

She laughs. The sound is hollow.

"It was all a game," she whispers, her lips curling into something between a smile and a snarl. "Wasn't it?"

Her shackles rattle as she shifts, her bruised wrists pulling against the restraints.

"Wasn't it!" she screams, slamming her arms forward, fury bursting out of her like a bomb. "You fucking pigs. You think you're any better than my family? You torture, you kill, you manipulate. You stalk. You prey."

Her voice climbs, cracking with emotion as her words pierce through the glass like bullets.

"Echo Kane," she growls. "Powerful, untouchable Echo fucking Kane. You got into my head. Made me think I could trust you. Made me feel safe. What was the plan, huh?" Her smile is deranged now, tears streaking down her cheeks as she loses control. "Kidnap me? Torture me? Use me? Fu-"

"That's enough, Katya," I bark, voice sharp as steel, stopping her before she can tear into the one word that would finish me.

But it's already too late.

Her voice lowers again, poisonous.

"So," she hisses, "it wasn't part of the plan."

Roman turns toward me, his jaw locked. "What is she talking about?"

My hands tremble. I curl them into fists to hide it.

"She's playing her games," I lie, the words tasting like rot in my mouth.

Katya grins, feral. "What does his face look like now?" she taunts the room. "Does he look scared?" She cocks her head, mocking. "Are his hands shaking?"

I dig my nails into my palms hard enough to break skin. Anything to stop the tremor from rising.

"What do you want?" I ask, the words barely holding together. Her eyes flash.

"For everyone but you to leave that damn room," she snaps. "I want to speak to you. Alone. No fucking cameras. No eyes. Think you can manage that, Echo?"

There's silence.

Roman shifts beside me, disbelief etched across his face. "Echo-"

"Everyone out," I say, voice low but final.

Roman takes a step forward, hand outstretched. "Echo, think about what you're-"

"Roman." My voice cuts through the room like a knife. My jaw tightens, my stare locked on the glass. "I said get out."

The room empties slowly, one shadow at a time peeling away until only silence remains. The hum of the overhead light buzzes in my ears, louder now that I'm alone. My hands tremble as I fumble with the lock, the key slick in my grasp. It slips once, twice, before I shove it in and turn it, the click echoing like a gunshot in my chest. I pocket the key, a final barrier between us erased. The door creaks open as I step into her space, into the wreckage I made with my own hands.

She doesn't flinch.

Her eyes lock onto mine the second I cross the threshold, bloody, glassy and dead. Her body doesn't move, but her gaze is a weapon sharpened on my throat. I swallow hard, drawing in a breath I don't deserve.

"Well, look who's listening to commands now," she whispers, voice soft but dripping with venom.

"Katya-" I start, but the name sounds foreign even to me, like I'm saying it from the wrong mouth. Her face twists before the second syllable escapes.

"Don't." Her voice cracks like lightning. "Don't fucking say my name. Don't say it like you know me."

Her words hit harder than any bullet I've ever taken. I step closer anyway. My body moves on instinct, but my soul recoils with every inch. I don't know what I'm doing, I just know I need to be closer. I reach out.

She doesn't stop me, but her eyes dare me to.

When my hand strikes her cheek, it's like the room explodes.

The sound is soft. Too soft. But my hand trembles where it falls. The shame hits instantly, rushing up my throat like bile. I can't look away, but I can't stand the sight of what I've done either. Not again.

"Stop," I snap, low and raw. "Stop running your fucking mouth before you get yourself killed."

She gasps, but not from fear. It's disgust. My thumb brushes her lip where blood gathers, smearing it away in a slow, shaking motion. My fingers graze her jaw like they're apologizing, but the damage is already done.

"Do you understand me?" I ask, quieter now.

She laughs, dark and unhinged. Her voice is a dagger she drags across my chest.

"Like you give a fuck."

She thrashes in the chair, rattling the restraints, teeth bared like an animal backed into a corner. "You used me," she spits. "You broke me down, inch by inch, and then you fucked me like I was nothing."

"I did not fucking use you," I hiss back, stepping closer, fists clenched at my sides. "You think this was all some kind of plan?"

"Yes," she screams, tears rising now, fury breaking into something deeper. "Look at me! Look at what you did to me!"

I try. I do.

But her face... bruised, bloodied, haunted. It's too much. I glance down, eyes stuck on the floor like a coward. She sees it.

"I protected you," she growls. "I could have run, more than once. I could've let Nikolai kill the both of you and walked away without a scratch. But I didn't."

"But you didn't," I snap, voice rising to meet hers, my chest caving in with the weight of it. "You didn't. You stayed with me. You stayed because you didn't want to leave me."

Her head jerks up, eyes blazing. "No. I stayed because you were in my head. You manipulated me. You made me think I was safe. Made me think you cared."

I step closer, breath ragged. "You don't think I care?"

She doesn't answer.

She doesn't have to.

Her silence says everything. And it carves me open.

"You're going to use me again," she whispers, almost childlike. "Just like you did before."

I stare at her for a long moment, my body numb and humming, my mind splitting in two.

Then, slowly, I kneel. The metal clinks as I begin undoing the shackles around her wrists.

She flinches. Her eyes widen, breath hitching, heart beating so loud I swear I can hear it.

"Maybe you're right," I whisper, not even sure if I'm lying anymore.

Because maybe I did use her. Maybe I still am.

And maybe I don't know how to stop.

22

Shame On You

Katya

The moment I try to rise, to reclaim even an inch of ground, Echo's hand shoves me back down with unforgiving force. My spine hits the chair, breath stolen from my lungs as he looms over me, a storm barely leashed behind his eyes.

"All I do is use you, right?" he growls, his voice a sharp snarl that vibrates through my bones.

"Yes," I snap, chin tilted high even as heat coils in my stomach, betraying me.

His smile is dangerous.

"Do you even know what using you looks like, Katya?" he hisses, my name dragged across his tongue like venom and silk. His body radiates heat, pulsing with a possessive fury that wraps around me like a vice. I can't breathe. I don't want to.

"Fuck you, Everett-"

His hand fists in my hair before I finish the syllable. He yanks me up with a snarl and drags me across the room, forcing me forward until my cheek smashes against the cold glass wall of the interrogation room. I scream, banging my fists against it, but his grip only tightens, one hand at the nape of my neck, the other pinning my hips back, holding me in place like I weigh nothing.

"There's no one in there, Katya," he murmurs into my ear, his voice low, lethal. "No cameras. No guards. No one watching but you and me. I have the only key to this room."

His hips press into me, and I feel it, hard and unforgiving, grinding against my ass with ruthless intent. My skin ignites beneath his touch, betrayal and desire crashing in my veins like thunder.

"No," I breathe. "No, I won't feed into this."

"Yes, you will," he growls. "Because you always do. Because you're mine, Katya. Mine to keep. Mine to ruin. Mine to fuck. Mine to remember. And tonight, I'm going to remind you just how real it was."

He drags my pants down with one hand, the other still anchoring me by the throat. My breath shudders, thighs clenching, but it's too late, he already feels it.

His fingers slide between my legs and pause.

"You're soaked," he whispers, a dark chuckle curling in his throat. "So tell me, why the fuck did you really ask to be alone with me?"

I don't answer. I won't give him that satisfaction.

He pinches my clit hard enough to make my knees buckle, my mouth opening in a cry I hate him for.

"Why, Katya?" he snarls, his lips right against my ear, fingers teasing, threatening, claiming.

My eyes sting, but I keep them closed. I grit my teeth.

"Fuck you."

His laugh is pure sin, and his hand...merciless.

And I already know I've lost. Again.

His fingers don't stop. They stroke through my folds like he's savoring every slick inch, like he already knows how far gone I am. The pressure is deliberate, taunting and possessive, familiar. My thighs twitch as he teases my entrance, not pushing in, just circling, dragging my arousal across swollen flesh like he wants to see how much I can take before I break.

"You know what I know," Echo growls behind me, his voice molten and vicious, each word pressed hot against the back of my neck. "You know this wasn't some goddamn act. You felt it, every time I touched you, every time you screamed my name. You knew I had to hurt you to keep Roman from putting a bullet between your eyes. You know the reason you asked to be alone with me is because you wanted this, you wanted me. All of me. Just like this."

I shake my head, but it's barely a twitch. My body's too busy reacting to him, too far gone to pretend otherwise. Heat blooms in my stomach, rising fast. I can feel myself getting wetter, can hear it now as his fingers glide between my folds, slick and needy.

My body wants him. Desperately. My mind is screaming. My pride is dying.

"You wanted me to find out how fucking wet you are for me," he snarls, "even while you're spitting hate through your teeth."

Then I hear it.

The buckle. The belt sliding free.

My breath catches.

"Tell me you want me," he commands, voice dropping to something primal. "Tell me, right now."

"I won't-" I snap, but my voice wavers. I can't stop it. I can't stop any of this.

His hand fists my hair. The other yanks my hips back with brutal precision, and then he slams into me.

A strangled scream escapes my lips as I lurch forward, my chest slamming into the glass wall. My hands fly up, palms slapping against the cold pane to keep from falling. My breath fogs the surface instantly, ragged and hot, while his cock stretches me wide, thick and pulsing and deep.

He doesn't ease into it.

He pounds into me from the start, ruthless and merciless, grinding his hips against mine with each thrust like he's trying to claim every inch of space inside me. My body jerks with every impact, my breasts pressed tight to the glass, thighs shaking as pleasure slams through me, raw and furious.

His grip is bruising on my hips. He's holding me in place like he owns me.

Maybe he does.

"Tell me you need me," he growls, his voice dripping with rage and want. His hand slips between my thighs again, finding my clit and circling it with maddening, punishing speed. My back arches, my mouth falls open, but I bite back the moan.

"N-No," I whisper, but my body's screaming something else entirely.

"Say it," he snarls, dragging his hand up my stomach to wrap around my throat. "Fucking say it, Katya."

He pulls me upright against him, my back to his chest, still buried deep inside me. His free hand moves up to grip my jaw, forcing my head to turn, to look at our reflection in the glass, me bent, fucked, undone.

"I'm in your blood," he whispers into my ear, his lips brushing the shell of it. "I'm in your fucking soul. You can hate me all you want. You can scream, curse, claw, but you need me. You'll never stop needing me."

Tears sting my eyes, fury and arousal warring inside me until I don't know which one will destroy me first. Every thrust sends sparks shooting through my veins. Every slap of his skin against mine pushes me closer to the edge.

I hate him.

I crave him.

I'm lost.

And worst of all?

I don't want him to stop.

I can barely breathe from the force of him pounding into me. Each thrust punches into me with punishing rhythm, and all I can do is take it. My hands are splayed against the glass, breath fogging the surface, my body caught between pleasure and war.

"Tell me," he groans, voice rasping with hunger. "Tell me you need me, Katya."

My eyes flutter. My mouth falls open. The sound that slips out is pure surrender.

"I do..." I whisper, broken on a breath. "I do need you."

His grip tightens around my throat like he's drinking those words in, letting them root inside his skin. But I'm not finished.

"...but you betrayed me."

The words hang in the air like a curse.

He hesitates. Just for a second. The rhythm of his thrusts stutters, his breath catching in my ear. And in that tiny pause, that flicker of vulnerability, I strike, jabbing my elbow hard into his ribs.

He gasps, stumbling back. His cock slips free, wet and twitching, and I hear the anger swell in his breath. But I'm already spinning, already diving for the pocket of his discarded pants. My fingers close around cold metal.

The key.

His fucking arrogance left it right there.

I lunge for the door.

"Katya!" he shouts, but he's still fumbling with his pants, still stunned.

Slamming the interrogation room door shut with a deafening crack, I don't hesitate. I shove the key into the lock, turn it hard, and trap him on the other side of the glass.

One breath. Two.

Then he's there, raging.

Pounding on the window like a caged animal.

His eyes are wild, his jaw clenched, pants halfway zipped, his chest rising like he's about to explode. His fists slam into the glass, the sound thunderous.

"Katya! Open the fucking door!"

I don't move. I just stare. He looks feral, hair a mess, shirt half-buttoned, cock still tenting his waistband. And for once, I have the power.

My gaze drops to the control panel beside the mirror. The mic blinks red, waiting.

Pressing the button, I lean in, whispering, soft and cruel.

Lean in.

"It's just business."

The effect is instant.

His face shatters.

The arrogance drains from him, his mouth parting, his fists falling limp against the glass. His eyes, those fucking eyes, go wide like I just ripped something out of him.

Good.

Let it hurt.

Turning, my legs still shake, my thighs still slick with him, my pulse crashing beneath my skin. I feel everything, ache, heat, triumph, heartbreak, and it all burns like fire as I move toward the exit.

Each step is heavier than the last, but I don't stop.

At the door, I slip the key in, twist it twice, and feel the bolt release.

Cool air rushes in.

I pause for half a second.

Then I walk out, leaving the monster exactly where he belongs. Behind glass, broken and alone.

23

You're In My Cage Now

Katya- Week's Later

"K atya?"

Nikolai snaps his fingers in my face like I'm some disobedient child, like he hasn't already disgraced himself beyond repair. The gesture is desperate, offensive, and unoriginal, exactly what I've come to expect from him. He's always trying too hard, puffing his chest like it matters. Across the room, the two guards posted by the door remain still, confirmation that he holds no real power here.

The aged scotch burns down my throat in a way that should bring calm. Instead, it stokes something low and hot in my belly, something I haven't been able to smother since I walked out of Catalyst. Every swallow tastes like regret. Like memory. Like him.

That thought should've been buried by now.

It should've died the moment I turned the key and locked Echo Kane behind glass.

But it hasn't.

It clings to me like his fingerprints still staining my skin. I down the rest of the glass anyway.

"Don't remember asking you to speak," the words leave sharp and clipped. Glancing across my father's desk, everything about this space is curated, pristine. Dominance built into the bones of the room. And still, it reeks of absence. My father isn't here. Which means I am the one they answer to.

Nikolai shifts uncomfortably under my gaze, his mouth twitching before he speaks again. "Your father asked you to look this over while he's away."

A folder lands with a soft thud in front of me, tossed carelessly across the polished wood. The emblem stamped across the front hits like a gut punch. *Catalyst.* That familiar sigil, clean lines, power etched into its design, is more than just a logo. It's a ghost. A memory. A warning.

And beneath it, the faint echo of his presence.

The file remains unopened as I study him, shoulders squared, face carefully neutral, the coward hiding behind new loyalty. After fleeing Echo's grasp with his tail between his legs, Nikolai returned to my father and spun a half-truth with just enough shame to be believable. Claimed I was hysterical, corrupted, fucked senseless into loyalty. Left out the part where he failed to kill me. Where he failed to control anything. Where he begged.

My father saw through it immediately. Called it what it was, cowardice. But loyalty, even from the weak, still buys time. So here Nikolai stands, still breathing, still offering reports like he's earned the right to be here.

"Is that all?" The question isn't really for him. It's for the men who allowed him into this space. For anyone who forgot that my word carries weight now.

Nikolai's lips thin. "No one's seen Echo in weeks. His house is quiet. Still guarded, but no movement. If he's there, he hasn't left."

The way he says Echo makes something shift beneath my ribs. That name alone drags heat and ache to the surface, uninvited. Images flicker, Echo's hand at my throat, his voice in my ear, the feel of him still imprinted between my legs.

But it doesn't show. Not here. Not to him.

"That's not your concern," I murmur, pouring steel into every syllable. "You're lucky you weren't castrated. Lucky you're still allowed to come and go with your pride intact."

His expression darkens, but he doesn't speak. He knows better.

"If that's all," I say smoothly, pushing my chair back with quiet grace, "our men will see you out."

A smile pulls at my lips, cold and practiced.

"Tell your father thank you for this month's generous contributions," the tone drips honey over the blade. "And do let him know I look forward to meeting his new pick for our families' union."

The scotch still lingers in my mouth, warm and bitter. The emblem still stares at me from the desk. And somewhere far from this room, behind glass and silence, I know Echo Kane is still waiting. Guarded. Hidden.

And despite everything, so am I.

The union was formally dissolved in the wake of Nikolai's disgrace. After his failure, his cowardice, his cruelty, there was no salvaging what little pretense had existed between us. My father and his agreed to sever the tie, quietly, cleanly, replacing it with a new arrangement bound to another name in the Sokolov house. Another pawn. Another promise. One meant to repair the fracture Nikolai left behind.

"Will do," he mutters, jaw clenched, eyes avoiding mine.

I offer only a nod. That's all he's earned.

My men move toward him, hands lifting to escort, but he yanks his arm away before they can lay a finger on him.

"I can see myself out," he snaps, wounded pride wrapped in false confidence.

The anger in his retreat is louder than his footsteps, his pace too fast, too tight. Practically running. Pathetic.

As soon as the door clicks shut, silence falls. I don't fill it. I let it sit.

Then I speak, calm and clipped. "Leave me."

The guards hesitate, only for a breath, then file out wordlessly, the weight of their boots disappearing down the hall.

Alone, I glance at the folder still sitting on my father's desk, the Catalyst emblem like a shadow bleeding across the cover. I open it, fingers slow, careful. Inside, documents, maps, and images.

Noah Ackerman.

Roman Briar.

Anastasia Burns.

Locations, last known movements, habits.

The weight of it makes something coil low in my stomach.

"Hmm," I murmur, tracing the corner of the page. "Interesting."

Names I know. Lives I've brushed against in fleeting moments, some more than others. Allies. Enemies. Echo's world, mapped out for my benefit. Or my manipulation.

My phone vibrates on the edge of the desk, the screen lighting with a single message that makes my blood cool despite the burn in my chest.

Can't wait to see you tonight!

So normal.

Only it isn't.

This is what healthy is supposed to look like. What safety should feel like.

But none of it does. Not really. Not anymore.

The text feels foreign in my hand, like someone else's life flashing across the screen. I stare at it a moment longer before slipping the phone into my coat pocket and exhaling a slow, deliberate breath.

This is normal.

This is what normal should be.

And yet, deep down, I know, nothing may ever feel normal again.

The keys rattle in the lock as I slip into the apartment, my body sore, my mind fractured in a dozen different places. Candlelight greets me first, casting golden shadows across the walls. The scent of clove and wax lingers, heavy and cloying. It's all too intentional. Too nice. This isn't mine. This isn't comfort. This is someone else trying to make a home where there never was one.

Garrett stands in the kitchen, lighting the last of the candles. His face is soft, his smile boyish, like he's proud of the ambiance he's curated. He moves with gentleness, as if we're something tender. "You've been working late," he offers, striking a match with one hand. "Didn't realize insurance paperwork could be so emotionally daunting."

There's something in me that wants to laugh at the irony. Instead, I stare, unmoved.

"When did fucking turn into gestures?" The words slip from my mouth like venom wrapped in silk.

He chuckles, mistaking my disdain for flirtation. "You're far too cold, Emma."

Emma. That name doesn't belong to me. It feels like wearing someone else's skin, tight and suffocating. He's been in my bed more than once, and still, he has no idea who I am.

Shrugging off my coat, I toss it and my bag onto the couch, the weight of them hitting like punctuation. "I told you," I say, voice low and flat. "You come. You leave. That's the deal."

Garrett approaches like he's about to press his luck again, leaning in, kissing me softly. It's a harmless kind of affection, light and meaningless, a touch that demands nothing but offers even less. For a moment, I let him.

Then the knock comes. Three short raps against the door.

My spine stiffens before I even register the sound.

"That must be the rest of the food," Garrett says, already heading toward the door, but my stomach is already twisting. Something is wrong.

A voice comes through the door, muffled but clear.

"I have an order for Katya."

My entire body locks into place. That name, my name, shouldn't exist in this space. Not with him here. Not like this. My hand instinctively moves to the waistband of my jeans, fingers grazing the hidden steel of my gun.

Garrett, oblivious, undoes the lock with a frown. "No Katya here. Are you sure you've got the-"

The door opens.

And there he is.

Echo.

The shadows cling to him like lovers. His hat is pulled low over those eyes, eyes I know better than my own. There's blood on his hands, smeared across his knuckles like war paint. His curls stick to his temples with sweat, and he holds a takeout bag like it means something, like it doesn't already drip grease onto the floor between them.

He doesn't speak at first. He just looks. At me. At Garrett. At the space between us.

Garrett, caught off guard, takes a step back. "Jesus, man, are you, are you okay?"

"Garrett," I say, voice low and flat. "You should go."

He turns to me, confused. "If you're not feeling well, I can-"

"She told you to leave," Echo interrupts, voice calm, edged with something sharp and volatile beneath the surface. He steps inside slowly, the takeout bag dropping from his hand. It hits the hardwood with a dull splatter, something wet and red leaking through the bottom.

Garrett straightens, posturing like he might defend something. "Who the fuck do you think you are?"

Echo doesn't respond.

He moves.

One swift motion, and the gun is beneath Garrett's chin, lifting him slightly onto the balls of his feet. Garrett stiffens, lips parting, his hands flying up as if that will save him. The cold metal under his jaw silences every breath in the room.

Echo presses in close, not just threatening, but invading. His presence wraps around Garrett like smoke, intoxicating and suffocating. His free hand comes up, thumb brushing along the underside of Garrett's jaw, not affectionately, but with eerie calm. Like he's choosing whether to end him or just leave a scar.

"You smell like her," he murmurs, the words meant for both of us. "Which means you've touched something that doesn't belong to you."

His eyes lift to mine, wild, dark and burning.

"Did you let him fuck you, Katya?"

I don't answer. My chest is tight. My throat dry. There's nothing in my body that doesn't remember what it felt like to be under him, his weight, his breath, his hands on my throat, his name on my lips like a prayer and a curse.

His smile curls wider.

To Garrett, he whispers, "You thought you were safe in her bed? Thought this was real? This isn't yours. She isn't yours."

The barrel of the gun presses harder beneath Garrett's chin. He trembles.

And Echo?

He just watches me.

Like I'm the only thing in the room that's alive.

"I'm not a fucking delivery driver," he mutters, the words gravel in his throat, thick with venom and whiskey.

"Don't," I breathe, barely audible, my chest rising too fast.

"Garrett," I snap louder, swallowing down the tremor in my voice. "Go."

He doesn't hesitate. Smart boy. Garrett bolts like the air just turned to poison, stumbling over himself in his rush to escape. I hear his feet disappear down the hallway, the slap of soles against tile fading fast.

Echo scoffs behind me, something feral flickering in his chest as he kicks the door shut with the heel of his boot. The lock clicks with finality, and it's just us again. Him. Me. This awful silence that hums with everything we never said.

His eyes sweep the room, taking in the candles, the soft light, the still-warm food cooling in its untouched containers. His hands are stained, slick and red, drying in the creases of his knuckles, and yet he doesn't bother to hide them.

"Candles," he growls, voice low and bitter. "A nice meal. Katya Romanov's got herself a fucking suitor."

My jaw tenses. "Where's the delivery driver?"

"Alive," he shrugs. "In his car."

"How the hell did you get out of your house without being seen?"

His smile is slow, crooked, and wrong. "I'm sure you'd love to know."

The moment stretches, breathless. My gun is already in my hand. So is his. Neither of us flinch.

"I'm not going back to Catalyst," I say, the words sharp and cold. "I'm not going back with you."

There's a glint in his eye, something twisted and hungry. "Did you fuck him?"

My laugh is brittle, hard-edged. "You came all the way here to ask me who I've fucked? Was it worth a bullet in your head, Echo?"

His gun lowers.

Mine doesn't.

He doesn't seem to care.

Sliding his pistol back into the holster at his hip, he steps closer, slow, unbothered, like my aim means nothing.

"You're not going to shoot me."

"Wanna bet?" I whisper, cocking the gun with a quiet click. My finger itches against the trigger.

"You're not going to shoot me," he says again, softer this time, more like a promise than a dare. He closes the space between us one step at a time, until the distance is gone and only heat remains.

"I'm not playing games with you anymore, Everett Kane," I snap.

"They were never games, Katya," he murmurs, slurring slightly, his breath thick with liquor. He's close enough that I can smell it now, smoke, sweat, and something sharper beneath it. Something dangerous.

"You're drunk."

"Liquid encouragement." He smirks lazily, dragging his tongue across his bottom lip. "Only got so much time before one of your daddy's little pets realizes your coffee shop fling bolted, and the driver's still sitting in his car wondering what just happened."

He steps again. I retreat.

"Echo-"

"Katya," he purrs, closing in until the muzzle of the gun presses to the center of his chest.

He doesn't stop. Doesn't blink. Just reaches up, slow, and curls his fingers around the barrel, dragging it down his sternum like it belongs to him. "You gonna shoot me?" he whispers, head tilted. "Hmm?"

I don't move.

His thumb brushes the side of the trigger. Teasing. Testing. Owning.

"Isn't that what you're supposed to do now that you're playing the part so well?" he hisses. "Daddy's little heir. Following his orders. Wearing his mask."

"I'm not following his rules-"

"Then whose?" he cuts in, voice guttural. "Whose rules are you following, Katya?"

"No one's."

"Wrong." His hand shoots forward, sliding up under the hem of my shirt. The heat of his palm sears my skin as he drags his finger over the name carved into my flesh. His name.

His breath shudders out against my neck.

"You know it," he growls. "You fucking know it. When I snap my fingers, you follow. When I speak, you move. When I touch you-"

He grabs my jaw with his blood-stained hand, tilting my face toward his.

"-you melt."

And god help me, he's right.

The crack of steel against his face echoes like a gunshot in the room. My grip doesn't falter as the barrel of my weapon slams into his cheekbone, sending him sprawling back onto the couch. He curses under his breath, stumbling, catching himself against the cushions, blood already blooming beneath his skin. That perfect face, flushed and dazed, tilts up toward me with a mix of fury and something far darker.

He should be afraid.

But he isn't.

I step over him slowly, deliberately, letting my shadow fall across his body like a warning. He groans, reaching for his side, but I move quicker. My fingers curl around the pistol holstered at the back of his waistband, and I wrench it free, flinging it across the room where it clatters uselessly against the tile.

"Not anymore," I murmur, a slow, dangerous smile curving my lips. Holstering my own gun, I reach down, sliding my fingers over the knife strapped to my thigh.

"I have an idea of my own, actually."

His eyes flick to the blade as it catches the low light, but his gaze doesn't linger long. It returns to me, always back to me, as if he can't help himself. Like even now, bleeding and breathless, he wants more.

I don't give him a chance to rise.

Before he can push off the couch, I lunge, grabbing him by the throat. My palm presses hard against his neck, driving him backward, pinning him down. His breath catches, sharp and involuntary, but I don't let up. I squeeze.

Hard.

The muscles in his jaw tighten beneath my fingers, his hands flying up to grip my wrists, but he doesn't fight. Not yet. His eyes flare wide, the whites showing, and still... he holds my gaze.

He watches me.

His legs shift beneath me, bucking once in resistance, then stilling as I tighten my grip. The veins in his neck throb against my palm, his lips parting as oxygen slips away from him like a lover leaving in the dark.

There's something erotic in the power. In the way he lets me take it.

His face begins to blur at the edges, the fight draining from his limbs as the lights behind his eyes start to flicker.

And still, I don't release him.

Not yet.

You're in my cage now Everett Kane.

24

You're Mine Little Butterfly

Echo

The first thing I register is heat. Not just the kind that comes from a flushed face or a pounding head, but the low, slow burn of shame and arousal twisting together beneath my skin. My throat is dry, lips parted around something soft and soaked. It fills my mouth completely, muffling every breath, every word I want to spit. Something damp clings to my tongue, laced with salt and musk.

Fucking hell.

I blink, the fog in my head beginning to clear, only to be replaced by a different haze that'd thicker, darker, and far more dangerous. My knees press into the soft rug beneath me, and my hands are bound behind my back, not with rope, but with silk, something that clings and constricts in a way that feels too elegant to be cruel, and yet... it *is*. My shirt is gone. My chest rises with each slow, ragged breath. And then I see her.

Katya.

She's no longer in jeans or leather. She's no longer playing the captive or the soldier or the heir to a violent empire. No, now she's something else entirely, something untouchable. The sheer black fabric of her gown kisses every curve of her body, leaving nothing to the imagination. Her legs are draped lazily over the arm of the chair, one heel dangling from her toe, her thighs spread just enough to drive me mad. There's no underwear to shield her, no modesty left to protect her. Candlelight flickers across her skin, catching the shimmer between her legs and the curve of her breasts. The gown is barely more than a whisper clinging to her nipples, which harden in the chilled air and my helpless stare.

A blade glides between her fingers.

She looks at me like I'm prey she's already sunk her teeth into, like she's not just toying with me, but feeding off the very act of control. Her expression is unreadable, lips parted slightly, amusement hiding just behind the venom in her eyes. And then she speaks.

"You know," she says slowly, running her fingers along the hilt of the knife as though recalling a memory she's learned to enjoy, "you fucked me with a blade just like this."

The words slam into me like a punch to the gut. I should look away. I *want* to look away. But I can't. My cock strains hard against my pants, twitching at the sight of her, the sound of her voice, the scent of her soaking my tongue as her underwear gags me in place. The weight of what's happening coils tighter and tighter around my chest.

She doesn't approach me. Doesn't rush the moment. She lounges there, legs open, gown hitched high, letting me *see* all of her but keeping me exactly where she wants me, on my knees, caged by silk and pride and the suffocating taste of her.

And she knows. *Of course she knows.* Her gaze flicks down to the tension bulging against my zipper, and the smirk that curls across her lips is nothing short of sinful.

She leans forward, slow and deliberate, the gown slipping off one shoulder. "Look at you," she purrs, almost pitying. "Drooling. Silenced. Harder for me now than you ever were when you thought you were in control."

Her legs shift again, spreading wider. The blade grazes her thigh, then disappears beneath the fabric. I can't breathe. Not because of the gag, but because of the way she *moans*, soft and low, as the metal dances across her bare skin. She doesn't look away as she plays with the knife, doesn't blink. She watches me unravel like a thread pulled too tight.

"I thought about this," she murmurs. "About how it would feel. You, gagged with the same thing you ripped off me. Me, finally getting to watch you *need*, while I decide whether or not you get anything at all."

I groan, half in frustration, half in awe. My whole body aches for her, every part of me straining for release, for contact, for *permission.*

Katya leans back, satisfied with the wreck she's made of me.

And I'm left kneeling in the flickering dark, bound by silk and drowned in scent, aching for the very woman I once believed I controlled.

"What was your goal coming here, Echo?" she breathes, her voice dripping with cruel amusement. "Hmm? Were you going to take me again? Fuck me? Drag me back to your house and slip me past my men like a dirty secret?"

She grins wickedly, then rises from the chair like sin itself. The sheer gown clings to her every curve, barely hiding anything. Her nipples press against the translucent fabric, the hem barely brushing the tops of her thighs. She's bare underneath. I can see the heat between her legs. And she knows I see it.

She *wants* me to see it.

God, what the fuck is she doing to me?

Each step she takes is slower than the last, deliberate and lethal, hips swaying like she's stalking prey. Me. "Garrett is a nice man," she says, circling me like a flame teasing gasoline. "Safe. He takes his time. Fucks me gently."

My vision goes red.

The idea of another man touching her, kissing her, sliding into her where only I've been, rage coils in my gut and I lunge. But she moves faster, that sadistic smile still painted across her lips. Her foot slams into my chest, sending me sprawling backward. I grunt from the impact, but I barely feel it. My cock is still throbbing, harder now, the pain only fanning the fire burning under my skin.

"You're dangerous," she whispers, crouching beside me, her fingers lazily trailing a blade over her bare thigh. "Unpredictable."

The tip glides higher, her other hand cupping her breast like it's nothing, like she owns every inch of me with the flick of a wrist. "You held me like a hostage," she says. "Kept me like I was something to be played with. And maybe I liked it."

Her fingers slide down her hip, stopping just below the curve of her ass. "Your name," she purrs, voice thick and heavy, "permanently carved into my skin. Like branding a cow."

My cock twitches at the memory, a smile creeping along my lips.

She doesn't flinch. Doesn't back down. Instead, she rips her underwear from between my lips, soaked with her scent and covered in my spit.

"What's so funny?" she asks, eyes narrowing.

I grin, with shameless possession. "You can run," I murmur, standing slow, closing the space between us, "hide, disappear halfway across the world... but that scar? Those marks?"

I lean in, breath brushing the shell of her ear. "They're a permanent reminder that you will always belong to me, Katya." I chuckle darkly. "That no matter how hard you fight it... your body remembers me."

She tosses the ruined lace to the side, venom flashing in her eyes. "Am I yours?" she whispers, stepping closer, too close. Her knees touch the ground, and suddenly she's at my feet, a goddess disguised as a weapon, her knife dragging down my chest.

"Or are *you* mine?"

Her eyes sparkle, deadly and divine.

Then she moves.

Hand on my throat, she slams me to the floor like I weigh nothing. My back hits hard, but she's already straddling me, her thighs tight against my ribs, her cunt pressed to my abs. *Hot. Wet. Hungry.*

She grinds against me, slow, torturous, slick heat spreading across my skin. I buck beneath her, groaning like an animal, hands flying to her hips. But she grabs my wrists, pins them above my head with one hand, blade still pressed against my hip with the other.

"Katya-" I rasp, my voice shredded with lust and fury and fucking need.

"That's right," she purrs, leaning forward until her lips brush mine, her breath like smoke and sin. "Say my name again."

Her hips roll again, this time lower, right against the bulge of my cock. I nearly lose it right there.

"You think you're in control?" she whispers, tongue flicking over my bottom lip. "Tell me, Echo... if I let you up right now, would you fuck me like you hate me? Or like you need me more than your next breath?"

My voice is gone. My thoughts are gone.

All that's left is her.

I try to sit up, barely. But her hand slams into my chest, knocking me flat again. The force stuns me, head reeling, stars dancing behind my eyes. I don't know if it's the blow or the rush of watching her work, but I can't move.

She straddles me like I'm a canvas, not a man. Her blade glints in the low light, and then, slow and merciless, she drags the edge across my skin. A hiss breaks past my teeth. Not from pain. No. It's pleasure in its rawest, most feral form.

Her eyes go wide, dark with delight, transfixed by what she's doing to me. The slice is shallow, precise, cruel. She carves like an artist, every stroke intentional, every flick of her wrist owning me.

And I can't do a fucking thing about it.

My arms are useless, pinned, limp with submission and shock. I'm stuck between pain and ecstasy, delirious. Drenched in heat.

"Now," she breathes, voice low and deadly, the words slithering into my bloodstream like poison. "You are no one's... but mine."

She lifts off me slowly, a slick trail glistening on my chest where her pussy just was, wet, warm, and absolutely soaked from the violence she just gave me. My head drops back, and then I see it.

The cut.

Her name.

Her fucking name, etched into my skin.

My cock pulses so hard it hurts. I can't stop it. Don't want to. I want her to see what she's done to me.

Her gaze drops to the obscene bulge in my pants, eyes narrowing like she owns every twitch beneath the fabric. Without a word, she leans down, lips brushing over the outline of my cock, barely, before trailing up.

Higher.

To the cut.

To her mark.

Then her tongue flicks out, slow and sinful, dragging across the open wound. My blood stains her mouth like a kiss from the devil. She tastes me like I'm her last meal, like she'd bathe in me if I let her. And I would.

Tossing the blade aside, she stands over me with her lips painted red, her grin twisted with triumph. My heart slams in my chest, hard enough to crack bone.

"Sit up," she commands.

I don't move fast enough.

Fingers tangle in my hair, tight and punishing, and she yanks me upright, dragging me onto my knees before her like I'm nothing more than a toy she's winding back up.

She lifts her gown.

Fuck.

Her pussy is right there. Inches from my mouth. Slick and swollen. The scent of her, heady and addictive, hits me like a drug. My mouth waters. My cock throbs against the constraint of my pants. She's dripping, thighs glistening with arousal that has everything to do with what she just did to me.

Her fingers curl beneath my jaw, forcing my eyes up to meet hers.

"Are you sorry, Echo?" she whispers. Her voice isn't mocking now. It's soft.

I can't think past the ache between us. The way her thighs tremble from the thought of my mouth, the way she's soaked just from controlling me.

Ignoring the sting bleeding from my chest, I speak the only truth I know.

"Untie me," I rasp, voice thick with hunger. "And I'll show you just how sorry I am."

Her smile deepens.

"Yes," she purrs. "You will."

She moves behind me silently, undoing the binds around my wrists one by one. The second the last one falls loose, blood rushes back into my arms, but I don't even flinch. My eyes are locked on her. Every part of me is coiled, waiting, ravenous.

She steps around to face me.

Slow. Commanding. Gown clinging to her body like a second skin, soaked between her thighs.

Her eyes burn into mine as she reaches out, gathering both hands in my hair, fisting it, before pulling me close like I'm hers to claim. And I am. I fucking am.

My lips part, and I taste her before I even reach her. The scent of her arousal wraps around me like smoke, dragging me under. My tongue finds her thigh first, hot and smooth beneath my mouth. I lick up slowly, reverently, my hands gliding from the back of her legs to her ass, gripping hard, squeezing, needing to feel every inch of her.

Her skin is velvet. Her thighs tremble as I slide the gown higher, bunching it around her waist.

And then, she's there. Right in front of me.

Her pussy, glistening, perfect, pink and slick, dripping with everything I've ever fucking needed.

I stare for a second, breathless. A man kneeling before his god.

"How much did you miss me?" she asks, her voice a soft, wicked sigh. Like she already knows the answer.

So much.

Too fucking much.

I shouldn't be here.

I shouldn't want this.

But I do.

I fucking do.

"More than you'll ever know," I whisper, voice low and cracked with need.

Then I bury my face in her pussy.

My tongue drags along her folds, slow at first, savoring the taste of her, the salt of her skin, the sweetness of her need. I lap at her clit like it's the last thing I'll ever taste, flicking it, rolling it, teasing until she gasps above me, her fingers yanking tighter in my hair.

I groan into her, sucking, licking, devouring.

She whimpers, her body pressing forward, hips rocking gently against my face, grinding into my mouth with helpless desperation. Her thighs start to shake. Her breaths come harder, faster, chest rising and falling like she's drowning and I'm her last inhale.

My hands grip her ass, hard enough to bruise, holding her right where I want her. Right where she belongs. I don't stop. I can't. Her taste is everything, intoxicating, addictive, mine.

I eat her like a man starved, tongue fucking her until her knees buckle and she has to brace herself on my shoulders, until she's panting my name between moans and needy little whines she can't swallow down.

I want to be inside her. I want to stretch her open and make her beg me to stop. I want to ruin her, mark her from the inside out, fuck her until she forgets every other man who's ever been between her legs.

How many have there been?

How many worthless bastards have touched what belongs to me?

The thought is poison. And it makes me hungrier.

I drag my tongue back up her slit, flick her clit, and press a kiss just above her pussy like a promise.

No one else gets this.

No one else ever will.

And the next time she moans, I won't stop at my mouth.

I'll bury myself so deep inside her, she'll forget how to stand without me.

I don't give her time to think, don't give myself time to breathe. The second her slickness coats my face and her thighs begin to tremble from the aftershock of my tongue, I rise. My movements are sharp, commanding, frantic with the kind of hunger that lives in my marrow. The kind that's been festering inside me since the first time I touched her.

I grab her by the back of the neck, not gently. My grip is firm, possessive, a silent vow carved into my skin and hers. She gasps as I turn her, and before she can speak, I bend her forward over the back of the couch, her breath catching in her throat as her hands splay out to steady herself.

The gown is already bunched around her waist, revealing the slick, swollen mess I've made of her. My mouth is still wet with the taste of her. My cock is thick and pulsing behind the zipper of my pants, so hard it aches. I can't wait, not even for a second. My hands fly to my belt, fumbling only briefly before freeing myself.

The air hitches in her lungs when she hears the sound of my zipper. Her head tilts, like she's trying to regain control, but it's too late. I step behind her, grip her hips, and in one fierce, desperate thrust, I sink into her.

She cries out, her voice cracked and feral, half-moan, half-scream.

Her walls tighten around me like a vice, hot and wet and fucking *perfect*. I nearly see stars. Every inch of her wraps around me like she's made for this, made for me. I sink deeper, groaning against the back of her neck, my breath heavy, my hands clutching her hips hard enough to bruise.

"Fuck," I growl against her shoulder, jaw clenched. "You feel so goddamn good."

I drag my hips back, just enough to feel the stretch, and thrust again, slower this time, deeper. Her body takes it, swallows me whole, and then begs for more. She keens when I shift my angle and hit that perfect spot, her fingers digging into the fabric of the couch like she's trying to claw her way out of this moment, like it's too much and still not enough.

I slide my hand up her body, along the slope of her spine, until I find her throat. Wrapping my fingers around it from behind, I lift her slightly, keeping her steady as I fuck her deeper, harder. Her back arches into me, hair sticking to the sweat building along her shoulders.

Every thrust is a claim. Every slap of skin against skin is a vow.

This isn't sex. This is a goddamn reckoning.

She can't speak, not with the way I hold her throat. Her moans turn guttural, helpless, her body grinding back into me with unspoken need. Her cunt grows slicker, tighter, greedier. And somewhere beneath the mess of it all, I feel the sting of blood, mine, hers, both. The cut along her hip must have reopened, mixing with the small tear across my hip, and now her ass is streaked with crimson.

It should be wrong. It should disgust me. Instead, it sends me spiraling.

The blood. The sweat. The sound of her falling apart underneath me. All of it blends together into something primal, holy, *sacred* in its filth.

I slam into her again, forcing a broken sob from her throat. "Say it," I growl, tightening my grip. "Say you need me, Katya."

She gasps, her voice barely a breath. "I- I need..."

Her words falter, lost in the force of what I'm giving her.

"Say it," I snap again, my hips snapping forward, the pace relentless, brutal.

"I- I need you," she whimpers finally, head falling back as her body trembles. Then, a small smile curls her lips, even through the ruin. "And *you*," she whispers, panting, "you fucking need me."

And with that, my control shatters.

I spill into her with a low, guttural moan, my cock pulsing inside her as I pour every ounce of need, fury, obsession into her body. My hands still grip her like I might break her apart if I let go. My chest heaves against her back, sweat dripping down my spine, my mind blank with the sheer force of release.

I don't move for a long moment, both of us trembling in the aftermath.

Then, slowly, I pull out.

My cum spills from her, thick and messy, dripping down the inside of her thighs. I watch, mesmerized, transfixed, as she straightens and reaches between her legs, collecting a strand of it on her fingers. She lifts it to her lips without hesitation, tongue flicking out to taste me.

Her grin is feral.

"Perfect," she murmurs, licking her lips like she's savoring every drop.

I can't breathe.

I step forward again, my cock already hardening with the promise of more, my body aching for a second round. I tilt her chin toward me and whisper against her mouth, voice low and ragged.

"Your bedroom," I say, kissing her with the hunger of a man unhinged. "I'm not done playing with you yet."

25

Mine To Ruin

Echo

Her body moves like silk and sin, rolling over mine with a control that makes me ache. Every motion is calculated, meant to break me down piece by piece, to teach me patience in the cruelest way. She sinks down on my cock with slow, torturous precision, taking me inch by inch until I'm buried so deep inside her, I feel her heartbeat thudding against mine.

I want to grab her hips, fuck up into her, claim back the rhythm. But I don't. I can't. Her rules still hang in the air like chains, and the way she watches me, like she'll punish disobedience with silence, roots me in place.

She rolls her hips slowly, grinding down, her warmth tightening around me as she moves in a slow, deliberate circle that has my jaw clenching, my breath hitching. Her fingers drag down my chest, nails leaving faint red lines in their wake. It's not pain, it's possession.

Her mouth lowers to my throat, tongue flicking over the pulse there before she bites, not hard enough to break skin, but firm enough to remind me, I'm hers right now.

"You feel that?" she whispers, her breath hot against my skin. "How tight I am for you? How fucking wet you make me?"

I groan, my head falling back against the mattress. Her pussy clenches around me, fluttering as she grinds down again, pulling a helpless moan from my throat that I can't swallow fast enough.

"I could ride you like this all night," she purrs, her voice syrupy and slow. "And you'd take it. Just like that. Quiet. Obedient. Desperate."

She leans back, one hand sliding between her legs, her fingers rubbing small circles over her clit as she rocks her hips forward again. The sight of her, completely bare, fucking herself on my cock while her own fingers tease her swollen flesh, is enough to make me dizzy.

The sounds, God, the sounds, are wet, obscene. Her slick clings to my skin, every thrust pulling a new moan from her throat, every grind making her thighs quiver just a little more.

"You like watching me take you like this?" she asks, tilting her head, eyes gleaming in the low light. "Do you like feeling my cunt milk your cock while you lie there like a good little toy?"

"Fuck, Katya-" I choke, the muscles in my thighs straining, my body trembling from the effort it takes not to flip her over and fuck her until she's limp.

She grins like she hears the scream building behind my teeth.

"Not yet," she whispers, dragging her fingernail down the center of my chest again. "You'll cum when I say. And not a second sooner."

My hands fist the sheets beside me. My entire body feels stretched taut, straining against invisible ropes. Her cunt pulses around me again, and my hips buck on instinct, just a shallow thrust, a desperate plea.

She stills instantly.

"You want to finish already?" she asks softly, mockingly. "You're that close?"

I nod, sweat dripping down my temples, breath coming in shallow pants.

"Good," she whispers. "Then hold it."

She starts to move again, this time faster, just slightly. Enough to make my vision blur, enough to send sparks exploding behind my eyelids. She rides me like she's sculpting her own pleasure, using my body like a throne, like a toy that only works for her.

Her pace builds.

Each grind is harder, wetter, messier.

Her moans get louder, deeper. One of her hands tangles in my hair, tugging just enough to make my back arch beneath her. She leans in, kissing me deep, open-mouthed, her tongue teasing mine with the same rhythm her hips deliver. My cock twitches inside her, and I feel the rush hit me hard, too hard.

I'm right there. At the edge.

"Katya, please-" I beg, voice completely wrecked.

Her eyes snap to mine, dark and sharp. "Not. Yet."

And then she tightens around me, deliberately. Her muscles clench, and her fingers return to her clit, rubbing faster, chasing her own release while mine teeters on the brink.

She's panting, riding harder now, her thighs slapping against my hips as she gasps out my name again and again, head thrown back in abandon. Her body starts to tremble, her moans break into whimpers, and I feel the telltale flutter of her orgasm creeping in.

And still, I'm not allowed to fall.

She leans over me again, sweat beading on her chest, her lips brushing my ear.

"Now," she whispers.

That single word is all it takes.

I explode inside her with a guttural groan, hips bucking as I spill into her, my orgasm ripping through me like a storm. Her own climax crashes over her at the same time, her body trembling as she rides out every wave, her pussy clenching and pulsing around me until I can't think, can't speak, can barely breathe.

We collapse together, her body draped over mine, our hearts beating like war drums in unison.

Her fingers trail lazy circles across my chest, her breath still heavy against my neck.

She doesn't speak. She doesn't need to.

She already knows she owns me.

And I'd let her do it all over again.

Her body lies beneath me, flushed and trembling, skin sheened with sweat, the faint ghost of bruises already blooming across her thighs and hips. Her mouth hangs open, breath coming in shallow gasps, her legs still spread wide, twitching with overstimulation. She looks ruined. Beautifully so. But I'm not satisfied, not even close.

I slide out of her slowly, her slick coating me, dripping down between her thighs in a messy trail that has my cock twitching again. She shivers from the loss of fullness, her brows furrowing like she already misses it, and maybe she does. Maybe she wants more, wants everything I've been holding back.

And she's going to get it.

I shift lower, dragging her thighs over my shoulders as I settle between them. My hands press to the insides of her knees, forcing them wider. She whines, tries to close them instinctively, but I growl low in my throat and grip harder until she's helplessly open beneath me again, glistening and swollen, her cunt raw from everything we've already done.

"You can take more," I murmur, voice dark and thick with need. "You want more, don't you?"

She bites her lip, eyes fluttering open to meet mine, hazy and unsure, but curious. Needy.

I spit into my palm, slow and deliberate, letting her watch the string of it drip from my lips before I bring it to her entrance. Her body jerks slightly at the contact, but I rub her slowly, soothingly, dragging slick fingers through her folds, teasing her clit with lazy strokes while my other hand presses flat to her stomach, holding her in place.

"I'm going to give you something else now," I whisper, bending to kiss the inside of her thigh. "I want to see you stretch for me. I want to feel you open so wide around my hand you can't think straight. You trust me?"

She nods once. Barely. But it's enough.

I start slow, two fingers pushing into her, curling up, stroking deep inside until her hips twitch beneath me. She's soaked. Her body gives easily. She's already halfway there from everything we've done, from the wreckage of her orgasms.

Three fingers slide in next. Her jaw drops, a gasp escaping her lips as I pump into her slowly, steadily, keeping her relaxed, her body clenching and fluttering around me.

Her hands twist into the sheets. She bites her knuckle to keep quiet, but I won't allow that.

"No," I growl, pulling her hand from her mouth. "I want to hear you."

I add a fourth finger.

She cries out, beautiful, broken, her pussy fluttering around the stretch. I slow my movements, coaxing her through it, easing her body open while she trembles beneath me.

And then... my thumb presses in.

She screams, truly screams, as I slide my whole hand inside her, my fingers folding slightly, the knuckles breaching as her cunt swallows me to the wrist.

Her back arches off the bed. Her hands claw at the sheets. Her legs shake violently on either side of my head, and I feel her muscles flutter and grip and fight the stretch, but she takes it.

She wants it.

I pause for a moment, buried deep, just breathing with her, letting her adjust. Her body clenches around me, so fucking tight, so full, and I watch her face shift from pain to awe to desperate, filthy pleasure.

"That's it," I whisper, watching her, studying every twitch of her body. "You're doing so fucking good for me, Katya. You're taking it like you were made for this."

I curl my hand just slightly and she wails, her body jerking violently against the bed. Her thighs spasm. Her chest heaves. I pump my wrist slowly, methodically, and every motion has her unraveling more, coming apart in front of me like I've split her wide open not just with my hand, but my need.

"Look at you," I pant, watching her stomach twitch beneath my other hand. "So full. So fucking open."

She sobs my name, over and over, voice cracked and wild.

I start fucking her with my hand, slow and deep, each drag of my wrist inside her bringing a new wave of cries, moans, curses. The slick, wet sound of it fills the room, echoing off the walls as I break her completely.

She tries to squirm, but she can't go anywhere. I have her pinned, locked, shattered. Her face contorts with every thrust, her body trembling uncontrollably, her cunt fluttering around the obscene stretch like she's trying to come, but can't.

Not yet.

Her climax finally hits like a bomb.

Her legs lock up. Her thighs clamp around my shoulders. Her whole body convulses, her pussy squeezing my hand so tight I can barely move, her scream choking off into something silent and raw as wave after wave crashes through her.

I stay buried in her through it all.

Only when the last tremor fades do I slowly, carefully slide my hand out of her body. The release is wet, messy, obscene, slick dripping from her hole like she's been broken open. Her legs fall limp to the bed. Her chest rises and falls in erratic gasps.

She's done.

Ruined.

Owned.

I crawl up over her, pressing a kiss to her throat, her jaw, her swollen lips.

Her eyes flutter open, glassy and dazed.

And I whisper against her mouth, voice soft now, reverent, like a prayer offered to the altar of her destruction.

"No one will ever touch you the way I do."

She's trembling beneath me, broken open in the most beautiful way. Her thighs are slick, her lips swollen, her pussy still gaping from the stretch I forced her to take. I should stop. She looks finished. Her breathing is shallow. Her limbs limp. Her eyes hazy with pleasure-drunk ruin.

But I don't stop.

I *can't*.

Because I'm still hard, still throbbing, still so deep in this place inside my head where nothing matters but making her feel *everything*. Again. And again. And again.

"You thought that was the end?" I murmur, dragging my fingers through the wreckage between her thighs, spreading her slick and cum and sweat like it's war paint. "I'm not fucking done with you, Katya."

Her eyes flutter open, barely focused. She shakes her head weakly, her body already overloaded, but her mouth parts in a moan when I rub her clit, two fingers teasing the swollen bundle of nerves with cruel slowness.

"I-I can't," she whispers.

"Yes," I growl, my voice like gravel. "You can. You fucking *will*. You'll cum until you cry. You'll scream until my name is the only word your body remembers."

I press my fingers back inside her, still sensitive, still wrecked, and she sobs at the intrusion. But her hips twitch up. Her cunt *welcomes* it. Greedy, even now. I curl my fingers inside her, rubbing hard over that spot that makes her legs jolt and her hands claw at the sheets.

Her body betrays her. Her slick is everywhere. She's dripping again, her walls fluttering around my fingers even as she shakes her head, begging for mercy that she doesn't really want.

"You love this," I whisper against her ear, grinding my cock against her thigh, my voice poison and silk. "You love being ruined by me. You love knowing that I'll keep going even when you think you've got nothing left."

Her breath hitches, broken and beautiful.

I shift her hips, dragging her to the edge of the bed. Her limbs are jelly now. Her body trembling with the aftershocks of everything I've given her. But when I press the tip of my cock back against her slit, her thighs part *just enough*.

"Please-" she gasps, but she doesn't finish the sentence. She doesn't say stop.

So I don't.

I *slam* into her.

She screams.

It's not a sound of fear, it's surrender. Raw. Guttural. Her body arches, her hands flailing before gripping the headboard again like it's the only thing tethering her to earth.

She's so fucking tight.

Even after everything, she clamps around me like it's the first time. Like her body *still* doesn't know how to take me. I fuck into her hard, relentless, no rhythm left, just force. Just need.

Her pussy makes the wettest, filthiest sounds as I ram into her, and her moans turn to cries, her cries to sobs, tears spilling down the corners of her cheeks as I pound into her, deeper and deeper, until my hips crash into her ass and the bruises from earlier darken under my grip.

But I don't stop.

I reach between us, rubbing her clit again, fast, merciless, dragging her up toward another orgasm even as her body shakes from the last.

"You said you couldn't cum again," I whisper, my lips against her temple, catching the salt of her tears on my tongue. "You fucking lied."

She's *screaming* now, eyes squeezed shut, breath ragged, hips bucking up to meet each thrust as another orgasm builds with violent force. Her cunt pulses like it's fighting me, sucking me deeper, trying to hold me inside her forever.

And then she *breaks*.

Her body goes rigid, then completely slack as she cums so hard she goes silent. Her throat strains, but no sound comes out, just the quake of her body, the pulsing of her cunt, the twitch in her hands.

I bite her shoulder as I cum. Hard. Brutal. Filling her again until she's overflowing, my cum mixing with the slick mess already ruining the sheets.

And still, I don't pull out.

I stay inside her, buried deep, grinding gently through the overstimulation, watching her twitch, watching her sob, watching her fall apart in the purest, rawest, filthiest way I've ever seen.

I whisper into her ear, a voice soaked in reverence and madness.

"This is how you'll remember me. This is how you'll wake up every night, aching. Empty. Wanting."

Her body is limp now. Her chest rising in shallow pants. Her thighs spread wide, her cunt leaking my cum, her lips parted in quiet, exhausted bliss.

I cradle her against me, still buried inside, kissing her cheeks, her forehead, her mouth. Worshipful. Possessive.

And then I lay her back against the bed and whisper one final truth:

"I haven't even started."

She doesn't move.

Her body lies limp across the sheets, chest rising in shallow, uneven gasps, her skin flushed and damp, marked everywhere I've touched. Her lips are parted, red and swollen, eyes half-lidded but still glassy, dazed. She looks like something holy. Like something that's been sacrificed.

And I'm the one who bled her dry.

But it's not enough. I want more.

My breath is ragged as I shift back, pulling her thighs apart once again. She whimpers, not from fear, but from that deep, raw place where pleasure starts to hurt. Her cunt is slick and open, a mess of our cum and everything I've already taken from her, and still, her body flutters when I slide two fingers back inside.

She gasps sharply, hips twitching involuntarily.

Her body knows mine. Even now, overstimulated and wrecked, it begs for more.

I kiss the inside of her thigh, slow, reverent. Then again, higher, near the bruise where I bit her. She trembles beneath me, her fingers twitching in the sheets, barely able to lift her head.

My hand trails up her side, pausing at her ribs, then her jaw. I cradle her face, thumb brushing gently over her cheekbone as I press another kiss to her lips.

"You're not done," I whisper. "Not until I say so."

She doesn't speak, can't. But her legs part wider.

That's all I need.

I reach for her nightstand, grabbing the toy she had set aside earlier, no doubt to help her finish with Garrett. The sight of it makes my cock twitch again, already starting to harden as I look down at her ruined body.

I settle between her thighs, grabbing one leg and pushing it up to her chest. The angle exposes her, opens her, shows me every slick, throbbing inch of what I've already claimed. I trail the toy between her folds again, dragging it slowly down, until it rests just below.

Her breathing quickens.

I press the tip to her tight rim again, this time slower, more deliberate. She twitches at the contact, moaning as the toy eases past the initial resistance. I take my time, working her open again inch by inch, watching her eyes flutter as the stretch builds.

I can see the strain on her face. But beneath it, desire. Her hips rise to meet the pressure, her breath caught between pain and want. She's letting me in. Trusting me to take her apart the way only I can.

Once the toy is fully seated inside her, I lean over her body again, my cock pressing against her soaked cunt. I don't thrust in immediately, just glide the head through her slick, letting her feel the weight of what's coming.

She whines, arching under me.

I slam into her in one violent thrust.

Her scream is pure devastation.

Her body clamps down around me like it's never known me before. The double intrusion has her writhing under me, legs locked around my waist, her cunt fluttering wildly as she tries to breathe through it.

I don't give her time.

I start moving, slow at first, letting her adjust to the overwhelming pressure. The toy shifts inside her with each thrust, and every inch of me drives the point deeper. I fuck her hard, my cock driving into her slick, wet heat while her body tenses, moans turning to cries that catch in her throat.

Her hands claw at the sheets, trying to find something solid to hold onto. Her walls squeeze me so tight, it feels like she's trying to pull me deeper, like she wants me buried in her.

I shift my weight and grab the backs of her thighs, forcing her knees to her chest, folding her open. She sobs when I slam deeper, the toy grinding inside her as I bottom out.

"You feel that?" I growl, my voice breaking apart. "You're stuffed so fucking full you can't even think."

She tries to answer but it's just a moan high-pitched and helpless.

Her cunt pulses again, and I know she's close. Another orgasm, building too fast, her body trembling violently beneath me. I drive in harder, the slap of skin on skin wet and filthy, echoing through the room with each brutal thrust.

I can't stop.

Not with her like this.

She looks ruined, and she's never looked more fucking perfect.

Her body spasms suddenly, legs locking, toes curling, her mouth open in a silent scream as her climax hits with brutal force. Her pussy squeezes around my cock so tight it punches the air from my lungs, and her ass clenches around the toy so hard it nearly pushes back out.

I growl her name, driving through her orgasm, grinding deep, cock swelling with release as I pour into her again. My cum fills her with no resistance, spilling out around my length, around the toy, painting the sheets, the backs of her thighs.

And still, I don't move.

I stay buried inside her, panting, forehead pressed to hers, her body twitching under mine, overstimulated and gasping.

She's incoherent. Drenched. Crying softly, but she's not afraid. Her hands reach for me weakly, fingers curling against my chest, as if to say don't leave. Not yet.

And I won't.

Not until she's certain no one else will ever fuck her like this again.

She doesn't speak...she can't.

Her mouth is open against the pillow, her breathing uneven and wet with sobs she's long since stopped hiding. The sound of her pleasure echoes softly in the room, broken by the rhythm of my hips slamming against her ass. Her body is a mess of overstimulation, slick, flushed, twitching.

Still, she takes me.

Every thrust drives her forward, her body pressing further into the mattress, her limbs too weak to resist. But her cunt grips me with a desperation that betrays her mouth. She says nothing, but her body screams yes.

I watch her closely.

The way her back bows when I slide deeper.

The way her thighs tremble when my hips grind down at the end of each thrust, pressing the head of my cock against the place that makes her sob into the sheets.

The way she moans when I drag my hand up her spine and tangle it in her hair, pulling her back just enough to hear her voice again.

She makes the most beautiful sounds when she forgets she's not supposed to want this.

I lean over her, chest flush against her back, my breath hot against her ear as I thrust slower, deeper, burying myself inside her inch by inch like I'm carving myself into her memory.

"You're so full of me you don't even know where I end and you begin," I murmur, lips brushing her cheek.

She shudders.

Not just from my words, but from the slow roll of my hips, from the way I grip her jaw and force her head to turn so I can watch her expression as I drag every last ounce of resistance from her.

Her lips are swollen. Her lashes are wet. Her eyes are glassy, unfocused, but they stay locked to mine as her cunt clenches down again, tight and hungry.

I pull back slightly, giving her just enough space to feel the absence of me, and then slam back in with force. The bed frame groans beneath us. Her whole body jolts, a cry ripping from her throat that sounds more like surrender than pain.

My hand slides down her side, then lower, cupping her between her legs. She jerks when I touch her clit, her thighs trying to close, but I pin her open with my weight.

Her body is sensitive.

But still she pushes back against me, still she spreads wider, her hips rising involuntarily as I rub her in slow, deliberate circles.

She's soaked again.

I feel her slick coat my fingers as I stroke her, as I fuck her deeper, as I break her apart piece by trembling piece. Her body doesn't know what to do anymore, caught between wanting to escape and begging for more.

She cums again.

Not with a scream this time, but with silence. A breathless, shaking release that steals the sound from her lungs. Her pussy clamps down violently, milking my cock, pulling me deeper as her body quakes beneath me, arms collapsing, face pressed deep into the mattress.

I keep moving.

Not out of cruelty, but necessity.

Because I need this.

Because I need her.

Because fucking her like this isn't just about sex. It's about being inside the only place I feel at home. It's about burning my name into her blood, into her skin, into the space behind her ribs where no one else will ever reach.

My thrusts slow, not because I'm done, but because I want her to feel every single second of what I'm giving her.

Every inch.

Every pulse.

Every claim.

Her walls flutter again around me, overstimulated and barely able to keep hold. But she tries. Her body tries. Even broken, she still wants to keep me.

When her hands clench the sheets again, I press my chest to her back, my voice a whisper against her ear.

"I'm going to cum inside you again."

She whimpers. Nods.

She doesn't speak, but her hips tilt up.

Welcoming me.

Begging me.

And I do.

I spill inside her slowly, grinding deep, my cock throbbing with the force of it. My cum fills her, mixes with what's already been left there. It leaks around me before I even pull out, dripping from between her legs, soaking the sheets, her thighs, my skin.

She's marked.

Inside and out.

I collapse beside her, my hand still on her waist, anchoring her to me even now. Her breath stutters. Her body twitches. Her skin is streaked with sweat and tears and everything I've given her tonight.

And she's never looked more perfect.

Her body is a mess of spasms in my lap, every tremble in her thighs a soft echo of the punishment I've already given her. Her skin sticks to mine with sweat and slick, streaked red in places where my grip had tightened too hard, too long. Her cunt, still wrapped around my cock, is red and used, puffy from overuse, pulsing with the slow, involuntary contractions of a body that's forgotten how to come down from climax. Her head rests limp on my shoulder, the strands of hair plastered to her temple sticky with tears and heat, her chest still stuttering against mine in breathless, shivering aftershock.

I can feel how close she is to unconsciousness. I know I've pushed her past the edge, have ridden her through every twitch and gasp until she's not thinking in words anymore. Her muscles twitch from pure reflex, not resistance. She doesn't speak. Her voice gave out two orgasms ago. But her cunt is still clenching around me, soft and warm and welcoming, even as her body shakes like it's begging for a break.

And I don't give her one.

I pull out slowly, watching her flinch from the drag, her raw walls fluttering in protest. Then I thrust back in, hard. Deep. A single, brutal grind that knocks a sob from her throat before she even realizes she's made a sound. Her arms twitch but don't lift. Her legs part just enough for me to take her again, even as her toes curl into the sheets and her jaw locks like she's fighting not to scream.

I grip her waist with both hands, tilting her hips just slightly, angling her until the head of my cock finds that spot that has her pussy spasming around me. I feel it, the way she clings, tries to resist the wave I'm forcing through her again. But she's helpless. She's already gone. All instinct. All reaction.

I fuck her slow. Deliberate. Cruel in the way I draw each thrust out, grinding deep until she's gasping quietly against my throat. I listen to the breath catch in her lungs. I feel her nails twitch against my chest like she wants to push me away but can't remember how. Her head falls back as another tear escapes the corner of her eye and rolls down her cheek.

She's not saying no. Not with her mouth. Not with her body either.

Her cunt is soaking me again. Dripping down my cock. Her muscles clench tighter the longer I hold her open, like she's trying to force me deeper. Her body knows what it wants, even if her mind's too wrecked to keep up.

I force her hips forward, keeping her arched over me as I grind in slow, bruising strokes. I want her to feel this in her womb. I want it to hurt. I want her to remember this, not just with her mind, but in every ache that'll stay with her tomorrow.

She starts crying again, softer this time, broken and hoarse. I lean into her ear, my breath hot and ragged against her skin, and murmur dark things she's too far gone to process, things about how good she feels, how fucking tight she is, how she's going to take every last drop whether she begs or not.

And she does.

Her breath shatters in her chest. Her cunt locks down, sudden and sharp, and I feel the tremble before I hear it, another orgasm tearing through her body without permission. She shakes violently in my lap, her body locking up, her mouth open in a silent scream. She falls apart against me, totally limp, totally fucked out.

I hold her there, letting her ride the full edge of it, keeping her stuffed full until the spasms fade. Then I start again.

A slow thrust. A deeper one.

Her fingers curl into my chest.

A sound leaves her mouth, just a whisper.

"I can't... I can't anymore..."

But her pussy still grips me. Still welcomes every inch of me. Still drips slick over my cock like it doesn't believe a word she's saying.

I cradle the back of her neck gently, pulling her head to rest against my shoulder, and I finish inside her, slow, grinding, deliberate thrusts until I come again, deeper this time, her body twitching in protest as I fill her one last time. My cum mixes with the mess already leaking out of her, spilling down her thighs as she whimpers from the pressure.

She's motionless for a long time.

Quiet.

Her breathing is shallow, but steady. Her body, still trembling, has lost all tension. I stroke her spine slowly, anchoring her back to the room, to the bed, to me. And I feel it, the moment her fingers twitch, the moment she pulls herself just slightly closer to my chest.

Then her voice breaks the silence.

It's not loud. Not even steady.

"Don't leave me."

My arms tighten around her instantly. I don't speak. I just breathe into her hair, pulling her fully into my lap, into my chest, holding her like something fragile and sacred.

"Please," she whispers again, softer now. "Don't leave me alone..."

Her body curls into mine with a quiet desperation. Her cunt is still leaking around me, still stretched open, still holding the memory of what I did to her. And yet, she clings to me, not to be saved, but to be kept.

I kiss the crown of her head and pull her tighter.

"I'm right here," I murmur, voice low and rough. "You're not going anywhere. And neither am I."

Her breath evens out. Her body, finally, stills.

And for the first time since this began, she lets herself fall, safe in the wreckage, safe in the arms of the man who broke her.

26

WHISPERS FROM THE DEVIL

KATYA

Morning seeps in through the window like a soft betrayal, warming skin that still throbs from the night before. The ache isn't gentle. It's deep, lingering in the marrow of my thighs, in the hollow of my spine, in the sting between my legs where his hands, his mouth, his everything, left their mark. Every breath brushes against bruises that haven't even begun to settle. Beneath the hum of pain, something deeper thrums: a memory I'm too wrecked to recall fully, and too full to forget.

Sheets tangle around my legs like restraints, soaked and twisted, the mattress damp beneath me in places I don't dare identify. His scent still clings to the linen, dark and primal. A musky blend of sweat and blood, sex and control. The evidence of his presence is everywhere, except for the man himself.

The spot beside me is vacant, still warm but fading quickly. Only the impression of his weight remains, like a ghost pressing into the mattress. Reaching toward that empty space, fingers brush only fabric and something foreign, paper, soft and crumpled, nestled where his hand should be.

The note is simple. Two words scrawled in dark ink, slanted and precise.

Your move

No punctuation. No signature. As if he knows he does not need one.

Breath snags in my throat. Not from fear. From the cruel intimacy of the message. It's not over. It never is. He didn't fuck me into the ground and walk away. He's waiting. Watching. Still playing.

The bed frame is cracked at the top, the headboard split where his grip turned savage, where I thrashed too hard against the ropes. One of them still dangles, frayed at the knot, bloodstained at the base where skin must have torn mid-struggle. Pain flares across my wrist at the sight, not from the injury, but from the memory it summons.

Between my thighs, the mess is unbearable. Slick, blood, and the thick, unmistakable drip of him spilling from inside me. The room smells like a sin that's settled into the walls.

A soft tapping draws my attention toward the window.

It's rhythmic, almost delicate. A flutter more than a knock. On the sill, a jar, small, cylindrical, and sealed tight. Inside, a single butterfly beats against the glass, golden wings flashing each time they strike the sides. Trapped. Desperate. A reflection, a mockery, a message.

Laughter breaks from my throat, rough and hoarse and far from sane. Not amusement. Just recognition. Of course he'd leave that. Of course he'd find a way to turn even something beautiful into a cage.

Movement is slow. Limbs resist. Muscles protest. Standing feels like surfacing from the bottom of a lake, every step a reminder of where his body was and where mine still responds. The silk robe clings where skin is tacky with sweat, grazes where the bruises ache most.

A knock at the door cuts through the room.

Not tentative. Not loud. Sharp and measured, three taps, then silence.

No name.

No voice.

Fingers tighten around the edge of the robe, blood humming under the surface. Whether it's him returning for more or someone else entirely, the aftermath clings to me in ways no fabric can hide.

He left me wrecked.

And still, some sick part of me hopes it's him.

The knock echoes through the room again, a sharp crack against the aftermath of silence. For a moment, I don't move. The air still carries the scent of him, Echo, along with blood, sex, sweat, and something rawer. Something that lingers in the pit of my stomach and burns low like a second heartbeat.

It's not just soreness that slows me as I approach the door. It's dread. It's instinct. A pull in my gut that says whatever is on the other side isn't safe. And yet, I go anyway, dragging myself across the room with a quiet grace that betrays the wreckage under my skin. Muscles ache. Thighs tremble. The robe I tied around myself clings to my skin, damp where bruises are beginning to bloom, silk catching along the stickiness between my legs where his cum is still slowly leaking out of me.

I open the door without ceremony.

Maria stands there, arms crossed like she owns the threshold. Her hair is pulled back into a sleek twist, not a strand out of place, her lipstick perfect, deep red, like fresh blood. She's smiling, but it's not friendly. It's the kind of smile women like us are taught to use when we want someone to know we're dangerous.

"What the fuck are you doing here?" The bite in my tone is intentional. I make no effort to hide the disdain curling off my tongue. Her presence alone is an insult. Her timing is worse.

Her gaze flicks across my face, down my neck, catching for just a second on the faint handprint on my throat. Her smirk sharpens.

"My brother sent me," she says casually. "To make sure you were ready for tonight's meeting. He said you asked your guards to leave last night. He was... concerned."

Concerned.

The word tastes like poison.

"Your brother doesn't give a shit about me," I snap, not bothering to hide the venom in my voice. "Try again."

She lifts one shoulder in a soft shrug, feigning innocence. But her eyes say something else. There's calculation behind them, perhaps even awareness. She knows. Not everything, but enough.

My attention slides to the phone in her hand, and that's when it clicks.

The meeting. The perfectly timed absence of my men. The silence that gave Echo the space to destroy me.

He got into my phone.

Fucking bastard.

Of course he did. Of course he played me before he ever touched me. The seduction started long before the first bruise. The moment he cleared my house was the moment he claimed me without laying a hand on me.

And now Maria's here like a messenger of fate.

"So," I mutter, voice tight, "what meeting are you talking about?"

The smile fades from her lips. Her spine straightens, posture going rigid with the weight of what she's about to say.

"Echo Kane," she announces like it's a name that still holds reverence. "Requested a formal audience with your father. Dimitri expects you there. And all the families have been summoned."

The air shifts.

Not just tension now. Power. The kind of power that drips slowly into a room and turns into something suffocating.

"When did this happen?"

"Last night." She licks her lips once, hesitating. "The bastard seems to have grown a pair after what he did to you and Nikolai."

"When?" My voice comes out smaller than intended. Not weak. Just... off-balance.

Maria tilts her head. Her tone softens just slightly, but the steel is still there.

"Tonight," she says, eyes narrowing. "Your father's hosting a dinner. One that Echo isn't expected to walk away from."

For a moment, I can't breathe.

Not because of the threat implied. But because of the way my body reacts to it.

The part of me that should feel relief doesn't. The part that should want him dead, doesn't. I can still feel him inside me, deeper than anything I can wash off. Still hear the things he whispered as he fucked me into something barely recognizable. Still taste the ghost of him on my tongue.

I should want vengeance. Should want blood.

But all I feel is a pull. A low, aching tether that won't stop tightening around my ribs.

Dimitri's setting a trap.

And something inside me already knows, if Echo walks in alone, he's not walking out.

And if he dies tonight, something in me might die with him.

Something's wrong. Not in the way that makes you panic, but in the way that coils low and tight, like instinct knows what logic hasn't caught up to yet. The kind of dread that doesn't scream.

It whispers. It strokes your spine like a lover's touch and tells you everything is about to change.

Echo... what the fuck are you doing?

Maria doesn't stay long enough for a goodbye. She just holds something out, a square black box, sleek and heavy in her manicured hands. There's no bow. No note. Just the unspoken weight of expectation.

"Black tie," she says, voice clipped. "A gift. Courtesy of your father."

There's venom in the word *courtesy*, but she's already turning on her heel before I can call her on it. Her heels click softly down the hall, each step getting quieter, until the silence is deafening again.

I close the door slowly, carefully, like shutting it too hard might break whatever fragile thing still holds me upright. The box stays in my hands as I lean back against the wood, the cool edge pressing into my spine.

It takes me a full minute before I move.

The silk robe rustles around my legs as I pad barefoot across the floor, the aftermath of Echo still clinging to every inch of my skin, every throb between my thighs, every unsteady breath. I haven't even cleaned myself yet, haven't washed away the scent of him. Part of me isn't ready to.

I set the box down on the vanity and stare at it.

A gift from my father. A black-tie event. All the families attending. And Echo, requesting a formal meeting like he hasn't just fucked me so hard I can barely walk. Like he hasn't carved his name into me with a blade.

None of this adds up.

And I know that voice in my head, that quiet, dangerous whisper, it's right. He's playing something bigger than seduction now. This is no longer about claiming me. This is about power.

And I need to know what he's planning before it's too late.

The box remains unopened on the vanity, but I already know what's inside. Something black. Expensive. Meant to soften the edges of my reputation in front of the other families. Meant to make me look tame.

Only, no one in that room knows the truth. Not the way I do.

Echo Kane doesn't play by anyone's rules.

Not even mine.

And if my father thinks he can use tonight to trap him, if Echo's really walking into a dinner that's meant to be his execution, then I have no choice.

I have to follow him.

I have to find out what he's planning.

Because the last time I underestimated Echo, I ended up on my knees.

And if he burns this world to the ground, I need to know whether I'm standing beside him... or in the flames.

27

That Four Letter Word

Katya

The morning air is cool against my skin, but it does nothing to steady my nerves. Each step is calculated, heels traded for soft-soled boots, the tight black fabric clinging to my body chosen not for vanity but for utility. Shadows swallow me easily in clothes like these. I blend in. I disappear. Just like I was trained.

But right now, stealth isn't about survival. It's about him.

Trailing Echo isn't something I should be doing. It's reckless. Dangerous. Foolish. And yet, the moment Maria walked away, the moment I read the words *Your move* in that note, I knew there wouldn't be peace until I understood what game he was playing.

He wouldn't be stupid enough to go back to his house, I tell myself again, eyes darting along the dim streets, scanning every turn like he might materialize out of the dark. *Not after formally requesting a meeting with my father.* That alone is a declaration of war, or something worse. A dare. And Echo Kane doesn't bluff.

My fingers curl tighter around the phone in my hand, screen lighting up with a soft glow. For a moment, I just stare at it. At the silent weight of my own betrayal.

I'd slipped the tracker onto his phone last night, sometime between the third orgasm and the moment he passed out, spent and buried in me so deep I wasn't sure where he ended and I began. He didn't even stir. Just sighed in his sleep like he owned the air between us.

He wouldn't have noticed. He never notices when I'm watching.

The app takes a second to load, the red dot pulsing against the digital map. My heart kicks against my ribs as I realize exactly what I'm seeing.

Not his estate. Not Catalyst headquarters. Nowhere secure.

An abandoned building. East of town. Remote. Isolated. Forgotten.

And he's there.

No guards. No cameras. No eyes.

A trap, maybe.

Or maybe it's something worse.

The urge to call someone flickers and dies just as fast. My father would send a team. He'd send guns and firepower and too many questions I don't have answers to. And Echo would vanish. Or bleed. Or kill.

None of those options sit right.

The car hums to life beneath my hands as I start the engine, headlights off until I've cleared the edge of the estate. The roads ahead blur into black as the city gives way to wilderness, and my fingers tighten on the wheel with every passing mile.

Because I don't know what I'm going to find.

Only that if he's doing something reckless, something violent, I need to know about it.

And if he's not...

If he's hurting...

If he's planning something I'm not part of,

Then *he's the one who needs to be afraid.*

The further I drive, the more the world seems to unravel behind me.

Streetlights vanish. Pavement cracks beneath the tires. Civilization gives way to rot, rusted fences, warped signs, buildings swallowed by time and ivy. The kind of place you're taught to avoid as a child, but taught to study once you learn the truth of our world. Because monsters don't hide in castles. They breed in forgotten places like this.

And now, Echo Kane is the one nesting in the dark.

The building comes into view like a specter rising from the earth, three stories of crumbling brick, boarded windows, and silence so thick it feels alive. My car slows as I pull to the edge of the lot, careful not to park too close. I kill the engine, let the morning shadows wrap around me like a second skin, and step out.

There's no wind. No movement. Just the hush of something waiting.

My boots crunch softly against loose gravel as I approach, eyes scanning the perimeter. No obvious guards. No surveillance. No movement through the broken windows, just the outline of rot and shadow.

And then I hear it.

A scream.

It cuts through the silence like a blade. Not a woman. Male. Ragged. Frantic. A sound that doesn't echo so much as it vibrates, as though it's clawing at the foundation of the building itself. Followed by something else, a thud. Wet. Heavy.

Then silence.

The hair on the back of my neck stands on end, every instinct in my body bracing for violence. But I don't move. Not away. Not back. I take a step forward.

Another scream follows. This one shorter. Hoarse. It gurgles before it cuts off entirely, and suddenly the air feels tighter, like the building itself is holding its breath.

He's in there.

Echo.

Not just fucking. Not teasing. Not seducing.

This is something else.

I inch closer to the entrance, staying in the shadows, trying to piece together what the hell I'm walking into. Blood hums in my ears. The metal door is cracked open slightly, just enough for someone to slip through.

Part of me wants to call out. To stop this before it spirals into something irreversible.

But another part... the part he's carved into me like a second skin...

Wants to see.

Wants to understand just how far he'll go when no one's watching.

Because if he's killing tonight, I need to know why.

And if he's unraveling...

I need to be the one to stitch him back together.

The door is cracked just enough to see him, only him.

Even with the blood, the ropes, and the broken man tied to the chair, it's Echo who commands everything. The room bends around him. He doesn't just stand there, he possesses the space. Like it belongs to him.

His shirt is rolled to the elbows, forearms cut with ridges of lean muscle and smeared with streaks of red, each movement fluid, purposeful. The knife glints in his hand, not erratic, not sloppy. He's methodical. Calm. So devastatingly calm it makes my stomach twist. That control, so cold and calculating, somehow sets me ablaze.

Garrett groans, low and breathless, slumped forward in the chair with his wrists bound in stained rope. His chest rises and falls with frantic, shallow gasps, and yet I don't feel sorry for him. Not really. Not when I see the way Echo tilts his head, studying Garrett like he's a puzzle with one missing piece.

"Fuck you," Garrett spits, blood flecking his lips.

Echo smiles.

Not wide. Not crazed. It's subtle...measured. A slow, curling thing that settles into the corners of his mouth like he's savoring every second.

"Fucking," Echo murmurs, voice smooth as velvet, "is precisely the reason you're in this predicament."

He steps closer, and I swear the temperature of the room shifts with him. The knife comes down with quiet finality, no rage, no shouting. Just the wet sound of steel sinking into flesh. Garrett screams, head snapping back. The blade's buried deep in his thigh.

I should recoil. I should run.

But I don't move.

Because it's not just the violence, it's the way Echo moves through it. The way he's perfectly composed, eyes sharp and electric, hair curling slightly at the nape from sweat. His chest rises slowly, deliberately, like he's meditating in the middle of a storm he created. Every breath he takes is power. Every word is a command.

He circles the chair, voice low and deliberate. "So tell me, what do you know about Katya?"

"Fucking nothing," Garrett gasps. "If I'd known her crazy-ass ex would be doing this, I'd have never gone near her."

He says my name like I'm a mistake. Like I'm something to regret.

But Echo doesn't even blink. Instead, he tosses Garrett's wallet to the ground.

Photos spill out.

I recognize them instantly, moments of me, stolen when I wasn't looking. Me ordering coffee. Me getting into my car, glancing over my shoulder, unaware I was being watched.

My blood runs cold. My skin burns.

"You were sent to watch her," Echo says softly, stepping in so close Garrett flinches. "You weren't some idiot barista with a crush. You knew who she was. You researched her. You joined her circle, shadowed her habits. So tell me... who sent you?"

The knife skims gently across Garrett's cheek now. Just a whisper of steel against skin.

It's maddening, how beautiful Echo is in this moment. Wild and contained all at once. His voice, low and intimate. His eyes, glinting with fire and calculation. The flex of his jaw, the faint scrape of stubble, the sweat painting his collarbone beneath the open edge of his shirt, it's all heat, and rage, and devotion. As if every brutal thing he does here tonight is an act of worship.

And I should be screaming. I should stop him.

But I can't look away.

Because somewhere in the pit of my stomach, in that dark place I never dare to touch, I want him to hurt for me.

I want him to ruin the world for me.

I want to walk into that room, step over the blood, and remind him exactly who he's doing it for.

The gunshot still echoes, trapped in the concrete walls like a ghost refusing to leave.

Garrett's body slumps forward in the chair, lifeless. Slack. Blood pools beneath him with a slow, steady rhythm, thick and metallic, the sharp scent of it saturating the room. It clings to the air, coats the back of my throat, and seeps into the pores of my skin like a stain I'll never wash away.

But I don't regret it.

I thought I would. I thought something in me would snap after the trigger pulled. That I'd shake. Fall apart. Collapse into some hollow version of myself and cry about what I just did. But instead, there's only stillness. A kind of silence that feels sacred. Solid. Like the moment I made that choice, I stepped into the version of me Echo's always seen.

I don't even remember reaching for the gun. One second, Garrett was speaking, naming the man who sent him. My father. Of course it was my father. The man who keeps pretending he still owns me, who thinks I need protection from my own darkness. The next moment, my hand was already steady, finger curled with certainty, bullet leaving the chamber before I could blink.

And now he's gone.

I lower the gun slowly, the weight of it heavier now. It doesn't tremble in my hand. I don't need to pretend to be strong. I am strong. This is who I am now. Not a pawn. Not a daughter. Not a victim. Just me, standing over the man who thought he could use me, manipulate me, sneak into my life like a parasite.

The silence that follows is deafening, not just from the shot, but from what it meant. From the fact that Echo hasn't moved. He stands there, just a few feet away, the same man who held a knife to Garrett's throat minutes ago, and yet the look he gives me now is different. Measured. Quiet. Almost reverent.

He turns toward me slowly, like anything faster might break the moment. His eyes don't blink. They trace every inch of me, from the blood on my cheek to the gun still hanging at my side. There's something unreadable in his face. Not shock. Not anger. Just... stillness. As if he's reassessing everything he thought he knew about me and finding he'd underestimated it all.

I meet his gaze without flinching.

I want him to see me. Not the woman he fucked. Not the girl he marked. But me, this version of myself that doesn't wait to be rescued or kissed or forgiven. The one who makes the hard decisions. The one who pulls the trigger.

For a long moment, he says nothing. Just breathes, slow, steady, reverent. His jaw tightens slightly, a flicker of something dark flashing behind his eyes. Pride. Arousal. Something hungrier than both.

His mouth parts as if to speak, but no words come. He takes a single step toward me, eyes never leaving mine, and that's when I realize, he's not afraid of me.

He's falling deeper.

Into me.

And for the first time, I feel the balance shift. Not away from him. But toward something shared. Something that no one else in this world would understand except the two of us standing here, soaked in blood, with the past rotting at our feet.

We are not lovers.

We are not enemies.

We are two ends of the same weapon.

And I think he knows it now, too.

He steps closer, slow and silent, like a storm crawling toward the shore. Every inch he closes between us feels like pressure tightening around my ribs, like I've swallowed lightning and it's crackling just beneath my skin.

I don't move. I can't. Not when his eyes pin me the way his hands used to, possessive, punishing, addictive. There's something volatile in the way he looks at me now, something feral simmering just beneath the surface, caged but ready to tear out the moment I give it reason. He glances toward Garrett's crumpled body on the floor, then back to me. And fuck, the weight of that stare is heavier than any chain he's ever wrapped around my wrists.

"You let him touch you."

It's not a question.

It's a goddamn accusation.

A wound.

I brace myself against the way the words slice into me. There's no room for lies, not here. Not with blood still thick in the air and the echo of a gunshot still clinging to my skin. Not when every pulse of my heart is screaming who I belong to. My jaw tightens. I don't flinch. I don't look away.

"I didn't know what he was."

Echo's nostrils flare. His jaw ticks, that muscle twitching with a fury he's barely holding back. "But you let him inside you."

The shame hits harder than the recoil of the gun I just dropped. It's acidic. Ugly. But under it, God help me, there's something else. Something darker. Hungrier. Not just guilt. Need. A need to crawl back into his grip, to be stripped bare and claimed until I remember who I am beneath it all. Who I belong to.

My breath shudders out of me as I drop the gun onto the concrete floor with a metallic clatter. The sound barely registers. That version of me, the one who needed control, who needed to feel like I had a choice, she already surrendered the second he looked at me like this.

And I follow.

I lower myself to my knees, the blood-slick ground biting into my skin as I slide toward him, slow and deliberate. It stains my thighs, streaks across my calves, but I welcome the chill. I want him to see the ache in my eyes, the devotion carved into my spine. I want him to know this isn't weakness.

This is worship.

His breath catches. Just a fraction. But I see it, the flicker behind his eyes, the hunger flaring into something wilder. His fingers twitch at his sides like he's deciding whether to thread them into my hair or simply watch me unravel beneath him.

My voice is raw, wrecked. "I need you to understand something," I whisper. "There's no one else. Not anymore. Not after this."

He crouches, slow and low, until he's eye level with me. His hand lifts, rough fingers dragging along my jaw with a touch that borders on punishment. His thumb presses beneath my lip, tilting my chin up until I have no choice but to look at him.

"I own you," he breathes, voice thick with heat and possession. "Say it."

The words fall from my lips like a prayer.

"I'm yours."

Something cracks between us.

His hand tightens. And then he's kissing me, no, devouring me, his mouth bruising, biting, claiming every inch of surrender I offered. His other hand fists in my hair, dragging my head back so he can feast down the column of my throat. I moan, needy and wrecked, as I press my body into his. I want him to see what he does to me, how quickly I come undone under his touch.

He drags me to my feet only to shove me back against the wall, mouth trailing fire over my skin. "You're mine," he growls again, his teeth grazing my ear. "And I'm going to remind you exactly what that means."

And God help me, I want every brutal, beautiful second of it.

He urges me back down, the pressure of his hand on my shoulder not rough, but commanding. I sink, my knees sliding against the blood-slick concrete, still warm in places, sticky in others. My breath trembles as I look up at him, and he doesn't even try to hide the way his gaze shifts, first to Garrett's crumpled, lifeless form sprawled just feet away, then back to me.

He smiles.

A cruel, delicious thing. One that makes my thighs clench and my shame coil tighter around my spine, twisting with something darker. Dirtier. Needier.

"You're going to suck my cock," he says, voice low and smug, like he's daring me to flinch. "Right in front of him."

My lips part, but no sound comes out. Not a protest. Not a plea. Nothing but the sharp inhale of someone who should be horrified, but isn't.

He leans down slightly, fingers tangled in my hair now, forcing my head back just enough that I can't escape the full weight of his gaze.

"And you're going to fucking love it."

God help me, I already do.

Heat floods my cheeks, my chest, the space between my legs. The humiliation should burn, should crawl over my skin like a rash I want to scratch away, but instead it blooms. Twisted and toxic and perfect. My breath hitches, and I nod, barely, because speaking feels too big for this moment.

Because my mouth already knows what it's about to be used for.

He unzips slowly, deliberately, and the sound alone sends a tremor down my spine. He strokes himself once, lazy, arrogant, already half-hard and swelling more by the second as he watches me tremble for him. The scent of blood mixes with the ache between my legs, and I swear I could fall apart from just the way he looks at me.

"Open," he says, voice dipped in sin.

And I do. Lips parting, tongue out, offering myself like a sacrament to the only god I've ever truly worshipped.

Echo.

And as the tip of him grazes my lips, as he pushes inside and his groan echoes off the walls like a death sentence and a promise in one, I know I'll never need redemption.

Only this.

Only him.

Even in front of a corpse.

Maybe especially because of it.

I open my mouth for him, lips soft, tongue flat and ready, because that's what he's turned me into, ready. Always. Even with blood in the air and death at my feet. Especially because of it.

He groans low as he slides in, slow at first, letting the head of his cock drag across my tongue like he owns it, like he's branding me from the inside out. And he is. Every inch he pushes into my mouth feels like a claim. A punishment. A possession.

His hand tightens in my hair, not guiding, controlling. "Look at him," he murmurs, fucking slowly into my mouth. "Look at what happens to the men who touch what's mine."

I try, even as he sinks deeper, my lips stretching around him, the taste of him intoxicating, salt, musk, and something uniquely Echo. But my eyes flick to the body on the floor. Garrett's mouth still slack. Eyes glassy. Skin pale. It should repulse me.

It doesn't.

Because Echo is watching me now like I'm art. Filthy, ruined art he's proud of defiling.

"Did he kiss you with this mouth?" he asks, breath ragged. "Did you let him taste what belongs to me?"

I choke a little as he thrusts deeper, spit sliding down my chin, pooling at the corners of my lips, but I nod, tears blurring the edges of my vision. I can't speak around him, not with the way he's holding me open, not with the brutal rhythm he's building, but I don't need to.

My shame is loud enough.

"Good," he growls, fisting my hair tighter, making my eyes water as he uses my mouth like a weapon and a reward. "Then I'll fuck it clean."

He thrusts harder now, deeper. The sounds are obscene, wet and slick and desperate, but I take it. I want it. The burn in my throat. The stretch of my jaw. The sting of his hand tightening every time I try to pull back.

Because this? This is absolution. My penance. My worship. This is how I show him I know who I belong to.

Spit drips down my chest, and I moan around him, the vibrations pulling another curse from his lips. He pulls out just long enough for me to gasp for air, to spit and pant and try to speak, but he slaps the tip against my cheek and pushes right back in.

"You'll take every drop," he says, voice almost tender beneath the cruelty. "You'll swallow every fucking inch until you forget what it was like to ever have someone else inside you."

And I do.

Because with Echo, it's not just sex.

It's devotion wrapped in degradation.

It's ruin disguised as reverence.

And I would kneel for him again.

Every single time.

He pulls out with a slick pop, the corner of his mouth curled in that cruel, gorgeous way that makes my knees want to stay on the floor forever. His cock glistens with spit and defiance. Mine. Not his. Not really. But it doesn't matter. Because he already owns me.

I'm breathless, ruined from the throat down, trembling in a puddle of spit and blood and something far more dangerous... want. But Echo's not finished with me. Not even close.

He grabs me by the throat and lifts me like I weigh nothing, shoving me back into the nearest wall with a force that makes the concrete cry out louder than I do. My head thuds against it, but I don't care. I burn beneath him. My pulse stutters as his body presses into mine, pinning me in place, his hand still around my throat, not choking, just holding. Like a leash.

"Tracking me, Butterfly?" he murmurs, voice a low threat against the shell of my ear.

"You left," I manage, my voice raw, lips swollen. "You went off the grid."

"Did I?" he hums, smiling. "Or did I just get tired of being watched by the men who claim to protect you?"

I struggle in his grip, but only because I hate the way he sees through me. "Why are you meeting with my father?" I hiss. "Would Roman approve?"

"Roman," he scoffs, his thumb brushing up my neck, right under my jaw. "Roman doesn't dictate what I do."

"You can't come over-"

"I will do what I please when it comes to you." His voice sharpens, cuts like glass. "And I won't ever let another fucking man touch you again."

I laugh, bitter and shaking. "You don't control that."

His eyes flash.

"Don't I?" he snarls.

His hand drops between us, pressing against the seam of my pants, rubbing slow, taunting circles over the fabric. I whimper, shame blooming like a bruise across my chest, but I still arch into his palm.

"Tonight," he breathes, leaning in until his lips ghost over mine, "I'm going to fuck you right in your daddy's house-"

His teeth nip my bottom lip.

"-and remind you exactly who you belong to."

He presses harder, grinding against me until I'm squirming beneath his hand, needing more. My breath comes in ragged gasps. I don't want this. I need it.

"I will show your father," he whispers, "that you belong to no one but me."

I shake my head. "I can't-"

His hand slides up to grab my chin, forcing my eyes to meet his.

"You will," he growls.

There's no room for negotiation. No space for choice. There never has been with him.

"You may be a Romanov," Echo murmurs, brushing his nose along mine, lips barely grazing my skin, "but when you're with me... you're a Kane."

The name carves itself into me like a brand.

And then, softly, dangerously tender, he kisses my forehead. Just once. Just enough to break me in an entirely new way.

"Consider this a token of my love," he whispers.

My breath catches.

Love.

The word rattles through me like a bullet I didn't see coming. Garrett's blood still stains the floor where I was on my knees. Echo's cock is still hard against my stomach. His hand is still cupping my cunt like it belongs to him.

But all I can hear is love.

And the terrifying part?

I believe him.

He doesn't release me. Doesn't let me breathe. He just stares, eyes locked on mine, watching me unravel beneath a single word. Watching me choose him, again and again, even when everything in me should be running the other direction.

He pulls away without another word. No gentle look, no soft touch. Just the sound of his belt sliding back into place and the satisfied exhale of a man who just claimed everything he ever wanted, and knows he'll take it again.

Then he walks away.

I stay where I am, cheek pressed against the cool concrete, the seam of my pants still tugged halfway up my thighs. My body aches in ways I don't even have names for. I can still feel the way he filled my throat, the slick warmth still leaking down my legs.

But all I can hear is the ghost of a single word.

Love.

He said it like a knife. Like a noose. Like a curse meant for both of us.

Love.

Not obsession.

Not control.

Not possession.

Love.

It shouldn't make me tremble like this. Shouldn't make my throat tighten and my chest ache and my mind spins faster than the toy he had inside me. But it does. Because Echo Kane doesn't say things he doesn't mean. He doesn't need to. His love isn't soft. It isn't wrapped in safety or tied with a ribbon.

It's fucking violent.

It comes with blood and bruises and graves.

And he gave it to me.

I reach up, fingers brushing the scar on my waist.

It doesn't feel like ownership anymore.

It feels like a promise.

28

BEHIND THE MASK

ECHO

They call it *Devil's Night*.

A night soaked in legacy, lust, and blood. The kind of night whispered about in corners of the world too dark for light to touch. A tradition among the Romanovs, one their inner circle lives for. A night that blurs the line between man and monster, pleasure and pain, predator and prey.

Katya doesn't know. Not really. She thinks this is just another tactic, me playing puppet master again, pulling strings to keep her close. She thinks this obsession is about control. And maybe, in part, it is.

But she doesn't know what they do behind those doors. Not truly.

She doesn't know what *Devil's Night* demands.

She doesn't know what kind of blood they drink, how young it is. How warm. How it's taken, not offered. How it's seen as sacrament.

And I sure as hell won't let them drag her into it.

They'd dress her up like a gift. Lay her bare in front of masked men and twisted gods, pretend it's all part of some legacy she was born into. Let her taste the wine, without telling her where it came from. Let her laugh, unaware of the screams echoing in the lower halls. They'd call it honor. They'd call it family.

But I call it what it is.

Evil.

And I'm willingly walking straight into it. Offering myself to Dimitri like a lamb too proud to bleat. No backup. No Catalyst. No Roman or Noah at my side. Because if they knew, they'd try to stop me. They'd call this what it is: suicide.

But this isn't about survival anymore.

It's about her.

It's about the way her body froze when I said it. The word I never thought I'd say again. *Love.*

That sick, cloying feeling that makes men soft. Makes them reckless. It's in my chest now, thick and unrelenting. It's the only reason I'm pacing like this, wearing out the floor, my mind circling her name like it's the only thing keeping me tethered to this earth.

Roman and Noah? They're drinking with their families tonight. Safe. Smiling. Blind to the fact that hell is opening its gates and Katya is standing at the edge.

But she's mine.

And if I have to offer myself, if I have to bleed for her, kill for her, burn for her, I'll do it without hesitation.

Because when Devil's Night calls for blood…

It won't be hers.

Let them take me.

That's the thought that keeps circling my mind like a vulture, hungry and patient. Let them use me. Let them shackle me to their legacy, bury me under the weight of their rituals and demands. I'll be their monster. Their blade. Their fucking slave if that's what it takes to keep her untouched by their poison.

I'll kneel. I'll bleed. I'll strip myself of every last shred of pride if it means Katya never learns what it feels like to be fed from.

They want a symbol of control? Fine. They can carve their crest into my chest and call it loyalty. I'll smile through the pain if it means her name never finds its way onto their altar.

But even in my madness, part of me still fights.

Pacing the room, my hands tremble. The scent of blood clings to me, hers, mine, theirs. I don't even know anymore. My jaw aches from grinding it too hard. My mind keeps screaming for me to tell someone. Loop someone in. Give Roman a damn heads-up before I get myself killed.

But I already know what he'll say.

He'll tell me this is emotional. He'll tell me I've lost control. That she's gotten too deep, that my judgment is compromised. And he'll be right.

Fuck, he'll be right.

Still, my fingers twitch toward my phone like they have a mind of their own.

She's all I see when I close my eyes. Katya on her knees, fire in her eyes, blood on her lips. Katya, trembling and broken and still strong enough to look me in the eye and call me out on everything I am. Katya, carved and claimed, with her name etched into my flesh like a promise.

I swallow hard, the silence around me deafening.

I can't let her be a pawn. I can't let them take her.

If I give myself to Dimitri, maybe he'll see the value in me as more than just a Catalyst threat. Maybe he'll call off his fucking dogs. Maybe he'll consider it a peace offering. A sacrifice.

A trade.

My phone screen glows in the dark, Roman's name pulsing like a heartbeat I can't outrun. There's no plan left, only instinct. A compulsion born from guilt and something far more dangerous: desperation.

Silence blankets the room, thick with the whisper of everything that's gone wrong. Every breath drags like gravel down my throat. The phone feels slick in my hand, not from sweat, but the dread that whatever happens next, there's no undoing it. No redemption arc waiting at the end of this.

The call connects on the second ring.

"Echo?" Roman's voice slices through the quiet like a blade, alert and already on edge.

His tone demands answers, but my mouth won't cooperate. The words swell, fight, stumble.

A swallow lodges halfway down. The weight in my chest doesn't budge.

"R-Roman..." The name barely makes it out. Slurred by the pressure behind my ribs.

A pause stretches between us, too short to be silence, too long to be safe.

"Echo, talk to me."

Teeth grind hard enough to threaten the enamel. Tongue thick behind the words that won't form.

"I..." A breath hitches in my lungs, useless. "I fucked up."

There's more to say. There always is. An explanation. A plan. A confession that Katya is no longer a mission but a heartbeat in human form. But even thinking it feels dangerous.

And Roman doesn't get another second.

The call ends with a final click.

The silence that follows doesn't feel empty.

It feels like judgment.

And now, there's no turning back.

The silence after the call lingers like smoke, clinging to my skin, seeping into the cracks of my resolve. Roman's voice still echoes faintly in my ears, that edge of alarm, that unspoken what have you done hanging in the space between us even after the line went dead.

Stumbling into the bathroom, the light overhead flickers to life, casting a pale glow across the cracked porcelain and rusted fixtures. The mirror stares back, unforgiving.

The man staring back is barely holding together.

Fingers fumble at my collar. The fabric is stiff with dried sweat and regret. With slow, mechanical care, the tie is straightened. The knot pulled tight like a noose. Jacket smoothed down. Shoulders squared. It's almost laughable, dressing for death like it's a fucking meeting.

A slip of paper catches the corner of my vision.

Tucked beneath the rim of the box Dimitri had sent, is a folded note. The handwriting is precise. Deliberate. The ink pressed deep into the page like a threat.

No mask.

Time for everyone to see the real Echo Kane.

A slow breath escapes my lips.

So this is it.

Not the monster behind the glass.

Not the executioner Catalyst built.

Not the savior Katya thought she saw buried somewhere beneath all the violence.

Just the raw, exposed truth.

No more masks.

No more lies.

Only the reckoning.

29

Devil's Night

Katya

The gown is a masterpiece of black silk and quiet control, stitched by someone who knew exactly how to cage a woman without chains. Selected by my father, delivered without a word, it waited in solemn wait in Maria's arms. Wearing it now, surrounded by candlelight and carefully curated decadence, it clings to my body like a silent contract, one signed in legacy, obedience, and blood.

The room pulses with elegance. Shadows swirl between chandeliers and lace-veiled faces. Each guest dons their mask with practiced ease, a crowd of strangers pretending to be friends, monsters pretending to be men. Voices hum around the dining table, laughter floating in the air like perfume, the sharp clink of silverware against fine porcelain keeping tempo. At a glance, this could be any exclusive gathering in the upper echelons of society, wealthy men, powerful women, aged wine and veiled intentions. But something festers beneath it all. Something ancient and grotesque, like rot masked with roses.

Something isn't right.

The glass in my hand catches the glow of candlelight, the liquid inside too red to be wine. Swallowed out of courtesy, it burns down my throat with the bitterness of something I don't want to understand. No one speaks plainly here. Every sentence is a riddle, every toast a threat wrapped in metaphor. The older men speak of "preserving the lineage," of "tasting power at its purest." They smile behind their masks like snakes curled in velvet.

A menu lands in front of me with a practiced flick of a waiter's wrist.

Fingers curl around the edge of the card as my eyes fall to the page, and everything stops.

No entrées. No delicacies. Just names.

Columns of them. Some accompanied by symbols, others labeled by vague descriptions. Sweet. Fragile. Cured. Aged to perfection. Each name is branded with an age, eight, ten, eleven. My stomach twists, a tight coil of nausea rising up the back of my throat. This isn't a dinner.

It's a *ritual.*

They've dressed it up in crystal and silk, hidden it behind tradition and generational wealth, but the truth is clearer than any wine: this night is a celebration of hunger, and the hunger they feed is unspeakable.

From the head of the table, my father raises his glass. The others follow. Their eyes, those I can see, gleam behind their masks with fevered reverence. He speaks in metaphors, references "Devil's Night" as if it were a sacred rite. He thanks us for our loyalty, our silence. Talks of sacrifice and rebirth, of removing the mask of society to reveal what we truly are. His smile tightens when he speaks of those "ripe with power," when he lifts his glass and references the "first taste of legacy." His voice is warm. Inviting.

It makes my skin crawl.

Then comes the moment.

With a proud grin and a hand lifted toward the doors, my father makes the announcement. "Now," he says, drawing every eye in the room, "let us welcome our *esteemed guest.*"

Stillness descends like a curtain falling over a stage.

The double doors part slowly.

And through them walks the last person I wanted to see tonight.

No mask. No disguise. No hesitation.

Echo Kane strides into the room like a man returning to a warzone, his presence magnetic, undeniable. Every movement is calculated, each step a weapon. Blood has been cleaned from his hands, but something darker clings to him still. His suit is pressed, his eyes blank, unreadable.

He doesn't search the crowd. Doesn't acknowledge the sea of masked eyes turned his way.

He looks only at me.

There's no smirk. No softness. Just silence between us, thick and strangling.

Whatever brought him here, it's not about saving anyone.

It's about survival.

And suddenly, I'm not sure who's wearing the mask anymore.

The room doesn't breathe as Echo crosses the threshold. Not a flicker of movement, not a whisper from the guests who moments ago laughed freely over their flutes of sin. The silence around him is thick, reverent. The kind of stillness reserved for saints and sacrifices. But there is nothing holy about the man walking toward the head of the table, only a dangerous kind of reverence, the same one given to predators in a den full of lesser beasts.

He doesn't look away from me. Not even once. And I don't dare look away from him. He moves like he owns the floor beneath him, like the very tiles bend to his will. But there's something off in his eyes, something dulled, almost hollow. The same sharpness is there, the same Echo, but faded... like the soul behind him has been scorched into submission.

A chill coils through me as my father rises slowly to his feet, his wine glass catching the light like a blade.

The clapping starts, slow, deliberate, mechanical. One by one, each masked face joins in, and the room echoes with applause. It's not joy they're celebrating. It's ownership.

"My friends," my father begins, his voice smooth and practiced, his hand sweeping toward Echo like he's presenting a prized stallion at auction. "It is my pleasure, my honor... to introduce a man many of you have heard of. A man who has operated in the shadows of power, steering the unseen with skill and silence. Tonight, he no longer hides. Tonight, he steps into the light, as one of *us*."

Whispers ripple through the room, approving nods exchanged behind masks. The mask I wear is suddenly suffocating, the velvet pressing against my lips like cloth meant for the dead.

"Echo Kane," my father continues, "former head of Catalyst. Weapon of the Briars. Architect of order in chaos. A man born in fire and sharpened by betrayal."

A sick warmth blooms in my chest. The name burns. *Former.* He said *former head.* My stomach turns.

"But tonight," my father says, his smile spreading wider, colder, "he sheds his past. He has seen our ways. He has looked upon the truth of House Romanov and not flinched. He comes to us willingly... *reborn.*"

The guests murmur with pleasure. Glasses rise. Blood-red wine swirls.

"You see, we do not just break men," my father says, walking toward Echo, who stands impossibly still, his hands at his sides, his jaw clenched tight. "We rebuild them. And tonight, Mr. Kane has made his choice. He has bent the knee, and in doing so, will be granted the highest gift a sinner can ask for...absolution."

He reaches into his coat.

A ceremonial blade. Ancient. Polished. Romanov-engraved.

My breath stalls as my father lifts Echo's shirt, baring his chest to the air, to the room, to *them*. And without hesitation, he carves. Slow, shallow. Not for pain. For permanence.

Blood drips as the symbol is etched into his skin, the House crest, precise and cruel.

Echo doesn't move. Doesn't blink. Doesn't even *breathe*.

"He is a servant to House Romanov now," Dimitri declares, raising the bloodied blade. "A child reborn."

More applause. The sound of madness dressed in civility.

No one questions. No one blinks.

Except me.

And Echo still won't look away. His eyes never leave mine, even as his blood stains the collar of his shirt, even as the brand still glistens fresh along his chest.

But whatever he's trying to tell me through those unblinking eyes, whatever piece of himself still fights inside that shattered shell, there's no saving either of us now.

Not tonight.

Dimitri's blade glints crimson in the candlelight, a slow drip of Echo's blood tracing down the curve of his abdomen. The air is thick with triumph and control, the silence among the guests not hesitation, but hunger. They feast with their eyes long before any toast is raised, savoring Echo's submission like the finest cut of meat.

And still, he doesn't flinch.

The applause fades, replaced by a dry, low chuckle. My father's hand hovers in the air before he lets the knife rest gently against a linen napkin, as if it were any ordinary utensil.

"Ah, Echo," he muses with amusement, his voice curling around the name like smoke. "I must admit, I never imagined you would be the one to come crawling to our doorstep. The infamous architect of Catalyst, groveling at the feet of the family you once hunted."

He turns toward the room, addressing the crowd now like a ringmaster welcoming the night's finale.

"How far the great have fallen. And yet... how beautiful they look once broken in."

A few masked guests chuckle, a toast is raised, and Echo's lips part, but no words come. His chest rises, slow and tight, the fresh wound pulsing with every breath. But his eyes, they never waver from me.

Dimitri follows the gaze and lets the silence settle before he speaks again, this time with a faux gentleness that sends a chill up my spine.

"Katya, dear," he says, as if this were any ordinary family dinner. "Would you do me the honor..." He pauses, savoring the pause like a course between wines. "...of serving our guest his first drink?"

Every gaze turns to me.

The velvet mask suddenly feels suffocating, the gown a noose. For a heartbeat too long, I don't move.

My father's smile doesn't fade, it sharpens.

"This is a celebration, after all," he adds, his tone coated in honey but laced with command. "He is one of us now. Let's toast properly, yes?"

A servant steps forward with a crystal tray. Balanced atop it, a single black chalice, ornate, heavy, ancient. The liquid inside is deep red, far thicker than wine.

The scent hits me first.

Rich. Metallic. Sweet.

Not wine.

God. Not wine.

The tray lingers in the air between us, and slowly, carefully, I reach out and take the chalice into my hands. It's heavier than it should be, weighted with symbolism, with consequence. Every inch of me screams to drop it. To run. To put a bullet in every man seated at this cursed table and never look back.

But I walk.

One step after the other. Across the polished floor, toward Echo, toward the man who once peeled the world open with his cruelty and held me in the aftermath.

He watches every step. Not with pride. Not with desire. Just that same unreadable stillness, his face a stone mask cracked only by the fresh blood glistening over the brand on his chest.

Stopping just before him, the cup trembling slightly in my grasp, I glance up.

He doesn't move.

"Drink," my father says from behind me. "Let the night begin."

And still, Echo says nothing.

He just stares, at me.

Waiting.

The chalice trembles in my hands, heavier now that I'm standing directly in front of him, Echo, stripped of his mask, his title, and whatever pieces of himself he once claimed to control. But something stirs beneath that impassive face. It's subtle, buried deep under layers of practiced stoicism, but I feel it like a wire pulled tight between us.

I shouldn't have stepped this close.

Before I can react, his hand shoots up and tangles in my hair, fingers knotting at the base of my skull. The gasp that leaves me isn't loud, but it's sharp enough to earn the attention of half the table. My body jerks slightly, the chalice sloshing just enough to lick the rim.

The room doesn't move. No one dares intervene.

Leaning forward, his lips ghost my ear, slow, deliberate, the heat of him coiling through me like poison laced in honey.

"I'd hate for the precious drink to be wasted," he whispers, voice low and rough. The kind of threat masked as seduction. The kind of tone that once made me weak. That still does.

His grip tightens, not painfully, but enough to remind me exactly who he is beneath all this pageantry. Or who he *was*. My body fights to stay steady, to keep the cup from tipping between us.

I can feel the eyes on us, their attention sharpening, their hunger mounting. This is a performance now, and we are center stage.

My lips part, but no words come out. There's too much heat, too much memory. My breath catches as his thumb brushes the side of my neck, grazing over the pulse that betrays every lie I've ever told myself about him. About what this was. What it still might be.

He releases me just as slowly as he grabbed me, the tension hanging between us like smoke over a fire not yet smothered.

"Let him drink, Katya," my father snaps, almost amused. "We wouldn't want to keep our guests waiting."

My hands move before my thoughts catch up, lifting the chalice to Echo's lips.

He never takes his eyes off mine.

And when he drinks, slow and savoring, like he's devouring something sacred, I feel it all unravel beneath my skin.

This isn't submission.

This is war, dressed in elegance.

And we're both bleeding.

The chalice is empty before I realize my fingers have gone numb from holding it. Slowly, I lower it. His lips are stained red, a smear of it at the corner of his mouth. Still, he says nothing. There is no thank you. No plea.

Only the fire of shame and something far more dangerous, smoldering beneath his silence.

My father claps his hands once.

The sharp sound cuts through the stillness like a gunshot, shattering the breath I didn't know I was holding.

"Echo Kane," he declares, his voice booming with theatrical reverence. "You are now a servant to House Romanov. Body, blood, and will."

A cheer rises from the table. Glasses clink. Laughter blooms like something sour, and still, Echo stands in silence, his eyes dark hollows beneath the weight of the room.

Dimitri turns his attention to me next, a serpent's smile playing at the edges of his mouth.

"Katya, dear," he croons. "Why don't you show him to his new quarters?"

My throat tightens.

Every eye returns to me. Every gaze a command.

My feet refuse to move. But I feel his presence beside me, Echo, still and waiting, like a knife left unsheathed.

The room watches. The mask on my face might as well be fused to my skin.

I nod once, barely.

And without another word, I lead him from the room.

30

Stolen Moments

Katya

The blood on his lips isn't wine.

It clings thick and dark, painting the corner of his mouth with a crimson sheen that doesn't belong in any glass. My fingers tremble as they brush it away, the warmth of it sticking to my skin like a silent warning. It tastes like iron and secrets, the kind of taste that seeps into your bones and never washes clean. The ballroom hums with laughter and clinking glasses just beyond the corridor, but in this stolen moment, we are suspended in something colder, heavier.

"Echo, what the fuck are you doing?" I whisper, my voice a broken thread as I wipe the blood disguised as drink from his lips. His eyes are dull, soulless in a way I've never seen before. Not even during the interrogations. Not even in the basement.

"Your father promised," he murmurs, tone low and distant, as if speaking through a haze. "So long as I did this, he wouldn't drag you in."

I don't wait. My grip finds his wrist and I yank him down the hallway, our footsteps muffled by ancient rugs and stained indulgence. The guest room door creaks as I shove him inside, slamming it closed behind us. The ornate lamp glows dimly on the wall, casting soft shadows across the fine furniture...a luxury prison.

"Drag me into what?" I demand, my heartbeat thundering beneath the surface of my skin.

He leans against the wall like he's seconds from collapse, the sharp planes of his face illuminated just enough to show the madness creeping in. "This," he breathes. "This night. The drinks they pass. The evil that feeds them."

My mouth goes dry. I want to scream, to hit him, to shake the truth out of him. "What was in that drink, Echo?" The words shake loose from my throat, ragged.

He doesn't move. His silence confirms what I already fear.

"I think you know," he says finally, and something inside me shatters.

Revulsion coils in my gut. "You need to call Roman," I hiss, urgency rising like bile. "You need to-"

Before I can finish, he grabs me. Slams me back into the wall with more need than violence, his breath hot against my face. He's trembling. Desperate.

"Roman won't keep you safe," he growls, voice raw. "No one will. No one but me."

I glare at him, breathing hard, trying to decide if this is madness or love or both twisted into something unrecognizable.

"The drink," I snap, struggling against his grip. "What was in it."

He leans in closer. His lips nearly graze mine.

"Let's just say your family doesn't mind bleeding the youth."

Revulsion turns to nausea. I shove him back, staggering as cold realization washes over me.

"Jesus Christ," I whisper. "Why would you come here? Why wouldn't you run?"

His laugh is bitter, hollow. "Because you needed to see it. All of it. Me. This night. Them. You needed to look me in the eyes and tell me you still stand with them."

He reaches for me again, not with anger, but with something molten and needy. His hands run down my sides, gripping with just enough pressure to ground me.

"I can't take down an empire without you," he murmurs, voice sliding over my skin like smoke. "And I sure as hell can't do it from the outside looking in."

My breath catches as his mouth hovers near the base of my neck.

"You want to take down my family?" I whisper, lost in the heat radiating between us.

His eyes meet mine, glassy but intense. "Don't you?"

Silence stretches between us, thick with truth I haven't wanted to face.

"Then what will I have left?" The question isn't just for him, it's for the girl I used to be.

His answer is simple. Devastating.

"Me."

That's all it takes.

He pulls me toward the bed, and I go willingly, heart pounding, pulse thrumming beneath my skin like war drums. The second we hit the mattress, everything else disappears. No logic. No betrayal. No blood. Just him. Just us. A tangle of limbs and fury and hunger.

His lips crush mine with reckless hunger, tongue pushing past my teeth like he owns the space, like he's staking a claim. His fingers tear at the black dress like it's a lie, a mask, something that needs to be ripped away until there's nothing left but bare skin and truth.

He groans into my mouth, a sound low and guttural, the kind that makes heat curl in my belly. His hands grip my thighs hard enough to leave marks, dragging me to the edge of the bed like he doesn't just want me, he needs me. Desperately. Violently.

"Here?" I whisper, breathless.

"In your father's house," he growls, voice thick with something darker than lust. "Where he can hear you beg for me."

His mouth is everywhere, neck, collarbone, chest, lower, burning a trail that makes my spine arch and my thighs fall open without thought. His stubble scrapes my skin, his tongue soothing it after like a damn apology he never means to keep.

"You're mine," he rasps against my stomach, before biting down just below my navel. "Always have been."

His fingers slide beneath the thin scrap of lace between my legs, tearing it aside like it's offensive, like it shouldn't be there at all. His thumb presses against my most sensitive spot, slow and brutal. I cry out, trying to keep quiet, but he catches the sound in a kiss, devouring it like it feeds him.

"You think your father would approve of this?" he murmurs, fingers sinking into me without warning, making my body jerk, breath hitching.

"Echo-"

"You should be afraid," he whispers, dragging his mouth back up to my ear. "But you're not, are you?"

"No," I pant, hips moving against his hand like I'm chasing salvation in the very man sent to destroy me.

He smirks against my throat, then flips me over like I weigh nothing. His belt clinks open behind me, pants hitting the floor, the blunt heat of him pressing against my entrance as he fists my hair and yanks my head back just enough for his lips to brush mine.

"Good," he mutters. "Because I'm going to ruin you in every room of this house until your father knows exactly who you belong to."

And then he thrusts, deep, punishing and raw.

Every thought leaves my mind. All I know is this: the way his body feels inside mine, the stretch, the sting, the fullness that makes my toes curl and my eyes roll back.

He fucks me like he's trying to bury himself in my bones, like the act itself is a brand, one that says *mine, mine, mine* with every ragged breath. The headboard slams against the wall. The bed creaks. And still, he doesn't stop.

"You'll scream for me," he promises through gritted teeth. "And when you do, you better hope your father's listening."

And I do.

God help me, I *do*.

His grip tightens on my hips as his thrusts turn feral, deep, fast, devastating. Each snap of his body into mine punches a moan from my throat, my spine arching as I shatter all over again beneath him.

He groans my name like it's the only word he knows, slamming into me one final time, burying himself to the hilt as he spills inside me, hot and thick, pulse after pulse, like he's emptying everything he is into me.

We collapse together in a tangle of limbs and sweat, his chest pressed to my back, his breath hot against my neck. My thighs are shaking. My skin is slick. My body aches in the best, filthiest kind of way.

But Echo doesn't let go.

His hand wraps around my throat, gently at first, just enough to make me aware of who's in control. Of what I've given him. Of what he's taken.

"You think I'm done with you?" he murmurs, his voice still thick with lust. "That was just the first round, Butterfly."

I whimper, trying to turn, but he pins me flat on the bed, his body stretched out over mine like a second skin. His fingers trail down between my legs, slow and cruel, gathering the mess he left inside me. My breath catches as he presses his soaked fingers between my lips.

"Taste it," he growls. "Taste what I've done to you."

My mouth opens automatically, tongue curling around his fingers. I moan, obscene and shameless, and that sound, it snaps something in him. His free hand fists my hair, yanking my head back so I'm staring up at him, jaw slack, drool on my chin.

"You're fucking perfect like this," he says, voice low and reverent. "Ruined. Owned. Mine."

I'm dizzy, high off him, drunk on the power he holds over my body.

But he's still hard.

Still hungry.

He rolls me onto my back and pushes my knees up, wide and trembling. My legs are coated in slick, my thighs marked with the bruises from his grip. He positions himself between them like a man ready to pray and then desecrate.

"This pussy," he murmurs, dragging his cock through the mess of me. "This is the only altar I worship at."

And then he's inside again.

Deeper.

Slower.

Possessive.

He watches every inch disappear into me like he's engraving the sight into his memory, one thrust at a time. His thumb circles my clit lazily, teasing, never giving me enough. My back arches. My nails claw at the sheets. I'm unraveling all over again.

"You'll never let another man touch you again," he says, like it's a fact, not a threat. "You'll be full of me every day. Dripping for me in every room of this house until your father realizes there's nothing left of his little girl."

"You're sick," I pant, eyes fluttering.

He smiles, dark and wicked. "I *love* you."

That breaks me.

The word I hadn't expected. The one that hits harder than any thrust or bruise.

He leans down, kissing the tears off my cheeks like they belong to him too.

"I love you," he says again. "And I'll show you every fucking day until you believe it."

He doesn't slow. Doesn't stop. His rhythm turns rough again, savage and all-consuming as he fucks the confession deeper into my bones.

I shatter beneath him, again and again, until I'm crying out, my legs twitching, my throat raw from screaming his name.

And still, Echo isn't satisfied.

He pulls out, slick and glistening, watching the mess leak out of me with a hunger that's *feral.* Then he leans in close, his breath hot on my ear.

"Now," he whispers. "Crawl."

I blink. "What?"

"You heard me. Crawl, Katya."

The sheets fall away as I move, humiliation and heat twisting together like a knife in my belly. I slide off the bed, limbs sore and shaky, knees meeting the cold hardwood floor. He follows behind me, slow and methodical, watching every sway of my hips like a predator.

"Crawl to the door," he orders. "Open it."

"Echo-"

"Do it."

Heart racing, I reach the door, my body on full display, ass high in the air as I unlatch the lock and open it. The hall is empty, silent. But I know anyone could walk by. One of the house staff. A guard. My *father*.

Adrenaline pulses with the threat of being seen. My pulse spikes. My cunt clenches.

Echo leans down behind me, pressing the head of his cock to my entrance, teasing, not entering. Just letting it *hover*.

"You like this," he breathes. "You like the risk. You like knowing you're dripping my cum down your thighs while crawling through your father's house like a pet."

"I shouldn't," I whisper.

"But you *do*."

He slides inside, achingly slow, stretching me open again with the thick drag of him.

I bite down a moan, fingers curling into the floor, trying to stay upright as he begins to fuck me right there in the doorway, deep, deliberate thrusts meant to make me squirm and whimper. His hand slides up my spine, then wraps around my throat, holding me still as his cock fills me again and again.

"I want them to see," he growls. "I want someone to walk by. I want your father to *walk by* and hear the sounds you make when you're mine."

"You're insane," I gasp.

"I'm in love," he snarls, biting down on my shoulder. "There's a difference."

My vision blurs, eyes glassy, body unraveling again as pleasure builds to unbearable heights. I don't even know how many times I've cum. I don't care. My body belongs to him now, wrecked, wet, ruined in ways no one can undo.

He slams into me one final time and stills, pulsing deep, emptying himself inside me again like he *needs* me full of him. Like it's not just sex, it's a message. A war declaration.

And then, with a dark smirk, he grabs a silk tie from his pants on the floor and wraps it around my throat, tight enough to feel, loose enough to breathe.

"Breakfast," he says, tugging the makeshift collar like a leash. "You're going to sit across from your father with my cum dripping out of you and your throat marked by *me*. You'll smile. You'll sip your tea. And every time you shift in that little chair, you'll remember exactly who you belong to."

My knees buckle, and still, I nod.

Because I'm already his.

And maybe I always was.

I'm a mess beneath him.

Wrecked.

Ruined.

Worshipped.

And still, he lingers inside me, cock twitching with the last pulses of his release, his body draped over mine like a shadow I'll never outrun. He doesn't speak at first. Just stares at me, like I'm some holy thing he defiled and now prays to.

His hand still wrapped in my hair, he pulls me back from the open doorway, guiding me through the shadows like something he owns. My knees nearly buckle with every step, slick and sore, but he doesn't stop, just walks me backward until the backs of my thighs hit the mattress.

"Up," he commands, voice rough.

I climb onto the bed, trembling, every inch of me raw and open. He follows, crawling over me like a storm, eyes locked on mine as he presses me down into the sheets.

His thumb brushes my swollen lip. His other hand cups the side of my face with a gentleness that doesn't belong in this house, in this room, in the aftermath of what he's just done.

"You feel that?" he murmurs.

I nod.

"Good. Because I never want you to forget it." He presses a kiss to my forehead, then my temple, then the hollow beneath my ear where his teeth bit down minutes ago. "Every breath you take, every step you stumble through tomorrow, I want you to feel me. Still inside you. Still *claiming* you."

My eyes flutter closed. I don't have words. Just heat. Just ache. Just the faintest glimmer of something terrifying in my chest that might, *might*, be love.

He lays beside me, pulling me into him, one hand still gripping the silk tie around my throat like a leash he refuses to drop. His lips brush my hairline. His breath tickles my skin.

And then he speaks, soft, dangerous, and certain.

"Tonight," he whispers, voice like smoke, "I claim you."

He pulls me tighter, palm resting possessively on my belly like he's already planted something there, an idea, a future, a war.

"Tomorrow," he finishes, "we bring down the empire... hand in hand."

31

Burn It All Down

Katya

I shouldn't have stayed the night at my father's estate, let alone stayed with Echo. Yet here I am, seated at the long, polished dining table between the two people who raised me, pretending everything is normal. Pretending I haven't just been claimed by the man they swore was the enemy.

Just like Echo said would happen.

My body still aches in all the right places, filled and stretched and marked in ways my father would gut him for if he knew the truth. I can still feel the way Echo kept me pinned to the bed this morning, refusing to let me leave without taking one more round from me, slow, messy, possessive. And now, I sit here like nothing's changed, even as the air vibrates with unspoken tension.

Across the table, my father cuts his eggs with deliberate care. My mother sits beside him, expression distant, as if she's not quite here, not really. Her hands move mechanically, lifting a teacup to cracked lips. No one speaks.

But I feel the weight of his stare, the question coiled on the tip of his tongue.

"Say it," I murmur, voice low, eyes never leaving his.

His fork pauses mid-air. "When did you plan on telling me you shared a bed with Echo Kane?"

He doesn't raise his voice. He doesn't need to.

Fingers tap against the side of my glass in a rhythm that keeps me grounded. The answer slips from my lips easily, too easily. "What better way to infiltrate Catalyst than to go after the head himself?"

A lie. A thin, paper one, cracked at the edges from the weight of everything I feel.

As if Echo's hands on my hips didn't make me forget every oath of loyalty I ever took.

As if I'm not falling in love with the man I was raised to fear.

My father turns to my mother, voice cold but soft. "Sounds a lot like you, hm, dear?"

She doesn't flinch. Just stares ahead, porcelain still, like she's forgotten how to speak. Or maybe she remembers too much.

"So," my father continues, knife gliding through his food with unsettling calm, "your time in Echo's confinement wasn't wasted after all?"

The corner of my mouth lifts, just enough to pass for a grin. "Apparently not."

I lean forward slightly, resting my elbows on the table, gaze sharpening. "Though, I do believe it's time you start involving me in more of the family's internal dealings. Starting with last night, specifically, where our drinks came from."

That gets his attention. His hand stills. His eyes narrow, flicking up to meet mine with a quiet calculation I know too well.

"Is this your request, Katya?" he asks slowly. "Or is it Echo Kane's?"

Before I can answer, a voice cuts through the room like a blade. "Not mine."

Echo enters like he belongs here, barefoot, shirt unbuttoned halfway, neck still showing faint scratch marks from the night before. There's no shame in the way he walks toward us. No remorse in the way he moves to stand directly behind my chair, his hand ghosting over my shoulder like a silent warning to everyone watching.

"Though loyalty," he says coolly, "is a narrow bridge, Dimitri. I won't insult your intelligence by pretending my fealty to House Romanov is anything but personal. But if you want my resources, my network, my men, you'll need to accept one simple truth."

He lowers his gaze, fingers brushing the back of my neck.

"My loyalty begins with her."

My father's jaw tightens. My mother shifts for the first time, eyes lifting to Echo, searching, perhaps, for any trace of the monster she's been told he is.

"This house was built on silence," Echo says, voice lowering just enough to draw everyone in. "But silence rots power from the inside. If you want results, we need transparency. We need unity."

He looks at me then, not with possession, but purpose.

"And she's not a pawn in your empire anymore. She's the hand that topples it."

A silence stretches over the room.

My father sets his utensils down with careful precision, the clink of silverware against porcelain far too gentle for what follows.

"If you intend to stand beside my daughter, Mr. Kane," he says, voice smooth as ever, "you should know something about our house."

He lifts his napkin, dabbing the corners of his mouth as if wiping away something distasteful.

"In the Romanov line, we measure loyalty not in declarations, but in endurance. In longevity. Promises mean nothing if they wither at the first sign of consequence."

His eyes drift to me, softening just enough to unsettle.

"My daughter has always been... passionate. But passions, as I'm sure you know, can be inconvenient and...temporary."

Echo stiffens behind me, his hand still resting on my shoulder, thumb dragging back and forth like a reminder: he's here. He's listening. But so is my father.

"Women, Mr. Kane, are precious things. Beautiful, brilliant, but easily broken." my father smiles. "And when broken, easily replaced."

My fingers twitch against the tablecloth. Echo doesn't move.

"But you already know that, don't you?" my father continues, leaning back in his chair like a man with nothing to lose. "So if you're going to make yourself a fixture in this house, I suggest you keep your end of the arrangement intact. Otherwise..."

His gaze slides toward my mother, still staring into her untouched tea like a ghost.

"...we both know how easily things can go quiet again."

For a moment, the air freezes. Then, as if the storm hadn't just rolled through the room, he exhales and gestures toward one of the servers lingering silently near the wall.

"Speaking of transparency, Katya, since you're so curious about the drinks from last night..."

He raises a brow, as though amused.

"I'd be happy to show you the source."

He lifts his teacup with mock cheer. "The vintage is rather rare, after all. Very small donors. Very fresh."

My stomach knots.

Echo straightens behind me.

My father sips. "You're welcome to see the lot yourself. A new shipment came in this morning. The little ones are kept below stairs, for now."

His smile doesn't reach his eyes.

"And they do prefer when their guests look them in the eye before drinking."

Echo doesn't flinch. Neither do I.

On the outside, we are composed and stoic. We wear the Romanov mask well, mirroring the same indifference my father perfected years ago. No tremble in my hands. No fire in Echo's glare. Just silence and control.

But inside?

I'm splintering.

Every breath in this corridor tastes like rot. Like blood. Like children's screams swallowed by stone walls. And still, I nod slowly as Dimitri gestures toward the next steel door, as if I'm admiring a fucking wine selection.

Echo plays the part even better, hands tucked behind his back like a soldier awaiting orders, eyes trained on my father like he's listening, learning. Obeying.

It's terrifying how easy it is to lie with your face when your soul is already on fire.

My father continues walking, pleased with himself, the heels of his shoes echoing in perfect rhythm against the floor. The deeper we go, the colder the air becomes. The less it feels like a home, and more like a tomb for the living.

He stops abruptly and turns, his eyes locking on Echo with a glint that isn't quite respect, but isn't contempt either.

"This is where you come in, Mr. Kane," he says smoothly. "Catalyst is... efficient. Organized. Ruthless, when necessary. It's time those qualities were put to use beyond your little rebellion."

Echo raises a brow, just enough to feign curiosity. "Expansion?"

"To begin with, yes," Dimitri replies. "More territories. More distribution centers. More donors. We've outgrown the old systems. The Black Veil is fractured, my men are disorganized, and your men have the infrastructure I need."

He steps closer to Echo, gaze hardening.

"If you have no fear fucking my daughter senseless under my own roof," he says, voice sharp as a knife's edge, "then I assume you'll have no fear doing what is necessary."

A beat.

Then the strike.

"Starting with getting rid of Roman Briar."

The name slams into the silence like a bullet. My pulse stutters, but I keep my expression blank.

Echo doesn't blink. "You want him eliminated."

"I want him erased," my father says, smile returning, slow and venomous. "Quietly. Thoroughly. His influence has become...

inconvenient. He's too beloved, too independent, and far too interested in preserving what should have been extinguished long ago."

His eyes flick to me then, like I'm some kind of test Echo has passed.

"He's a relic of an old world," Dimitri continues. "One your generation will bury, one way or another."

Echo nods once, measured and thoughtful. "And if I do this?"

"Then Catalyst becomes more than a tool," my father answers. "It becomes legacy. A dynasty carved in blood and silence."

My stomach turns.

But I force a smile.

Echo slips his hand into mine, casual, warm, reassuring beneath the cold.

"We understand each other," he says, voice calm. "Consider Roman Briar handled."

My father grins.

And I swallow the bile in my throat.

Because beneath the mask, beneath the practiced stillness and pretty lies, I'm already plotting how to burn it all down.

The heavy steel door shuts behind us, sealing the Romanov horrors back in the basement where they belong. For now.

We don't speak as we walk. Not through the hallway. Not past the staff with their lowered gazes. Not as we climb the stairs and put distance between ourselves and the cold, sterile hell below.

But when the bedroom door finally closes, Echo locks it.

Not out of fear, but of necessity.

He pulls his phone from his pocket, screen lighting up with a relentless stream of missed calls and messages.

Roman Briar (27 new messages)

3 missed calls

> Answer me.

> What the fuck are you doing?

> I swear to God if you've gone dark…

Echo exhales, tossing the phone on the bed like it's buzzing with live ammunition.

His jaw is tight. Muscles coiled. The composure he wore like armor downstairs is already cracking around the edges.

"Roman won't stop," he mutters, pacing. "He knows something's off. And he's not wrong."

I sit on the edge of the bed, blood still pounding in my ears from everything that just happened. The images. The doors. The children.

"They want him dead," I say softly, as if saying it out loud might make it more real. "He knows too much."

Echo doesn't look at me right away. He stares at the floor, the wall, anywhere but my face.

Then finally, "We meet him. Today. I'm done keeping him in the dark."

"Echo-"

"I already set it up," he says. "Catalyst. Vault floor. No signals. No recordings. Just us."

He grabs his phone again, fingers flying over the screen, sending one short, sharp message back to Roman:

> Two hours. Be ready. Bring nothing.

He turns to me.

"You're coming with me."

My brows knit. "You want me at a meeting with Roman?"

"I need you there," he says, stepping closer. "Because this isn't just about me anymore. You heard your father, this isn't a game of power moves and family politics. They're planning genocide wrapped in legacy. They want to use Catalyst as the knife."

He drops to one knee in front of me, resting his hands on my thighs, firm and grounding.

"I won't let them turn you into a symbol for their sick empire. I won't let them use us to start their war."

A beat passes, and something in his voice softens.

"But I'm not doing this alone."

He looks up at me, gaze sharp, unwavering.

"We face Roman together. No secrets. No masks. If this burns down, we burn it down hand in hand."

32

Let's Bring Down An Empire

Echo

The vault floor at Catalyst is silent, the kind of silence that doesn't just press on your ears, it gets under your skin. This place was built for war. For secrets. For blood. And now it's the stage for the most dangerous conversation I've ever had.

Roman's coming. I know that by the way my chest feels tighter with every tick of the clock. The missed calls, the barrage of messages, it's not just anger. It's fear. Not of what I've done, but why.

I stand alone in the center of the room, the lights above casting a cold, sterile glow over the concrete walls. I made sure the cameras were off, the weapons locked up, the exits secured. Roman may be furious, but he's not stupid. He'll want answers, and I'm done hiding them.

Minutes later, the door bursts open with the force of his fury behind it. He doesn't hesitate, his gun is drawn before the sound of his boots even registers on the floor. Roman moves like a man who's already decided how this ends.

"Don't fucking move."

His voice echoes, sharp enough to slice through bone. He crosses the space in three long strides, eyes locked on me like I'm a traitor he never thought he'd have to kill.

I stay still, arms at my sides. I don't flinch. Not because I'm unafraid, but because I need him to see this isn't cowardice, it's strategy.

"You go silent for thirty-six hours," he growls, rage simmering beneath every word. "Then I hear you've been at the Romanov estate? Sleeping in their fucking home? You think I wouldn't hear about that?"

"I wasn't hiding," I say, my voice level, steady despite the storm radiating off him.

Roman's lip curls into something that's not quite a snarl but close. "Then what the fuck do you call this, Echo? Silence? Disappearing? You think I'm just going to stand here and pretend like you haven't crossed a line?"

I raise one hand, not in surrender, just to slow him, to give him one reason not to pull that trigger.

"There's someone you need to see," I tell him. "But if you're going to make a decision right now, at least see her first."

That stops him.

His brow furrows, gun still up, but his stance shifts slightly. "Her?"

I don't answer. Instead, I glance toward the door on the far end of the vault. My steps are slow, deliberate, as I knock once and step back.

The door opens.

Katya steps through.

She doesn't hide behind me. Doesn't cast her eyes down or act like she doesn't belong. She walks into that room like it's hers, like she's earned the right to be there just as much as Roman or I. Hair down, shoulders square, lips set in a line that doesn't waver. The soft silk blouse she's wearing is a far cry from battle gear, but there's something just as lethal in her posture.

Roman stares at her like he's looking at a ghost. Like something impossible has been dragged into the light.

She doesn't say a word.

She doesn't have to.

It's all written on our bodies, the subtle way she moves toward me, the tension in my shoulders when she's not at my side, the fact that I let her in here at all.

Roman's mouth opens, then closes again, like he's trying to piece together a puzzle with blood-stained hands.

"You're fucking her," he finally says, not a question but a grim conclusion.

My jaw tightens. "It's not like that."

But it is. And we both know it. It's exactly like that. And more.

He lowers the gun slightly, not out of trust but because it's pointless to keep pretending this is about one betrayal. This is about all of them. Every rule I've broken. Every line I've blurred.

Roman lets out a bitter laugh, one that holds no humor. "You've completely lost your mind. All this time, you've been the one lecturing me about restraint. About choosing the mission over the mess. And now you're wrapped around her like a leash you want to wear?"

Katya steps forward then, breaking the invisible line between them. Her voice is low but steady. "If I wanted Roman Briar dead, he'd already be in the ground."

That makes Roman stop.

Not because he believes her, but because he's finally listening.

"I didn't come here to kill you," she says, lifting her chin. "I came here to help you aim."

His eyes narrow. "So that's it? You're Catalyst now?"

"No," she replies. "I'm not yours. I'm not my father's. I'm not Echo's. I'm me. And I know what's coming."

Roman's gaze flicks back to me, this time slower, less anger, more calculation.

"What did Dimitri offer you?"

I step forward, voice grave. "Access. Power. Legacy. If I help them take you out, I become the right hand of the next regime."

"And instead, you brought me here," he mutters. "You could've sold me out."

"I still could," I remind him. "But I didn't."

He exhales, eyes dark. "Then say it. Why am I here?"

I glance at Katya.

"To choose whether we fight this together, or die on opposite sides of it."

The room stills.

Roman watches me like he's trying to decide if I'm a threat he can reason with, or one he needs to put down. I can see the calculation behind his eyes, the way he's turning every piece of this over, trying to find the angle where it doesn't end in betrayal.

But then Katya speaks.

Her voice cuts through the air, clear and unflinching.

"I love him."

Everything freezes.

Even Roman goes still.

I turn to look at her, but she doesn't meet my gaze. She's staring at Roman, like she's making the confession to the man who'll judge her for it, not the one she's giving it to. Her hands tremble slightly, but she doesn't hide them. Doesn't try to pull the words back.

"I love Echo," she says again, softer this time. "I shouldn't. God knows I shouldn't. Everything about this... it's wrong. It's violent. It's broken. But I do."

She finally turns to me then, and the look in her eyes, fuck, it wrecks me. Because it's not lust or loyalty or the carefully measured manipulation she was raised on. It's raw.

"We don't get to pick the families we're born into," she says, voice tight, "but I can choose the one I have moving forward."

My chest goes still, like something in me forgot how to breathe.

She turns back to Roman, stepping into the center of the space like it's a courtroom and she's laying down judgment.

"Those children in the cellar? They're not leverage. They're not supply. They're innocent. And if we don't do something, they die. My father wins. Catalyst becomes his machine, and every ounce of blood he spills will be because we let him."

A beat passes. Her voice cracks, but she doesn't stop.

"He needs to pay."

The silence that follows feels endless.

Roman doesn't speak.

He just watches her with a look I've never seen on his face. It's not pity. Not anger. It's something heavier, like he's seeing her for the first time, not as a Romanov, not as a pawn, but as a weapon she sharpened herself.

Then, slowly, he lowers the gun completely.

"You love him," he repeats, almost like he's trying to taste the truth of it.

She nods.

And for the first time since he walked through the door, Roman's eyes flick to me, not with rage, but something closer to reluctant understanding.

"You better not fuck this up, Kane," he mutters.

I don't say anything.

I just take her hand.

Tightly.

Like I never intend to let go.

Roman stares at our joined hands for a long moment. Not with disgust. Not even with disappointment.

With recognition.

That's what it is, recognition. Like he's looking at something he's already lived through. A decision he once made. A line he once crossed.

His jaw ticks, and then he sighs, a slow, tired exhale that seems to deflate some of the anger still bracing his spine.

"I'm no stranger to loving someone I shouldn't," he says quietly, not looking at either of us. "It doesn't go away, you know. That guilt. That weight. Doesn't matter how right it feels in the dark... when the lights come back on, you still have to face the wreckage."

There's a flicker of something in his expression then, something old and bruised. His gaze drifts toward the floor like he's seeing ghosts.

"You spend years convincing yourself you're doing it for the right reasons," he mutters. "To protect her. To use her. To save her. Doesn't matter. In the end, it always feels the same when the world turns on you."

He finally looks up, locking eyes with Katya. "So if you're going to choose him, you better be ready to bleed for it. Because there's no going back after this. Not for you. Not for him."

Katya doesn't blink. "I know."

Roman nods once, like that's the only answer he'll accept. Then he turns to me, all softness gone.

"Alright, Kane. What's the plan?"

It's a challenge.

A test.

The past few minutes might've cracked something open between us, but that doesn't mean the war is over. Trust, if it's going to exist between us again, needs to be earned. Brick by bloody brick.

I tighten my grip on Katya's hand, then release it, stepping forward toward the projection table in the center of the vault.

"We take over from the inside," I say, tapping the screen to reveal the underground schematics of the estate. "We isolate the loyalty cells, strip Dimitri of his leverage, and expose the blood supply line. If we make the children disappear, we collapse his hold on the donors. His empire bleeds dry from the root."

Roman steps beside me, eyes scanning the blueprint.

"And Dimitri?"

"He dies screaming," I answer. "But not before we rip everything he's built down around him."

Katya moves to my other side, her voice quiet but razor-sharp. "He'll never see it coming. He thinks we're loyal. He thinks I'm still his little girl."

Roman glances at her again. "Then I hope you're ready to break his heart."

She doesn't look away. "I'm ready to crush it."

33

Kill The Boy Echo Kane

Katya

I've never seen Catalyst this quiet.

Not when it's awake.

The underground war room buzzes with low light and static screens, the sound of shifting paper and fingers tapping keys filling the air like distant thunder. No one's yelling. No one's panicking. But there's a charge in the air, one that coils in my chest like a storm waiting to strike.

They're planning how to dismantle my father.

Echo stands at the center of the table, shirt sleeves rolled up, neck still red from where I kissed him hours ago, but his eyes hold nothing of that softness now. He's sharp angles and colder intentions, focused and calculating, the leader I've only just begun to understand outside the bedroom.

Roman stands to his right, arms crossed, jaw tight. He hasn't spoken much since the vault, but he doesn't have to. He commands presence without words. Whatever pain he confessed, whatever ghosts he cracked open for a moment back there, are gone now. This is the soldier in him. The weapon.

Across from them, Ana flips through aerial schematics, her red hair pulled into a severe braid, lips pressed into a line that says she doesn't trust me, not entirely. But she's here. And that says something.

Noah leans against the wall beside her, the glow of the screen illuminating the scars flecking his skin. Unlike the others, he's watching me more than the table. Not out of suspicion, but curiosity, like he's wondering where I'll be when this all starts burning.

I haven't spoken since they called me down here.

I just listen.

Watch.

Try not to think about how the walls on this screen, the outer perimeters of the estate I grew up in, used to feel like home.

Echo is speaking again. "We go in through the garden utility gate, east side. Minimal guard rotation, and Dimitri won't have them watching the greenhouse tunnels. He's arrogant, not stupid. He'll fortify the front, not the roots."

Roman taps the map. "Once we're inside, we split. Noah and I will sweep the upper levels, trigger the security loop, and wipe the interior grid. Ana and Echo head to the lower cells, extract the children first. Quiet. Fast. If we're seen, we abort."

Noah speaks up. "What about the blind girl in Cell Five?"

The question lands like a blow to my ribs. My stomach tightens.

I swallow. "She's mine."

Four pairs of eyes snap to me.

"I'm going with you," I say. "To the cellar. To the children. I'm not sitting behind a monitor while someone else walks through the hell my father built."

Ana raises a brow. "You sure you can stomach it, princess?"

I meet her gaze, voice steady. "I grew up above it. I think it's time I walk through it."

Echo doesn't interrupt. He watches me with something unreadable in his eyes, maybe pride. Maybe fear. Maybe both.

Roman exhales and looks to him. "Your call."

Echo looks at me for a long moment, then nods once.

"She goes."

The room shifts again. Back into motion. Back into planning.

But I feel it in my bones, this is the moment everything changes.

Because I'm not just betraying my father anymore.

I'm becoming the weapon that breaks him.

Ana clicks something on the tablet and the schematics shift again, rotating into a wireframe of the Romanov estate from beneath. There it is, the garden gate, tucked into a slope of ivy and old stone walls I used to hide behind as a child. I remember picking mint leaves there. I remember feeding the birds. I never knew there was a tunnel right beneath my feet used for smuggling blood.

No one speaks as the layout loads fully. The tunnels twist like veins beneath the manor, branching paths leading into darkness, some blocked off, others pulsing red where Catalyst scouts have marked security hotspots.

Echo leans forward, hands braced on the table. "The eastern greenhouse tunnel is our best entry point. It runs under the main ballroom and out toward the wine vault, which sits just above the cells. It's unguarded because no one's used it in over a decade. If we time it right, we'll get through without tripping the pressure sensors on the ground floor."

Roman eyes the map. "Time it wrong, and we'll trigger the silent perimeter lockdown. The house'll seal like a tomb."

"That's why we go during the gala." Ana speaks up, her voice crisp. "There's one scheduled three nights from now. He'll be too focused on the show to monitor the old pathways. Half the estate will be buzzing with political pawns and blood donors. Noise is cover."

I clench my fists against my thighs. That's how they talk about it, *blood donors*. Not prisoners. Not children. Just... supply.

"We'll have twenty minutes, tops," Noah adds. "Roman and I hit the estate security first, loop the feeds, spike the backups. We take out the exterior comm relay in the west corridor. If we're clean, we ghost the whole upper system."

Echo nods. "Once the grid's down, Ana, Katya, and I drop through the wine vault access hatch and get to the cells. There's a steel partition separating the older donor blocks from the new ones, Katya, you'll get us through."

I nod once, already feeling my pulse beginning to quicken. "The keypad in the third corridor, he uses my birthdate as the override."

Roman scoffs. "Cute."

"I know the codes. I know the layout. I know the staff schedules. He never thought I'd turn on him."

"That's because he still thinks he owns you," Echo says without looking up. "We'll make sure he doesn't walk out believing that."

Ana gestures to the far-right screen. A rotating digital model of the underground cell system appears, layered with blinking tags: Cell 1 through 12. Red means occupied. Two are flashing yellow.

"Those two," she says, pointing. "Children with irregular vitals. One's been moved from extraction protocol twice in the past week. If he's draining them that fast-"

"He is," I cut in quietly. "The girl in Cell Five... she has Romanov blood. I overheard him tell one of the handlers he's trying to refine her."

Echo turns his head toward me, slow and deliberate. "You're saying she's family?"

"I'm saying she's leverage."

A beat of silence falls again, heavier this time.

Then Echo straightens and squares his shoulders, his tone turning steel. "We get the girl. We get them all. Then we burn the place down."

Roman snorts. "We blow the tunnels after we're out. Send a message with it. No more quiet disappearances. No more whispers."

Ana's eyes flick toward me. "You sure you're not going to hesitate when it's time to put your father in the ground?"

The question lands like a slap, but I don't flinch. I meet her eyes, steady and cold.

"I won't hesitate," I say. "But I *am* going to look him in the eye when it happens."

Echo's hand brushes mine under the table, brief but grounding. A silent promise.

Roman closes the tablet with a snap. "Three nights. Be ready."

After the meeting ends, no one speaks for a while.

We just *know.*

The countdown has started.

Three nights.

Three nights of silence. Of shadows. Of pretending.

Echo and I won't be returning to Catalyst. We'll go back to the Romanov manor. Back to the halls where blood is currency and power is spoken in whispers. Back to the place where I was raised to obey, and now plan to betray.

It's the only way this works.

We stay inside.

We stay close.

We wear our loyalty like a second skin until it's time to tear it off and strike.

To my father, we are exactly what he needs us to be, his daughter, reclaimed; and Echo Kane, the wolf collared at last. He thinks Echo has shifted his allegiance from Catalyst to House Romanov, and he thinks I've fallen right into place, eager to serve the legacy I was born into.

We let him believe it.

We let him *feed* on the illusion.

Because the closer we stay to him, the easier it will be to gut him.

Echo and I have rehearsed every angle. Every entrance. Every exit. We've mapped out the estate in silence, marking routes for extraction and escape. There's a locked servant passage behind the wine vault, a second access point through the garden cellar, and a hidden stairwell that connects the west wing to the lower levels. I memorized those walls as a child. Now, I'll use them to tear his world down.

We communicate in looks, in touches, in half-muttered lies between the sheets. At night, we lie in the same bed just a few doors down from Dimitri's chamber, our skin still warm from his hands, our mouths still full of secrets.

We don't sleep. Not really.

We stay sharp. We listen.

We exist in this careful choreography of trust and deception, of hunger and hatred. Echo touches me like he needs the reminder that I'm still here, that we're still *us*. I kiss him back to remember what we're fighting for.

It's a strange kind of intimacy, to plan a man's downfall while sleeping under his roof.

To share meals with a monster.

To call him Father while plotting his execution.

But I've learned to survive on performance.

Now, I'll survive on vengeance.

Because the clock is ticking.

And when the moment comes, when the system goes dark and the security grid drops, Echo and I won't hesitate.

We'll take the keys. Open the doors. And unleash hell from the inside.

Dinner at my father's table always feels like a performance.

Tonight, it's a symphony of silverware on porcelain, quiet sips from crystal glasses, and silence dressed in civility. The chandelier overhead throws fractured gold light across the table, catching the sharp edges of Echo's profile and the glint of a blade resting beside a barely-touched steak.

My father sits at the head, calm and composed, dressed in his usual black-on-black tailored to perfection. His rings glint with each movement of his fork, his wine untouched as usual, he's never trusted what others drink.

I force myself to eat, each bite tasting like ash, my throat raw with the weight of the lies I'm about to feed him.

But Echo speaks first.

"Catalyst will be yours in three days."

His voice is smooth. Steady. Laced with quiet conviction.

The lie slips from his lips like he's telling the truth.

Dimitri looks up, amused, his gaze drifting from Echo to me. "So it's done, then?" he asks softly, as if the idea of conquering the most formidable resistance cell in the country is as simple as pouring a second glass of wine.

"Roman's lost the reins," Echo replies. "The fractures were already there, we just widened them."

I nod once, adding to the illusion. "The loyalty cells have started responding to new leadership. We've given them someone more... decisive to follow."

My father smiles, slow and sharp.

"Good. Catalyst has been wasted on idealists for too long. Soldiers who think sentiment is strategy."

Echo lifts his glass in mock agreement, but I can feel the tension behind his calm. He's wearing it like a suit of armor tonight, polished, silent, ready to draw blood the second it cracks.

"And Roman?" Dimitri asks, voice soft but expectant.

"Handled," Echo answers.

The word is a lie soaked in blood, but it lands exactly the way Dimitri wants it to.

He leans back in his chair, the shadows collecting in the hollows of his face, satisfied. "You've done well, both of you. You make a powerful pair. Loyalty and love, dangerous when aligned correctly."

He raises his glass, but still doesn't drink.

"To the beginning of a new era."

Echo and I lift ours. The glass is cool in my hand, but the wine burns on my tongue.

"To legacy," I murmur.

"To control," Echo says.

We drink.

And every swallow feels like swallowing glass.

My father watches us over the rim of his untouched glass, and I wonder, just for a second, if he suspects.

But he doesn't.

Not yet.

Because tonight, we've convinced him the empire is already his.

And in three days, we'll reduce it to ash.

34

I LOVE YOU

Katya

T he room is quiet when we return. Too quiet.

The door clicks softly behind us, locking the outside world away, the war, the deception, the venom coiled beneath my father's smile. Gone are the lies we fed him, the promises Echo made with a voice soaked in betrayal. All of it is behind that door. For now.

I don't move. I stand in the middle of the room, still wearing the light dress that made my father say I looked like my mother, still wearing the necklace that carries the weight of our name. The silence stretches like a thin wire, threatening to snap.

But Echo doesn't speak.

Not yet.

Instead, he walks to me slowly, as if approaching something fragile. As if touching me too quickly might break whatever this moment is becoming.

He stops just in front of me. No rush. No command.

His hand lifts, fingers brushing a strand of hair behind my ear, then resting on my jaw like I'm something delicate he's not sure he's worthy of holding.

"You were perfect," he murmurs, voice hoarse with restraint.

I open my mouth to say something, to deflect, to deny, to shift the weight of his praise elsewhere, but his thumb traces my bottom lip and the words die there.

His touch isn't demanding.

It's gentle.

And it wrecks me.

"You looked him in the eye," he whispers. "And promised him a kingdom we're going to destroy."

I exhale, shaky. "It didn't feel brave."

"That's what made it brave."

His eyes are molten when they meet mine, not with fire, but with depth. With knowing. Not the man who claimed me in the shadows, who pressed me into sheets and whispered filth into my skin, but the man who's been quietly learning me all along.

"I need to say something," he breathes. "And I need you to believe it."

I nod, barely.

His fingers trail down my cheek, brushing the side of my throat, skimming over the faint mark he left nights ago with teeth and hunger.

"I love you."

The words land like a knife, not in pain, but in precision.

He could've said it while he was inside me. Could've groaned it against my throat or choked it out between thrusts. But he says it now.

Quiet. Steady. Undeniable.

My breath catches.

"I should've told you sooner," he continues. "I didn't want to. I didn't think I could. But somewhere between you spitting blood and defying every fucking person who's ever tried to own you... I fell in love with you, Katya."

His hands find my waist and still don't pull. They settle. They stay.

"I don't want your pain. I don't want your allegiance. I want you."

I'm trembling before I realize it. Not from fear. From something deeper. Something older than both of us.

Echo leans in, forehead resting against mine. His breath mixes with mine, warm and soft. When his lips brush mine, it's not a kiss. It's a question.

And I answer it by stepping into him, arms around his neck, mouth pressing back into his with something unspoken and heavy. My fingers tangle in his hair as his hands finally pull me closer, gently, reverently, like he's afraid I'll vanish.

When he walks me backward, it's slow. Methodical. He doesn't throw me onto the bed like he has before. He lays me down like something precious.

The dress falls from my shoulders inch by inch, his fingers dragging the silk with care, not haste. His mouth follows, pressing kisses across every inch of newly revealed skin. My collarbone. My sternum. The top of each rib like he's charting a map only he gets to read.

When he pulls the dress fully off, he pauses.

Just stares.

Like I'm the most dangerous and beautiful thing he's ever seen.

His hands skim down my sides, his thumbs pressing lightly into the curve of my hips. He kisses my stomach, then lower, soft and warm, nothing like the sharp, hungry man I've known. His mouth moves as if worshiping, not claiming.

I reach for his shirt, and he lets me undress him slowly, each button undone revealing skin I already know but need to touch again. This time differently. This time real.

When we're both bare, he doesn't rush.

He crawls over me, nose brushing mine, eyes locked to mine. His hand cups the side of my face as he lines himself up, and when he finally presses inside, I gasp, not from the stretch, but the way it feels.

Like coming home to something I never believed could be mine.

There's no feral pace. No bruising need.

He moves with devastating slowness, hips rolling into mine like he's savoring every second inside me. His breath hitches when I moan, and he swallows the sound with a kiss so soft, it makes my chest ache.

"Say it again," I whisper against his lips.

"I love you," he breathes. "So fucking much."

I wrap my legs around him tighter, arms clinging to his back, nails pressing into muscle as he thrusts deeper, each movement drawing sounds from me I didn't know I could make. Moans. Whimpers. His name.

His hands find mine and lace our fingers together, pinning them above my head as he sinks in deeper. Slower. Deeper again.

I break apart beneath him. Quiet, trembling. Overwhelmed by the slow, rhythmic drag of him inside me. It's not just physical. It's everything.

He doesn't stop when I cum. He keeps going, hips rocking into me with the kind of control that makes my entire body shake. My second release creeps up slower, building heat in my belly, spiraling until I can't think, can't breathe.

"I need you," I gasp. "Don't stop. Please, Echo, don't-"

"I won't," he groans, thrusting harder now. "I'm not going anywhere."

And when he finally cums, it's with a low, guttural moan into my neck. His body shakes above mine, spilling deep, his arms tight around me like he's afraid I'll slip through his fingers if he lets go.

But I don't.

Because I'm here.

And for once... so is he.

He collapses onto his forearms above me, chest heaving, his breath still tangled with mine. His face is buried in my neck, lips pressing into the sweat-damp skin beneath my ear, and I think, for a moment, it's over.

But it isn't.

He doesn't pull out. Doesn't move away. He just *stays* there, deep inside me, like he belongs.

And then he kisses me.

Not my lips this time.

My throat.

The slope of my shoulder.

The curve of my breast.

Each kiss is soft. Lingering. Not driven by lust, but by something softer. Warmer. He doesn't move his hips. Just touches. Just *sees* me.

"You don't know," he whispers, voice shaking, "how long I've wanted to love someone like this."

His hand trails down my side, not with hunger, but reverence. Fingers glide over the dip of my waist, the bruises he left nights ago, the curve of my hip. He kisses the inside of my wrist, right over my pulse.

"I love you," he murmurs, again and again, like saying it once wasn't enough. Like saying it is a vow.

"I love you when you lie."

A kiss to my collarbone.

"When you fight."

His lips press just above my breast.

"When you cry."

Another kiss, lower. Slower.

"When you scream my name like I'm the only thing holding you together."

His mouth traces the skin beneath my ribs, and my breath hitches.

"I love you when you pretend not to need anyone."

He moves farther down, spreading my legs again, not to take, but to taste.

"I love you when you let me in."

His mouth meets my dripping cunt with the kind of patience that makes my head tilt back, my spine arch. He's not rushing. He's not proving anything. He's *worshipping*.

He licks me slowly, tongue moving in slow, perfect circles as his arms wrap beneath my thighs and hold me like I might float away. I sob his name, already too raw, too wrecked, but he doesn't stop. He moans into me, lips devouring me like I'm the first god he's ever believed in.

Every time I try to come down, he pulls me back to the edge. Every tremor, every breathless gasp, he *wants* it. Not for dominance. Not for control.

For *me*.

Because this is his way of saying it.

Over and over again.

I come apart on his mouth, shaking, legs locking around his shoulders, tears slipping down my cheeks from the sheer intensity of it. But *still*, he doesn't stop.

He only lifts his head when I can't take anymore, when I'm shaking so hard I'm afraid I'll fall through the mattress. His lips are slick with me, and his eyes, god, his *eyes*, are dark and reverent and full of something I never thought I'd see on his face.

Devotion.

He crawls back up my body, one kiss at a time, until he's above me again, brushing hair away from my face, his palm cradling my cheek.

"I will burn every man that tries to take you from me," he whispers. "I will ruin every man who looks at you like you're his to have."

I reach for him, pulling him into another kiss, softer now. Slower.

He shifts his hips, still hard, still aching, and when he slides back into me, slow, deep, perfect, I gasp, overwhelmed all over again.

"I love you," he says again, right against my lips. "I love you when you fall apart. I love you when you fight me. I love you every way there is."

He moves in me like a promise, like he's not trying to fuck me, but *keep* me.

And I let him.

Because I love him too.

Because for the first time in a life full of chains and control, I feel *free*.

And it's with him.

Always him.

He's still inside me when he lowers us gently onto the bed, his body pressed to mine like he can't bear even an inch of space between us. His lips graze my cheek, then my jaw, then the corner of my mouth, and for a moment, neither of us says a word.

There's only breath.

Heartbeats.

Sweat-slick skin and the sound of the sheets shifting as I move beneath him.

But something stirs in my chest, warm and unbearable. I want more. Not of him *on* me.

Of him *beneath* me.

Not to reclaim control, not to prove anything. I just want to *see* him. Every inch of him. I want to take my time. To feel what it's like to love him back—not with words, but with every part of me.

"Lie back," I whisper, voice hoarse but steady.

His brows lift, just a little. He studies my face like he's searching for hesitation. There isn't any.

Wordlessly, he shifts onto his back, hands falling away, giving himself over to me without resistance. His chest rises and falls with the kind of anticipation that makes my thighs ache all over again.

I straddle him slowly, palms splayed against his chest, my legs trembling with the sensitivity of what came before, but needing him again, deeper this time. Different.

His cock slides against me, still hard, slick with the remnants of us. I sink down slowly, inch by inch, gasping at the stretch, the way it fills me again like I've been empty without him.

His hands grip my hips, not to guide, just to *feel*.

But I don't move. Not yet.

Instead, I rest my hands on either side of his face, thumbs brushing his cheekbones. He looks up at me like I'm gravity itself.

"I love you," I say.

His eyes widen, not with shock, but something softer. Something like awe.

"I love you, Echo." My voice breaks on his name. "I shouldn't. God, I *shouldn't*. But I do. And I don't care what it means. I don't care how it ends. I just want *this*. You. Us. Even if it's only for a little while."

His hands slide up my waist, slow and reverent. "Say it again," he whispers.

I lean down, lips brushing his. "I love you."

And then I start to move.

Slow at first, grinding down, hips rolling in a steady rhythm that makes us both gasp. My palms brace against his chest, and his hands stay at my waist, gripping hard enough to anchor me, but gentle enough to let me lead.

He moans beneath me, eyes locked on mine like he doesn't want to miss a second. I ride him with everything I am, every scar, every scream, every piece of broken glass I've ever carried. It's all here, laid bare between us.

Each movement is a confession.

Each grind is a promise.

He rises to meet my pace, thrusts getting deeper, slower, perfect. My hands find his, fingers lacing together above his head. I lower myself until our foreheads touch, our mouths sharing every shaky breath.

"I love you," he says again, and again, and again, like it's the only truth left in a world full of rot and fire.

When I cum, it's not loud. It's not desperate.

It's *complete*.

And when he follows, spilling into me with a broken moan and his hands gripping me like he'll never let go, I know, *this* is real.

No lies.

No power plays.

Just love.

Raw and terrifying.

And ours.

The world is still.

The air hums with our breath, slow and uneven. My body rests atop his, every inch of skin flushed and damp, my head tucked beneath his chin like it belongs there. His hands move slowly over my back, just fingers trailing across spine and shoulder blades, like he can't stop touching me even now.

It's quiet. Not the kind of silence that weighs like guilt or fear, but something *softer.* A kind of silence that settles into the bones. A peace I've never known.

Neither of us says a word for a long time.

His heartbeat is steady beneath my cheek, echoing into my chest like a metronome that finally found its rhythm.

I could fall asleep like this.

But then his voice breaks the stillness, low, raw, and quiet, like he's saying something meant only for the shadows between us.

"I kept you in my cage," he murmurs, fingers still tracing my spine. "And somehow... you kept me in yours."

I lift my head slowly, meeting his eyes in the dark. There's no smirk. No arrogance. Just a kind of broken honesty that makes my heart twist.

His fingers tuck a strand of hair behind my ear, lingering there like he's memorizing the shape of me. "You were supposed to be leverage. A way in. I told myself that from the start."

He swallows, eyes scanning mine. "But it stopped being about tactics the second you looked me in the eye and didn't flinch. The second you saw the monster... and didn't run."

"You were never a monster to me," I whisper.

A faint smile tugs at his mouth, but it doesn't last. "I was. I am. But with you, I feel like I could be more than that. Or at least... less."

I press a kiss to the center of his chest, right over his heart. "You're already more."

He pulls me in tighter, arms wrapping around me like he's afraid I'll disappear if he lets go. "I don't know how to love gently, Katya. I don't know how to do this the right way."

"There is no right way," I murmur. "There's only *this*. Us."

His lips brush my temple. "Then I'm yours. Whatever happens next... I'm yours."

The words fall into the space between us like a vow.

And I believe him.

For the first time in my life, I believe someone who's sworn to stay.

We lie there in the dark, tangled in sweat and love and whatever strange fate has pulled us together. Outside these walls, the world is still a battlefield.

But right now, wrapped in his arms, it feels a little less cruel.

Because he's not Echo, the commander.

Not Echo, the weapon.

He's just *him*.

And somehow... he's mine.

35

MINE

KATYA

The gown fits like a noose.

Tight at the ribs, cinched at the waist, the fabric gleams with golden thread woven into the black silk like veins of power stitched straight into my skin. It's one of my father's favorites, picked not for my comfort, but for how it frames me. How it reminds everyone in the room whose blood I carry.

And whose future I've been promised to.

I don't look at myself in the mirror. I've seen enough reflections in this house to know they lie.

Two of my father's attendants circle me like vultures, their hands cool and detached as they finish adjusting the clasps on the back of the gown, brushing invisible lint from the bodice, smoothing my hair with clinical precision. I feel like a doll in a box. Pretty. Perfect. Hollow.

One of them leans in to adjust the low-cut neckline and I barely suppress the urge to slap his hand away.

They don't speak to me. Not really. They speak around me. About me.

"Dress is flawless."

"She'll turn every head."

"Dimitri will be pleased."

The words slide over me like oil. Cold. Unclean. I stand still, jaw tight, wondering how many more lies I'll have to wear before I can finally tear them off and breathe.

A knock sounds once. Sharp. Commanding.

Before either man can react, the door swings open.

And then he's there.

Echo steps into the room like he's claiming territory. Dressed in a black suit that fits him like a second skin, the collar of his shirt open at the throat, his eyes darker than the shadows he walks through.

The moment he enters, the temperature shifts.

He doesn't bark or raise his voice. He doesn't have to.

"You're dismissed," he says, low and final.

The two attendants hesitate, barely, but one look from Echo has them moving. Fast. They disappear down the hall, the door clicking softly behind them, leaving only silence in their wake.

And him.

I don't turn. I stay facing the mirror, my heart hammering now, not from fear, but from something hotter. He watches me from behind, and I feel it like a current running under my skin. The weight of his stare. The quiet reverence in it.

"You clean up nicely," I murmur.

He doesn't answer right away. Instead, I hear the soft shuffle of fabric as he reaches into his jacket, withdrawing something I don't have to look at to recognize.

His steps are slow, deliberate, and when I finally turn, he's already standing in front of me with the compact silver pistol cradled in his palm. It gleams under the low chandelier light, sleek, feminine, deadly.

"It's time," he says softly. "We go in armed. Always."

I nod, heart thudding harder now for an entirely different reason.

He lowers himself to his knees in front of me, like a knight in devotion, and my breath stutters. There's something unholy about the way he kneels. Something *dangerous* about a man like him bowing for a girl like me.

Not in submission.

But in worship.

His hands slide up my calf, slow and reverent, gathering the hem of my gown until the cool air kisses the bare skin of my thigh. His fingers ghost over my inner leg, and I swear my pulse migrates there, drumming wild beneath his touch.

He wraps the leather holster around my thigh, firm but gentle, his thumb dragging over the soft flesh just below the strap. His breath hitches when his eyes flick up to meet mine and find me watching him.

"You can't think of any other use for it?" I ask, my voice a soft dare, honeyed with heat.

He freezes.

The question hangs between us, heavy and charged.

"You can't think of any other use for it?"

He freezes.

And then, something shifts. The air thickens with tension, the kind that makes my thighs clench and my breath stalls. He looks up at me slowly, still crouched at my feet, his hands resting just beneath the hem of my gown. His eyes burn with something darker now, need laced with reverence. Hunger laced with restraint.

His fingers trace the line of the holster strapped tight around my thigh, then slip under the leather, tugging the small silver pistol from its place.

For a moment, he just looks at it. Holds it in his palm like he's weighing not the steel, but the *moment.*

And then his gaze lifts to mine.

"You trust me?" he asks, voice low. Controlled.

My pulse pounds in my ears. "Always."

That one word unlocks him.

He stands, slow and deliberate, the pistol still resting in his hand. The weight of it looks obscene in his grip. Wrong and holy all at once.

Without a word, he backs me toward the bed, hand slipping around my waist. When the backs of my knees hit the mattress, I sink, heart racing, skin burning. He follows me down, pushing the skirts of my gown up until they pool around my waist, baring my thighs, my hips, my heat.

He kneels between my legs again, and the look on his face is almost reverent, like I'm something sacred. A battlefield and a church.

He sets the gun on the inside of my thigh.

Just the cold press of the barrel, resting against the soft skin there, makes me gasp. I shift, but he grabs my hips with firm hands, holding me still.

"Stay," he murmurs. "Let me worship you with this."

I nod, breathless.

His touch is slow, precise. He trails the gun up the inside of my thigh, the cool metal dragging against overheated skin, and my breath stutters. It's not the danger of it, it's the trust. The obscene intimacy of letting him this close with something that could ruin me.

He presses the barrel against the thin lace of my panties and watches me squirm.

"You're soaking," he murmurs. "From this."

"Yes," I breathe.

He moves the gun in slow, teasing strokes, dragging it up and down my slit through the lace, the metal slicking quickly with my arousal. The sensation is maddening, cold steel against swollen heat, the edge of the barrel pressing into the thin barrier of fabric like a promise.

I arch against it, needing more.

Needing *him*.

"Beg for it," he growls, voice ragged.

"Please," I whisper, legs falling wider. "Please, Echo...fuck me with it."

His breath catches.

And then he tears the lace aside with one sharp tug.

The first press of the barrel inside me is slow, so slow I cry out from the stretch, the chill, the sheer filth of it. He watches every inch disappear, his thumb rubbing slow circles on my inner thigh as he thrusts the gun in and out, using it like he knows exactly how to unravel me.

Every glide is precise.

Every twist deliberate.

My hands claw at the sheets, my head falling back as my hips grind toward the rhythm he sets. The pressure builds fast, sharp and overwhelming, as my body pulses around cold steel and unbearable need.

"You feel that?" he whispers, leaning in close, lips brushing my ear. "That's mine. All of it. Every part of you...*mine.*"

I moan, loud, broken, completely undone.

He curls the gun just right and my world snaps. My body jerks, release crashing through me like fire. I cry out, trembling, thighs clenching around his shoulders as he fucks me through it, letting me ride the wave until I'm limp beneath him.

Only then does he pull it free, slow, wet, glistening.

He places the gun, slick and warm now, back into the holster at my thigh, his hands lingering.

"You're armed," he says, voice husky. "And thoroughly fucked."

I blink up at him, dazed. "That's one hell of a pre-op ritual."

He smirks. Then kisses me, deep, slow, claiming.

"Next time," he murmurs against my mouth, "you'll beg me to use the silencer."

36

MY SALVATION

KATYA

Applause rings through the ballroom like shrapnel, hollow and performative, echoing between crystal and gold. My father basks in it, standing at the top of the staircase like some blessed monarch giving his people permission to breathe.

My heart pounds behind my ribs. Not with nerves. Not even with anger. With dread.

Something's coming.

Echo must feel it too, because his arm shifts against me, tightening just slightly, protective without drawing attention. His body remains still, but I can feel the subtle coil of violence rolling through him like a loaded spring. His patience is measured. His restraint, razor-thin.

Dimitri raises his glass again, and the room hushes.

"Tonight marks a turning point," he says, smiling that smooth, manufactured smile. "The union between House Romanov and Catalyst is not just a strategic move, it's a legacy in motion. A bloodline strengthened. A future secured."

I feel Echo exhale slowly beside me, like he's counting every breath. Every second until this all falls apart.

"But there's more," my father continues. "Something I must speak plainly of."

The crowd leans in, not physically, but mentally. You can feel it. The air tightens like a noose.

My father's eyes find me.

I stand straighter, jaw clenched, every muscle locked beneath the silk of my gown.

"For much of her life," he says, tone shifting into something softer, dangerously soft-"I didn't believe my daughter would offer anything meaningful to our cause."

Echo bristles. I feel the movement ripple through his frame.

My father goes on, his voice taking on a mockery of affection. "She was... sensitive. Emotional. Obstinate. But what wounded me most, was the discovery that, after a certain punishment, she would likely never bear children."

The words land like a blade, twisting.

All the air leaves my lungs.

I don't move.

I don't blink.

But something inside me cracks.

Echo turns his head sharply toward me, his brows knitting, but he says nothing. He's watching me now. Reading me like a loaded dossier. Every detail. Every wound.

Dimitri smiles faintly, tilting his glass. "A regret of mine, truthfully. I should have tempered my methods. But discipline must be taught, and obedience must be earned, even if the cost... is legacy."

The crowd doesn't know how to respond. There's a moment where the hush becomes suffocating. Some guests murmur into their glasses. Others look politely away. A few even glance at me with something close to pity.

I'd rather be shot.

Beside me, Echo doesn't move for a long beat. Then, slowly, methodically, he reaches up and adjusts the cuff of his shirt as if to keep from breaking something.

Dimitri's voice sharpens once more. "And yet... now with Echo Kane at her side, perhaps the Romanov line may continue in other ways."

Another ripple of laughter, hollow and unbearable.

I feel my throat tighten, breath shallow. I want to run, scream, break glass, but I do none of those things.

Because I know how to survive my father.

And I won't let him win this moment.

Echo finally turns to face me. One hand lifts to brush a curl from my cheek, gentle where the rest of the world has always been cruel.

His voice is low, just for me. "He's wrong."

My lashes flutter, vision blurring for the first time tonight. "You don't know that."

His hand slips lower, to my jaw, grounding me with the steadiness of it. "I don't need you to be something *useful* to be something *worthy*, Katya."

A breath shudders out of me.

"And if he ever touches you with words like that again," he adds, voice barely containing the violence beneath, "I'll do more than break hands."

My father raises his glass once more, oblivious to the storm forming just below him.

"To legacy," he toasts.

But all I can think about is the moment that's coming, when this marble palace cracks, when blood pools beneath the crystal chandeliers, and when the father who once beat the future out of me stares down the same pistol Echo used to worship me.

Not as a daughter.

Not as an heir.

But as a reckoning.

The glasses lift again.

"To legacy," My father says smoothly, voice rich with pride. But that pride is hollow, sharpened at the edges by cruelty.

And yet, somehow, he isn't finished.

"My daughter," he continues, "has always been a puzzle, fragile in the worst of ways. But perhaps her purpose has finally been revealed." His smile curls. "Not through obedience, nor brilliance. But simply... by who she now spreads her legs for."

That's it.

That's the moment the storm breaks in Echo's eyes.

His jaw tightens so hard I can see the muscles twitch. One hand balls into a fist at his side, the other clenched tightly around the stem of his glass. But when he moves, it's with terrifying control.

He releases my waist and steps forward, not toward my father directly, but to the foot of the marble staircase where the host still stands smugly above the crowd.

The room stills. No more laughter now. Only silence.

Echo lifts his glass.

"May I offer a toast?" he asks.

Dimitri looks vaguely amused, a hand gesturing with casual permission. "By all means, Echo Kane. You've earned your place at the table."

Echo climbs the first step. Then another. The crowd shifts, eyes locking onto the two men now standing side by side, Romanov patriarch and Catalyst commander.

Echo stands just one step below, but in presence, in force, in *gravity*, he towers.

He turns to face the room, raising his glass.

"Legacy," he echoes, voice clear and dark. "A word we cling to when our names are too soaked in blood to mean anything else. A word cowards use when they're too afraid to change, and monsters use when they've run out of excuses for the bodies buried beneath their floors."

A murmur rolls through the ballroom like distant thunder.

My father stiffens.

Echo continues, not looking at him. Not yet.

"I've served many empires. Brought them to heel. Burned others to the ground. But none have ever tried to disguise their rot with the perfume of lineage quite like this one."

Now he turns, facing my father fully.

"And tonight, in front of every trembling mask in this room, I want to make one thing clear."

He raises his glass higher, then tips it toward me.

"To the only Romanov I'll ever kneel for."

I can't breathe.

The crowd doesn't move.

My father's expression twists, confusion and fury flickering behind his eyes like static. He opens his mouth to respond, but Echo beats him to it, leaning in close, his voice low enough only we can hear.

"And one day soon," Echo murmurs, "this toast will be for your fucking funeral."

He knocks his glass gently against my father's, the crystal *clinking* between them like a bell tolling for the dead.

Then he turns and descends the stairs, glass untouched.

Back to me.

Back to war.

The second Echo squeezes my wrist twice, I know.

There's no turning back.

Not from the plan. Not from the blood. Not from the war that's about to rip through the Romanov estate like rot surfacing beneath polished wood.

He steps back from me without a word, hand brushing my hip one last time beneath my gown, as if to remind me I'm armed. I am. I have the gun Echo pressed against my thigh. I have my conviction. I have *him*.

And I have a father who is about to choke on the last lie he ever told.

Across the room, Roman nods from behind his mask, disguised in servant black, hands steady at his sides. On the upper balcony, Ana watches everything like a hawk perched above the battlefield, hidden beneath velvet shadows. Noah is already out of sight, slipping into the back corridor with a tray of flutes no one noticed him replacing.

And then-

Darkness.

The chandeliers stutter twice. A flicker. A warning.

Then black.

Gasps fill the room. Chairs screech backward. The quartet cuts off mid-note. A glass hits the floor and shatters. Somewhere across the ballroom, someone screams, not loud, but sharp. The kind of scream that sounds like someone trying not to scream.

My heart slams against my ribs.

And then the red lights pulse on, bloody and artificial. The backup generators flood the room with emergency lighting, casting every guest, every pillar, every sculpture in a wash of violent crimson.

For one suspended breath, the world seems still.

And then the bodies begin to fall.

It's not a fight. Not yet.

It's a reckoning.

The poisoned champagne, Noah's doing. He must have worked through the list himself, targeting every loyalist with surgical precision. There's no flailing. No cries for help. Only the dull *thump* of bodies collapsing onto the floor. A man near the fountain slumps into a seated position, eyes wide and glassy. A woman in a glittering emerald gown lets out a garbled gasp before her knees give out beneath her, fingers clawing at her throat as she crumples like discarded silk.

All around us, people are dying. Quietly. Elegantly. Exactly the way this family built their empire.

Echo doesn't flinch.

He's already moving, eyes sweeping the room for threats, hand slipping into the inner lining of his coat to draw the pistol holstered there. My feet move of their own accord, skirts of my gown swishing through the marble-drenched chaos, but I don't feel weightless anymore.

I feel *anchored*.

Because I know what's happening. I helped plan it. Every hallway, every weak point, every locked door, we mapped it out. We practiced it in whispers and glances, in late-night meetings lit only by Echo's smirk and Roman's growl. This isn't revenge.

It's precision.

Up above, there's a sharp report of a rifle firing. A guard drops near the entrance, skull snapped back in an instant. Ana. Her position is perfect. Her aim, deadly.

Below, Roman steps into the center of the chaos and rips off his mask, firing a single round into the air. The sound is deafening, and the entire ballroom freezes.

"This is a hostile takeover!" Roman's voice booms over the confusion. "Drop your weapons and live. Raise them, and you won't."

Some guards falter. Some shift toward cover.

Others, fools, move to draw.

Three more shots ring out, clean and synchronized. Ana again. She's not missing. Not tonight. One falls by the wine table, another near the stairs, another half-raised his gun before his kneecap shattered beneath him.

Echo reaches back for me and pulls me in tight to his side, eyes scanning like a machine. "Stay with me. Do not hesitate. Shoot anyone who touches you."

"I won't be the one hesitating," I reply, voice low and steel-edged as I lift my skirt and draw the pistol from its thigh holster.

All around us, the ballroom is descending into calculated chaos. The survivors flee toward the exits, only to be met by Catalyst operatives storming the doors from the outside. Silencers, stun rounds, and red gas. It's like watching a machine devour itself.

And I don't look away.

I *won't*.

Because I was raised inside this house. I know the walls, the secrets, the ghosts and tonight, I'm helping tear them apart, brick by gilded brick.

"Katya," Echo says, tugging my arm. "We move now. We're going for your father."

"Where?"

He looks at me, voice cool and final.

"The panic room."

Of course he would have one.

Dimitri Romanov always assumed the world might one day turn on him.

He just never imagined it would be *his daughter* leading the charge.

The air inside the panic room feels heavier than the rest of the manor, as if even the walls are holding their breath.

My father is slumped against the far stone wall, coughing blood down his shirt, his pistol long forgotten on the floor. His pride is cracked wide open now, and for the first time in my life, I see him for what he truly is. Small. Human. Pathetic. All the bravado, the speeches, the violence, it all fades when you're faced with your own mortality and no one left to command.

And he knows it's coming.

That's why he looks at me with hollow, almost pleading eyes.

Not at Echo. Not at the man who slammed him against the wall and nearly crushed his windpipe.

He looks at *me*.

Because he knows I'm the one who gets the final word.

Echo stands beside me, vibrating with fury, gun still drawn. His chest rises and falls in sharp bursts, like each breath is a war he's barely winning. I can see the storm in his eyes, the craving to end this. To empty a clip into the man who made me bleed. Who carved scars into my skin and called it love.

But he doesn't.

Not until I speak.

"Katya," he murmurs, voice low, teeth clenched. "If you don't want to do it... I will."

I shake my head once, slow. Not because I don't want to. But because I *have* to.

He steps back, jaw tight, and lowers the gun.

He lets me.

My heels click softly across the floor as I approach my father. Each step feels deliberate, like I'm walking across every year he stole from me. Every humiliation. Every slap. Every whisper behind closed doors that I was a disappointment. That I was broken. That I was a failed vessel.

He tries to sit up straighter, but the pain folds him in half. I stand over him, gun resting against my thigh.

"You could've had a daughter," I whisper. "But you wanted a soldier. A machine. A womb."

He grimaces, blood staining his teeth. "You were never strong enough."

A bitter smile plays at my lips. "I was always stronger than you. You just couldn't stand the thought of it."

I lift the gun. He flinches.

But I don't fire.

Not yet.

I kneel beside him, level with the man who taught me everything I should never have learned.

"You punished me for not giving you an heir," I say softly. "You carved that punishment into my body. And now? The bloodline ends with you."

His expression wavers. Something shifts behind his eyes, not fear. Not regret. Just the sinking realization that I was never his to control.

The gun rises.

I don't hesitate.

One shot. Clean. Center mass.

His body jerks. Then slumps.

And that's it.

Just like that... it's over.

The silence that follows is suffocating. Not because I feel guilt. But because I feel free. Light. Like I've cut the tether that held me underwater for far too long.

I don't cry.

I don't collapse.

I just stare at him, heart steady, breathing even.

Behind me, Echo moves. His footsteps echo softly in the chamber as he walks toward me, not fast, not frantic. Just sure.

When he reaches me, he drops to one knee, cupping the side of my face with hands still trembling from restraint. His thumb brushes across my cheek. Not because there are tears, but because he wants to touch. To connect. To *know* I'm real. Here. Alive.

"I wanted to be the one," he murmurs, voice low, wrecked. "But watching you... Katya, you were...*fuck*. You were every-thing."

I lean into his touch, fingers curling into the lapels of his shirt.

"I needed it to be me," I whisper. "I needed to be the one who ended him."

"You were," he says. "And you were magnificent."

He leans forward and kisses me, slow and reverent. Not a kiss of dominance or hunger, but of awe. His lips press to mine like a promise. Like a prayer.

"I kept you in a cage," he whispers, pressing his forehead to mine. "And somehow... you kept me in yours."

A small smile ghosts across my lips.

"You saved me from the real monsters," I whisper. "You were the salvation I dreamed of."

37

Cleanse It With Fire

Echo

The Romanov manor doesn't breathe anymore.

It groans.

The kind of sound old bones make when they're left in the cold too long, cracking, brittle, rotting from the inside. The walls aren't walls now. They're tombstones. Plated in gold. Painted in family portraits that are going to burn the second I give the order.

Catalyst moves through it like a pack of wolves, disciplined and deliberate. Every room is accounted for. Every loyalist body is tagged. Every hard drive, ledger, blood-stained ledger, and secret compartment ripped open like the guts of a dead animal. We're not just clearing the estate.

We're dissecting it.

And for the first time in years, I don't feel the weight of my name pulling me in two.

Because she's here.

And she's still breathing.

I spot her from the corridor that leads into the conservatory, what used to be Dimitri's favorite room. A glass atrium where he played god. Where he cut roses at the stem and admired the way they bled on marble tiles.

Now, that same floor is covered in blankets.

In children.

And in Katya.

She's kneeling between them, her once-immaculate gown torn and soaked at the hem, her palms bloodied in ways I know aren't hers. The moment she leans forward and wipes a child's tear with the sleeve of her ruined dress, my throat closes. Her fingers are trembling, but her voice, though I can't hear it, is steady. Reassuring.

One of the boys clings to her sleeve like she's the only solid thing in the world. She doesn't flinch. Doesn't move. She lets him.

She lets them all.

And maybe that's what wrecks me more than anything. I've seen her powerful. Seductive. Weaponized. But this? This quiet kind of strength, the way she holds broken things like she was made to put them back together, makes my hands ache just to touch her.

I start toward her.

And that's when the shot goes off.

Crack.

Not an echo, not a warning.

A bullet.

I turn, but I already know.

Nikolai.

Noah stands behind him, arm still extended, smoke curling from the barrel of his pistol. Nikolai's body hits the marble like a sack of wet meat, blood spraying in an arc across the ivory floor. The back of his skull caves, just like I'd always imagined it would.

He doesn't get a last word.

He doesn't deserve one.

Noah doesn't blink. He just lowers the gun, slides it into the back of his waistband, and looks at me like he's asking if we're done here.

I nod.

We are.

Roman's footsteps approach before I speak. He smells like smoke and steel. His knuckles are torn. One sleeve is soaked in someone else's blood. When he stops beside me, neither of us says anything at first. We both look toward the conservatory, where Katya is still holding the boy.

Still breathing.

Still *there.*

"She's not the same girl you brought into this," Roman finally says.

"She's not a girl anymore," I murmur. "She's fire. All of it."

He glances sideways at me, expression unreadable. "You love her."

It isn't a question.

And I don't need to answer.

Because it's in the way I look at her. In the way I haven't exhaled since she walked into that ballroom hours ago. In the way her voice could cut through the worst of me and still sound like absolution.

"She told me she loved you," Roman adds.

That makes me pause.

"She said it," he clarifies, folding his arms, watching the way my jaw tightens. "To both of us. Said she chose you over blood. Over family. That those kids meant more to her than legacy."

My chest aches.

"I knew it was real," Roman continues, "when she said you were her family now."

I swallow hard, watching her run her fingers through a little girl's matted hair, her voice soft, patient.

"She's not just mine," I finally say. "I'm hers."

Roman nods once. "Then let's give her the world she burned this one for."

We both stand in silence a moment longer, watching as she gently lifts a child into her arms and rises to her feet.

And in that moment, covered in ash, bruises, blood, and softness, she's not a Romanov.

She's a new dynasty.

The one we'll bleed for.

The one we'll rebuild everything around.

I've seen death in a thousand variations, quiet, violent, pathetic, cruel.

But what I see now isn't death.

It's something worse.

She stumbles into the conservatory like a ghost, one arm clutching her ribcage, the other reaching for something that isn't there. Her gown is shredded, pearls torn from the collar and scattered like teeth along the hallway. Her hair, once always pinned, polished, immaculate, is matted and streaked with ash. Blood seeps from the corner of her mouth, and when her eyes land on Katya, they widen with something that looks like recognition... but not relief.

There's no relief left in her.

Only ruin.

Dimitri's wife.

Katya's mother.

The woman I've barely heard speak since the first dinner I sat across from her.

She staggers once more, then collapses to her knees, frail arms reaching forward, and Katya catches her before she hits the marble. Dropping to the floor with her, Katya's arms wrap around her mother's too-light frame, holding her like she's trying to keep the pieces from crumbling all over again.

"Mom," Katya whispers, voice breaking.

The sound of it is a blade.

Her mother doesn't respond at first. Her body trembles. Her fingers dig into Katya's back with surprising strength, as if something inside her is finally waking up after years of sleep. Her mouth moves, lips parting against Katya's shoulder.

"I tried to protect you," she rasps. "I tried, I swear. I never wanted him to take it that far."

Katya stiffens.

But she doesn't pull away.

She holds her tighter.

"I know," Katya whispers, voice ragged. "I know."

Across the room, I stay still.

Frozen.

Watching.

Because what I'm seeing isn't just a mother and daughter.

It's a reflection.

Of what could have been.

Of what almost *was*.

That could've been Katya, if I had left her. If I hadn't dragged her out of the dark. If she had stayed under Dimitri's roof, letting the weight of Romanov legacy grind her down to dust. She would've become this: glass bones, downturned eyes, a hollow voice that only knows how to whisper apologies into blood-stained air.

And the thought of it *guts me*.

Because she was never meant to survive like that.

She was meant to *live*.

And now she does.

Because she fought.

Because she *chose*.

Me.

Us.

Katya lifts her mother's face gently in her hands. Her own tears are silent, tracking down her cheeks as she brushes damp hair from her mother's brow.

"You're free now," she whispers. "You're free."

Her mother's body sags into hers. Not dead. Just... done. Like she's finally allowed herself to fall apart now that the monster's gone.

Katya rocks her slowly, eyes closed, lips pressed to her mother's temple.

And I swear, in all my years of violence, rage, power, I have never seen anything more devastatingly beautiful than the way Katya holds a woman who never got to fight back, and says:

"It ends with me."

And it *does*.

Because she made sure of it.

The air shifts.

Not because the blood is gone. Not because the silence is peaceful now, it isn't. There's nothing peaceful about the way this place dies. But it shifts... because something is *done*.

Katya's mother goes quiet in her arms, head resting against her shoulder like she's returned to a place she never thought she'd see again. Safety. Warmth. Maybe even forgiveness. Her body is light, too light, and when Katya finally exhales and lets go, she does it slowly. Carefully. Like putting down a porcelain doll that's cracked but still precious.

She wipes her cheek with the back of her hand, eyes red but burning with clarity.

"She can't walk," she says softly, and I'm already moving.

I lift the woman in my arms without protest. She doesn't resist. Just closes her eyes and leans into my chest like she's already halfway gone. But I don't carry corpses. Not today. Not now.

We walk together, Katya at my side, toward the long corridor that leads out of the west wing, the one we cleared first. The hallway smells like smoke and victory. Faint gunpowder and fading screams.

At the end of it, the children are waiting.

Blankets wrapped around thin shoulders. Eyes too wide, too old for their age. Noah is crouched in front of one of the younger girls, speaking low and calm, while Ana checks over another boy's bandaged arm. Roman is there too, pacing, protective, his face unreadable, but his stance makes it clear: if anyone tries to come through that hallway, they won't make it three steps.

The moment the kids see Katya, they brighten.

Not in the way children usually do, but in the way soldiers see a flag rise on the battlefield. She walks to them like she was always meant to lead. Drops to her knees again, arms open, and they move toward her like they've *been* waiting.

Like she promised she'd come back for them, and she did.

"Everyone ready?" she asks, voice gentler now.

Most nod.

One little boy steps forward, blanket falling off his shoulder. "Where are we going?"

Katya lifts her chin. "Home."

"But where's that?"

She glances at me. At Roman. At Ana, who gives her a small nod. Then she looks back down at the boy and says, "Anywhere he can't hurt you again."

The boy's mouth wobbles. Then he nods. Slowly.

I feel something hard in my throat.

We guide them in a line, twenty-two in total. Some too young to understand, others far too old in their eyes. Katya keeps them close, touching shoulders, ruffling hair, keeping them *anchored*.

I walk behind them, carrying her mother, sweeping the rear like we always planned. My gun's still warm at my side. My heart heavier than it's been in years.

And still, somehow, it feels *right*.

As we step through the broken threshold of the Romanov manor, sunlight cuts through the haze of smoke and dust. It's dawn. The storm passed hours ago, and now all that's left is what we saved.

What we *chose* to save.

Katya turns back once, just for a moment, and looks at the place she once called home.

Then she turns away for good.

And we walk.

Out of the house that tried to kill her.

And into the world we'll build from the ashes.

Together.

The last child steps past the threshold, feet dragging slightly as Katya squeezes his shoulder and sends him down the long gravel path where Ana and Noah are already helping load them into waiting vans. Roman gives a nod from the tree line, watching, always calculating, but his stance has softened.

The worst is over.

But Katya doesn't move.

Not yet.

She stands just beyond the archway, where the ornate marble floor gives way to dirt and broken stone. Her spine is straight. Her chin high. Smoke clings to her like memory. The wind tugs at her gown, now stained and frayed, yet she looks like something carved out of the bones of goddesses. Not fragile. Not clean. But holy in her rage.

I watch her from a few paces behind, the weight of her mother no longer in my arms, now resting gently in the van, wrapped in warmth and care Katya never had growing up.

And still, she doesn't look back.

She lifts a silver lighter from her pocket. Not flashy. Just simple. Familiar. I'd seen her twist it in her fingers before, nervously, absently, back when this place still had power over her.

Now, she flicks it once.

Flame.

Small. Controlled. Alive.

She kneels at the threshold and places it beneath a torn piece of curtain soaked in alcohol—one of the first things Catalyst rigged when we swept the room. It catches quickly. Smoke curls up like a whisper.

Then the fire spreads.

Up the velvet, across the wall, licking at the banisters and the tapestries, devouring years of secrets and blood rituals, greed and quiet pain.

She watches it rise like it's a performance she's waited her whole life to see.

And then she turns to me.

No tears. No words. Just eyes that burn brighter than the inferno behind her.

"Ready?" I ask.

Her fingers slide into mine.

"I've been ready since the day he put a lock on my bedroom door," she murmurs.

I draw her closer, the heat curling against our backs like a dragon exhaling its last breath. Her chest rises and falls. Her pulse beats steady beneath her skin.

She doesn't look back.

Neither do I.

Together, we walk forward. Away from the Romanov name. Away from the graves we never dug. Away from the girl they tried to break and the man they never saw coming.

The manor burns behind us.

And Katya Romanov, no, *Katya Kane*, walks into her rebirth, hand in hand with me.

Not a prisoner.

Not a pawn.

But a queen made of ash and vengeance.

And I will follow her anywhere she leads.

38

New Beginnings

Katya

It's been twenty-four days.

I've counted them, each one carved into my memory with the precision of a scalpel. Twenty-four days since I stood in the rubble of my father's empire with ash on my face and smoke curling behind me like a crown. Twenty-four days since the name *Romanov* began to unravel, thread by gilded thread, until there was nothing left of it but whispers and dust.

And still, I wake up waiting for the weight of him to return.

The silence is louder than it should be.

Sometimes, I find myself listening for the familiar creak of his footsteps, the harsh sound of his voice at my door, the metallic click of the lock sliding into place. I listen for the phantom pain of obedience and punishment, proof that maybe this freedom is still a dream I'll wake from.

But it never comes.

The empire he built, the one that raised me like a weapon and praised me when I bled for it, has been dissolved. Dismantled with brutal efficiency by the very man he underestimated. By Echo Kane, and by me.

Every safe house has been seized. Every corrupt Romanov enforcer captured or killed. The bribes, the payoffs, the offshore blood-trafficking networks, the compounds with sterilized walls and shackles, all gone. Catalyst stripped the house bare, and anything they couldn't use to rebuild... they buried.

The accounts are frozen. The properties turned over. Even the families who once begged to be married into Romanov prestige have gone silent. Legacy doesn't mean much when it's drenched in the screams of children and the scent of fire.

And I... I don't know who I'm supposed to be now that I'm not surviving him.

The children are safe, at least as safe as they can be. They stay in temporary bunkers, converted Catalyst wings turned into makeshift sanctuaries. The walls aren't pretty. They're not lined with gold or silk like the ones I grew up in. But they're clean. They're warm. They *don't lock.*

Sometimes at night, I sit in the hallway and listen to them laugh. Not always. But some nights.

That's how I measure progress now.

In laughter.

In breath.

In the space between heartbeats when I realize no one is coming to drag me back.

There are days where I feel nothing. Like I'm just a hollow echo of the girl who burned her father alive. I go through the motions, tending wounds, checking inventory, moving children from location to location. Everyone calls me *Katya Kane* now. The name fits more every time someone says it. But I still keep my Romanov ring in a small black box under my cot.

Not as a keepsake.

As a grave marker.

I don't wear it. I don't open it. I don't even look at it.

I just need to know it's there. That I'm the one who put it away.

That *I* chose.

That I still can.

From my place on the windowsill in the east wing, I can see the tree line stretching out past the compound. The forest beyond looks untouched, quiet and indifferent. Like it doesn't care who rules, or who dies. It just continues. Unbothered. Unyielding.

Sometimes, I envy it.

Echo's voice floats down the hall again, low and rough, giving orders to Roman and Ana as they plan the next transition group. He sounds like himself again, not the weapon forged by revenge, but the man I met beneath all the rage. The man who touched me like I was sacred after spending years believing he could only destroy.

And he's *mine*.

God help me, he's mine.

There are moments when he looks at me like I'm still glowing from the fire I lit, like the ash never settled. And when he touches me now, there's no control or conquest behind it.

Only reverence.

Only love.

It terrifies me more than anything else ever has.

I close my eyes and press my forehead to the cold glass. The air smells faintly of copper and medicine. Somewhere down the corridor, someone laughs again. One of the little ones, I think her name is Megan, chasing Ana down the hallway, giggling in oversized socks.

I don't smile.

But my chest doesn't hurt quite as much.

There's still so much to do. Still enemies who haven't yet crawled out from their hiding places. Still names on lists. Still holes in the world I don't know how to fill. I don't know what comes next.

But I know this.

My father's empire is gone.

And I am *still here.*

Still standing.

Still choosing.

And for the first time in my life, I don't feel like I'm bleeding for someone else's crown.

I feel like I'm building my own.

I find him in the lower wing, tucked into one of the old Catalyst map rooms. The lights are low, the walls still lined with worn-out tactical schematics and field reports from a war that now feels like it ended years ago. He's standing over a table, fingers splayed on either side of a spread blueprint, sleeves rolled up, shirt half unbuttoned like he forgot to finish dressing once the adrenaline wore off.

He doesn't hear me at first.

Or maybe he does, and he just wants me to speak first.

"Planning a war?" I ask, voice softer than it's been in days.

His head lifts.

And just like that, his whole body shifts.

The tension drains from his shoulders the second he sees me. Like I'm not just Katya to him anymore. Like I'm the calm after a storm he never thought he'd survive. He straightens, and in three long strides, he's in front of me.

But he doesn't touch me.

Not yet.

"You've been quiet," he says, his voice rough like he hasn't used it for anything but orders.

"I've been thinking," I murmur. "About what comes next."

He nods. His eyes trace mine for a long moment, like he's waiting for something, permission, maybe. Or confirmation that I'm *still here.*

"I don't want you in a bunker," he finally says.

That catches me off guard.

"What?"

He exhales slowly, reaching up to tuck a piece of hair behind my ear. His hand lingers at the curve of my neck, warm, steady.

"I know this place is safe. Secure. But it's not a life. It's just a landing point between fire and flight. You don't belong between walls anymore, Katya."

"And where exactly do I belong?" I whisper.

His thumb brushes my jaw.

"With me."

The words hit harder than I expect.

Not because of how he says them.

But because of how *sure* he sounds when he does.

"No more hiding. No more pretending you're just an asset or a temporary ally." He leans closer. "Move in with me. Not as a gesture. Not as a power play. As you."

I blink, caught in that strange stillness that happens when everything you've ever wanted is suddenly real.

"You're serious," I murmur.

"Dead serious."

His palm flattens over my lower back, tugging me closer, until our bodies align in that quiet, perfect way that never feels like enough. My hands curl into his shirt. I feel the heat of him everywhere. The grounding weight of his presence. The heartbeat of something soft in the middle of all the sharp.

"I don't have a place," I admit. "Not really."

"You do now," he says, no hesitation. "Mine."

A silence stretches between us, not tense, but deep. Like the ocean holding its breath.

"I don't want to just survive with you," I say after a beat. "I want... more."

"You'll have it," he promises, and when he finally leans down to kiss me, it's not rough. It's not hungry.

It's *home.*

His mouth is still on me when I pull him up.

Not roughly, *deliberately.*

My fingers thread through his hair, tugging until his lips part from the mess he's made of me, his breath hot against my thigh. His eyes, those storm-dark eyes, lock onto mine as I guide him upward, my body aching and flushed, my breath ragged. I feel him tremble against me, every muscle tight with restraint, like he's holding himself back from unraveling completely.

Not tonight.

Tonight, I want him undone.

When he rises, I don't let him speak. I push him backward, slow and steady, until the backs of his legs hit the edge of an old couch. He sinks without a word, lips parted, pupils blown wide, hands flexing like he doesn't know where to put them if he's not worshipping me.

I step between his knees, straddling his lap without hesitation. My dress is still hitched high around my waist, and his shirt is hanging open, chest bare, jaw tilted up as if in offering.

"You're quiet," I murmur, letting my hands slide down his chest, tracing the defined lines like I'm memorizing scripture.

"You make me that way," he says hoarsely. "Every damn time."

My fingers reach for his belt, slow, deliberate. I don't rush, don't give him the satisfaction of urgency. I want him to *burn* with it. Want him to sit in the weight of what it means for me to be the one taking my time.

He watches me, his eyes following every movement, reverent and possessive, his mouth parted as if he wants to say something but can't find the words.

I roll my hips once, slow and teasing, the friction between us enough to make him groan.

"Katya..." His voice is a growl, hands gripping the arm rest, like touching me would be the end of him.

"Shhh," I whisper, pressing a finger to his lips. "You begged for this. So let me give it to you."

When I finally lower myself onto him, I don't look away. I want him to see it, the way my body takes him in, inch by inch, slow enough to be cruel. His eyes flutter shut, jaw tightening, a string of curses hissing past his teeth like a prayer he's too far gone to finish.

I start to move, slow, purposeful, grinding against him in a rhythm that's more worship than war. My hands brace against his chest, and his finally lift, trembling, reverent, one on my waist, the other cradling my jaw like I'm something holy.

"You feel like sin," he whispers. "And I'd burn in you a thousand times over."

I smile against his mouth, biting his bottom lip before I kiss him hard, swallowing every broken breath, every groan. We fall into a rhythm, fluid and hot and devastating. He lets me lead. Lets me ride him into oblivion, hands never straying too far, like he's afraid he'll lose control if he grips too tight.

And when I lean down, lips brushing his ear, I whisper the words that wreck him completely.

"I love you."

His body shudders beneath mine.

"I love you," I repeat, hips never slowing. "You're mine, Echo. Every broken, beautiful piece."

His arms wrap around me then, tight, possessive, anchoring me to him as if we're both afraid the world might rip us apart again.

But not tonight.

Tonight, we make something sacred out of the ashes.

39

Can You Hide From Your past?

Katya

The house is quiet when I arrive.

Not the sterile quiet of locked rooms and cold walls, the kind I grew up in, but something warmer. Intentional. Like the silence was chosen, built into the space like a secret.

The door creaks shut behind me, and for a moment, I just... listen.

The faintest flicker of something sweet hangs in the air, smoke, honey and sandalwood. The scent winds its way through the foyer like it's leading me somewhere.

And then I see it.

Candles.

They're everywhere.

Small white votives flickering along the floorboards, trailing up the staircase, their golden glow casting shadows that dance across the walls like ghosts with secrets. There's no overhead light, just that warm, pulsing amber glow drawing me deeper into the space.

My shoes come off without a thought, the silence in the room somehow demanding bare feet.

There's something reverent about the way it's all laid out. Thoughtful. Measured.

This isn't just romance.

It's *control.*

It's *invitation.*

And it's him.

I follow the trail, heart pounding faster with every step, the soft hush of candlelight brushing against my skin like a prelude to something darker. Something *earned.*

When I reach the bedroom, the door is cracked just slightly.

Inside, it's more of the same, candles lined along the windowsill, the edge of the dresser, the nightstand. Everything glows with soft gold light. The bed is made, sheets crisp and dark. My breath catches as I take it all in.

And there, on the edge of the bed, is a single note, folded and precise.

I step closer, fingers trembling slightly as I lift the paper and open it.

Put on the mask.

That's all it says.

Just four words.

But it feels like a dare.

My eyes lift, and that's when I see it. A black velvet half-mask laid out across the pillow. Sleek. Ornate. Almost ceremonial in the way it gleams in the candlelight.

A slow, pulsing heat coils in my belly.

He's not here yet. That much I know. I would feel him if he was. The air would shift. The shadows would tense. *I* would tense. But all I feel now is the *want*.

Not just to obey.

To *offer*.

He set this up for me. For us.

And I want to play.

The mask feels heavier than it looks.

Lifting it from the pillow, the velvet is cool against my palms, plush, but firm in shape. It's not a cheap thing thrown together for spectacle. The kind of item meant to conceal and reveal all at once. The edges are smooth, but the inner lining carries warmth already. As if it's been worn before. As if it knows where it belongs.

My fingertips trace the curve of the eye cutouts, the sweep of the nose bridge. He chose this for me. Not just as an accessory, but as a command.

Put on the mask.

Not *will you*. Not *if you're ready*.

Just, *do it*.

My pulse stirs at the finality of it.

I cross the room slowly, trailing my fingers along the edge of the mattress as I move toward the mirror. The soft glow of the candles paints my reflection in amber and gold, skin kissed in firelight, shadows gathering in the hollows of my collarbone and along the inside of my thighs where my dress has begun to slip. I didn't notice until now just how exposed I already am. The fabric barely clings to my body, whispering down my arms as if it's ready to fall.

Standing in front of the mirror, I hold the mask up to my face and breathe in deep.

Then I lower it, press it gently into place, watching my reflection shift with it. My eyes remain visible, sharp and dark beneath the satin frame, but the rest of me is cloaked in mystery. Softer. More dangerous. Like a secret waiting to be told in screams and sighs.

I don't tie it yet. Not until I've taken in the sight of myself. My bare legs, the open robe, the flicker of firelight skimming every curve like his hands already have. The way my pulse throbs at my throat. I've never felt more visible than I do now, half-covered, half-masked, all exposed.

Slowly, I tie the mask into place, the ribbons whispering across my cheeks as I knot them behind my head. A shiver races down my spine, not from fear, but anticipation.

He told me to wear this.

He told me nothing else.

Which means he'll do the rest.

The silence stretches.

Each candle flickers as if it senses what's coming.

And then-

A soft click from the front door.

My breath catches.

I don't move.

The footsteps are deliberate. Slow. The kind of pace Echo only uses when he knows you're waiting. When he wants each step to be a warning.

I remain by the bed, spine straight, chin lifted, hands folded at my front like I'm about to be examined.

Judged.

Claimed.

The bedroom door creaks open behind me, and I watch him in the mirror as he enters.

Dark suit. No tie. Shirt collar open. Hair still wet from the rain.

His eyes find me in a breath, and he stops just inside the doorway.

Doesn't speak.

Doesn't blink.

His gaze trails from the mask down the line of my bare shoulder, over the open part of my robe, to the place where my thighs meet.

He inhales slowly.

And then the door clicks shut behind him.

The mask makes me feel like someone else, but the way he looks at me?

That makes me feel like *his*.

The door clicks shut behind him, sealing the room in warmth and flickering gold. The candlelight doesn't flinch. It just sways, soft and slow, casting shadows like dancers across the far walls. My breath is still and shallow, held in my chest as if even exhaling too loudly might disturb the ritual he's clearly set in motion. I don't speak. Don't move. Every muscle in my body is tense with anticipation, every nerve aware of how bare I am beneath the silk robe hanging loose around my hips.

I expect him to speak. To say my name the way he always does, low and reverent like a prayer just before it turns blasphemous. Or to hum something smug beneath his breath, the way he does when he wants to watch me squirm, knowing I'll respond without even meaning to. Echo never enters a room quietly when I'm waiting for him like this. He drinks in the moment. He owns it.

But the silence stretches too long.

There's no teasing breath against my ear. No scrape of belt buckle. No quiet sound of shoes being kicked off in haste, like he's too eager to bother with patience.

Just stillness.

Too still.

His footsteps are slow, but they don't creak the floorboards. They don't make a sound at all, like he's gliding across the room without the weight Echo always carries, the heaviness of his presence, the storm he brings with him wherever he goes. This feels lighter. More precise. Measured in a way that sends a chill skimming across the surface of my skin.

I hear him behind me, not by sound but by pressure. The weight of a gaze I can't see but feel, crawling up the back of my neck like something cold and wet. His breath fans the air, soft and even. No tension in it. No rasp.

I try to breathe around the tightness blooming in my chest, but something isn't right. I can feel it now, blooming slowly under the veil of warmth and intimacy like rot beneath roses. Still, I stay frozen in place, as if moving will make it worse. I try to listen, to latch onto any detail that might settle the dread rising like bile in my throat.

His hand touches my hip.

It's gentle. Fingertips only. Tracing the curve like he's uncertain, or worse, *curious*. The contact should ground me. Should remind me this is real, that it's Echo, that I'm safe.

But it doesn't.

His other hand moves higher, gliding up the side of my waist, brushing the edge of my ribs, then higher, toward the ribbon of the mask tied behind my neck. He stops there, fingers ghosting across the knot. He doesn't pull. Doesn't tug. Just lingers.

Watching.

Waiting.

Echo would've gripped me by now. Would've tilted my chin back, forced eye contact through the mask and reminded me exactly who I belonged to. He would've said something filthy, something dangerous. Something mine.

This man, this *presence*, says nothing.

When he finally does speak, the words land wrong in my ear, sliding beneath my skin like oil.

"You wore it for me..."

The voice is low. Controlled. But clean.

Too clean.

No rasp. No strain. No gravel curling around the consonants like a bruise. Echo's voice is lived-in. Rough from war, worn from smoke and screaming and too many nights he didn't sleep. This one is smooth. Precise. Like it's been trained to charm and cut in equal measure.

My lungs freeze.

For one long, aching moment, I try to pretend I didn't hear it. That the air between us is warped, the acoustics wrong. That it *must* be Echo and my mind is just playing tricks on me. But then he speaks again, and this time, there's no denying it.

"I wonder," he muses, voice thoughtful, as if turning me over in his mind, "if he knows how easy you are to dress up."

My spine locks. My heart starts pounding, too loud, too fast, thudding against my ribs like it's trying to escape. My skin goes cold beneath the robe, the firelight suddenly too dim, the shadows too thick. Every detail begins to warp in on itself. Every flicker of candlelight feels like a warning I didn't see in time.

I turn.

Too late.

He's already stepping back, just far enough that I can't see his face clearly through the low light. The shadows cling to his jaw, his cheeks, the corner of his mouth where a smile is blooming, sharp, cruel, and somehow worse than violence.

He wears a mask too.

Not velvet. Not soft.

Black leather, carved to cut, sculpted with precision like a second skin. The kind of mask meant for anonymity. Meant to hide the monster underneath, not invite it forward.

I don't recognize him. Not fully. But he knows me. The way he watches me, *owns* the moment, tells me everything I need to know.

This isn't Echo.

It never was.

He never intended to touch me.

He only wanted me *vulnerable.*

"You should see yourself," he says, tilting his head. "A little candlelight. A velvet mask. And all that loyalty just melts away, doesn't it?"

I don't speak. I can't. My mouth is dry, my body frozen, still reeling from the violation of what I let myself believe. What I invited in.

"You looked so pretty standing there. Waiting." His tone is light. Pleased. "I almost didn't want to ruin it."

He starts walking toward the door, not rushed, not even careful. Confident. He's made his move, and he doesn't need to stay to see the damage it caused. My silence is confirmation enough.

At the threshold, he glances back over his shoulder. I see the faintest glint of his eyes beneath the mask, inhumanly calm.

"I'll see you again soon," he says softly, almost sweetly. "When Echo's not home to protect you."

The door shuts behind him.

No echo. No footsteps.

Just silence.

The moment the door shuts, I collapse forward. Not onto my knees, not in surrender, but in recoil. My arms shake as I brace them against the mattress, trying to steady myself, trying to *understand* what the hell just happened. The air around me still smells like smoke and sandalwood, the warmth of the candles licking my skin like some cruel afterthought, as if the room hasn't realized that the ritual is over.

That it was never real.

The mask lies in a heap on the floor now, crumpled and accusing, its velvet form stained by my own sweat and shame. I want to scream. I want to rip it apart, destroy every soft reminder of how I stood here, bare, trusting, *waiting*, for a man who never even stepped inside.

I should've known. Should've felt it sooner. But I'd let my heart cloud my instincts. Let the scent of him, the idea of him, be enough.

I force myself to stand.

I'm halfway across the room before the world goes silent again, not warm, not reverent, just *still*.

Still in the wrong way.

Still like something is holding its breath.

My spine prickles. The hairs on my arms rise.

I don't hear the door open again. I don't hear the footsteps. There's no sound to warn me, just the *shift* in the air, the kind you feel before a storm hits and tears everything apart. It's in that heartbeat of silence, that razor-slice of knowing, that I realize, I'm not alone.

I spin, but too late.

A hand wraps around my wrist and yanks.

Hard.

My whole body lurches forward, and I hit the dresser with a dull thud, the edge biting into my hip. My free hand lashes out, nails catching cloth, skin, something. The scent that hits me isn't Echo, it's sharper, metallic, threaded with sweat and something sterile. The grip tightens. His other arm snakes around my waist, pinning both of mine to my sides before I can even get enough air to scream.

My throat burns.

I open my mouth, just enough to yell, just enough to cry out his name, but I don't even get that far.

He shoves something between my lips. It's thick, cotton maybe, and laced with something bitter. My jaw aches as it stretches to accommodate the gag, my scream strangled down to a pathetic muffled sob. I thrash harder, twisting my body, trying to drop to the floor or kick out behind me, but he's strong, brutally so, and frighteningly silent.

No curses.

No gloating.

No sound at all except my own ragged breathing and the sharp shuffle of feet on the wooden floor as he drags me back toward the hallway.

I slam my heels against the ground, claw at his wrists, elbow his ribs. He stumbles once, I feel his balance shift, feel a sliver of hope slice through the fear, but it's not enough. He adjusts too fast. Traps my wrists with one hand, yanks them behind my back so hard I nearly cry out around the gag, and clamps his other arm tight around my throat, not choking, not yet, but *controlling*.

Possessing.

The hallway spins as he forces me down the stairs. My feet barely find the edges of the steps. I stumble, crash against the wall, but he holds me upright, herds me with precision, like he knows the layout of the house as well as I do. Like he planned this. Like every step has been choreographed in advance.

The candles flicker behind us. The flames distort and dance as if they know what's happening, but they offer no protection.

No witness.

Just heat.

Just shadows.

He doesn't speak until we reach the bottom of the stairs. Until he slams me up against the wall just past the threshold of the kitchen, knocking the wind out of my lungs. My legs buckle beneath me, but he's already pulling something from beneath his coat. A small syringe. A cap. A glint of silver.

Terror floods me so fast I can barely see.

I try to scream again, louder this time, but it's no use. My throat burns, my jaw aches, and the sound dies in the folds of the gag.

That's when he finally leans in, pressing his masked face close to mine.

His breath is steady.

His voice colder than the steel he's about to sink into my skin.

"You should've stayed quiet."

40

Run Echo Run

Echo

I hadn't planned to be gone this long.

That thought hits first, sharp and dismissive, like an aftertaste I want to spit out the second it forms. I know better. Timing matters. Precision matters. I should've been here an hour ago, maybe two. I'd planned every step of the night with the kind of scrutiny that keeps people alive. But I let myself relax, let myself believe we had time. That she was safe. That this house, *my* house, was the one place on earth no one could touch her.

Now the second I step through the front door, every nerve in my body tells me I was wrong.

It isn't immediate, no shattered glass, no alarms. Nothing loud or obvious.

It's quiet.

Too quiet.

And the air… it's wrong. Warm. Sweet.

There's a scent curling through the space that doesn't belong to this house. Not to me. Not to her. Wax, maybe. Smoke. A soft, sickly sweetness like vanilla left too long in the sun. I follow it into the hall, where the flicker of firelight paints the edges of the walls in gold.

I don't own a single fucking candle.

But there they are. Lined up on the hallway table, flame by flame, burning low like they've been lit for hours. The wax is dripping steadily down onto the surface, creating glossy little puddles on wood I keep spotless.

None of this is mine.

Every step toward the bedroom feels heavier. Slower. My boots barely make a sound, but the air gets thicker with every breath, like I'm descending into something I can't quite see.

The closer I get, the more I feel it, *presence*. Not energy. Not movement. But *intent*. This isn't just a setup. It's a message. Every carefully placed candle, every softened light, the scent still clinging to the air… it was all arranged with one goal in mind:

To draw her in.

And now it's drawing me.

I reach the doorway and stop.

The bedroom is still bathed in that same low golden glow, soft and romantic like a scene from a dream. The bed's unmade. The sheets pulled halfway to the floor, her silk dress twisted in a heap, the sash torn loose beside it. It would look like foreplay, like a perfect, delicate mess, if not for the silence.

If not for the fact that *she's not here.*

And then I see it.

Her mask.

The one I left on the pillow this morning, untouched, waiting. It's not there now. It's on the floor, crushed at the bridge like someone gripped it too hard, like it was torn off in a rush.

My eyes scan the room, cataloging every inch like a sniper sighting targets. The chair near the vanity is pushed back at an odd angle. One of the candles has toppled onto its side. And there, just beside the window, almost like an afterthought, a single black glove.

Placed.

Deliberate.

Like a signature.

I move slowly, not because I'm afraid, because I'm *calculating.* Because if I let myself feel for even one goddamn second, I'll start tearing this room apart until there's nothing left but splinters and rage. My hand hovers near my weapon as I walk to the glove, crouching to examine it. No initials. No markings. No blood.

But I already know what this is.

This wasn't a robbery.

It wasn't a mistake.

It was an *infiltration.*

Someone planned this. Someone got into my house. Past my security. Past every measure I set in place. Someone walked into my territory, looked at the woman I love, and decided they could *take* her.

And they did.

My vision goes dark at the edges. I'm aware of my breath, how shallow it is. A knot twists deep in my gut, not panic, but *grief.* The kind of grief that becomes fire. Becomes rage. Becomes the *end* of whoever was stupid enough to think they could touch her without dying for it.

I back out of the room slowly, keeping my gaze on the floor as I trace the faint scuff marks from her heels, dragged, not walked. Every detail confirms what I already know. She didn't go willingly. This wasn't seduction. This was force. Silent, surgical, and personal.

Someone knew where to hit me. Knew exactly when to strike. And they left the scene just messy enough to twist the knife.

I reach for my phone, already barking commands into the line before it fully rings.

"Lock the compound. Sweep the perimeter. Pull every camera within a ten-block radius. Anyone moves, I want them flagged. If they're breathing, I want them on their knees."

There's no need to say who I'm looking for.

They know.

She's gone.

The room has been stripped of safety. Every familiar detail, the sheets she curled up in, the pillow she stole from my side, the robe I left draped over the chair for her comfort, has been transformed. Twisted. Turned into part of a spectacle I never gave permission for.

This was supposed to be *ours.*

But the moment I step fully into the bedroom, it feels desecrated.

My boots stop at the edge of the bed, the soles grazing across the faint smear of blood on the hardwood, *hers,* without question. That iron-rich scent is faint but distinct, and it coils up into my sinuses like a taunt. I track the trail, small, deliberate spots, not enough to kill her, just enough to *tell me* she bled. To let me *know.*

And then I see it.

Not tucked away.

Not hidden.

Right there, bold as a fucking slap.

A note.

Placed neatly on the center of the bed like a calling card. White, stark against the muted grays of our bedding. The handwriting is tight, slanted, and deliberate, each curve and angle more of a threat than any weapon.

I don't touch it right away.

Just stare.

I want to believe, for a fraction of a breath, that maybe she left it. That it's from her. A whisper, a warning, *something.* But the longer I look at it, the more I know. She wouldn't leave her blood on my bed. She wouldn't disappear without a fight. And she sure as hell wouldn't leave a note written in something that smells like rust and revenge.

When I finally pick it up, the paper is heavier than it looks.

No frills. Just a message.

Thought your past wouldn't come to haunt you?

Time to clip her wings.

That's it.

That's all they needed to say.

And yet it's everything.

My hands don't shake. Not visibly. But my breath shortens, tightens in my throat, the same way it did the first time I held a blade to a man's neck and realized I wasn't doing it for orders, I was doing it because it felt *necessary*.

This?

This feels worse.

Because someone thinks they've reached back into a part of me I buried long ago. The version I've kept chained, starved, half-dead behind layers of cold logic and control. They think they can dig him up and puppeteer him. Use my history like a knife.

But what they don't understand is, I buried that man for a reason.

Not because he was weak.

Because he was *too efficient*.

And now?

Now I'll become him again.

Not because they dragged me there.

Because they threatened *her*.

They touched something I built with blood and grit. They broke into the only home I've ever let myself *want*. And they left behind a fucking *invitation* to war. A message written in her blood, daring me to remember exactly what I used to be.

And I will.

Every brutal second of it.

Because this time, I'm not fighting for Catalyst.

I'm not fighting for orders, or control, or legacy.

I'm fighting for *her*.

And when I find them, whoever they are, wherever they're hiding, I won't ask questions.

I'll just burn the world until she's back in my arms.

Because if they clipped her wings, then I'll teach them what it means to die by the hands of a man who knows how to fly without them.

The paper crumples in my fist.

I don't even feel the burn of it cutting into my skin, don't register the blood where my nails break through flesh. All I can see is that goddamn line, still burned into my mind like a brand.

Time to clip her wings.

I stare at the bed, the sheets we shared, the fabric that still smells like her. And then something inside me just... *detonates.*

A roar tears from my throat, guttural and raw, the kind that hasn't left my body in years. Not since before Catalyst. Not since I was the monster they trained and then tried to bury. It echoes off the walls, rattles the picture frames, vibrates through my ribs like a bomb went off behind them.

And then I move.

The first thing to go is the nightstand. I rip the drawer clean out and throw it across the room, contents shattering against the far wall in a burst of broken glass and useless bullets. The lamp follows, glass exploding as it hits the floor. A candle gets kicked sideways, wax splattering up the wall like blood.

The dresser doesn't stand a chance. One solid boot and it tips, crashing sideways with a wooden groan that almost sounds like protest. I drag the rest to the floor with both hands, not even feeling the splinters slicing my palms as it goes down in a thunderous heap.

The mirror above it cracks when I slam my fist into it, once, twice, three times, until my knuckles are split open and the reflection staring back at me is fractured, distorted. Unrecognizable. A dozen shards of my own face, all twisted with fury. All helpless. All *too late.*

"FUCK!"

The word rips through the space like a gunshot, but it doesn't make a dent in the grief thudding beneath my sternum. It doesn't do a damn thing to quiet the sound of her voice in my head. The way she whispered my name last night like it meant something. Like *I* meant something.

And now she's gone.

Stolen.

Used to get to me.

Used to *hurt* me.

My hands slam against the walls as I pace the room like an animal trapped in a burning cage, fury blurring my vision. I want to destroy more. I want to raze the fucking building. Tear down the ceiling, rip through the floorboards, scream until the sound breaks *something* other than myself.

But even as I wreck everything around me, it isn't enough.

Because I can't break the thing I want to most.

The one who took her.

The one who dared.

The one who thought I'd come undone.

You don't get to take her from me and live.

You don't get to leave her blood in my bed and walk away.

You don't get to leave a message unless you're ready for a reply.

And mine?

Mine will be delivered with a body count.

ACKNOWLEDGEMENTS

I had far too much fun with Katya and Echo's story to not continue it. Throughout the duration of Devil's Night we really got to see Katya's past and present, but what about dear Echo Kane? A man as sexy as him is sure to have many skeletons in his closet.

Now, time for the sappy sappy.

During the writing of Devil's Night, I found out I was pregnant with my first, and as you read this, the little miracle is still inside my tummy. Everyday I sat town to write this book, it felt like I had a little co-author guiding my thoughts, helping me craft this story into something wonderful. I want this kiddo to be proud of their momma, able to one day say their mom is a badass author. So, thank you little bean for motivating me more than ever.

To Jazzy, my very best friend, you are literally my rock in this world. I don't know what I would do if I did not have you by my side everyday. You quite literally make life bearable sometimes.

On top of being the best mom and the best friend, you are one creative badass woman and I am honored to call you my best friend. Love you always Jazzy boo.

To my father and my husband, thank you for your continued support throughout my literary journey. You both made a dream feel like a reality until it could be. I love you both endlessly.

To Sami and Nikki, you girls have been rocks in my life for so long. I can't imagine a life without you. I love you both so so much.

Thank you everyone who has supported this silly little dream.

Now, who is ready for more spicy tales here in the near future? I know I am.